THE BREEDERS

THE BREEDERS

BY MATTHEW J. BEIER

AN EPICALITY BOOK • EPICALITY BOOKS

Minneapolis

Library of Congress Control Number: 2012933133

ISBN-978-0-9838594-0-6

FIRST TRADE PAPERBACK EDITION
Also available in eBook format
Epicality Books, LLC, 2012
www.epicalitybooks.com

For my parents, Walter and Mariana Beier, the ones who created me, loved me unconditionally, and encouraged me to follow my dreams.

PART ONE:

ENGILUTION

"A STORM IS COMING."

—The National Organization for Marriage,
2008

CHAPTER 1 ✳ (HER)

For Grace Jarvis, the threat of banishment came at Garland's Food Emporium on Monday, the twenty-ninth of October.

She was reaching down for an empty grocery basket when a stabbing sensation twisted in her abdomen. Mr. Dietrich, a wrinkled old fag who had been running the nearby sample station for as long as Grace could remember, frowned as she stopped, put a hand on her stomach, and lurched forward. The pain came again—a violent cramp, like nothing she had ever felt before.

This only happens to carriers, was the thought that crossed her mind as Mr. Dietrich took a step away from his pineapple chicken mini-skewers.

"Everything all right, Miss Jarvis?"

Grace stood up to full height, trying to cover her sudden panic with a polite smile, and approached his table. She grabbed one of the skewers and said, "Must have been something I ate at lunch." Then, with a smile, "Maybe one of your samples will help. They usually do."

"Only $4.99, and they're already skewered. I'm telling you, they're *fabulous*."

"Well, we both know I have a weakness for good food." Grace winked at Mr. Dietrich, slid a pineapple bite off the skewer with her teeth, then continued on to the produce section.

The pain grew worse with each step, and the first trickles of concern sank into her chest. With defiant resolve, she grabbed a head of broccoli.

Stop it. You're being paranoid. They're not going to send you to Antarctica just for having weird cramps.

But the concern turned to terror as she picked out a bundle of cilantro. The herbs were wet, and just as Grace was shaking them off and enjoying the mixture of pleasant aromas around her, a peculiar warmth touched the inside of her underwear. She looked down.

On the sparkling white floor was a red circle. There was no spatter around it; for a second, Grace hoped it was dried paint.

Then another drop fell from under her skirt. And another. It was thick, almost viscous looking, and the fact it was her own blood registered with a final burst of wishful disbelief.

This is impossible. Absolutely impossible. The engineers can't have messed me up.

She swiped one of the blood drops with the tip of her shoe, trying to wipe it away, but this only transformed it into a garish smear. She glanced left, where a lesbian couple (Regina and Bear, their names were—she knew them from last year's Union Day Fest) had stopped in front of the dairy section, ten feet away. Bear was looking at the floor; Regina was staring straight at Grace. Neither wore a threatening expression, and both—bless them—seemed to be registering her panic.

"*Get out now,*" Regina mouthed.

"*I'm sorry,*" Grace whispered, now dripping tears as well. She set her half-full basket on the floor, gave Regina and Bear a pleading glance, then made for the market's exit as fast as she could. Her gait became a conspicuous waddle in the effort to keep her legs pressed together, and Mr. Dietrich furrowed his eyebrows. "Left my com in the car," Grace murmured to him as she stole a glimpse backward and saw Bear hurrying to wipe up the blood.

A moment later, she was outside. The gusty October night sent her straight dark brown hair into a fitful dance, clashing with the sticky heat spreading inside her skirt and down her legs. It turned cold as she ran from the grocery store, past the Atom Clean fuel station, and into the train station lot where her car was parked. But here was a shred of luck: buried in her trunk were a backup running jacket and an unused beach towel from her last outing on Lake Minnetonka. Grace wiped herself clean, wrapped herself in the towel, then sat in the driver's seat on the waterproof jacket.

I'm as good as dead if anyone sees this, she thought. Her knuckles were white; her legs were numb. The pain in her abdomen throbbed as she forced herself to start the hydro engine and drive toward home.

It began to rain.

The Jarvis mansion was dark when Grace turned into the driveway—a second shred of luck. She rolled past the main courtyard and stopped in front of her fathers' small brick guest house. It had been her home since moving out at age eighteen, but tonight, its small frame and aging brick walls left her feeling exposed and susceptible. By morning, it could all be a figment of her past, never to be seen again.

Grace dashed through the rain and into the house, then hurried to the bathroom. Dropping the soiled beach towel to the floor, she fumbled out of her clothes and into the shower. All that mattered—and it could be life and death, really, if the Bio Police decided to forego the legal process of banishment in favor of simple execution—was getting the bleeding to stop.

In accordance with Mandate 11, her fathers had engineered her to be sterile, just like all other females. She was not supposed to ovulate, not supposed to menstruate, and certainly not supposed to create life. Any of those three things were absolute grounds for banishment; all it would take for the Bio Police to make a decision was a simple medical test to see what was causing the bleeding. She had never heard of any woman passing it. Genetic mistakes and legal carriers were the only types of women who bled like this, and she sure as hell was not a legal carrier.

The water swirling around her feet turned from red to pink to beige before finally stopping. Grace turned the shower off and stood there, bare, until the drops trickling down her body grew cold. But her heart was on fire, beating faster than it ever had in her life.

The New Rainbow Order had come to an innovative balance of punishment for illegal fertility, even if it was accidental—no more forced abortions, no more forced hysterectomies. Expulsion to the Antarctic Sanctuary was the real and only deal now, in the interest of both humane treatment and foolproof control of humanity. The threat of being stuck at the bottom of the world, in an artificial bubble full of excommunicated breeders, was what kept society in line.

And now I have to find a way out, Grace thought.

Here in Minneapolis, she was landlocked. All inhabited spots on Earth were now controlled by the worldwide government, and the places that had disintegrated during the Bio Wars—the coasts here on the North American continent, much of South America, much of mainland Europe, and most of Asia—were impossible to survive in. If the terrorist plagues hadn't wiped people out, the military bombs used to obstruct them had, and the ruins that remained were more treacherous than any natural jungle. They were called the Unrecoverable Territories for a reason.

The smartest thing would be to kill myself. Do it easily, somehow. Painlessly.

But no. It would be unfair to her fathers, her brother, and Linda Glass, her best friend. Grace was the luckiest heterosterile she knew of: rich parents, an education, a solid job. Ending her life would be a poor display of gratitude.

Trembling, she wrapped herself in a towel, returned to her bedroom, and stood alone in the darkness.

Tomorrow was her final meeting with the Minneapolis Neighborhood Development Council to make one last case for an overhaul of the Obesaland slum. It was the city's only true cosmetic atrocity, and there was no way she could miss the meeting, not unless she wanted the poor fatties living there to rot in their misery. Fitness was a virtue, yes, but even those who didn't subscribe to the homosexual-male-driven ideal of perfection deserved a shred of dignity. Grace wanted nothing more than to be an advocate for them, and tomorrow was her last chance. The meeting was at nine o'clock— just twelve hours away.

But it no longer mattered. It couldn't. She could find some sort of absorbent material to block further bleeding, but if it failed during her plea for funding, the Bio Police would be on her within minutes. That was the awful truth.

Father might turn me in if I ask for help, but Dad won't. He can't. Not his little girl.

Her dad, Stuart, was a doctor. He had no love for government-imposed standards, and he would be able to identify the problem. Even so, diseases were rare, and chronic irregularities would have been identified during her engineering. Judging from what she had heard about carriers, bleeding and pain of this sort seemed too sudden to be menstruation. This left one likely scenario, however absurd it might be:

She was—or had been—pregnant.

It could only have happened during the orgy with Todd Bender and his five friends: Hannah, Peter, Elena, Fletch, and the short but muscular man whose name had remained a mystery, the one she had gone all the way with. His salt-and-pepper-colored hair had given him an air of maturity she had melted under—the first time since the Dyke Patrol had attacked her outside Pommie's Pub that she allowed herself to publicly embrace her sexual orientation. She had succumbed to the urges engineered into her—lost control, really—and now, life as she knew it was over.

Standing in front of the mirror, Grace let the towel fall. She stood naked, aware for the first time of her body's frightening power.

The potential to create life was the very reason breeders didn't stand a chance when natural conception happened by accident—which of course was the only way it could happen at all these days. The homosexuals had won the Bio Wars, plain and simple. Twenty generations later, they had perfect, worldwide control. Few questioned the sense in controlled homosexual reproduction—the medical breakthrough of same-sex chromosome combination had marked the end of spiraling populations, children born to unfit parents, and heterosexual recklessness.

"Too many mistakes!" Secretary General Vincent Metzer had said during his last address to the world, when he had become so excited that his gaudy blonde wig had fallen off. "Too many chances for the world to fall back into its old ways!"

He had already been in office three terms past his legal limit, blaming the unprecedented extension on a recent resurgence of God's Army terrorists. Now, in just three weeks, his homosexual government assembly would be voting on Mandate 43, a new law rumored to be his final attempt to squelch human birthing from society completely. People called him the Queen, but the only sparkly things about him were his signature blue dress and matching eye shadow. The man was ruthless—the first true dictator since the Bio Wars, though nobody had the courage to say it.

Grace stared out her bedroom window. The tree branches in her dad's garden thrashed in the darkness, as if to remind her that life, as finished and nullified as it seemed right then, had not ended just yet. She returned to the bathroom, gathered her clothes, and dragged them down the shadowy hallway toward the living room fireplace. It would be the only sure way to dispose of her secret, at least until it happened again.

Just as she passed the kitchen, another cramp circled her abdomen. The same warm feeling followed between her legs. More blood. She ran to the shower for a second time, and it came out with sobs of shock, pain, and confusion. Hot, red, sticky, horrible.

As of that night, Grace Jarvis was, by the New Rainbow Order's definition, a biological fugitive.

CHAPTER 2 ✻ (HIM)

EIGHT MILES PER HOUR. Nine. Ten. Eleven and a half.

Intervals were Dex Wheelock's favorite running exercise, as they had been since childhood: maximum cardiovascular benefits and fat loss, minimum time spent slaving away on a treadmill. Today, the gym's roof was retracted, and the Indian summer sun beat down on him. Only another month before the roof would be up every day, keeping out the winter. From this treadmill, the skyscrapers of Minneapolis were visible. Most of them glinted in subdued but obvious rainbow colors, a century-old construction trend symbolic of society's bright future.

Bright future if you're normal, Dex thought. *And that will never be me.*

Heterosexuals made up exactly 8 percent of the New Rainbow Order's population, and he was among the 2 percent who were fertile and male. The reality of this—of the sheer number of homosexuals pressing him into society's corners, believing him to be inconsequential—made him feel like spit in a churning ocean. It didn't help that the only heterosexuals working in those skyscrapers were the ones cleaning the toilets.

Dex finished his warm-up, hopped off the treadmill, and approached the weight room. Here, he always looked as good as (and sometimes better than) the homosexuals in this gym's crop, despite his short height. He had joined Flip Fitness because it allowed males and females to comingle, unlike the other gyms near his apartment that tolerated heterosexual clientele. The females at this particular location also tended to be interested in men. If it wasn't obvious due to the general but often correct stereotype that lesbians avoided gyms, it was obvious because of the eye contact they would make with him: *Yes, I'm hetero. And available.*

Diana Kring had been one of them—a sparkle of a woman who had worked at the front desk. She had not been shy in telling Dex the night they met that smaller men, graying hair, and bulging muscles turned her on, so he had escorted her right back to his apartment and done things to her his mothers would be ashamed of. Three months later, they were in love. It had taken thirty-seven years, but Dex had finally found in Diana a queller for his loneliness.

And then she had disappeared. Apartment empty, coworkers shrugging, one aging father left scratching his head. Either Diana had duped everyone she knew, or some unexpected desperation had forced her to run. It was enough to show Dex for the first time ever how a broken heart could both define and unravel him, in one swift emotional gust.

Despite being a constant reminder of what he had lost, Flip Fitness had since become his prime spot for grief evasion. In the weight room today were two shirtless fags pumping dumbbells with blank concentration, one on either end of the long weight rack. The closer of the two, a gym regular, had an erection under his tight shorts. Dex approached a bench facing the middle of the rack, maintaining a wide berth on either side of himself, hoping the fags would leave him alone. But the one with the erection nodded hello. His eyes flickered over Dex's body as he set his dumbbells back in their allotted place.

Dex had just begun a warm-up set of seated shoulder presses when the fag approached him from behind. A second later, he felt the erection press against his upper back.

"Shorty, you don't have a husband, do you? I don't see a ring."

Typical.

"Uh, no. Not quite interested in anything today though."

"Oh, come *on*!" The fag flicked his wrist forward, and it landed on Dex's shoulder. "You know, I give *really* good head. Just saying."

"Maybe another time."

The bulging erection circled Dex until it was pointing him in the face. Dex looked up at the fag, whose eyes were still vibrating back and forth over his muscles. Come to the gym when there weren't many lesbians or heterosteriles present, and this was what any attractive failsafe got. It was normal for fags to assume every other male was homosexual and wanted to have sex, as if they had somehow forgotten about the government's mandate that some males remain hetero. It was ingrained in social etiquette, which left failsafes like Dex with the awkward challenge of having to explain themselves while also avoiding potential threats. He had to be careful, always.

"Hey, I'd rather just do my workout. Thanks, though."

"I'm Glen."

Dex sighed. "Hi, Glen."

"I've seen you around here before. Never seen you leave with anyone, though. What gives?"

To their left, the other fag dropped his hundred-pound dumb-bells to the floor and looked at Glen. His muscles were rippling and dripping with sweat. "Honey, he's a *failsafe*. I've seen him make eyes at women before. Trust me, you can do better."

Glen stepped back, his face contorting as if he had bit into a lemon. It was only a matter of seconds before the tent in his shorts started to recede. "Sorry. Not really going to put my mouth on a dick that wants to breed, even if it's a hot one."

Dex felt his cheeks burning. "And I never asked you to."

"He left with that Diana chick once," the other fag said. "She worked here for a while."

"Oh, I know her!" Glen's arms flailed up at nothing. His wrist flowed in an arc, then settled with the rest of his hand into a pointing gesture aimed at the other fag.

Dex almost dropped his dumbbells. Erection boy knew Diana.

"Mark, wasn't she the one who was, like, bleeding all over a couple months ago? I swear, it was disgusting. I saw it coming through her pants, like she was a carrier in pre-fertilization mode or something. I mean, you hear about that happening to carriers, but who really wants to see it?"

The musclehead—Mark—took a quick, inward hiss of air as he grabbed the ninety-five-pound dumbbells and began shrugging them. "Maybe she got the Lrh1 switch. She would've made a pretty carrier, even if she was a hetero. Unless maybe she was a genetic mistake. I haven't seen her around since."

Glen giggled with a flamboyant smile. "And we all know what Queen Vincent is doing to those illegal breeders!"

Panic had drained Dex's strength in a matter of seconds. If Diana had somehow accepted the procedure to become a carrier, the Bureau of Genetic Regulation would have registered her for a ration of tampons. She would not have bled in public.

"How long ago was this?" he asked.

Glen pursed his lips and turned back to him. "Oh, well look at you, all interested in talking now! Looks like she's moved on, honey. Haven't seen her in weeks. Nice girl, though, for a breeder. Too bad she's going to lose that stomach when they insert her with an embryo, you know? Those things, like, *grow*. Of course, they'll probably abort it anyway once Mandate 43 passes."

Despite Glen's having at least eight inches of height on him, Dex jumped out of his seat, threw the dumbbells back onto the rack, and stepped into his face. He was close enough to smell sweat through the fag's cologne.

"*Piss off.*"

But it was Dex who abandoned his workout and stormed toward

the locker room. It would be dangerous to come back to this gym anytime soon, lest he risk being cornered in the showers.

He changed clothes as fast as he could. Dread raged in his chest.

Saturday, the fifteenth of September, had been his last day of contact with Diana. He had woken up next to her in his apartment, kissed her, and risen to make coffee. After leaving momentarily to run to the corner store for cream, he had returned to an empty apartment. Her overnight bag was gone, and she had left the bed unmade. No note; no "I love you"; no hint, except for the obvious one: when Mandate 43 passed, females, even lesbians, would be needed only for the shells of their ova, because test tube gestation would replace human carrying completely. The law, proposed by Sanjay Raghuvanshi of Srinagar (but conceived of by the Queen, surely) was now up for vote in just four weeks' time.

Diana had been nervous about the implications of Mandate 43, but mostly for Dex's sake. If the Queen were to abolish society's natural reproductive backup plan, heterosexuals—especially failsafes like him—would officially become disposable.

Dex squinted again at the city's glaring skyline as he left the gym. Just when it had seemed apparent that answers would never come, here was this, a clue. Diana had suffered the worst fortune an innocent heterosterile could ask for:

She had bled like a carrier.

A MEMORY ✳ (HER)

*F*OUR YEARS OLD *is very young to be reading as well as she is, and Grace is of course very proud. It doesn't matter that she is making Abraham feel bad, and she cannot help it if he is seven and still on easy readers. It's dinnertime on Friday, her favorite day, and her father swirls his wine, the way he always does. Grace is curious how it tastes, because the purple color reminds her of the flowers in her dad's garden—the same garden her father says looks overgrown, even though that's how it's supposed to look.*

All day, she has been itching for dinner so that she can make her announcement:

"I read today how babies used to be made!"

She screams it over the clanking of silverware on dishes, careful not to look at her father James. Instead, she focuses on her dad Stuart, who is always nicer about things like this.

Across the table, Abraham claws a fork through his potatoes in slow, jealous strokes. But how can Grace help it if he doesn't like school? The teachers say he never pays attention, which is why he has trouble learning.

"And where, pray tell, did you read about that, Grace?" James says. Whenever he sips his wine, he looks like a curious snake, which makes Grace think of snake bites and sucking out the poison.

"On the com," she replies.

The com: a gateway to anything and everything, even for a four-year-old. She can type in anything and learn. Oceans? It would have information. Africa, that far-off place only the military goes to? She could learn about it. Snakes? Well, that's how she knows about sucking out the poison.

"Tell us what you learned, Pix," Stuart says, setting the salad bowl at the table's center.

James rolls his eyes at his husband's nickname for Grace, as always, which never makes sense to her. She beams at her dad and tells him what she knows:

"Before the Bio Wars, failsafes and carriers used to press their bodies together, and the penis would go in the vagina, and women back then weren't heterosterile, and the penis would shoot out stuff called sperm, and it would magically combine with female eggs, but not the kind we eat, obviously, and then the egg would just start growing, and then a baby would come out! And when the babies weren't going to happen, females had to use things to plug up the blood, because it would hurt and come out of the vagina!"

Her dad smiles, but her father looks stern.

"And why do you think that was wrong, Grace?" James asks. Now, he reminds Grace of the hawk that was sitting on top of the guest house last week. First he is a serpent; then he is a hawk. She doesn't know why this makes her nervous.

"Wrong?"

"That was a horrible thing that used to happen in the world, and human beings have come far enough in their technological advancements to stop it and control it. Why do you think they wanted to do that?"

"Because of the blood?"

"Because of population. The world has only so many resources, and those failsafes and carriers, even though they were not called that back then, were destroying the world by having too many babies. Now,

only same-sex people can make babies together, and everyone is happier, even you! Those silly heterosexual breeders almost destroyed the planet!"

"It said something about genes." *She pronounces the word with a hard G. Geens.*

"Oh, genes," *her dad corrects with a chuckle, leaning over to help Abraham with his artichoke hearts. Dad always reminds her of clouds, not scary animals.*

"Genes," *Grace repeats, thrilled at the pronunciation.* "Genes made it so that those magic eggs couldn't work anymore. Which means carriers couldn't make babies by rubbing together with failsafes. But I watched a video of it, so I know how it used to be!"

James seethes. "Don't they have parent lock on that type of stuff? I told you she shouldn't be allowed on the desk com, Stuart. Call me old-fashioned." *He lets out an exasperated sigh and swirls his wine.*

Abraham's face twists into a jealous, angry scowl, which makes him look just like their father. "But you let the engineer make Grace a heterosexual!" *he screams, as if he's somehow won a game she forgot they were playing.* "That makes her bad!"

James raises his eyebrows at Stuart and smiles as if he's the reason Abraham won the game. Stuart's face turns red, and he slams the potatoes down in front of his husband. They don't speak for the rest of dinner.

CHAPTER 3 ✳ (HER)

Heterosexuals. Babies. Rubbing together. *Dirty.*

Today, Grace realized it was a gross overstatement. The world would have gone on, even if humanity managed to destroy itself. It had almost happened during the Bio Wars, and the planet pulled through, somehow. Didn't it always?

She was in the grungy women's bathroom at her office, sitting in the stall farthest down, letting blood trickle from between her legs into the toilet water. Its flow was nowhere near as heavy as the previous evening, but it would still make a mess if she wasn't careful. Sanitary wipes had held it at bay during her meeting with the Neighborhood Development Council, where her boss, the new executive director Devon Shemple, had all but cancelled the Obesaland project she had spent the last two years planning. Today's meeting had been a last-ditch effort to rejuvenate the rotting slum, and Shemple had put the project on hold until the New Rainbow Order's General Assembly voted on Mandate 43. It had been only two months since he accepted the executive director post, but it had taken Grace only a day to realize he had no interest in helping the less respected members of society. He was a foot soldier of the Queen through and through.

I shouldn't have believed I could make a difference, she thought, arching her spine on the toilet and wincing at the pain squeezing the small of her back. Obesaland did not matter now, of course, but Grace was not yet ready to call it quits with her old life. That she had nobody to turn to with her questions about the last twenty-four hours (*What was causing the bleeding? If it really was a pregnancy or miscarriage, how had she become fertile?*) made it easier to imagine that nothing had really changed.

It was a stupid way to think, but the more Grace thought about trying to disappear, the more impossible it seemed. If she were able to make a run for the Unrecoverable Territories to live in the wild, she would need to scan the TruthChip in her wrist at some point along the way. This would brand her a heterosterile to every vendor, government agent, or law enforcement officer she might come across. If they were to find out she was a fugitive, the escape effort would be wasted. Better options would no longer exist.

The night of the orgy, Todd Bender—the man she had been brave enough to start dating two weeks prior—had handed her a little green pill. It was just over two months ago now.

"Come on, take it."

"I'm not sure I want to."

"Come on, you're hot as hell. This will make you hotter. Take it."

"Okay, fine."

No backbone. She had wanted so badly to recover from the trauma caused by the lesbian attack outside Pommie's Pub that embracing her desires publicly, without fear or shame, seemed to be a logical step in the right direction.

There had been sex. Lots and lots of sex: Todd working magic with his fingers, pulling out, then letting Fletch and Peter do the same. Then Hannah and Elena had licked every part of her as Fletch and Peter fucked them, all while the mysterious Salt and Pepper man watched. "You're so fucking hot," they all said as they devoured her, except the silver-haired stranger, who remained quiet and contemplative, even as he escorted her to the couch after Todd disappeared into a bedroom with Fletch and Hannah. What followed was the most intense sex of Grace's life. Salt and Pepper made her forget Todd Bender completely.

But he had been gone in the morning. Probably for the best, because she looked like hell. Felt guilty, too, for having given into drugs and thoughtless judgment like everyone else. Instead of feeling empowered, she had crept to the train station with the sunrise, afraid anyone she passed would immediately know what had occurred the night prior and punish her for it.

Now, this: the biggest of all possible accidents, all because she had acted against her instincts and insecurities to fit in with the crowd. All Grace wanted was to forget it had ever happened, but by the time she left work to meet Linda Glass for coffee, the bloody puzzle pieces were aligning themselves against her willful ignorance. The obvious had been showing itself, despite what she now recognized as her own subconscious denial: she had been sick in the mornings; it had been happening almost daily since the orgy; she had seen bits of blood on underwear in recent years, as if her body was showing signs of unnatural menstruation. Today, Grace knew she had seen the possibility all along and been stupid enough to brush it off. What she didn't know was how long life would hold together before it decided to unravel.

LINDA EYED HER CAREFULLY when they found a table at the Union Café in Wayzata, just two miles down the road from where they had grown up. She was a classic lipstick lesbian—ravishing blonde hair, a tight, feline physique, and lips so red they just begged to be kissed. It was no secret she had borne a crush on Grace since childhood. Still best friends, they joked about it often. "Want to make out?" Linda always asked, clearly half-serious. Grace always laughed in response, saying, "Not today, baby." Had she been normal, they would have been married, no question.

Today, Linda's hair glistened against the waning afternoon sun. "What's up, honey? I thought we talked about that gloom and doom face you keep wearing out in public. You're too pretty for that. You've got to put that dyke gang shit behind you."

Was it worth the risk to tell Linda?

No. As much as it grieved Grace to evade the truth, she did. "It's not that. I'm just feeling tired. I haven't slept much this week. Spent all my time prepping for that Obesaland pitch."

"Oh yeah, how did that go?"

Grace told her, forcing the proper amount of frustration into her voice, putting on a show worthy of the old Hollywood movies. She even wrapped in a psychological thread relating to fear of being herself among homosexuals, which solicited an expected—yet somehow sympathetic—eye roll from Linda. Not once did she mention her bleeding, suggest that she might be a genetic mistake, or hint that their friendship might soon go the way of Antarctica. Linda, none the wiser, responded with stories about her daughter Rita, her wife Celine's drinking problem, and the new bra she had found at V-Barn. Typical girl talk.

So there it was; there it went. A social encounter, a regular instance in Grace's normal heterosterile life, a sign that things had not yet changed irrevocably. But the cramps, those little nightmares, were starting again.

CHAPTER 4 ❋ (HIM)

A Bio Police car crept onto Spruce Place and parked across the street from the rundown apartment complex where Diana Kring had lived. Dex saw its approach reflected in the building's front entryway.

For the third time, he scanned his wrist on the resident panel and buzzed Diana's neighbor, Trinka. Trinka had birthed eight children for seven different male couples after being forced by the Bureau of Genetic Regulation to become a carrier. Worn ragged by age twenty-seven, she had purposefully become addicted to hard methamphetamines in order to fight the system, and the last child to come out of her had been deformed. Trinka hated the New Rainbow Order more than anyone Dex knew, and she would have no problem letting him break into Diana's apartment—for a second time—to check for new leads.

He dared a glance toward the police car while waiting for the woman's answer. The bearish officer behind the wheel was peering sideways, in Dex's direction. Here the brute was in his purple uniform, outside Diana's home, two and a half months after her disappearance. Why now? Had Trinka finally become cause for concern, or was he here for some other reason?

Dex was due at work in just forty minutes. He buzzed Trinka again, scouring his brain for places in Diana's apartment he had forgotten to search the first time, wondering if there might have been clues about her bleeding incident all along.

His spirits had spiraled downward for two weeks after she stopped answering com calls and door knocks. The message had seemed clear: she did not love him, and this was her way of showing it. The orgy at Fletch Novotny's apartment had been a good way to blow off steam, and the drugged-up woman he had finished with had been beautiful enough to be proper revenge against Diana—an idealist-type who worked for the Obesaland slum, if he remembered correctly. Under her lush, dark hair, however, she had an innocent face and an air of sexual inexperience about her. Fucking her had made him feel as if he was crushing a fledgling under his heel, simply to snuff away his own pain.

And it had not brought Diana back.

Not long after the orgy, it became obvious *nobody* had seen her. When he had finally searched her apartment, Dex noticed her pink suitcase was missing, as were most of her favorite outfits. Diana's father Joshua was not prejudiced, so he made no mention of Dex to police. Associating his daughter's disappearance with heterosexual activity might have become dangerous for both of them. While both Civic and Bio Police were much more brutal in Chicago and certain other metropolises in the Recovered Territories, heterosexuals like Dex—and the people who cared for them—were still at risk here in Minneapolis. Avoiding the police rendered Diana's trail even colder, but it was just as well. If this bleeding incident meant she was a genetic mistake, the shadows would be her safest refuge.

The com in Dex's pocket vibrated. He grabbed it and looked at the screen.

A holomessage from Fletch Novotny. It was the perfect excuse to start walking toward the Twin Cities Com studio. If the officer decided to stop him, Dex would have a good excuse: the midday news, for which he was a camera operator. Trinka did not appear to be home, so with a final glance into the window's reflection, he turned and started on his way. He kept his gaze locked on his com.

"Hey, Dex," said the tiny hologram of Fletch. "Just wanted to say 'I told you so.' Remember that chick Sheila Willy I told you about? She sent me a link to this news story on WorldCom. There's a rally going on in New Zealand about the Sanctuary, so I wasn't completely out of line about my conspiracy theories last week. Some heteros down there are actually standing up to the NRO. Looks like it's getting pretty intense. You should check it out. Totally buried in the 'society' section of the WorldCom site, so I guess there's still *some* freedom of the press. Made me think of Diana. Hope you're not listening to this in public or whatever. I'm getting nervous again. Ciao."

Fletch's face disappeared. Dex touched the WorldCom menu on the com screen, which brought up a host of stories. He scrolled through them, and there it was, a hologram link. He tapped it with his finger.

A lisping WorldCom reporter sprang to life.

"We bring you an amusing report today from Christchurch, in the territory of New Zealand, where straight rights protestors are gathered in Old Cathedral Square, demanding answers about rumors surrounding the NRO's much-famed and celebrated Antarctic Sanctuary."

The gaysian journalist wore a smirk under his perfectly sculpted black hair. Behind him was a line of grungy protestors who were shouting and holding signs.

"The protestors are adamantly opposed to Queen Vincent's efforts at human progress, voicing concerns that the new breeding laws passed in the last two years have *already* filled the Sanctuary beyond capacity, and the quality of life for illegal carriers and failsafes who have been deported with their offspring is dwindling. Some even claim the quality of life doesn't exist at all."

The hologram cut to a red-haired, bearded man who was screaming at the camera in fanatical bursts.

"There never was a Sanctuary, and they're just *killing* the carriers 'n' failsafes they bring down there! Vincent Metzer is a Satanist who wants nothing more than to rid the world of everything natural! It's a *conspiracy*! God's Army had it right during the Bio Wars! We need to *fight the homosexuals*!"

Spit flew from the man's mouth just before the hologram cut back to the reporter.

"A conspiracy indeed, and boy, could *he* use a brow wax," came the gaysian's sum-up. "While myths concerning the Wilkes Land Sanctuary have been running amok since the Queen's term was extended after the terrorist attacks in Salzburg three years ago, this demonstration is a first for the territory of New Zealand, the gateway through which illegal breeders travel before final departure for Antarctica. For the past seventy-six years, despite the significant political polarization it has inspired, the Sanctuary has been a stimulus for the territory, whose economy previously relied solely on tourism, hetero pornography, and exports. Now, both Sanctuary staff and future residents pass through the country, providing an ample backbone for the local economy. But contrary to what these protestors are arguing, the number of reproductive criminals has been reduced significantly since Queen Vincent passed Mandate 42 two years ago. From Christchurch, this is Erik Milam with WorldCom."

The gaysian disappeared, but his report triggered an entirely new brand of alarm in Dex. After nearly a century, it seemed the Sanctuary's original purpose was starting to fizzle. What frightened him most was that it did not come as a surprise. On three occasions since Diana's disappearance, he had woken in the dead of night to the drumming of fists on doors and harsh but muffled male voices—the Bio Police, making their rounds. If they had begun arresting and disposing of innocent heterosexuals, it was still happening in the shadows.

Maybe Diana knew something I didn't, Dex thought. *Maybe she'd want me to disappear, too.*

A line of preschool children, tethered by a rainbow-colored leash and led by two smiling and flamboyant teachers, passed him as he reached the corner of West Grant Street. He took the opportunity to glance back down Spruce Place to see if the police car was rolling behind him. But no, it was gone already, which suggested an even worse life development:

The Bio Police officer had been there because of him. For whatever reason, he was now under their scope.

CHAPTER 5 ❄ (HER)

B Y SUNDAY EVENING, thinking ahead became Grace's only option.
Dinner with the family was a weekly tradition, despite simmer-
ing tension over value differences regarding the Queen's looming
agenda. Grace had become the unacknowledged elephant in the room
over the past thirteen years, since everybody (though they never
mentioned it) had realized her place in society was slipping through
the cracks. It would come soon now, considering both her bleeding
and Mandate 43: a reckoning, a fight to save her—or let social progress
snuff her out.

Her thirty-two-year-old brother Abraham, now once divorced,
once widowered, and sporting a pale, eleven-year-old son named
Lars, was bringing his new boyfriend Daryl to dinner. Lars had taken
a liking to Daryl, a copywriter, snobby as they came, who worked for
the Bureau of Sexual Progress. Abraham claimed Lars liked Daryl
more than he himself did but that it was good for the boy to have a
second father figure in his life. Grace knew her brother better than
that, however. Daryl filled a psychological gap for him. Abraham did
not enjoy being alone.

With a creepy son like Lars, I can't blame him, Grace thought.

She walked out of the guest house, past the pool, and up the brick sidewalk toward the patio. The crabapple trees—her dad's favorite—arched over her, gliding behind with each step. Stuart Jarvis had a passion for tending gardens, and during summer, this one was a spectacle to behold. Now, it was barren of color, swallowed by the growing cold of autumn. Grace slowed to savor each step as she realized the plants might never again bloom in her presence, if banishment truly was a risk she now faced.

During dinner, the bleeding happened just after Abraham had taken a scoffing Daryl into the kitchen to slice dessert (Daryl had deemed the fruit torte too fattening, to Stuart's face). Lars, who was sitting with his usual shrewd expression across from Grace, was wearing a subtle but unmistakable grin.

"You like fruit torte, don't you Lars?" Stuart said.

"I agree with Daryl," the boy said. "Too fattening."

"You could use some meat on those bones," Stuart muttered, ignoring the warning eye from his husband.

Grace decided to inject some neutrality into the conversation. "I'm going to go wash my hands. Got some olive oil on them."

She stood up, turned, and started walking. Suddenly, Stuart whispered, "Oh, my God, *honey.*"

Blood had soaked through the rear of her brand-new skirt and smeared on the plush dining room chair seat. Dark red, no mistaking it. There had been no pain to warn her, and her latest stuffing of sanitary wipes had failed.

"James, give me that extra napkin!" Whispers, all whispers, because of Daryl. On the other side of the table, Lars was staring, calculating.

"Honey, she's bleeding! Give me that napkin!" Stuart hissed at his husband. James's eyes widened in confusion, and he grabbed the extra napkin. Stuart slammed it onto the chair, then jumped up and rubbed it into the seat's fabric. He pointed a sharp finger at James, but his eyes were flicking in a concerned manner toward Lars. "Grace cut herself on the steak knife, and it got on the chair. We have to go look at it. Keep that blood covered, and cancel dessert. Too fattening after all. *Honey, if you question me on this, I'll regret I ever took your name.*"

James nodded, but there was a nagging disapproval in his expression, just as there had been in the hospital, the night Grace had been attacked by the Dyke Patrol. She caught a glimpse of it just as Stuart ushered her out of the room, blocking the view of her skirt from Lars.

"She wasn't using a knife," Grace heard her nephew say.

THEY WERE RUSHING DOWN THE FAR HALL, toward the bathroom.

"I don't know, Dad, I don't know, I didn't want to tell anybody—"

"When? When did it start?"

"Four days ago, only a couple times, but it hurt—"

"Why didn't you tell me? I'm a doctor, for God's sake! You're sure it's been bleeding from your vagina? Like menstruation? Christ, that isn't even possible."

But they both knew it could be.

He slammed on the bathroom lights, opened the toilet, and forced her down. Grace's breaths were sharp, her tears running with fear and humiliation. "But Daryl! He's here! What if he sees? Lars already knows I didn't cut myself on the knife! I could have made up something else!"

"What, an anal fissure?" Stuart growled, not out of anger but out of absolute concern. "Actually, that could work. Say you were experimenting with regular sex and it got a bit rough. I can cover Lars. I'll tell him I made the knife excuse so you wouldn't be embarrassed."

"But will Daryl buy that? Fissures wouldn't make me bleed like that, would they?"

"He doesn't have to see the blood, and neither does Abraham. Christ, Grace, this is just the type of thing that'll give the Queen an excuse to start his genocide!"

It was the first time either of them had used that word about the Queen's agenda.

Stuart put a hand on his daughter's shoulder. For some reason, Grace's gaze was glued on his wedding ring as it moved toward her. "Now, let me ask you, and be totally honest with me! I won't judge you, even though it would make no sense since Metzer is about to pass Mandate 43, but have you been menstruating? Did you get the gene switch procedure to become a carrier?"

Grace buried her face in her hands, too frightened to shake her head. Her dad gaped at her, wide-eyed.

"*Did you get the procedure?* Honey, it's okay if you did! Just tell me so I can know how to go about this—"

"No!" Grace choked back a sob. "No, I didn't get the gene switch! I just started bleeding!" Now, a stab of pain in her abdomen made her wince and double over.

Stuart caught her. "Jesus Christ," came his whisper.

"I'm sorry, Daddy."

"Morning sickness?"

"I was throwing up for a while in the morning."

"What, Grace? Did you think it was a *disease*? Diseases don't happen anymore! What did you think it was?"

"I didn't want to think!"

She hoped her father had followed through as inconspicuously as possible and kicked Abraham, Lars, and Daryl out for the night. Even if it worked, they would still wonder what happened to her, and she would be lucky if Lars had not already piped up that smart little voice of his.

No, this definitely wasn't menstrual bleeding, Stuart told her, but—here came the shock—it might not be a miscarriage either. It very well could be, but unless this was something other than a pregnancy, it was possible the baby was still alive.

"In the olden days, you'd have been in the hospital right away. I'm no expert in bioengineering, but I know the basics. I've had pregnant carriers visit my clinic before."

"Like Bonnie Henderson."

"Yes, like Bonnie Henderson. She had bleeding when she was carrying for Bill and Don, and it actually was quite heavy. Her engineer was the primary caregiver, but I saw her file. A number of things can cause bleeding. In her case, it was a partially detached placenta. That's the part that connects the baby—"

"To the carrier. I know."

"In any case, I'll have to examine you at the office. We'll say it's just a routine checkup for non-pathogenic abnormalities, because you've been having headaches."

It was embarrassing to hear her dad's questions. Had there been any signs other than morning sickness? On what occasion was it likely she had conceived? Could there be more than one possibility? Had she ever taken any strange drugs?

And then the answers: yes, apart from the morning sickness, there had also been fatigue on and off. ("Classic symptoms of pregnancy," her dad muttered as he checked her pulse.) It could only have happened that one night during the orgy, with Salt and Pepper. And the drugs? No, they had been standard, as far as Grace knew. Just typical party drugs that would not cause unpredictable genetic problems. Virus-based mutating solutions came in syringes; there had been no syringes, and even so, no street drug could perform the zinc finger switch that activated a female's ovarian $Lrh1$ genes. That happened with vectors, Stuart explained, altered viruses that carried genes engineered to produce the zinc finger proteins. These then bound to DNA in a woman's ovaries to activate the $Lrh1$ gene responsible for ovulation. The process was extremely complex, nothing a woman could instigate on her own.

Breathe, Grace. Breathe, Dad.

But this was quite the quandary.

The Lrh1 gene switch could happen only once in a woman. It was a one-way procedure to trigger fertility in a heterosterile. Geneticists had yet to find a way to reverse fertility after gene switches, because the DNA manipulation it required always caused severe or deadly mutations. Furthermore, it would be impossible to pass her off as a carrier in any official sense, because the TruthChip identification plate in her wrist was clear. Grace Emilia Jarvis was registered as heterosterile, and only an unforeseen genetic mutation or a zinc finger switch could have made her otherwise. If she had somehow been born a genetic mistake, the option of illegally switching her from fertile to sterile was also riddled with obstacles. As a general practitioner, Stuart Jarvis was not qualified to authorize experimental gene switches, even when they were legal. As a genetipsychologist, however, his husband James was.

"But even if your father *could* authorize an experimental procedure like that," Stuart said, "the decision would have to go through a hundred different people, both at the clinic and in the local and intercontinental branches of the NRO. They'd know you were a genetic mistake, and you'd be banished. I don't know how long we can hide this!"

Grace had seen her dad panic only once, the night of her attack. To see it again was unnerving.

"What about tampons or pads, those things carriers use?" she asked, feeling sick with worry. "Is there any way for me to get them? If I did miscarry, doesn't it mean I might start menstruating all the time, like a carrier?"

"Once a month, give or take. And tampons and pads are only sold under strict supervision by the BGR, and you, my dear, won't have the proper identification to receive those from any clinic."

"*Your* clinic, though? Do *you* have access to them? Does Father?"

"Neither of us would. It's not part of my Wellness Care Jurisdiction, and your father doesn't have clearance to prescribe them to carriers. He just . . . picks their brains to make sure they're good candidates. Besides, each pad or tampon package is tracked by the Bureau, so it'd leave a trail of red tape. Damn it, Grace!"

"I didn't try! I didn't know, Daddy!"

But he had not meant it as a scolding. A moment later, he grabbed her into a hug and whispered, "Well, you can always keep using sanitary wipes."

Grace chuckled, burying her face into his slippery silk shirt. "You're not going to turn me in?"

Stuart Jarvis squeezed his daughter extra hard. "Not on your life, Pix. But we need to find you help, and fast."

He let her go and began pacing back and forth. Grace sat back on the toilet, then folded her hands and looked down at the limestone floor tiles. It was a creeping mixture of uncontrollable selfishness and lonely dread that brought Salt and Pepper's face to mind.

"If it really is a pregnancy, should I try to find the father?" she whispered.

Stuart stopped. He looked at her with a wary expression. "Would you really want to put a failsafe in that sort of danger?"

What frightened Grace most, right then on the toilet, was that, for this all-important question, she had no immediate answer.

A MEMORY ✳ (HIM)

*T*HE WORLD IS AN EASY PLACE *for little Dexter, because all he has to worry about is what and who he'll play with on any given day. He loves the sun, and he loves it even more when his mothers take him to the community center in Nowthen. It has a bright and shallow pool with a large, mushroom-shaped umbrella where water rains down onto him and the other children.*

Today, his parents have him in the women's locker room, and they are changing into their swim-suits. His mother Karen is fixing her hair and checking messages on her com with a frown. As always, something is making her feel to Dexter like a rainy day. His mom Roberta is busy socializing with Susan and Jessica Claiborne, both of whom are naked and drawing Dexter's three-year-old eyes.

"He's getting so big!" Susan says, beaming down at Dexter, who hides behind Roberta, neither confused by the fact nor noticing that he is watching the spot between Susan's legs, where it looks different from his own and there is hair. It pleases him, somehow.

Her boy Tommy smacks Dexter on the head.

"Tag, you're it!" he screams, but Dexter doesn't understand the game, so tears form in his eyes.

"Tommy, play nice!" Susan says. "Go find your brother!"

There's something about all of this that makes Dexter want to keep hiding. Susan leans down, and her breasts tumble into his face. She is oblivious that Dexter is for some reason noticing them. "Honey, are you okay? Don't mind Tommy. He's not as well behaved as you are!"

She has made it all okay. The swat on his head is forgotten.

Tommy's other mother Jessica is just as beautiful as Susan. Red hair falls over her face in a way that sends a warm feeling through Dexter. The woman smiles, but he can tell (the way he can with his mother Karen) that it isn't the same kind of smile his mom and Susan have.

Jessica says, "I still can't believe you guys let him be a surprise. Doesn't it make you nervous?"

An ant on the floor catches Dexter's eye, and he runs from his mom's side and follows it down the length of the changing bench. He passes his mother Karen just in time to see her look up at Jessica and let out a sigh, the same one she does when she has helped him build a tower of building blocks, and he knocks it over on purpose.

His mom Roberta, however, looks at Jessica and stands a bit higher. "I'm being optimistic," she says. "Call me a dreamer, but I think the world was better off when things like who a child was going to be could be a surprise."

"Yeah, but won't that do a number on his mind, once he gets older? Finding out he's only here to be . . . a backup plan?"

The ant has disappeared. Dexter listens to the conversation, but it is made of grownup words, so he settles next to the bench, watching a group of older boys by the door who are waiting in uniform patience for their mothers. Some of them are touching each other's swimming suits and giggling. All Dexter can think of are the pool sounds and bright sparkles coming through the door, and he wants his mothers to hurry up, because it is sunny and hot outside, and the cool water awaits.

CHAPTER 6 ✳ (HIM)

"I T'S THOSE FUCKING FAGGOT *MEN*," Fletch drunkenly spouted to Dex before taking another sip of whiskey. He had bags under his eyes and, for the first time since Dex had known him, smelled slightly of body odor. "Men have always had the upper hand of power, but since the homo ones took over the world, mothers like *yours* had to get the short end of the stick! First they engineered bisexuals and trannies right out of society, then they cut out almost all the heteros, and now they're going after females! The whole lot of them! How the fuck do they expect humanity to survive?"

It was Wednesday, the fifteenth of November, and they were each on their fourth drink at Sterile Me Susan's. Fletch had left a message with his fellow government dissenter friend Sheila Willy three days before to ask if Diana's supposed bleeding episode might mean anything to her. The woman had not yet returned his calls, so he and Dex were spending this Wednesday's whiskey session discussing the next best thing: political and sociogenetic progression. It was Dex's mom Roberta's birthday, so their angle on the topic was lesbians.

"Hell, I almost feel *safe* around them, compared to the fags," Fletch continued. "I feel like they've been suppressed enough to know what it's like for us. Except for the biker gangs, obviously. Thank God men still tend to be stronger."

Lesbians did not as a rule carry a stigma (despite there being a relatively small ratio of them in political and medical power), but as individuals, they were considered lesser citizens when it came to reproducing. Why? Because females carried two X chromosomes, which could only produce females, and males carried both X and Y chromosomes, which could produce either sex. Over the past thirteen years, the Queen had reduced the engineering quota of females to only one fourth of what it had been before his rise to power, and it was getting lower every year. As a result, most lesbian couples were being forced to engineer males, which was impossible without their borrowing Y chromosomes from male donors. Never mind that all human embryos still needed an ungeneticized ovum shell to develop, and this rendered males just as dependent on females for reproduction. It was as if the post-Bio War world had forgotten that the science behind this modern process was extreme to begin with; all combined same-sex genes inserted into an egg also had to undergo extensive manipulation in order to mimic the natural developmental process dictated by male and female genetics. But people turned a blind eye.

Now, Mandate 43 was about to change everything. Soon, genetic material and eggs would be the only necessities. Female carriers, even homosexual ones, would be cast aside in favor of test tubes.

The music in Sterile Me Susan's was still low enough for Fletch's voice to carry across it. His rant was becoming dangerous, even for a hetero bar.

"Seriously, this stuff is getting scary, Dex! There's no balance of power anymore. People, especially lesbians, have to stand up and do something about it! Do you realize Mandate 43 will single handedly put us all out of commission? They're not just making heteros unnecessary, as if they are somehow immune to making a mistake and ever needing us to breed again, but they're making *females* unnecessary. Where are the female politicians to stand up against this shit?"

"Too scared to run for office," Dex replied. "Ever since Luna Vega."

Luna Vega had been a lesbian who ran for the chair seat of the Intercontinental Social Council six years earlier. She won it, then was found dead in her apartment a day later. To this day, not even WorldCom had reported any official explanation of her death.

Fletch shook his head. "They can't *possibly* go through with it. I mean, phasing out carriers? That means they'll just breed lesbian females and use them to harvest eggs! Doesn't anyone *care*? You grew up seeing that discrimination happening, right? Weren't your moms, like, some of the first dykes to be bred sterile?"

"Yeah, at least in Minnesota," Dex said, sipping his whiskey. The bar's dim, red lighting was starting to spin. He felt both weightless and heavy. Drunk, or at least getting there.

The extraction of mature female eggs had always been simple, the first part of the process either homosterile or heterosterile carriers-to-be went through to make their bodies viable for gestation. Fifty to a hundred eggs were always harvested, emptied of all their genetic material to become mere shells, and then frozen until the carrier's body, six months off the Lrh1 gene switch, was menstruating and ready for embryos. Genetic re-engineering had become a well-oiled process.

The seed for homosexual rule had been planted in the early 2000s, as far as Dex knew. While genetipolitics had always interested him as far as they concerned current events, his interest in political history had just recently blossomed. All he really knew (or needed to know) was that homosexuals had once been a repressed sector of society, a tarnish on what old-fashioned breeders had blanket termed "the family." While the hushed-up United Nations mission to thin out Earth's population by infecting humans with HIV had helped reduce the number of homosexuals, it had failed on a broader scale. Families in the developed world had still ballooned in numbers, eaten up the planet's resources, and caused an international social collapse.

It wasn't until the development of God's Army and the Bio Wars, however, that the effort to curb population actually succeeded. Again, the heterosexuals had been at fault; this time, they had perpetuated outright murder and terrorism in an effort to fight back against the homosexuals who had risen to power and begun to suppress them. Entire regions—continents, almost—had fallen to chemical and biological plagues that, in those final months, would have spread far enough to wipe out most of humanity were it not for the obstructer bombs dropped by the military to stop them. Cities that had once been power centers of the planet—New York, Los Angeles, London, Hong Kong, and countless others—were still in ruins.

A history lesson not to be repeated.

Fletch ran a hand through his black hair, which hung to his rounded shoulders. "I want to get my TruthChip replaced so nobody knows I'm a failsafe. People are talking, man. You know that group I was telling you about before? They said the NRO is going to stage a terrorist attack and use it as an excuse to blame it on heterosexuals, so it's okay to round us up for mass killing. And you know what? I wouldn't be surprised. I think we all know it's coming, if it hasn't started happening already. The Sanctuary won't be able to handle *everyone*, you know? It's big, but not that big. That's why I want to beat the NRO to the punch. Cause some motherfucking damage!"

Dex turned back to the bar to sip his drink, feeling his face flushing with self-consciousness. Not only was the possibility of genocide still a taboo subject to discuss in public, but any mention of resistance, particularly terrorism, could land the Bio Police on their backs in a matter of minutes. Dex drank, then said to Fletch in a low voice, "Shut up, Fletch. I mean it. Wrong person hears you talking like that, and we're both fucked."

It was as if he had spoken the words to a brick wall.

"I mean, look at what the fucking NRO is capable of, man!"

"I said *shut up*," Dex hissed.

"They're evil! Think about HIV, Dex! The fags used that shit to make chicks sterile, just to get back at the heteros. It was an RNA virus, and that United Nations group used it with gene therapy or whatever. This was, like, *way* before they figured out the whole zinc finger switch thing, but it just goes to show—"

"I don't really know the technicalities of genetics," Dex said with a hushed voice, leaning over his drink. In his peripheral vision, he noticed the bartender Clara watching Fletch like a cow in heat.

"Dex, dude, it's *history*!" the man slurred. "You've got to know it, or you can't back up your opinions about the *now*. I bet you don't even know why mitochondrial DNA restructuring is important!"

"You're drunk, and no, I don't. I bet you don't either."

"It's, like, that thing," Fletch said before taking a gulp so large it barely stayed in his mouth. "I mean, so the chromosomes read right, and everything develops normally when they put same-sex genes together! Proteins, man! You gotta know this shit!"

"Yep, proteins."

A hand, followed by an arm, floated through the air behind Fletch and tapped his shoulder. It looked like some sort of sea creature.

I'm drunk, Dex thought.

"Fletch, right?"

A woman. Nervous voice, the meek type.

He and Fletch turned at the same time.

Standing behind them was a woman in a black pants suit— perfect breasts, not too large, not too small, a trim body, and a round face that complemented the innocence in her voice. Dex recognized her right away.

It was the woman from the orgy two months ago.

CHAPTER 7 ✳ (HER)

Here Grace stood, in front of Salt and Pepper, about to destroy his life.

What kind of awful person had she become?

Their baby was perfectly alive. Her dad had confirmed the pregnancy the previous week. The bleeding, he thought, had been caused by a marginal placenta previa and subchorionic bleeding. Stuart had cared for enough carriers over his career to have a clue. His examination with the ultrascope had been hasty; he had not even given her a chance to look, because another patient had been due any minute. But he had seen the living being inside her, behind the ultrascope's electronic glass visor. The vision had brought him to tears.

Grace had found herself in the late hours of sleepless nights longing to talk with Salt and Pepper, to share the desperation and terror. Both had changed her. Anger had wrapped around fear and tricked her into justifying the desire to divide this burden. Salt and Pepper was half responsible, after all. Despite her dad's recommendation to rest as much as possible, she had begun frequenting Sterile Me Susan's. She knew Fletch Novotny was a regular patron, because the bartender had known him by name the two times she had met him here with Todd Bender. She had hoped to find him in order to learn more about Salt and Pepper.

And yes, in the back of her mind, she had also hoped for this: to meet the beautiful, horrible stranger face to face.

But anger and fear were not tools Grace had ever used to manipulate her world. She could no sooner hope ill for this man than watch herself sour from within. What had she planned to say? How had she ever thought this would be good, right, and satisfying?

When Salt and Pepper recognized her, guilt began to run its course.

CHAPTER 8 ✳ (HIM)

E VEN IN THE DIMLY LIT BAR, the beauty that had drawn Dex to this woman two months ago was striking; only now, there was something melancholy coloring her expression. He had never learned her name. Embarrassed, he turned his face back to the bar, as if he had been in the process of waiting for another drink, despite the refill sitting in front of him.

"Oh, it's you," he heard Fletch say in drunken surprise.

"Yes, Grace Jarvis," she said. "We met a couple of months ago through Todd Bender."

Grace. It was a nice name. Simple, to the point.

"Of course," Fletch said. "I remember. We all had some fun if I recall."

Behind the bar, Clara glared in Grace's direction. Fletch was probably smothering the poor woman by now, so Dex turned to follow Clara's glower.

Grace was staring straight at him. A magnetic rush passed between them immediately: a trace of the lust that had brought them together the night of the orgy, but also something more. Something deeper. Heat rose in Dex's face.

Grace dipped into a nervous smile, then shook her head. "Sorry," she said, "Maybe I shouldn't have—"

"No, sit!" Dex jumped off his seat to offer it, but his foot curled around its wooden leg, and he went flailing into Fletch's lap. Grace erupted in laughter as Fletch pushed Dex back toward the stool. Dex found his feet, but he knew there was no way he could hide the wobble in his legs. "What I meant to say was . . . I'm sorry I didn't say goodbye that night."

He was making a fool of himself, but Grace appeared to soften with relief. Despite her polite smile, however, there was a tightness in her face, as if her sudden jollity were masking some hidden anxiety. Grace reached for her rear left hip and itched it as she sat in his seat. *A nervous quirk*, Dex thought. *She did that the night I had sex with her.*

"So, what brings you out tonight?" Dex asked, thankful for the tipsy grin helping to mask his shyness. "Looking for another party like last time?" The words spilled out as a joke, but they sounded perfectly horrid as they hit Grace's gentle face.

"Hot, you studbucket. Really hot," Fletch said, chuckling.

Grace swallowed, then offered a restrained grin. "Actually, no. I was just meeting with a coworker here, and I saw you two and wanted to say hi."

Fletch leaned forward and placed a hand on the woman's knee. "What is it you do again, Grace Jarvis?" His eyes were flitting back and forth between her face and her breasts. Seemingly unaware of his need for a shower, he rested his free arm on the bar and tried to draw Grace's gaze with a ripple of his bicep.

Grace closed her eyes and shook her head, as if warding off tears. "Actually, it's not looking too good. I work for the Minneapolis Neighborhood Development Council as a preservation specialist in charge of Obesaland."

Fletch shook his head and scoffed with an unbecoming spray of saliva. He tried to hide it by taking one last sip from his empty glass and using a napkin to wipe his mouth. "Obesaland? Christ, honey, let's get you drunk. Or we could all go back to my place and do what we did last time." Now he was staring straight at the crotch of her pants suit. "You need something nice to get that hellhole neighborhood out of your mind. Ugly people aren't good for the soul. You game for some action tonight?"

The young woman stiffened at this and dragged her legs out from under Fletch's hand. She turned to her right, checking out the rest of the bar.

"Fletch, get the hell off her." Dex leaned carefully in toward Grace and pushed Fletch away. With a scowl, Fletch turned his flirtation to Clara while ordering another whiskey. "Sorry," Dex continued. "Fletch can be kind of a prick."

Grace let out a nervous chuckle, then shook her head. "It's okay. Just embarrassing."

"What's embarrassing?"

"Us, here. I mean, having come to say hello."

"Why, because of our . . . night together?"

"Kind of. Group sex has never been my thing."

"It's okay. We've all been there."

"I hadn't."

Grace turned to him and smiled. She couldn't be much older than twenty-five, unless she was simply extra good at looking vulnerable. He was closer now and could see her face jittering with nerves.

Fletch scampered off to the back room, leaving them alone. Grace straightened a strand of her dark hair, twice. "So, you're good friends with Fletch, then? The guy I was dating ran off with him and another girl that night, before you swooped in."

Dex sat on Fletch's stool now and maintained a healthy but friendly distance from Grace. "Friends? I guess. More like acquaintances who just happen to hang out every Wednesday. Otherwise, I pretty much just keep to myself. Kind of hard being a failsafe these days. Don't want to be caught in the wrong crowd."

With a hint of trepidation, Grace said, "Does Fletch know a lot of radicals then? He seems to."

"He talks like he wants to be one of them, but I'm not sure how serious he is about any of it. And I'm sorry he was hanging all over you."

Grace smiled, but it looked strained. "You seem like a gentleman. I thought that was something I'd only ever see in the old novels and movies. What did they call it . . . *chivalry*? Something like that."

An educated girl. But he could tell the small talk was an act.

"Yeah, chivalry. A dead art of heterosexuals past." Dex smiled, and Grace looked down at the bar top and traced the grain patterns in the wood with her index finger. Dex followed the tender motion, watching the finger blur lightly as Clara mixed a drink in the background.

"I didn't come up here to say hi to Fletch," Grace said suddenly, clenching her hand into a fist. She was crying.

Dex glanced around the bar, hoping for Grace's sake that people were not already staring. "Whoa, whoa, did I say something? Are you all right?"

"I shouldn't be doing this. I need to go home," was all she said before turning around and running out of the bar. Fighting his dizziness, Dex hopped off the stool, grabbed his jacket, and followed her. The crowd of people filled Grace's wake almost as quickly as she left it, but when he finally made it through them and stepped outside, she was under the street light, looking up. The first snowflakes Dex had seen all season were falling from the sky. Despite her tears, Grace seemed to be taking a moment to appreciate them.

Dex hailed her a cab. Because he was drunk, he climbed in as well.

A MEMORY ✳ (HER)

GRACE IS SIX YEARS OLD, *walking through her dad's garden, which is nothing less than a magic wonderland, filled with beauty, secret passageways, trees that might just lean over and whisper in her ear, and flowers she imagines might someday start to sing. In her imagination, there are always little tiny people living in the garden, ducking out of sight whenever a normally-sized human comes trampling about. If she never sees them, how can she know they aren't there?*

It is morning on a Sunday, and the garden sparkles under the rising sun. A rainbow hovers inside the spray of Stuart's hose as he waters the bright orange lilies. Grace is walking over a brick pathway with her arms spread like wings, pretending the garden bridge is a tightrope over a craggy canyon.

"Why do you like gardens, Daddy?" *she says.*

"Because they keep me in touch with what matters most in the world," *Stuart answers.*

"And what matters most?"

"Life!"

"What's that even mean?" *Grace giggles.* "Why does life matter?"

"Because, without it, the world would be a cold, meaningless place. Don't you think? What if there weren't any people? What if we had never engineered you?"

"I'd be sad," Grace says, jumping off the stone walkway onto the cold, dew-covered grass. A butterfly passes in front of her, and she imagines being one of those tiny people, riding on its back. The garden must be a jungle to them.

"You wouldn't be sad, because you wouldn't exist!" Stuart says, twitching his wrist so the hose water chases Grace for a moment. She giggles again and runs from it. A loose tooth moves as she presses her tongue against it. Today could be the day it comes out, and then the Tooth Fairy will visit. Maybe the Tooth Fairy lives in the garden!

"I'd still be sad," she insists.

"Maybe you would be. Or maybe the world would be sad without you. How's that for an argument?"

"I like arguments."

"Yes, Pix, I know you do. That's why it's impossible to get you to eat beets when we make them."

"Abraham can eat mine." This makes Stuart smile. Then: "Daddy, do you think I'll be a carrier when I grow up?"

From the corner of her eye, she sees her dad grimace and turn toward the daffodils. He thinks he is hiding the reaction from her by turning away, but he isn't. "Being a carrier can be sad," he says. "You have to say goodbye to the babies you bring into the world. Once you're a carrier, the NRO has a lot of control over you. Would you like that?"

"No, I don't think so." Grace jerks her head toward the snapdragons, her favorite flower. One of the tiny people had been peeking out of a flap on the petal; she will swear it to anyone who asks. "But Daddy?"

"Yeah, Pix?"

"What would happen if the NRO sent me to the Sanctuary?"

"They won't send you to the Sanctuary, honey."

"But what if they do?" There, another tiny person, climbing up the rope on her garden swing! It had to be! She was close to seeing it this time. And they might very well so send her to the Sanctuary. Her dad is just making light of her question. Everyone knows girls are always at risk of being sent away. That's just how things are.

"If they took you to the Sanctuary, I'd come and find you and we'd fly back home on a penguin!" Stuart says, making the kind of joke a parent makes when the conversation becomes uncomfortably serious. He thinks Grace doesn't know why he did that, but she does. It is because her questions scare him.

They scare him.

CHAPTER 9 ❄ (HER)

THE LIGHT FROM THE OPEN CAB DOOR made Salt and Pepper's eyes more visible: grayish blue with a spark of kindness. He closed the door, and his face turned black against the street lights. Grace's pulse quickened, but not out of fear. It was just unexpected, even though she had been ordering mocktails at Sterile Me Susan's every night for the past two weeks. Here he was now, in the flesh: all her imagined, hypothetical scenarios made real. Either he was too drunk to ask why she had just broken down into tears, or he was too polite.

"I'm Dex, by the way."

Grace turned and caught his eye, hoping the blush on her face was invisible in the darkness. "Thanks. I never quite caught your name."

He chuckled. "Yeah, we were a little busy last time, weren't we?"

Dex drummed his fingers on his knee, staring downward, looking shy. He was older than Grace, a very fit late thirties. Attractive though, in a gentle way most men lacked, except perhaps for her own dad.

"Wayzata," she told the driver. "Ferndale Woods Road."

They left the city.

WAYZATA WAS ONE OF THE LAST SUBURBS of Minneapolis to have

maintained the natural landscape that had borne it. It was also one of the oldest "upscale" areas in the Twin Cities region, having been home to some of the most prominent businessmen in the region's history as far back as the 1900s. As doctors, Stuart and James Jarvis were on the lower crust of Wayzata's social ladder, but they were still on the upper crust of luck. James's father, trained as a nutritional geneticist, had also pioneered a startup venture called DoMe Clinic, which provided safe, simple, and one-time gene modification sessions that would increase the body's ability to regenerate muscle tissue, ensuring men a simplified path to physical perfection. The business had earned him nearly half a billion dollars.

The home his money had afforded the Jarvis family was a perfect throwback to the olden days, before survivors of the Bio Wars had sought refuge in the Midwest and forced an unprecedented amount of suburban sprawl to be constructed. The mansion's cobblestone driveway stretched through a grove of maple trees, then looped back in a circle, ringing around an aging fountain depicting a nude Zeus. His phallus pointed outward in erect sexual reverence, and Grace would never forget the sparkle that had lit her Grandpa Jarvis's eyes every time he passed the statue. "My favorite sculpture," he always said. "His member looks just like the one your Grandfather Soren had, God rest his soul."

Grace had always smiled widely, loving Zeus's penis, too, solely because it made her one living grandparent so happy.

Men. All they think about is sex, she thought now. *I wonder if Dex is the same.*

The cab driver whistled and leaned forward, peering out the window with a jealous glower. "Nice place you got here, sister. Funny how someone like you can still have it so good."

"I'm sorry, I forgot to tell you I live in the guest house," Grace replied, leaning toward the wraithlike fag, who for some reason smelled like pork. "You can just drive around past the front door, then drop us off by that smaller driveway around back."

"How about you get out right here?" the driver sneered.

Dex opened his door and gestured for Grace to do the same. Following his lead, she climbed out and shut her side of the cab. Dex leaned down, into the driver's face. "How about we don't pay you?" he yelled, then slammed his door. When the taxi sped away, he turned to Grace and laughed. "I don't have a lot of patience for people like that anymore."

"Do you want to come in?"

"Do you want me to?"

Risk it, she thought. *Feel him out. See if telling him will do any good.*

TWO HOURS LATER, Grace wondered how it was possible they were still talking. Dex Wheelock, mysterious and beautiful, had suggested after a quick tour and a round of small talk that they make tea. Herbal, so as not to upset their eventual sleep. There, at her kitchen table, he grew sober, looking more and more comfortable in the transition. Dex's smile had different forms, but it was always there. Drunk, he could not hold back an edgy brand of silliness: jokes about hetero bars, fleeting over-dramatic swooshes of his thick eyelashes, fingers dancing like ballerinas on the granite tabletop. Sober, his gentleness remained, though it was underscored by something serious. Loneliness, perhaps? Soon, Grace had the skinny on his life. Born to two lesbians, he had been self-outed as a failsafe at fifteen, had lost his best friend to a hate crime eight years later, and still had one mother who wished he had been engineered normally, even after thirty-seven years.

Only nine years my senior, Grace thought. *Not yet old enough to make this creepy.*

Dex was also a camera operator for Twin Cities Com and usually worked from ten in the morning until seven at night, for the noon and early-evening newscasts. He liked chocolate macadamia nut cookies; they were a rare indulgence. He had once posed in an underwear commercial without having to scan his TruthChip and thereby divulge his sexual orientation, only to be removed from the ad once an acquaintance from the newsroom saw it and ratted him out to the marketing agency in charge. He enjoyed exercise and being physically fit, and not just for the usual reasons of vanity instilled in their culture by the New Rainbow Order. It gave him a sense of peace in a world that often felt like a giant maze of sameness.

"Work, exercise, women—wash, rinse, repeat," he said.

Hmmm.

Grace told him about herself: the social development work with Obesaland, her teenage weight problem, her politically polarized fathers, and the recent attack in front of Pommie's Pub. Her privileged life had still managed to hand her lemons, and now she was trying to make lemonade. Dex chuckled at the ancient cliché. For the second time that night, his laughter made Grace nervous. Her imminent revelation was about to make him the victim. If he was wise, he would then run as far away from her as possible. Wash, rinse, repeat.

"I'm a genetic mistake, and you got me pregnant." The words were desperate, stuck in her throat. To utter them now would mean giving up the comfort growing between them. *"Sorry, I can't get involved,"* he'd say. *"If the Bio Police find out, they'll take you, and they'll take me too. I can't risk throwing my life away."*

"You're a beautiful woman, Grace Jarvis."

She blinked, covering for the spark that jumped to life in her heart.

"You're just saying that because you want to screw me again."

Dex smiled. "I'd be a lucky man to have you twice. I'll keep that ball in your court. I've been going through some stuff lately anyway, so it might not be smart."

Oh, really?

The story of Diana Kring came out suddenly and left Grace in shock: a girlfriend who had disappeared, a mysterious bleeding episode witnessed by others, a cold trail left to the caverns of speculation. The woman had bled, then disappeared from society without a trace. Nobody but Dex and her father seemed to care.

"I don't know why I'm even telling you this. I shouldn't be putting you in this position." Dex placed a slab of cheese on a cracker and put it into his mouth. He chewed and swallowed. "I mean, either the Bio Police *took* her, or she disappeared on her own. I just don't know. I keep thinking, though, that if Diana was some sort of genetic mistake and the Bio Police got her, they'd have come for me, too. And with a lot of her clothes and stuff being gone, it makes me think she *did* leave on her own, you know? Maybe to get an underground abortion or something, before anybody found out she was a genetic mistake. If that's even what the bleeding was. I'm hoping Fletch's friend might have a clue, if she ever returns his calls. God, you must think I'm insane."

Grace could only shake her head no; she was too frightened to speak.

Dex seemed to take the gesture as sympathy. He ate another cracker, then buried his shimmering eyes in the heels of his hands and rubbed outward, leaving his forehead red. "I'm sorry. It's just . . . I don't really have a lot of people to talk to."

Confusion and dread had replaced Grace's guilt over having lured this man into her life. Dex Wheelock, whom she had remembered for the past two months only as Salt and Pepper, had just become inextricably woven into the fabric of her life. With her next words, Grace tied the final, frightening knot. "If I tell you something, do you promise to keep it to yourself?"

Dex nodded, and Grace spoke.

CHAPTER 10 ✳ (HIM)

This was never supposed to be my context. I was never supposed to create life.

Dex was on the train back into the city, purposefully a different one than Grace would be riding to work in half an hour. They had spent the night together but not slept, ultimately agreeing on something simple but obvious: they needed a game plan before moving forward together publicly, if they were going to do it at all. The options were all horrible, and at one point in the night silence of Grace's bed, she had whispered something terrifying: *"I just don't think I can bring myself to kill it."*

The irony was almost comical. Dex's ability to create life was the very reason he was the way he was. Failsafes were nature's backup, in case society crumbled and the survival of the species depended on old-fashioned breeding methods. If he had not been meant to create life, why was he sexually attracted to women at all? Why had his engineer even bothered to mix him this way, when his mothers had asked for a random surprise?

NRO quota orders, Dex thought. *Even the government knew its plan had inherent pitfalls.*

Now, Grace Jarvis was almost nine weeks pregnant, and he was a father. *A father.*

It left him at a toilsome crossroads. There was no way around it. He was half responsible for putting both their lives in danger, but he also now had to choose either to support whatever decision Grace made about the life growing inside her or to disappear and save his own skin. She had promised not to expose him if he decided to run, but what kind of man would do that? A weak one, surely. Was he weak?

It might not matter what I think if the Queen has his way, Dex thought. *He already has enough military power to back his agenda.*

Furthermore, if government officials really were killing off people at the Antarctic Sanctuary instead of offering them a chance to exist as old-fashioned breeders, fighting the system was not just the noble option but also the smart one. In a way, it was the perfect time to fight, because people might finally be scared enough of the New Rainbow Order to start an uprising. At worst, they would be captured and possibly face persecution or death. At best, they could hide, maybe even retreat to the Unrecoverable Territories and hope to survive in the wild.

And there was another angle to all this, one that sent Dex into the clouds. Who was that little human being growing inside Grace? It was quite literally the result of something as simple and pointless as an orgasm. The very implications of it were astounding: they, Dex and Grace, really were like every other animal after all. It was comforting somehow. For all humanity's collective intellect, there existed a primal beauty in life still untouchable by power and suppression.

What would this baby look like? When would it take its first steps? Experience its first kiss? Would it ever fall in love?

The thoughts brought tears to Dex's eyes, there on the train, as he approached the towering, rainbow-tinted buildings of downtown Minneapolis. If there was going to be any hope for this child, if they really wanted to do the brave thing and fight, Grace needed to find a way to hide. Or disappear. Which led to one final question: Would he have the courage to follow?

CHAPTER 11 ❋ (HER)

A T FAMILY DINNER THE FOLLOWING SUNDAY, James Jarvis cornered his daughter in the kitchen as she was shucking fresh corn from their communal greenhouse.

"You've been avoiding the house, Grace. Hasn't your rectal bleeding stopped by now?"

Grace closed her eyes, pasted nonchalance onto her face, then turned to her father. "Sort of. Dad didn't tell you the details of the appointment, did he? That would just be embarrassing."

"He could have set you up with Dr. Spriggs."

"I'm not going anywhere near a lesbian I barely know. At least I can trust Dad."

James reached around her, coming closer than was necessary. She heard him breathe in as he did so, as if he were trying to sniff out a lie. "That makes one of us, at least."

The kitchen's cool air danced on Grace's heated, damp palms.

Goddamnit.

"One of us? What do you mean?"

James sighed in an overly dramatic manner as he dumped the corn cobs into the kettle. He pretended to loosen the top of his dark magenta turtleneck. "You know, I would think it ill if your dad were to have examined you for one real reason and disclosed to me something completely different."

Play dumb. Just play dumb!

But Grace's voice cracked as she spoke. "What? What do you mean?"

"You know very well what I mean, Grace."

"Anal fissures? Father, I really don't want to be talking about this, especially with Lars in the next room. It was embarrassing enough having him witness that and know what I was doing with my . . . boyfriend." To her credit, her nervousness looked identical to embarrassment, and her face complied with an appropriate blush. But this was close. Too close.

James nodded with a tight, unconvinced smile, then delicately lifted his wine glass and sipped. "Boyfriend? Was this the gray-haired man I saw sneaking out of the guest house on Thursday morning?"

"Sneaking? He wasn't sneaking. He had to get back to the city. He works for Twin Cities Com."

"And he walked to the train, did he?"

"As a matter of fact, he did. He had a lot of things to think about."

"Oh?"

"It's really none of your business, but he felt horrible for having hurt me with his huge…talent." As straight-laced as James Jarvis was, he was just like any other fag. His concentration would quiver at the mention of a large penis.

The bluntness in her lie seemed to catch him off guard. When his eyes cleared of their momentary lust, his entire face contorted with the type of shattered naiveté only a father could show for his daughter. Perhaps his image of Grace as a beautiful, laughing child did not mix well with the image of her being stretched into the realm of anal sex.

But James Jarvis's guard never stayed down for long. He lowered his voice but spoke in the singsong way that implied stupidity on the part of his listener—his way of imposing intimidation. "Promise me one thing," he said.

"Okay. What?"

James swirled his wine. "Promise me that if your bleeding two weeks ago was indeed what it looked like, not to mention the weight you've put on recently, which is unflattering I might add, you'll do the right thing and find a way to get it taken care of. Or turn yourself in before someone does it for you. I'll give you this one chance."

Grace's defensive act flirted with terror, and for a moment, it almost faltered. Then, some primordial force helped her maintain it. It was a protective instinct she had never felt before. Her words came out solid, convincing, and angry.

"If you would willingly destroy your own daughter's life in favor of helping a humanity-hating dictator rise to power, you don't deserve my company. The next time you deal a threat like that, it'll be the last time you ever see me."

James turned back to the boiling corn cobs without a response.

Grace suffered through Sunday dinner with her family, sure now the tradition would soon be ending. At one point, her father, as always sipping his wine like a curious snake, silently shook his head at her in arrogant disapproval.

CHAPTER 12 ✳ (HIM)

A T THE EXACT MOMENT Grace was standing up to her father with a lie, Dex was in downtown Minneapolis, readying holocamera B for recording that evening's Twin Cities Com broadcast. He studied the two shirtless news anchors being misted down in front of the green screen. They were perfect: Adonis bodies, shallow grins, sex drives that were visible with every ripple of their muscles. They rarely made eye contact with Dex, and when they did, the message was clear: *Either fuck me, or get the hell out of this world. Failsafes like you don't belong.*

With the headliner of today's broadcast, such common prejudices could now incorporate not just failsafes but all heterosexual people, including heterosteriles and carriers. They were, as of Monday morning, Sydney time, no longer necessary.

Dex adjusted the camera as Lyle Winston and John Electra primped themselves. This report would first run live, then loop as filler for at least the next two days.

Five. Four. Three. *Two. One.*

"We're headlining today with a new development from the NRO Summit taking place in Sydney," Electra began, "where members of the Intercontinental Bureau of Genetic Regulation have made a historical vote to further standardize reproduction methods around the world.

This comes close on the heels of a straight rights demonstration in New Zealand having turned deadly four days ago, as Antarctic Sanctuary protestors killed four policemen with illegal automatic weapons before being gassed and incarcerated in Canterbury Regional Prison. Today, Chair of the IBGR Nolan Beauvais issued a statement saying that Mandate 43, the first addition to the Rainbow Charter to be passed under that prestigious title since Mandate 42 two years ago, is an even larger social restructuring than has been rumored amongst the general public."

Electra flashed his teeth at Winston. The holo and standard dimension cameras recorded them without judgment or pretext, but their glee was barefaced and unabashed. Anyone watching Twin Cities Com News would see it within seconds.

"That's right, John," Winston said. "To be phased in over the next ten years, Mandate 43 has piggybacked on nearly a century of research and development work for a potential system of nonbiological gestation. Well, that potential is now a reality, and IBGR members have presented a plan and budget for the construction of nearly three thousand gestation clinics across the entire span of the Recovered Territories. Also ruled under the new mandate, expanses still under reconstruction from the Bio Wars, particularly the East and West Coasts of the old United States, western Europe, the Ganges Delta, and the Sichuan basin of old China, will eventually host the development of further clinics in what is to be a hundred-year effort to rebuild once and for all the society that was all but obliterated by God's Army in the twenty-second century."

Dex's gut tightened, sending a burst of worry to his throat.

"Again under the umbrella of Mandate 43 comes news that not only will the NRO oversee construction of these new gestation clinics, but they will also bring the concept of the Wilkes Land Antarctic Sanctuary mainstream by rehabilitating a number of old civilian work camps not used since the period of martial law following the Bio Wars. The camps will be refurbished into self-sufficient reserves in isolated but accessible areas of the Unrecoverable Territories around the world, and as clinical reproduction slowly takes over, ex-carriers, heterosteriles, and failsafes will be given their own sections of society to live in. These reserves will be fully functional and funded by the NRO as long as they are needed, then integrated into regular society once the recovery effort catches up with them."

Once we all die, Dex thought.

Carrier or not, Diana Kring had disappeared without a trace. Was the government already clearing the way for its new utopia? Actively deleting this residual class of people from its perfect system and rebuilding a new, pure world?

Electra took the reporting reins once again. "Mandate 43 is to be the second of two steps in the NRO's effort to re-energize and repopulate the regions of the world most challenged since the Bio Wars," he said. "The first, being Mandate 39, successfully began the process of cleanup and recovery for these key regions they are hoping to repopulate. Thus far, nine years of effort have barely been enough to set the stage for recovery, but the Queen says the goal *is* reachable, step by step. Critics of the effort have not been silent, however, and concern over whether cities like Los Angeles, New York, London, Shanghai, and Tokyo will ever thrive again is rampant. Even so, NRO leaders are confident support for Mandate 43 will be widespread, despite the issues that are sure to be raised by straight rights activists and underground remnants of God's Army, who have, according to the Queen, been difficult to weed out. An attempt to do so will be phased in as early as February, when all registered heterosexuals and carriers will be called to their nearest Bio Police field office for social assessment."

Dex's chest was hot. *Social assessment.* He felt as if all eyes were suddenly on him. He was the only failsafe in the studio.

Just do your job. Record the report. Worry later.

"Furthermore," Electra continued, "as an addendum to the mandate, heterosexual males and females will no longer be able to display affection for one another in public. Those who resist this law will see immediate arrest. Secretary General Metzer explained himself that, and I quote, 'We cannot show the younger generations that it is okay to accept such flagrant disregard for the proper structure of love, sex, and family. Tolerance is destruction.'"

The heat in Dex's chest boiled into a rage. Human life in its most natural form of conception was already a thing of the past, and soon, even birth would be an extinct concept, at least in civilized society. But the construction of new sanctuaries? They would be nothing more than death camps, just like those European dictators built during the twentieth century.

How much time did heterosexuals really have left? If Grace did decide to fight the New Rainbow Order by letting her pregnancy continue, and if Dex followed her, did they or their unborn child really stand a chance?

Doubt clawed at his throat, like a serrated whisper saying no, no, *no*.

CHAPTER 13 ✸ (HER)

FINALLY, MANDATE 43 GAVE Devon Shemple the permission to discriminate openly.

"Your funding request for the Obesaland overhaul has been *denied*, Ms. Jarvis, but don't you pretend for one second that it was just the committee's decision. Mandate 43 changed everything, particularly NRO funding allotments, and there's just no money now to forward the project."

"No money, meaning it's not a priority," Grace said. The world seemed to be falling down around her, and here she sat, in Devon Shemple's office, listening to the incongruous sounds of his cheap coffee table fountain running over the low but incessant dance track playing through his desk com speakers.

Shemple studied his fingernails, holding his bottom lip tight. "Truth be told, it isn't a priority and never has been, Ms. Jarvis. These fatties make no effort to curb their problems and be of use to society. They've been a lost cause for centuries now, but there have always been people like you trying not to make it so. As lovely as such idealism is, it was never realistic. Not to mention heterosteriles just aren't taken seriously anymore. A woman like *you* in charge of a project to save the fat people? Minneapolis would be a laughing stock."

"Then why string me along all this time? It seems silly that the Neighborhood Development Council would have promoted me last year just to give me something to do."

Shemple waved his wrist, then looked out the bright windows. "You had your supporters. Suffice it to say, most of them only wanted to keep in good standing with your parents, because they host some of the most fabulous soirées in the metro."

It was a lost cause, but anger rose in Grace nonetheless. It was akin to that primal, defensive feeling with which she had faced her father. "I had more than just my supporters. I had the NRDA branch already approving forced closure of all stores that sell junk food in the area, not to mention Allied Fitness's cooperation in sponsoring an energizing program for those who need an extra boost. Obesaland needed only sixty thousand dollars to help pay for the project's peripheral costs. *Sixty thousand dollars.* Not much, considering the new heated sex cubes the city just installed outside last month. *And* what the NRO will be spending on their concentration camps."

It was not a joke, but Shemple smiled anyway. "Mandate 43 is forcing realignment with all NRO local and intercontinental government bodies, and Obesaland just needs to find its place."

Grace's fingernails were digging into her palms. "You don't even question the morality of this," she said. "It's astounding. You're just following along with the new mandate, no questions asked."

"And aren't *you*?"

Shemple's accusatory question hit Grace square in the chest, but instead of making her afraid, it ignited an ember of pride in her growing womb. But she had to curb the feeling and curb it now, or he would report her as a probable resistor.

"Of course. I have to go along with it."

"Then you'll understand why I'm going to have to eliminate your position with the Neighborhood Development Council, effective immediately. We've already taken a vote and decided you are not a person who can adequately help deliver this branch of Minneapolis into the new era."

"The new era," Grace repeated. Through the window, her civilization's rainbow-striped flag caught the wind, as if on cue. She chuckled. "You've wanted me out of here ever since you met me, because I was heterosterile. How long do you think it's going to be, Devon Shemple, until all of this crumbles? Until your men in power move this suppression onto lesbians too and use them only for eggs? How long do you think humanity will be able to sustain itself?"

"Sustainability is *not* the question here, Ms. Jarvis. *You* are. See to it your office is cleared by the end of the day."

"It'll be done in ten minutes, *sir.*"

Leaving City Hall and seeing the rainbow flags surrounding the fountain in its courtyard, Grace's throat constricted. Here it was, the storm people had once, long ago, called the gay agenda: rainbow flags, homosexual male dominance, and nothing to check and balance it. History was repeating itself, as if new social orders, attempts at restructuring social psyches, and genocide were somehow new and improved methods of fixing a broken planet. It had been hundreds of years since the last major dictators of the world had succumbed to the factions willing to fight them. Where now, in this rainbow-flagging, wrist-waving global state, were the dissenters? God's Army had failed. Who now would rise?

Grace stood on the City Hall steps, hand on her abdomen, holding her secret.

This is it, she thought. *The time when I have to make a choice. My ideal world is burning alive, and I've been given a gift to put out those flames, at least in a small way.*

She walked across the courtyard to the train platform, where three transparent sex cubes for waiting train passengers were blasting their usual dance tracks. Inside them were nearly two dozen businessmen, some kissing each other, others giving and receiving fellatio. Their suit jackets were thrown on the ground, near their feet. Grace averted her gaze as she always did, and by the time her train sped away three minutes later, most of the men were too busy to catch their ride home.

A MEMORY ✳ (HIM)

*T*HE NEW NEIGHBOR GIRL IS PEEING *in the dirt, out in the woods behind their houses. Dexter is watching from behind his bedroom window, fascinated, hoping desperately his mother and mom won't see. He has very few friends, because he doesn't enjoy playing house and dress-up like all the other first grade boys he knows. Summer vacation is lonely.*

The girl is beautiful. Dexter watched from his yard two days ago as the two dads, the boy, and the girl moved in. The boy is older, and he spent the day complaining at having to help haul things into the house. Obviously they aren't that rich. Only one family on their street has ever hired movers—the people in the big house at the end—but Dexter is curious, because he saw one of the dads push the other out of his way when the boy and girl weren't in the yard. Neither one looked very happy to be moving.

The girl pulls up her shorts and darts off into the woods. Her brown hair is long, curly, wild—like Sally Mushroom, the cartoon character.

Five seconds later, she emerges from the woods and runs straight through the yard to Dexter's back door, then pounds on it.

He freezes.

"What on earth is that?" comes his mother Karen's voice from the kitchen. "Dexter, did you lock yourself out?"

But the door isn't locked, and the girl has already let herself in. She is wandering around the living room when Dexter finally gathers the courage to go meet her.

"Excuse me, can we help you?" Karen says, swinging her wooden cooking spoon at the girl.

"I'm wondering if you have anybody here to play with!" she says, her back to Dex. "I'm Matilda Liverpool! I'm new."

"Yes, you obviously are," Karen says. She gestures toward Dexter, as if to shoo Matilda toward him, and the girl spins around and walks right up to his face. Dexter immediately notices a light layer of hair covering Matilda's top lip, but for some reason, the furry quality fits her perfectly.

"What's your name?" she asks.

"Dexter," he says.

"Dex!" she screams, then grabs him in a hug that knocks his wind out. "I'm going to call you Dex! Let's go play in the woods! Dex, Dexy Dex Dex!"

"Not until you eat lunch," Karen says, giving Dexter her favorite stern look, which is to widen her eyes and squeeze her lips together so it looks as if the bottom of her face is falling in on itself. Then she turns to Matilda. "I suppose I'll be feeding you as well?"

"My dads are at work. My brother watches me during the day."

"And how old are you?"

"Six and a half."

"Jesus, Mary, and drill bits," Karen says. "I'll have to have a talk with your dads."

Dexter notices that when she feeds Matilda lunch, his mother smiles for the first time in over a week. Is it because she wishes Matilda were her own? He never makes her smile like that. Maybe it doesn't matter, because Matilda will be his friend, and his mother can give her all the food she wants.

CHAPTER 14 ✳ (HIM)

November rolled toward December, and as Mandate 43 began to seep into the social psyche, Dex and Grace slowly became lights in each other's darkened world. There were decisions to make, and none of them presented a simple or obvious path. Grace's dad Stuart had begun the process of finding an illegal solution to his daughter's problem, urging her to remain as invisible as possible now that she was unemployed and to stay off her feet to avoid further bleeding. He had identified and informally reached out to an ex-doctor and heterosexual rights activist named Aiden Parsons, who was heterosexual himself and a rare example of one who had risen to society's upper echelons. Now, his nonprofit organization called Failsafe Rise was under scrutiny by the government, rendering his future uncertain. To Stuart and Grace's relief, Parsons had agreed to join them for a discreet lunch on the fourteenth of December.

Dex welcomed Grace into his small apartment so she could avoid the prying eyes of her father, brother, and nephew. Grace's excuse to them was simple and practical: Dex was her new boyfriend, and neither of them wanted to have sex in the guest house, under everyone's nose. It helped that her sexuality was already offensive to certain people on the premises—namely her father James.

Dex and Grace discussed their options, but sometimes, they

simply played games, read in silence, or cooked meals. Dex had not been misguided the night of the orgy. His attraction toward Grace was even stronger now, and the comfort he felt with her was as genuine as it was soothing. One cold night, as Dex held her in the darkness of his bedroom, he considered—just for a moment—that if they eventually found a way to survive together, perhaps keeping the baby would be okay. Joyful, even. It was as if they were running straight for a cliff, hands together, facing questions more significant even than the choices: Could good come out of any attempt to resist the government? Was the life growing inside Grace truly worth the fight?

They decided to let Fletch Novotny in on the secret. If his friend Sheila ever returned his calls and could somehow help, it was worth risking exposure. Dex met him at Sterile Me Susan's for a late drink on the nineteenth of November. Fletch already seemed on edge when they sat down at one of the back tables, and as the information about Grace came out, he tightened his lips and shook his head.

"They're not going to get her too," Fletch whispered. "I've been dabbling in some resistance shit the past few weeks but haven't done anything heavy yet. I think I just needed a motherfucking reason. Now I've got one." Dex started to give him a warning look, but Fletch held up a hand. "Don't worry, I'll be careful as hell."

He agreed to try contacting Sheila again. In the meantime, he would sniff around his social circles for other potential options, and he would tell no one about Grace's condition without first getting permission.

Dex returned home to find Grace sleeping. He joined her in his bed, but sleep remained elusive as the night progressed. Two sides of him were fighting a cataclysmic battle: recklessness and complacence. Recklessness would be to join Grace and search out a way for their child to be born, even at the cost of their freedom. Complacence would be to sit back and let the New Rainbow Order unleash his future for him, whatever it might entail.

"You don't have to choose now," Grace told him over breakfast on the third of December, a Monday. She was dressed in a pair of his flannel pants and a large T-shirt, looking particularly rosy in the cheeks.

For the first time in his life, Dex was finding it difficult to be honest with himself. The fear that he would be too weak to face the consequences head-on showed his true colors, and they were dull and muddy. Later that day, however, Grace broke down in his arms for the first time. It came on the shoulders of terror, uncertainty, and the prospect of evaluating morality's murky spectrum for the sake of their unborn child. It gave Dex hope for himself when he realized he wanted nothing more than to console her.

He did so in the form of strawberries and a hot bath, in tandem.

While Grace's bath water was running, Dex ran downstairs and across the street to the kitty-corner Target Express for the strawberries. In all of four and a half minutes, he was back in the bathroom, naked, kneeling next to the bathtub, holding a berry out to the mother of his child.

"This, my friend, is the answer to all your woes."

He climbed in next to her, and they fed the strawberries to each other. Succulent, perfect, like rain on pain.

They made love. Dex was careful at first, until Grace told him it was okay to go further, that sex used to be encouraged during pregnancy. Around them, the cooling water rose and fell in slight bursts on the side of the bathtub.

"I don't like what's happening to the world," Grace whispered when they finished.

Dex had spooned himself around her. He kissed her head now, then held his lips against her dark, wet hair. Grace used her foot to turn on the faucet, and heat from the new water moved around them. Dex was still aroused, still inside her. As the bath grew warmer, she made no effort to force him out.

Grace put her hand on his and rested them both on her abdomen.

"I think . . . I think I want to make it last as long as possible before they take it away from us. Make *this* last. But like I said, I won't blame you if you decide to save yourself and run. Just give me the word, and I'll figure it out myself."

The faucet dripped in front of them, hitting a small pool between the mess of their feet.

"I had a dream," Grace continued. "That I was raising a little girl. It's a girl, I think. She was running through the yard, laughing, turning around to see if I was laughing, too. That was all. Except she had salt and pepper hair, like you, even though she was just a tiny kid."

Dex burst into laughter, and he felt Grace's cheeks smile against his arm.

"I'd never been so happy in my entire life. Our daughter was alive, and it was all that mattered."

Dex's laughter dwindled, but the exhilaration at the thought of his child running around, being alive, happy, and unharmed, remained. His choice to help it survive would boil down either to bravery or to fear—recklessness or complacence. With either choice, he would forever wonder what the alternative could have brought. But life was life, even sliced small, and this child was innocent in the world's mess. Therein lay a spark of clarity and courage, the right choice. He just had to grab it, hold it close.

ON THE NINTH OF DECEMBER, Dex joined the Jarvis family for their Sunday dinner at James's request. The entire night, James spoke to him in his smug, sing-song voice, dripping phony friendliness, keeping his teeth at bay, but only just.

"You must like *real* sex quite a bit if you thrust hard enough into my daughter's anus to make her *bleed*," he said, grinning over his pinot noir. "Even though experimenting with anal sex *won't* make you normal, however much you might wish it."

Lars was grinning, twirling shredded cucumber salad around his fork. Grace had been right: he was a frightening child, pale, brimming with intelligence, and as of the previous week sporting the rainbow arm band of the Gay Youth, a newly formed and worldwide pre-military group for teenagers of the New Rainbow Order. But Dex noticed the boy's gaze wandering over his body whenever nobody was looking. Lars was attracted to him, and it was the boy's only hint of cerebral weakness. He did not say a word to Dex all night.

It was obvious nobody in Grace's family had yet tipped off the Bio Police to her condition. She was safe for the moment, and dinner passed under a constant but bearable wash of discomfort. Afterward, Stuart beckoned Grace and Dex into the kitchen to do the dishes. They spoke nothing of Grace's pregnancy, but Dex could tell Stuart was feeling him out with every pleasantry they exchanged; he wanted to know if Dex had what it took to be reliable. When Stuart accidentally set one of the knives too close to the counter's edge and it flipped off, toward his foot, Dex caught it.

"Good boy," Stuart whispered. They exchanged their first real smile.

As they cleaned up the kitchen, Lars watched from the living room doorway, standing like a sentry over the older clashing family members populating his world. His dark hair and clothes blended with the charcoal-colored cabinetry behind him, making his face float like a white theatre mask. It was impossible to tell whether the slight twist in his mouth was a frown or a smile.

LATER, DEX AND GRACE lay in bed in the guest house. It was calming to know this warm, brick bungalow would be surrounded by Stuart's vivid gardens in the summertime. The very thought of staying here with Grace, of living out this pregnancy in peace and building a future, inspired a bloom of tranquility in his heart so potent that he felt, in those moments, a seemingly mystical closeness to the soul growing inside her, to the life that had bonded them to begin with.

Dex was not religious, but he did believe in a soul. Christianity, the world's only government-endorsed religion, was a set of superstitions the homosexual majority used to justify their ways of life. With Christmas coming up, it was a constant reminder of their dominance. Since archeologists and biologists discovered through an unearthed blood sample in 2117 that Jesus of Nazareth had been a homosexual (and ancient Aramaic scrolls accompanying the sample claimed he was an active one at that, as had long been postulated), Christmas had become a rainbow-flared celebration, yet another way to suppress heterosexuals. But the idea of God, of a soul, still appealed to Dex. It gave him a sense of hope.

Yet there, as their calm nighttime breathing masked the thunder clouds billowing on their horizon, he asked Grace one last time: "Are you sure about this? Going against the law to keep this baby?"

They were facing each other in the darkness. Visible in the moonlight, Grace's contemplative expression remained stoic. It was as if she had not heard his question. He was about to ask again when her eyebrows scrunched. "Killing it would be the easy option, wouldn't it? The sensible one. Risk the complications of an underground abortion, or hell, I'm sure I could find a way to cause a miscarriage. Don't think I haven't been thinking about it constantly." Dex grimaced and nodded. She was right: getting rid of the baby would be easy and sensible. The only option, if they were to preserve what remained of their lives. When she continued, however, there was nothing easy or sensible in her expression. "But then I think about the dream. I think about killing the baby and telling myself it's to save it from being harmed or murdered or having a horrible life, and I realize I'd be bringing on those very things by snuffing it out myself. That reasoning is completely flawed. I can't know the future. I can't know what's in store for this baby. I've devoted my entire life to helping those who don't have a choice or a chance, because of the suppression the NRO has brought on everything. But this little person is my own flesh and blood. *Ours.* It's *somebody.* What would I be if I just erased that to save myself?"

Dex found himself nodding as Grace finished.

"A coward," she said.

They were both lying in fetal positions with hands touching lightly near their pillows. Outside was the rest of the world, blissfully unaware of the momentous moral dilemma resolving between them.

"Do you think we could ever love each other, Dex Wheelock?"

Grace's question sank into him, causing the heat of vulnerability to rise in his chest, then filter out to his limbs. Love? Time had not yet been ample enough for him to feel such a thing for Grace Jarvis. But there she lay with her brown hair falling over her shoulders, her warm feet reaching out to touch his somewhere deep in the sheets.

"I think I love what we created already, as scared as I am," he answered, knowing it might not be enough to instill nobility in him or crush any potential gutlessness. He was creating an opportunity for abdication, for that future, decisive moment when he would have to make this critical choice. "As for us," he continued, already feeling guilt swallow him, "I suppose we won't know until it happens. I think what matters most right now is doing our best. And whatever happens after that . . . just . . . happens."

Dex was not proud of his answer, yet it seemed to satisfy Grace. Her round face relaxed, and her gaze fell to the empty bedroom air between them. "Well, then . . . here we go."

A MEMORY ✳ (HER)

*G*RACE IS LYING ON THE GROUND, *and her nose is bleeding. Running across the school yard into the golden afternoon sun are Ben Bradley, Shia Madloff, and Kenneth Bon. It was a good day up until ten seconds ago.*

They punched her because of Social History. It is the first time she has ever been persecuted for being herself.

Social History is one of Grace's favorite classes, but Mr. Sobaski sweats in his armpits every day, so it tarnishes the experience somewhat. Today, he gave them an overview of their upcoming two-month unit called Homosexual Progress. For a fifth-grade teacher, he expects a lot from his students. Grace privately knows she is one of the few who actually understands what he is talking about, at least most of the time.

He told them earlier this morning that in 2026, the old United States (which, despite some stains on its reputation due to what Mr. Sobaski called "superfluous wars" and "environmentally unfriendly industrial addictions") had progressed on the social front and legalized marriage for homosexuals, who as a social group had fought decades for the "legitimacy of their relationships to be recognized in a legal manner."

At this, Grace actually laughed aloud, to her own embarrassment. Heterosexuals—breeders—being in charge of the world and not allowing homosexuals to marry is the exact opposite of her world. The thing she found funny was that homosexuals today say the type of restraint they suffered back then was unacceptable and inhuman, even though they now treat heteros that way all the time. Her chuckle at this incongruity had been loud and out of place in class, and everyone—most of whom were normal homosexual boys—stared.

Despite what she found funny, the things Mr. Sobaski told them next about the droughts, mass famines, overpopulation, and the Sterilize Yourself! liberal movement in the late 2060s were fascinating to Grace. In fact, she was the only student in the room to ask questions, even though she knew people were rolling their eyes at her. Did those first heterosteriles of the sterilization movement know that what they were doing would inspire fear in old-fashioned thinkers? That it would cause them to form the rebel group God's Army and start the twelve-year reign of biological and chemical terror the world now remembered as the Bio Wars? And when did homosexuality finally become more normal than heterosexuality?

"You'll find out all in due time, Miss Jarvis," Mr. Sobaski said. He looked at her in a curious way, as if suspecting she was indeed a heterosterile. She would have confirmed it had he asked.

Now, Grace realizes that being open about who she is might not be so smart. She is lying on the ground, mortified, knowing that blood is running right down the side of her face.

They snuck up behind her, spun her around by her backpack, and each hit her in the nose once. Ben, Shia, and Kenneth.

She has no idea why they did it, and all she can think is that it was because she laughed out loud in class and made it obvious she had understood something funny that they had not.

CHAPTER 15 ✳ (HER)

IT WAS A BRIGHT AND SUNNY FRIDAY. The first snow of the year had fallen the previous night, and rooftops and trees lining I-94 between Minneapolis and St. Paul reflected white against the ravishing blue sky.

It's beautiful, still, the world, Grace thought. *If anything, there's that.*

She was on her way to Kincaid's Revival, a classic American restaurant in St. Paul, where her dad and the straight rights activist Aiden Parsons had reserved a curtained nook for what Stuart hoped would appear to be a private business meeting. "Best to make the meeting look unremarkable," her dad had told her that morning. "If anybody recognizes us, we can say we're catching up with an old family friend."

The melted snow reflecting the sun on the freeway was blinding, and Grace had to shield her eyes to see the road ahead. She had driven today because of an afternoon meeting with Linda Glass, whom she had been avoiding ever since their last coffee date. Her avoidance was now bordering on suspicious, as her friend had pointed out on a com message the day before.

"Grace, it's me," Linda said. "I saw your father at the store, and he told me you're out of a job, which means you're helping me with Rita's school decorations tomorrow. No questions! I'll call you."

Rita was Linda and her wife Celine's seven-year-old daughter, who was a first grader at Deephaven Elementary. Abraham also lived in Deephaven, which meant there was a chance she might run across Lars, who was a sixth grader at the school.

The less he sees of me the better, Grace thought, exiting off I-94 and making her way toward Kincaid's Revival. *Either way, it's going to be an interesting day.*

"I'm meeting Stuart Jarvis for his party of three," she told the host after stepping inside. The black-haired fag gave her an approving once over, then led her to a secluded corner of the restaurant. The warm, meaty smells clashed with the cologne wafting off his thin body and bouncing walk. The fag held back the red curtain of one of the four nooks. Inside it were her dad and a hawk-faced man with slicked-back, graying hair. Aiden Parsons, surely—the failsafe who could and did, until the Bio Police had brought him down.

"Well hello, my dear," Stuart said, playing up the casualness in his tone, making it clear he had not yet mentioned anything of the pregnancy to Parsons. They had a plan: Stuart would lead the conversation, feel Parsons out, and if it seemed wise, reveal the necessary information about the pregnancy.

Both men's chairs squeaked outward as they stood up to greet her. Stuart kissed his daughter on the cheek, and Parsons reached across the table and shook her hand, looking her straight in the eyes, unflinching. "Pleased to make your acquaintance," he said. The man looked and acted like a classic successful failsafe: well-dressed enough to fit in with the homosexual majority, but also self-conscious in a heightened sort of way, as if he were scrutinizing his every action for mannerisms that might draw attention. Parsons stared at Grace as she sat down, holding a toothpick between his grinding teeth. He was on edge; that was clear.

Or maybe he just finds you attractive. He's a failsafe, after all.

"So, I've just been talking with Mr. Parsons about the closure of his organization," Stuart told Grace in the overly polite, small-talky tone he might use with one of his patients.

"Failsafe Rise, right?" Grace asked, keeping her voice purposely low.

Parsons sat with perfect, businesslike posture and rested his folded hands on the tabletop. "Unfortunately, not anymore. The NRO found my organization in conflict with Article 7 of Mandate 43. Were it to remain in operation, it would be considered a terrorist organization."

Stuart shook his head. "Ridiculous."

"I've spent the past fifteen years trying to use my clout with the local governmental establishments to promote compromise between the homosexuals and heterosexuals, and until very recently I was successful. But Mandate 43 is a setback. Possibly a permanent road block."

"What do you think is the future of straight rights action, then?" Stuart asked.

"I think advocacy is going to fall away more than we've ever seen before." Parsons shook his head, and for the first time, his wary self-assuredness wavered. He took a long time to take a single sip of water, and Grace could tell he was scrutinizing them. When the man seemed convinced they were on his side, he continued. His voice was low, almost dire. "May I step onto a soap box for a moment?"

Stuart gestured with his hand. "Be our guest."

Parsons sighed, then spoke. "What we have here is a classic dictatorship, disguising itself as a necessary one-world government and forcing its ideals by creating scapegoats for all the world's problems. It's the Second World War all over again, but on a grand scale, with a bit of genetic relevance thrown in for good measure. Yes, the world is right to be taking a new approach to the threat of over-population, but that threat is all but gone now. Snuffed out by genetic engineering. So, one has to ask: what is the difference between a homosexual marriage and a marriage between a failsafe and heterosterile? The answer is *nothing at all.*"

"Meaning...?" Stuart was not seeing Parsons's unfolding point.

But Grace understood. Genetic engineering could produce sterile heterosexuals just as easily as homosexuals, and if all humanity could agree on a form of population control, what made homosexuals better rulers? Nothing at all.

"It's the homosexual agenda that found its footing back when the old USA's President Gold came out of the gay closet in 2041. There are many out there who believe it was a planned political move, seeing as there were already a number of gay politicians in high levels of their old government. Along with them, other governments around the world continued to plant the gay seed early, even before the problem of population control took Earth by force. After the droughts in the 2050s, though, it became glaringly obvious that societies would soon have trouble sustaining their skyrocketing numbers. It jump-started a new wave of thinking in heterosexuals."

"'Sterilize Yourself!,'" Grace said, remembering clearly the day in school she had first learned about that era, the day those three boys had beat her up.

"Exactly," Parsons said. "At the time, it was considered a *liberal* movement. Normal heterosexuals sterilizing themselves in an effort to save the world. Only they were forwarding the gay agenda all along. And do you know who introduced that movement? The first president those old Americans actually elected, knowing full well he was gay."

"Lindon Trendy," Stuart chimed in.

"Lindon Trendy. He pushed sterility and shunned anyone, particularly those in religious groups, who disagreed with it. Liberals, whether now or then, have often used one thing above all others to forward their opinions, no matter how irrational or unrealistic they are: *anger*. They get mad about an issue and refuse to hear any arguments against it, and the logistics necessary to make the called-for reform successful take a back seat. Vote now, think later. That's what happened with sterilization, and the problem is that it simply continued so strongly that nobody thought twice about it until God's Army finally decided to start an uprising. Then, after the Bio Wars almost destroyed us *completely*, people just forgot what the world used to be like. Homosexuals usurped political power when it was, pardon the pun, "trendy" not to procreate, and they've let the very nature of humanity die in the shadow of terror."

Parsons was growing more and more passionate, as if he was thrilled to his bones that Grace and Stuart were offering him this opportunity to make a speech. But there was logic in it. The man's face was red and breaking a sweat.

"So, here we are today, forgetting that sexual orientation has nothing to do with the logistics of running the world, of defining people's value. Humanity would be controlling population regardless. People are forgetting this, and the NRO is using sexual orientation as a concept to blur people's perceptions of what is right and humane. But sexual orientation itself and the humane resolution to the population control problem are no longer even related, because engineering solved it long ago!"

"I couldn't agree more," Stuart said, looking flustered himself. He turned to Grace and widened his eyes slightly, as if he were about to let slip the big news. But he held back. "Mr. Parsons, I am a homosexual like most other people, but I absolutely do not support what is happening in the world, and I think there are other homosexuals like me out there. At the same time, it's becoming more and more dangerous to step up and take a stand."

"Oh, there surely are others like you," Parsons said. "The problem is that, for homosexuals, society has come to rest in a rather peaceful place. Economies are once again becoming intercontinental. Quality of life has improved vastly since the first few decades after the Bio Wars. People are comfortable, and taking a stand means risking that comfort. I don't think many people are willing to do that."

"*I'm* willing to." Stuart pounded the table with his fist.

Just then, the waiter walked in to take their orders. They all adopted cheerful expressions. For effect, Stuart even waved his wrist and lisped while ordering. The waiter seemed none the wiser, and he even flirted slightly with Aiden Parsons (who simply returned it with a nod and a tight smile) before swinging through the curtain and leaving them alone once again.

Until the food arrived twenty minutes later, Parsons continued poking holes in the government's social rationale. He was a brilliant man, Grace realized, the type who carved his way through the world around him, forming his own channels and tunnels through life's socio-economic fabric. He had grown up a middle-class failsafe in La Crosse, Wisconsin, the son of Kevin and Kirk Parsons, who owned a bed and breakfast on the Mississippi River. He had been an only child, the result of his fathers' choosing to be surprised by the engineer. As in Grace's own family, there had been one open-armed parent and one not-so-kind parent. The latter, Kirk Parsons, was the only one to survive past Aiden's fifth birthday. His husband had drowned that day when their sailboat capsized on the Mississippi, and he had swum after Aiden to keep him from drifting into the current. Kirk forever blamed the boy for it, often telling him in drunken bursts that they were no longer a family, that he, Aiden, should have been the one to drown instead. Once Aiden was old enough to clean rooms, keep track of guests, and direct the cook, Kirk would often leave the bed and breakfast in his hands and disappear to circuit parties for days at a time. Contrary to what could have been, Aiden used the responsibility to learn the ropes of business and economics. By the time he finished high school, he was top of his class, with honors. He attended the University of Minnesota on a full-ride scholarship, double majoring in premedical engineering and business administration. He went on to bioengineering school from there before establishing himself in the hierarchy of Minnesota geneticists.

"And here I am now, a lonely president of a snuffed-out not-for-profit." Parsons brought his fingertips to the table, resting them with the posture of a pianist on either side of his medium rare steak, which had just arrived.

Stuart glanced at Grace, straightened his glasses, then coughed. "Now, I hope this is not too straightforward, and if you would rather not discuss this, be honest. You mentioned last time we spoke that a colleague once accused you of genetically sabotaging the NRO's biological agenda. We—my daughter and I, that is—are wondering what exactly this refers to. You see, we—"

"We're wondering if you might know of any engineers who could have made it possible for heterosteriles to get pregnant," Grace interrupted, speaking in a whisper. Outside the nook, far away, the restaurant clanked and clattered. "We were just thinking that, if this was the type of biological 'sabotage' you were accused of, then you might be able to give us some insight."

It was a dangerous step to expose this secret so blatantly. Grace's entire body was rolling with a nervous heat.

Aiden Parsons stared into her eyes. "Why are you asking me this? Are you—?"

Neither Grace nor Stuart moved.

Parsons, frozen in his chair, studied them for a moment, his gaze fixing first on Stuart, then on Grace. "And you chose to tell me this *here*?"

"We're not telling you anything, as you can very well see," Stuart said in an overly cheerful manner, looking toward the curtain again to make sure the waiter had not slipped back into their nook. "Now, with that in mind, what might you be able to tell us about this topic?"

Parsons appeared for a moment as if he was considering

dismissing them completely and walking out, but then he grimaced, shook his head, and leaned forward. "Do you know what you're asking?"

"We just need something. A name. Somebody who can help us. Grace's engineer died almost thirteen years ago, and even if he were alive, it wouldn't be safe to just prance up to him and ask crazy questions." Now, Stuart looked desperate.

Parsons leaned back and pressed his palms to the table, as if it might keep him in orbit. "I guess it would mark me a coward if I ran from your question. And it's technically no secret what happened. My operations have been watched closely by the NRO since they removed me from my engineering practice. Still, they never had any proof, because my name was never officially attached to the project."

Adrenaline tingled in Grace's chest. "The project?"

"Tell me, assuming we're talking about what I think we're talking about, were you engineered locally?"

Grace turned to her dad. Realizing the platform was now his, Stuart blinked his eyes rapidly and fumbled over the answer. "Oh, um . . . it was the Minnesota Bioengineering Clinic over in St. Louis Park. Strict NRO supervision, just like all the private clinics. The engineer was Bozarth. Theodore Bozarth. We met with him three times. The BGR referred us. But only for you, Grace." He turned to her. "We made Abraham at the university."

Parson's eyes widened, and with the slightest exhale, he brought his fingertips together in one silent motion. "It worked," he whispered.

"What worked?" Grace asked.

Now, Parsons spoke even more quietly and quickly. "First, and let me be frank, I suddenly appreciate this meeting more than either of you will ever know. Second, today is the only time we will ever speak of any of this out loud. None of what I'm willing to reveal to you is anything the NRO doesn't already know about, but I've spent the last thirteen years avoiding any sort of resistance or sabotage activity for fear of being incarcerated, or worse. I purposefully let this case slip my mind. I don't want to die a victim. As for what I'm about to say, I'll let you surmise the parts I don't make obvious. How is that?"

"Perfect," Stuart said. "Continue."

Parsons took a sip of water. "Theodore Bozarth was in charge of all heterosterile engineering in the Twin Cities from 2354 to 2369, at the request of Sam Janken, who was head of the Minnesota branch of the Bureau of Genetic Regulation. They were friends, and Janken pulled strings to get Bozarth solely in charge of heterosterile engineering. Grace, you are, what, twenty-six? Twenty-seven?"

"Twenty-eight."

"Good enough. You were one of the early ones, then. There were only eight thousand heterosterile females bred during the fourteen-year period Theodore Bozarth ran that branch of engineering. He was an engineer for seventeen years before that, but those fourteen years were key. Rumor had it that he had found a way through protein engineering and gene sequence manipulation to introduce delayed fertility into his heterosteriles in an attempt to fight the continually suppressive ideals of the NRO. Rumor *also* had it that I was the outsourced geneticist he had worked closely with on this endeavor. It's true that the Bureau of Genetic Regulation once outsourced much of its fringe research divisions, and I *was* one of those divisions. I had my own engineering clinic at the time and was permitted by the Bureau to engineer two thousand homosexual females per year. That was my profession, but, as suggested by the rumors, I may have had a penchant for side research. Also, perhaps, an interest in restoring natural order to society. These *rumors*, then, ended when Bozarth was assassinated at the end of his run. The year 2372, it was. I say assassinated, because, from what I gathered, he was found with bullets in his chest and head. They never held a proper funeral, because they cremated him immediately."

Parsons's face was burning red, and the anger in his voice hissed out in sharp, warm breaths. "Of course, none of this was publicized, because it would have made people *think*. None of it was even proven. According to a source I had inside the Bio Police's walls, all of Bozarth's com and hardcopy files were removed and probably destroyed at some point before he was found dead. They thought he had destroyed it all himself to cover his tracks and keep the project intact. All the research gone, except the walking specimens he had released into society."

Specimens, Grace thought. She was nothing more than someone's little science project.

Her dad grabbed his water to take a sip, and the ice floating in it clinked steadily against the glass. His hand was shaking. When Grace looked at him, she saw it was not fear causing him to tremble, but scarlet-faced anger.

"Didn't you both think about the danger you were putting these young women in?" he hissed at Parsons.

Grace placed a hand on his shoulder. "Dad, please. Mr. Parsons can't—"

Stuart shook out of his daughter's hold. "No. *No.*" He pointed a finger at Parsons, who neither shrank under it nor appeared altogether proud. "This is unacceptable. My husband and I put the life of our child, knowing she would be heterosterile, in Theodore Bozarth's hands, and he did nothing less than mark her for banishment or death. *You* helped him do this! Not just my daughter, but thousands of women like her as well!"

Parsons nodded. If it was guilt causing his face to contort with anxiety, his words did nothing to address it. "Mr. Jarvis, what you first must understand is that the NRO had not yet put in place the mandates that are now all but causing an extermination of heterosexuals, sterile or not. Theodore and I suspected such edicts were coming, and—again, it was *rumored*—we did everything in our power to fight it. And yes, that included trying to secretly engineer women who could successfully breed with failsafes and potentially, when the time came, offset the frightening path the NRO was setting for itself."

"When the time *came*?"

"I'm talking about *now*, Mr. Jarvis. As I said before, I've done my very best to avoid anything related to this resistance effort, including finding out whatever became of all these women, but I know Theodore had friends on the inside helping him see it through. We weren't the only ones working against the—"

The nook's curtain scraped open, and the waiter pranced in. The prissy expression on his face suggested nothing out of the ordinary. Unless he was a great actor, he had not heard a word. "Are we all finished?"

"We were just leaving, and I'll get the tab," Aiden Parsons said, standing and holding out his wrist to the waiter, who scanned it with the restaurant's credit reader before thanking them and walking away. Parsons grabbed his coat and threw it over himself, then adjusted his collar. "I suggest you both keep this meeting to yourselves, for all our sakes. I may be able to offer you more at a later date, but not here. If you'll excuse me." He ducked through the curtain, leaving Grace and Stuart alone, shocked, and with plates still half full.

CHAPTER 16 ✳ (HIM)

WHEN DEX ARRIVED HOME FROM WORK that afternoon, a purple police sedan was sitting outside his apartment, fifty yards up on the street's opposite side. Through the dim window was a chiseled fag dressed in uniform. A Bio Police officer sipping on something, watching Dex with cool alertness.

Walk to the door. Don't look suspicious.

As he held his wrist to the door key to scan open the lock, he glanced quickly at the police car. The officer was looking down now, into his lap. Suddenly, a second officer rose from that spot, wiping his mouth. The first officer, looking preoccupied, jerked his gaze to the street again, as if he had let his subject slip. Dex turned away and stepped into his apartment door. Was he under surveillance? It was impossible to know just yet, but if his sudden association with Grace Jarvis had already alerted the police to possible illegal behavior, they were definitely quick on the draw.

Just do what you normally do. See if they're outside again tomorrow.

It was only when he was safe inside his apartment, however, that he noticed one of his kitchen cupboards, which he had used only to store cat food while owning a cat, was ajar. It was a cheap apartment, and the cupboards all stuck shut with magnetic hooks. Dex made a close examination of the door, then shut it. The magnetic hitching sound was cold and sharp, like a period halting a sentence. He glanced at the floor and saw the outline of a shoe, left by a trace of winter dirt.

Someone had been inside his apartment.

CHAPTER 17 ❄ (HER)

GRACE ARRIVED AT DEEPHAVEN ELEMENTARY at 2:30 p.m. She walked past classroom after classroom, seeing the perfectly gelled hair of all the little school boys, who appeared to outnumber the girls at least ten to one. She was no longer sure which classroom Lars was in, but he was in the sixth grade, most likely on the school's upper level. Grace wondered how many of the boys here were failsafes in the process of learning their lives would soon be meaningless.

"Hey there, dear," Linda said when Grace stepped into the empty gymnasium. The bright LED lights seemed to flatten everything in it, save for Linda, who jumped up to get a hug. "You actually showed up! Now you can tell your nephew Lars that you really do care about his school decorations. God, I've been almost sure lately that you were trying to disappear on me or something. Chalk it up to all this Mandate 43 crap."

"What, you think I don't want to help you make the decorations these kids should be making themselves?"

"Please. We all know it's the parents' job to do it. Kids these days don't give a shit about silly things like holidays. Besides, my decorations will look better."

Grace chuckled. "How's the wife? Any progress?"

"Oh, acting like a bat from hell. She got so drunk two nights ago that I had to take her to the emergency clinic. That was a first. And you'd think she'd take that as a hint, you know?"

Linda's wife, Celine, was the more rugged lesbian in the pair, almost twice the size of her spouse in bone structure. It never failed to amaze Grace how Linda could have fallen for Celine Melville, the dyke who had been senior quarterback of their high school's varsity football team when they were just giggling freshmen. The rough and cocky lesbian jock had grown into a woman who left Grace on edge every time their paths crossed, and she had recently developed a full-blown addiction to alcohol. The arguments resulting from this had led to violence exactly twice, but Linda was tougher than she looked. Not to mention stubborn.

"I keep telling her that she needs to keep the weight off, or the law firm might fire her, but will she listen? No, not at all." Linda unrolled a massive sheet of paper and spread it like a banner on the gym floor. "So, basically, the wife is causing me hell, and little Rita isn't exactly feeling the love. She said last night, 'Mommy, are you and Mom going to get a divorce?'"

"Oh, no."

Linda had hunched over the banner and was outlining the phrase **Bred By God!** in pencil. "She's only eight, for Christ's sake, and now she's having to deal with two dykes who don't have their shit together. Not to mention all the boys in her class are telling her she's going to Antarctica for being a girl, and it's scaring her half to death. Oh, well, just in time for Christmas, right? Say, can you fill in these letters with red?"

Grace opened a container of red paint and began following Linda's progress with her own. Linda was a talker, the mile-a-minute kind. Even though she always made room for other people to speak, part of Grace hoped she would talk through their visit today and save her from having to face the thorny truth that any meeting now could be their last.

But no such luck.

"So, what's this I hear about a boyfriend? Tammy Grekko said your father told her dad that you're seeing somebody. Is that true? I'm going to kill you if it is. You didn't tell me!"

Grace forced a smile, but inwardly, a snake was wrapping around her heart. *If I think too hard about saying goodbye, I'll cry. If I don't say goodbye, I'm going to be the worst friend in the whole world.*

"His name is Dex," Grace choked out, hoping it would sound to Linda like a dry throat. She coughed to cover the wave of grief washing through her.

"*Dex?* That's kind of a hot name, no?"

"If you saw him, even you'd want to jump his bones." It was a weak joke. Juvenile, like during their high school days. And nothing in Grace's tone sounded cheery.

Linda stopped outlining her letters and looked up. "Honey, is everything all right?"

Grace was about to cave in, but she screamed inwardly at herself. *Keep it together! Keep it the hell together!* She would have to employ the tactic she had used with Dex. Feel Linda out. She was liberal, but was she liberal enough? When Grace spoke, the words were fragile as glass about to shatter.

"What do you think it's going to be like when we have to say goodbye, Lin?"

"What do you mean, 'say goodbye'?"

"I mean, like, Mandate 43. The camps they're making for heterosexuals. I've heard rumors it's going to happen sooner rather than later."

Linda lowered her voice to a healthy rasp. "They're not going to fucking round you guys up. They can't! Nobody is going to stand for it. If they actually do, I'm taking Rita and getting the hell out of here. Off to the mountains in Alberta, or something." Giving a dismissive wave of her pencil, Linda turned back to the Christmas banner.

"I'm serious, Lin. What could you possibly do but watch it happen? I think we both know this whole gay world just tipped over into something pretty serious. There's nobody to check the power, and nobody but the NRO has access to weapons. So . . . what could you really do?"

A lock of Linda's beautiful blonde hair fell over her eyes. She stopped writing again, gathered her hair back behind her ear, and stared at the banner on the gym floor. What followed was the first instance of verbal calculation Grace had ever witnessed in the woman. "You know, I think I'm actively avoiding it all. I don't want to think about it. I think *nobody* wants to think about it."

Grace watched her own hand spread the red paint into Linda's big, bubbly **R**, feeling completely detached from it. "I guess I meant to say . . . I might not be around much longer. I've been scared to see you, because it might mean goodbye. A *real* goodbye."

Linda's chest, full under her blue wool sweater, rose and fell as her breathing became heavier. She kept her gaze glued to the paper. "What are you saying, Gracie?"

"I'm saying that something's wrong. I can't really say anything else."

"Of course you can!" Linda jerked her neck around and looked Grace in the eyes. Hers were suddenly full of tears, as if she already knew what Grace was about to tell her.

"I think it's safer for you if I don't."

"Bullshit. Grace, is this whole Mandate 43 thing about to get real and affect my life directly? In a bad way? Tell me. Tell me *now*."

"It's not just Mandate 43. There's something else."

"Did this Dex guy drag you into some rebel shit or something?"

"No. Not directly. It's more like . . ."

Just tell her, Grace thought. *If you don't, you're going to regret it forever. She'll never stop wondering what happened to you once you disappear.*

"It's not fair," Grace whispered. "Lin, I'm . . ."

"Wait. Don't say it. Don't tell me."

Relief flooded Grace, but— "What? Why?"

"Because I get it. If there's something you can't say and you're keeping it quiet to save me from those fucking faggot Nazis, it's okay."

"Okay."

But Linda was fuming. She hunched over her letters again and began tracing stars around them with a furious sort of gusto. "Promise me one thing."

"Anything."

"Promise me you'll say goodbye if something happens and you need to disappear. Until then, let's pretend you never even brought this up."

"*You* brought it up. You asked about Dex."

Linda shrugged, let out a chuckle that did not match her panicked expression, then fell backward, onto her rear. She sat cross-legged, her face now waxen. Decorating Deephaven Elementary seemed to have lost its appeal. "Grace Emilia Jarvis, you're not scaring me for no reason, are you?"

Grace shook her head. "I wouldn't do that."

"Then what do we do, here? I have a pretty good guess as to what's going on, because only one thing scares a heterosterile enough to talk like this. But do I pretend I have no idea? Do we just spend this time like it's any other, like they *won't* ship you off to Antarctica if they find out?"

There. She said it. She knows.

When Linda finally turned back to her letters, Grace followed along in silence, wishing she could have had one more day with her, just the two of them, friends forever without a care in the world.

CHAPTER 18 ✳ (HIM)

CHRISTMAS APPROACHED, and on the nineteenth of December, Dex, Grace, and presumably all of society's registered heterosexuals received via com their Bio Police summons. Social assessments would begin on the first of February, and those who were not present on their specified date would face arrest and incarceration.

Grace was slated for February twenty-second; Dex, for March ninth.

Dex accompanied Grace, her fathers, Abraham, and his boyfriend Daryl to Lars and Rita's Christmas program the following Friday. At the reception in the school cafeteria, Dex met Grace's best friend Linda Glass, who shook his hand with tepid enthusiasm before suddenly grabbing him into a monster hug. "Be careful," the blonde beauty whispered, almost inaudibly. Just before she escorted her sprite of a daughter out of the cafeteria, Linda hugged Grace as well, then gave her a voluptuous kiss, right on the lips. It was an inside joke of some sort, and Dex watched both women laugh until tears shone on their faces. Amid the clamor of the children and their parents, few others noticed the bittersweet exchange.

Christmas dinner with the Jarvis household came and went without a single mention of the social assessments, but there was a Bio Police car sitting on their tranquil Wayzata street all afternoon, just outside the driveway. Stuart pulled Dex aside to help him prepare the living room fireplace.

"What is that police car doing out front?" There was a tremor in his voice.

Dex had no good response. When the fire was blazing, he joined Stuart and Grace on the couch, and they watched in silence until it was nothing more than a pile of glowing embers.

Later that night, Dex received a call from a scrambled com address. It was Fletch Novotny, and he had two things to say: First, his friend Sheila had finally answered his com messages—quite enthusiastically, but he wouldn't explain why—and demanded he set up a meeting with Dex and Grace for the morning of the twenty-seventh. Second, he had experienced an altercation with the Bio Police three Thursdays prior and been charged with a petty misdemeanor for verbally accosting an officer who had unlawfully initiated questioning of Sterile Me Susan's' patrons. It was his second offense since August, and if the Bio Police were following routine protocol, they would again be monitoring his com and investigating all his known contacts, which could include Dex.

"I think they've been doing just that," Dex confirmed. "And just so you know, you're a dipshit for not telling me all this sooner." He had to be cautious with his words. The Bio Police would be able to run a voice filter on his side of the conversation but not on Fletch's, due to the scrambled address from which the man was calling. "Either way, tell me where we'll be meeting this chick. She sounds like fun."

"The Fallopian on Thursday," Fletch said. "11:00 a.m. sharp."

When Dex hung up, the only thing he could think to do was clean out his apartment. It started as a minimal attempt at creating order out of his possessions, but by the end of the night, he had discarded everything that might soon become a trace of who he once was.

THE FOLLOWING AFTERNOON, Dex drove the forty minutes to Nowthen and visited his mothers.

"It's about time you showed up for Christmas, Dexter!" Roberta said, rushing like a bull to the door for a hug. Dex grabbed her closer than usual. His mother Karen, who came to greet him with far less enthusiasm, fostered their usual tension by patting his back while he hugged her.

As it had snowed the night before, Dex shoveled their driveway before going inside. Their home was modest but functional, and the ones around it all looked identical save for the decorative choices that distinguished them from one another. Beyond the houses stretched what surely had once been farmland: low, rolling mounds that would simply look flat from a distance. Dex preferred this to the city; it felt more peaceful, less tarnished.

When he finally settled into a chair at his mothers' kitchen table, the words came more easily than they had in his imagination. Perhaps it was a good sign.

"I've had to face some significant life choices in the past few months, and I'm here to say goodbye."

Even Karen's knuckles turned white as she clenched her coffee mug.

Roberta's eyes widened, and she held her own mug to her chest with two hands. "What do you mean 'goodbye,' honey? Did you . . . are you getting sent to . . . ?"

"No, not Antarctica. Not yet. It could come to that, unless the rumors are true that something's gone wrong there. The Mandate 43 concentration camp thing makes me wonder. Nothing is for sure, yet."

With a stony expression, Karen pushed her chair out and stood up. "I can't hear this. I won't." She turned her back to them and began walking toward the living room.

"Mother, sit down. You might not have to deal with having a failsafe son for much longer."

At this, Karen stopped. With a slow turn, she revealed a tortured expression. Dex could swear the lesbian who never cried was on the verge of tears.

"I know I haven't visited as much as I could in the past twenty years, and I'm starting to realize that it didn't do me any good," he continued. "I don't have a lot of people in my life whom I can call close, and now the only ones I have are ones I might never see again. I wanted to give you both the benefit of knowing how much you'll always mean to me."

"Dexter, honey, what happened? Why are you saying this?"

"I don't want to say, because if things go wrong, the NRO might come here and ask about it. They've already called me in for the new 'social assessment' measure, and the rumor is they're going to start branding us as heterosexuals in a more obvious way than our TruthChip does, or worse. If they're getting ready to ship us off to these new and separated communities, like they say they are, then I'll be in a load of trouble anyway."

"It's just a protective measure," his mother said with harsh resilience.

"Who's to say they won't do the same for lesbians next?" Dex retorted. "It happened with sterilization. It could happen here. You know the fags in charge are looking for an excuse to have an all-cock world, if they're going to keep humanity around at all."

"Honey, don't talk like that!" His mom blushed, but it appeared to be more from her fear than from embarrassment at Dex's crassness.

"I'm not sure what my timetable will be," Dex continued, "but there's a chance I might be accompanying someone to the very end, if that makes sense. At least that's what I hope I'll have the balls to do. If it somehow turns out okay, and judging by the NRO's track record, I can't see how it will, I will come visit you both every day. That's a promise."

Roberta was crying now.

Then, the simple truth sounded almost elegant as Dex said it. "I like my life. Even the hard parts. Except saying goodbye. I don't even know how that part is possible."

It was Karen who stood up to fix an early dinner. Working in the kitchen had always been her way of processing life's conundrums. Dex and his mom continued to sit at the table, making circles around the facts of the situation he refused to reveal. In the space and time that passed between them, Dex evaded the terror threatening to consume him. It circled him with every breath, trying to get in his face, jeering at him over the futility of the courage he was projecting in front of his mothers. When his mom grabbed his hand, begging with her tearful eyes for something, anything, even a shred of a reason for his fateful visit, the notion he dreaded crept up behind his neck and took him like a frozen vice:

Hope really is dead.

An hour later, Dex and his mothers ate. By nightfall, he was driving away, watching them through his rearview mirror. They were standing under their front porch light, holding one another, just two women trying to cope in a rotting world.

CHAPTER 19 ❄ (HER)

T HE BELL ON THE FALLOPIAN'S DOOR JINGLED, and heavy boots stomped away snow. Fletch, who looked surprisingly unkempt, looked over Grace and Dex's shoulders. "There she is. She's a peach. You'll love her." Yet his eyes were exuding nothing but anxiety.

The Fallopian was one of the scrappiest bars in town. Grace had been waiting with Dex and Fletch for nearly an hour, picking over a grubby-looking breakfast that was now cold. She had spent the morning milling about Wayzata's greenhouse farmers' market, hoping to avoid any possible police surveillance, before taking the train into the city. On the corner of Washington and First Street she met Dex, and together they had bussed to the fringes of Obesaland to meet Fletch's contact.

The woman was thickset and short, not obese but clearly on the edge of acceptable attractiveness. Her dense and dry red hair didn't help, as it made her look like a Halloween scarecrow. But her eyes, sea blue, were those of a muse—beautiful, observant, and wildly experienced. What Grace noticed in them first was a level of fear that told its own story. Not only was this woman unhappy, but she had seen the side of life that could scar a person forever. Grace wondered if she would bear similar marks were she to come out of this pregnancy alive.

"Dude, this is Sheila."

Sheila gave Fletch a sour look as she took a seat on his side of the booth. When she turned to the two breeders, she did not extend a hand. Her gaze lingered on Grace for a moment before shifting to Dex.

"You're Dexter, I presume?"

As blunt as Sheila immediately was, Grace liked her. Something in those blue eyes.

Dex nodded and did extend a hand. "You can call me Dex. Nice to meet you." He and Sheila shook, slow but firm.

He didn't introduce me, Grace thought. Perhaps it was just to stay careful, but he seemed distant this morning, afraid.

Eyeing Dex, Sheila grabbed a toothpick and stuck it in her mouth. "You were the one in love with Diana Kring."

Grace blushed at this, but Dex did not seem to notice. Nor did he refute Sheila's statement. Fletch had finally explained upon their arrival at the Fallopian that not only had this woman known Diana Kring, but she was also involved in some sort of large-scale resistance effort against the government. Grace wondered if it was a faction of the one Theodore Bozarth had already made her a part of.

"So, you knew Diana then?" Dex asked. "How come I never knew you?"

"We were secret friends, if you get my drift."

Dex glanced at Grace, then looked at Sheila again. No, he did not get her drift.

"She found me at an underground abortion clinic I sometimes visit, in the last month before she left. She was pregnant, just like you thought, Dex. We did a lot of talking, and I introduced her around my circle. She had already found her way pretty far into the underground, but not quite far enough. Fletch, hon, can you go buy me a mint julep—extra sugar, no water?"

It was eleven-thirty in the morning. Fletch glanced at Dex, then at Grace, then at the bar, where a lone male patron was swirling a martini. The bartender was nowhere to be seen. Fletch threw a peculiarly submissive smile at Sheila, then rolled off the table to hail him down.

"That's my good little follower," Sheila said. "He's a lousy fuck, though. Thinks he's all that until he cums, and then it's abundantly clear he's just a little boy trying to find his way back to the mommy he never had."

A chuckle escaped Grace's mouth, then jumped back in. She smiled at Dex, who grinned with a sparkle in his eye.

"We should have guessed," he said.

As it turned out, Sheila Willy was a trove of secrets, one in particular she had not revealed to Fletch: she had been an accidental carrier, too. Her words were clear—not a genetic mistake, but an accidental carrier. This meant the switched-off Lrh1 genes accounting for sterility had been correctly engineered prior to her conception, and there were post-birth records to prove it, yet fertility had somehow slipped through the cracks.

"But first things first," Sheila told them. "I'm sure you're most interested in what happened to Diana." The woman twirled a strand of her arid red hair. "She started getting her periods about four months before you started dating. Periods, you know? Menstruating? Always hiding it from everyone, even to the point of being abstinent, at least up until she met you, Dex. But it happened out of nowhere, from what she told me. She was terrified. Any heterosterile would be. Same thing happened to me five years ago, but I had only one period before getting pregnant. I thought I was a genetic mistake. Anyway, I was too scared to do anything but let the baby grow until it was impossible for me to hide, and then the Bio Police arrested me, gave me an abortion, and even showed me the parts of the baby after their doctors took it out. 'So I'd never do it again,' they said. Apparently they thought I'd gone and had an underground Lrh1 reversal procedure so I could secretly start popping kids out for myself. Of course, that was right before

Mandate 42, so I had a choice between an abortion and Antarctica. I chose the abortion."

She looked back at the bar, where Fletch was still waiting to get her a drink, next to the failsafe with the martini. When Sheila turned around, Grace noticed tears in her eyes.

"Then the faggots took out my uterus. No questions, no choice. They said I was a threat, and they gave me six months in the old prison up near Sandstone. And that was immediately after the surgery. Barely gave me time to heal."

Under the table, Grace felt Dex squeeze her hand.

"So, I came back to the Twin Cities, right? Started doing some poking around. I was confused as all hell, and man, I was crazy-fuck angry about what they did to me. I *wanted* to have a baby then, just to spite them and fight the system, you know? If I could, I'd risk it again. But they took that away from me. It was a beautiful feeling, knowing I had the ability to do that. To create *life*, you know?"

Before she could stop herself, Grace nodded. "I've been feeling the same—"

Just as Dex held up his hand to hush her, Fletch slapped a mint julep in front of Sheila. But the woman ignored it, and her eyes were wide with enthusiasm, first boring into Dex, then burning into Grace. Energy sizzled in the air between them as Fletch inched back into his seat.

Still looking at Grace, the woman smiled. "So, this dickpuppet wasn't bullshitting me. Fabulous." She turned to Fletch. "Honey, good work. I didn't know you had it in you." Turning back to Grace, she finally extended a hand. "I don't believe we've been properly introduced. What's your name?"

It came out like an admission and a sigh of relief. "Grace Jarvis."

Sheila's blue eyes sparkled. "How much do you know, Grace?"

"About what?"

"About your engineer."

"I know his name was Theodore Bozarth."

"Then we had the same one. I'm assuming you're, what, thirty?"

"Twenty-eight." An innocent mistake, but Sheila seemed to be the type who liked to make them on purpose.

"Makes sense, then. And do you know what Theodore Bozarth was a part of?"

Dex brought up his hands, folded them, and rested his elbows on the table. His body language suggested to Grace an increasing level of anxiety. "Grace met with a man who was rumored to be one of Bozarth's lead researchers," he said. "She heard enough to know that every regular and Bio cop in this metro should have the names of every heterosterile Bozarth mixed up. So why haven't they done a roundup?"

Sheila snapped a finger and pointed it at Dex. "They *are*. And that's the crappy part. But the Bio Police still need proof that Bozarth's girls actually succeeded in being fertile. Thus far, it just looks to them like an abnormally high number of genetic mistakes, but nothing concrete. They've been keeping a lookout, but they've also been keeping it under wraps, because the Bio Police don't yet want to publicize the Opposition and give their good citizens a reason to question why other people are resisting. If people start thinking with their own heads, they'll start understanding what the NRO is becoming, and they, too, might want to fight back. We're living in a time when the freedom we've worked so hard for since the Bio Wars is on the verge of disappearing again, only this time for no tangible reason. Feel lucky we're still on top of that fence, not on the other side. We're still free enough to have secrets, which is why a lot of Bozarth's girls are finding a way to disappear."

Here it was, the moment Grace had been waiting for. Instead of being relieved that Sheila might actually be able to offer help, however, she was terrified.

"Where do they go?" she whispered.

Sheila grinned. "I'm not the one to tell you that, but let me ask you something, Grace and Dex. What do you plan to gain by keeping this pregnancy and trying to hold onto an ideal you'll never be able to preserve?"

Dex turned to Grace. Across from them, Fletch wore a confounded expression, as if the can of worms he had opened by introducing them to Sheila was far deeper than he had realized.

"Hope," was all Grace said, glancing into Dex's eyes.

But her hope came crumbling down when she saw the trepidation radiating from him. There it was: a verdict, even if Dex himself did not yet realize it. Terror sprang from every nuance of his face.

Grace knew it then. She would be walking the rest of her path alone. Perhaps it would be best to feign faith in Dex in the off chance she was wrong. But despair sank into her, and Sheila's next words poured forth like a death sentence.

"Fletch, you've earned a place in this. Tomorrow night. All three of you, meet me at Sterile Me Susan's. Eleven o'clock."

A MEMORY ✳ (HIM)

*T*HERE IS A STRIP OF WOODS *behind the house Dex lives in, and it is a year-round fort for himself and Matilda Liverpool. A small creek flows through the trees, often carving for them a path of lava, a castle fortification, a mysterious force field, or a border between the civilized world and the Unrecoverable Territories. Sometimes, it simply serves as a small channel of water to assist in the construction of roads, pools, or castles in the mud. On winter days like today, they like to play Sanctuary, because there is snow on the ground to make it feel like Antarctica. Of course, the trees don't help.*

It is growing late in the afternoon. Dinnertime is soon, and tonight, Matilda is planning on eating over.

"You had a baby!" she screams at Dex, attacking him from behind and binding his arms in her own. Even though she is a tough little lesbian, she always smells like the tropical mango shampoo her fathers buy. The scent is perfect, like heaven, and being ten years old, Dex has begun to feel a little bit funny when he looks at Matilda. The way the boys who play sex together probably feel, the way he has always wondered about.

But to feel it for Matilda is not normal.

"You're gone! You're going to the Sanctuary, and ain't nothing you can do about it!" Matilda screams, thrusting Dex across the frozen stream, over the boundary between Antarctica and the rest of the world.

"You can't keep me here!" he screams back, reaching over the stream and tugging on Matilda's arm.

She pulls her arm back and loses her soldier-like demeanor, in favor of bossiness, which is how she always acts. "Dex, stop it! You can't do that! Not when you're at the Sanctuary! Don't you know that you can't just escape?"

"I'm always the one who goes to the Sanctuary," he complains. "Can't we do it different?"

"Don't be stupid," Matilda yelps. "Now get back in there!"

"But what if you're my heterosterile, and we both made a baby, and we're both in the Sanctuary?" Dex poses. It would be a new way to play Sanctuary for them. No enemies, just both of them together, doing whatever it is grown-up men and women do when they get banished.

To Dex's delight, he can see Matilda soften through her scowl. She likes the idea, even though she doesn't want to admit it. "Fine. That means I'm the one having the baby."

Until the sun gets so low in the sky that the woods grow dark, the two play Sanctuary. They pretend to garden in the big communal gardens, just like they have seen on WorldCom. Matilda is pretty sure that people at the Sanctuary sleep in bunk beds stacked seven high, with ladders to get up and down. To illustrate, she climbs a tree.

"Honey, I can't get out of the bed!" she screams. "Our baby is hungry, but I can't get to the cafeteria for food! Can you bring some? Find the ladder!"

Dex finds the ladder by climbing the tree. There, he sits with Matilda, loving every inch of her, smelling her tropical mango shampoo, even in the icy crisp air. This is what everything should be like, and if he ever gets sent to the Sanctuary (because he knows, deep down, that his mothers have kept something from him, a secret that maybe he isn't going to be like the other boys), it better be like this. With Matilda.

Dex hands her a chunk of ice that he has carried up. "Here's the food, honey."

He leans in and kisses her.

It is warm, wet, and perfect, even though it tastes like the peanut butter and banana she ate after school. Matilda lets the kiss linger for just a second longer than normal pretending. Then, she pulls away and almost coughs up her snack.

"What'd you do that for? That's disgusting!"

Dex grows so red in the face that he cannot speak. The kiss felt so good, so right. He has spent curious but lonely nights hoping Matilda might actually like boys, but judging by the look on her face, she is disgusted with him.

"I think I'm going home," she says, climbing around Dex and down the tree. He sits there, shocked and ashamed of himself, sure his life is forever spoiled.

CHAPTER 20 ❄ (HIM)

DURING TRIPS TO THE BATHROOM on his Wednesday-night visits to Sterile Me Susan's, Dex had always noticed a closed door at the far end of the rear corridor. Only a handful of times had he seen anybody enter or exit it, and never would he have guessed that it was a gateway to the rebels.

It was the twenty-eighth of December, a particularly cold night.

Dex had an arm around the small of Grace's back as he ushered her into the bar. Few were able to read his emotions, but yesterday at the Fallopian, he had seen Grace recognize the dread that had been building in him over the past several days. He touched her now in an effort to show a bit of courage. Tonight's bartender, a burly, middle-aged man named Leo, watched them carefully as they crossed through the tavern.

Fletch and Sheila were sitting in the far back corner, in the shadows. The pink lights from the bar area were diffused to almost nothing, rendering the unlikely pair inconsequential against the establishment's more lively patronage.

"Are you sure you lost the cops on your way here?" Grace asked Dex, stepping around a shirtless man and pantiless woman who were gyrating against a free table.

"I think so. Did my best, anyway."

"Well, well, well. The fox and the hound arriveth!" Sheila stood up into a shaft of light falling in from the restroom hallway. She was sporting a bubbly turquoise blouse that, combined with her brilliant eyes and orange hair, reminded Dex of a walking coral reef. Fletch was a different story. Dex had never seen the man so ungroomed. His long hair was greasy, and his stubble was several days past sexy. Life among the rebels seemed to have transformed him completely.

After making small talk with them for five minutes, Sheila stood up. Fletch copied her, and much too quickly. She glared at him. "Fletch, be nonchalant, or get out of here." She turned to Dex and Grace and gestured sensually toward the bathrooms. "This way," she said with a wink.

As they walked down the rear corridor, two women and a man were walking back toward the bar. Judging by the women's chatter and their distance from the man, Dex presumed they were separate parties. The man he recognized as a Sterile Me Susan's regular, but another slice of recollection suddenly plucked his consciousness. The man had also been stirring a martini at the Fallopian the previous morning. Tonight, he looked Dex in the eyes with a brief nod as he passed.

Color Dex paranoid, but he swore there was lust in the man's gaze. If there was lust, there was sexual attraction, which suggested the man was a homosexual.

What would a homosexual be doing at two of the most heterosexual bars in town? Dex wondered.

Later, he would wish he had stopped for an answer, but right then, anxiety was chasing him from one second to the next, and all his focus was on outrunning it. Sheila took them through the door at the end of the hallway, which led to a storeroom filled with cleaning supplies, liquor, chairs, two extra tables, and an assortment of odds and ends. Lit by a large neon "Open" sign on the far right wall, the room glowed a musty purple color. Only when Sheila led them straight for the sign did Dex notice another closed door.

"Out we go," she said, opening the door, which led to a small courtyard blocked in on all sides by tall, windowless brick buildings. It was like an alley walled in on both ends, illuminated by the frozen night's dazzling moon. Twenty feet ahead of them, sitting against one of the towering brick walls, was the quadrangle's only interruption in uniformity: a cellar entrance with two rusted doors.

Sheila led them to the cellar. "Here's where we split up. Fletch, go back to the bar, by the bathroom hallway. Stand guard. Leo knows you're back here, so it'll just look like you're coming out of the store room. Call me if you see anything suspicious, particularly people hanging out in that hallway. I'll call you before we come back up."

"What's down there?" Fletch asked.

But Sheila shook her head. "You earned your role, which is up here. Now play it. Close these doors behind us." She ushered Grace into the cellar, then Dex. He clapped Fletch on the back before stepping onto the first stair in a series that faded downward, into the depths of the city.

"See you soon, bud," he told Fletch.

Their feet scraped the cement steps, and once they were all underground, the cellar doors creaked closed, shutting out what remained of the moonlight. Keys jingled in the darkness, then suddenly there was light from Sheila's LED keychain. Moldy bricks lined either side of the wall, smelling musty despite the cold air filtering down from above. Perhaps it meant heat was rising from below. The stairway brought them down at least two stories, to a small landing faced with another metal door. A strip of white light shone from under the crack at its base.

"Now, they know you're coming," Sheila told Dex and Grace, not caring to reveal the identities of "they." "Even so, you're going to have to go through some tests in order to proceed. Grace, that means *you*. Dex, you'll more or less proceed by default once we confirm Grace is pregnant. I know neither of you enough to actually trust you, but the Opposition is on a time crunch, and they're getting desperate to round up as many pregnant women as possible, so I'm taking my chances that you're legit. As silly as Fletch up there is, though, I do trust him. He wants to fight, and as he vouches for you, I think there's a good chance you're real. If you're somehow working for the Bio Police, I regret to say that the people down here are *not* going to let you out, just like Fletch wouldn't if you turned and ran right now. He's armed."

Dex gulped back the knot of discomfort in his throat as Sheila knocked three times on the door. "Queen of Sheba," she said.

From the other side of the door came the high-pitched beep and roll of someone's TruthChip opening a lock. Dex held up a hand to cover his eyes as the slab swung open into a wall of blinding light. His vision adjusted to reveal a white brick wall jutting out of a cement floor, five feet past the threshold. Standing to the side and holding the door was a man with mussed sand-colored hair, a scraggly goatee, and crooked wire-rimmed glasses. He was holding an old-fashioned automatic rifle, the illegal type that shot bullets.

"For Christ's sake, hurry," he whispered as Sheila led them into the chamber, which stretched left into a long LED-lit hallway.

"Guys, this is Barry, and he's dramatic," Sheila said. "We've come to see Dr. Trojan. This couple needs testing and approval for transfer to the Cliff House."

"These are your supposed referrals from that Fletch Novotny twerp?"

"Yes, as it so happens," Sheila said. "Barry, meet Grace Jarvis and Dex Wheelock. Grace is one of Bozarth's, and Dex is the father." She did not wait for Barry to lead her down the hallway. Dex tried to place a hand on Grace's back again as they followed, but this time, she sped up before he could reach it.

Sheila's hair and turquoise garments were an explosion of color against the stark white walls. Where Dex, Grace, and Barry's shoes left muffled sounds behind, Sheila's heels left sharp echoes. They approached another door, this one a metal blast door of sorts that looked far stronger than the previous two access points. Barry scanned his wrist against the code reader, and Dex heard a powered lock release somewhere within. It grated open horizontally from two sides with a deep mechanical groan.

"Try not to do anything stupid," Barry said.

They left the man behind to resume his guard duty. The door led to another stairway, this one a far more industrial extension of the stark hallway they had just left. Dex counted as they descended four more stories.

"This was a safety bunker during the Bio Wars," Sheila said. "They built the buildings on top of it about six years in, and lucky us, ownership passed along to Opposition supporters. Do you happen to be familiar with the clean liquid hydrogen tycoon and North American NRO Representative Frederik Carnevale?"

The last Dex had heard, Carnevale had been pushing for same-sex-education-only programs in all regional schools. Throughout the territory, he was the New Rainbow Order's most powerful footprint. "He's, like, premiere-fucking-fag around here, isn't he?" Dex said.

"And head orchestrator of the largest social rebellion in human history," Sheila said. "The NRO's agenda following Mandate 43 is *big*, but Carnevale is on the inside, leading us."

Grace shook her head in disbelief. "*Frederik Carnevale?* You can't be serious."

"We have information filtered straight down from him. He's the eyes and ears of the Opposition, Grace Jarvis, and he's smack-dab in the middle of the NRO's upper echelon. I know people who know him, and it's his Cliff House on Lake Superior you'll be going to. And if you both happen to be snitches for the NRO and try to rat me out for telling you this, nobody will believe you. Carnevale is as far in as they come. Rumor has it he's been considered for Secretary General once the Queen . . . leaves office."

A tremor of foreboding colored Sheila's tone. The Queen had no visible plans to relinquish his leadership. Dex glanced at Grace, whose wide eyes and sweating brow suggested she was finally absorbing the dire reality of this mutinous path. They were at the bottom of the stairs now, under the wintery gleam of the LED lights lining the ceiling.

"There's so much more to this thing than just biological resistance by people like Theodore Bozarth," Sheila said. "But just like the Opposition has a plan, so does the NRO. Mandate 43 is just a cover-up, according to the lines of communication coming down from Carnevale."

From what the woman had gleaned by listening to those who were closer to the Opposition's higher ranks, the mandate for the "social assessment" of heterosexuals scheduled for implementation on the first of February was one of the government's last tactics in the plan for a staged terrorist attack. "They're going to initiate a massive strike and blame it on fringe remnants of God's Army who are trying to stop the social assessments," Sheila told them. "This will lead to a declaration of martial law, and then anything even resembling the assessments will no longer be necessary, because they can then start arresting and removing failsafes, heterosteriles, and carriers on the grounds of intercontinental protection." Sheila claimed not to know any further information than that, because the Opposition's different branches functioned under unity by secrecy. "All I know is the Opposition is huge, and we're scrambling to gather as many failsafes, carriers, and accidental carriers as possible—not just Bozarth's, mind you—in order to form a colony of heterosexuals once whatever they're planning is all said and done."

Dex grappled at his mental strings to understand the scope of it all. If this woman was to be believed, the resistance effort was not only worldwide but also oiled so well that it was thriving right under the New Rainbow Order's nose.

"And Diana knew about all this?" he asked.

"She didn't know a thing until she got pregnant and we found her. The TruthChips Bozarth planted in his girls after 2359 were equipped with wireless biological activation devices. When a woman became pregnant, the chip would read it in her blood and alert whoever might be watching. You and I were too old to have them, Grace, so nobody could track us down. Thank the stars you were lucky."

"You mean they were breaking the Spatial Privacy Act by making chips traceable?" Dex asked. "Do you think the NRO has been doing that too?"

"I can't say. I wouldn't be surprised, but I doubt it's the case with any of the older chips. You can easily run tests to figure it out either way, but of course they all operate on particular frequencies, and there are a billion different frequencies, so identifying one for any given chip can be difficult. Bozarth passed his custom tracking system down to the right hands, which is why we even have access to it today."

"Lovely."

"In a matter of speaking," Sheila said. "In any case, the Opposition is already starting the underground evacuation before the NRO reaches a point of martial law, which is why you both are here. As I said before, we're scrambling."

One final doorway, this one air-locked but equipped with sheets of what Dex could only assume was bullet-proof glass, slid open before them. A heavy breeze of warm air washed over his face.

"Welcome to the Opposition," Sheila said.

Stretching before them was a cave of technology that looked like a cross between a hospital and an office building. Glass cubicles, some empty and some occupied, lined the walls to the right. To the left, Dex saw men and women milling past rooms filled with wall and desk coms, each set to a different channel. In front of some sat people talking digital face to digital face, and on others were what appeared to be the everyday WorldCom newscasts. As Sheila led them along the main corridor, past the cubicles and com rooms, the walls on either side disappeared, only to be replaced by blue-curtained medical stations. Some of the curtains were open, showing off clean hospital tables, equipment sterilizers, ultrascopes, and desk coms. Each partition also held an assortment of physician's materials: ultra-violet sterilization rods, cotton swabs, speculums, heartbeat monitors, and bottles of disinfectant. Other sections were closed, and Dex could hear voices behind the curtains. They sounded like women asking questions and male doctors responding.

"You mean overseas?" one of the women said just before a man answered, *"Yes, but you'll be completely safe, I assure you. Now please, if you could sit back on the table for me . . ."*

Dex struggled to hear more, but Sheila grabbed his arm and pulled him forward. She stopped them at the last curtained medical partition on the right. Farther down, the facility stretched into a darker hallway that veered left, into some unknowable quarter. Dex turned to Grace and saw she was already watching him with an exhilarated expression. There was fear in it, of course, but it was clear Grace had bravery on her side. This was her future, and she seemed to have accepted it with open arms.

She's the one carrying our child, Dex thought. *It's more real for her. It always was.*

Now, he came face-to-face with his true nature.

This has gone too far.

He turned away from Grace, toward the air-sealed door now at the far end of the facility. It was his only way out.

"Come on, Dex Wheelock," Sheila said, apparently noticing he had stopped moving. "If you're coming, you're coming now. We've got to run Grace's tests."

But there it was, crawling up his throat, reaching the back of his lips: weakness. In its tracks was self-loathing. "I . . . I don't think I want to do this."

He was not even facing Grace, but he could feel her shrink behind him. A mother alone, left to fight the evils of the world and, possibly, die while society watched and laughed.

"Dex?" Grace's voice. Crushed, but not surprised?

"I just don't think I'm ready."

"Well, fuck *ready*," Sheila said, suddenly irate. "You mean to tell me that you, a graying failsafe of almost forty with no visible meaning in his life, are going to crawl back to that hole of pathetic loneliness and, what, *wait* for your day to come? *Wait* for the NRO to just take you while you could be putting up a fight? Are you fucking *serious*?"

Tears of shame crept into Dex's eyes. He turned to Grace. "I honestly don't think I have what it takes. I'm so sorry."

Grace's expression told him more about himself than he ever wanted to know. She did not need words; her feelings were clear enough. She had hoped to see more strength in him, hoped he would have fought harder for their child.

Sheila was already talking into her pocket com, summoning someone to escort Dex away. Grace took a step back, toward her new ally.

"Go," she told him. "Just go. Be safe, and good luck. I won't try to contact you."

"Grace—"

But Sheila had been quick. A forceful hand grabbed Dex's shoulder. He turned to see a massive man staring down at him. Whatever muscle existed underneath his clothes had Dex's out-massed by threefold. His hips were equipped with not just one but three guns, and the boots on his feet looked steel-toed, the type that could land a deadly kick.

"Take him, Blitz," Sheila said. "Keep him in the holding room until I get back and try to talk some sense into him. If I don't come back, bring him downstairs. He's a risk."

"Wait, what? Downstairs?" Dex asked, but the man pushed him forward, past Sheila and Grace. "Where are you taking me?" Dex demanded. "Grace, wait—*wait*!"

"I hope you'll get another chance," he heard Sheila say as the monster named Blitz pushed him deeper into the bunker.

CHAPTER 21 ✳ (HER)

S HE HAD SENSED IT ALL ALONG, that underlying fear in Dex. He was both intelligent and simple, and these were traits that made stepping out of oneself very difficult. Father or not, Dex Wheelock had a life and personal experience to preserve. Grace understood this, but it did not stop anger, disappointment, and embarrassment from burning through her.

Like a little boy, crawling back to the womb, where he'll be safe, she thought.

Only he wouldn't be. Not in the New Rainbow Order's world.

When he disappeared around the corner, Sheila nudged her along, into the medical partition. The only place to sit was the poly-covered examination table, so Grace decided to stand against it.

"I'll go find Dr. Trojan," Sheila said. Before Grace could respond, the scarecrow woman whisked the blue curtain closed. Grace was left with the sterile smell of the medical room and the noises filtering in from the outside: clicks and clanks from the other curtained rooms, WorldCom News, Twin Cities Com News, people laughing in hushed voices, and wheels of a push cart running along the cement floor, toward the darkened hallway Dex had disappeared into.

Grace scrunched her hands into fists. *Serves him right. It'll be his loss not to see our baby be born.*

But the thought left her feeling stupid and alone.

The curtain rings scraped open with a quick, jingly rip, and a square-jawed, middle-aged man in an unbuttoned white lab coat stepped in. He was wearing an ultrascope eyepiece and holding the accompanying wireless probe, much like the one her dad had used to test her. "Hi there. Grace Jarvis?" he said without waiting for a response. He adjusted the probe's pulse controls. "I'm Dr. Trojan, but you can call me Ben. Let's *not* pretend we're not all here for the same reason, shall we?"

"Are we?" Grace asked. A slight flightiness in Ben's voice would have suggested the telltale if his Helovan shoes hadn't already. He was a homosexual.

"What? Because I'm a queen, you're thinking I'm not on your side? Please, princess, we're all in this together. I hate the NRO as much as anyone else in here, so let's get something straight: not all fags are out to eradicate you breeders. In fact, my own father worked for Theodore Bozarth. I assume you know who—"

"I know who he was, yes. I got that far."

"Well, good. Now, let me take a look at you."

Dr. Ben (as Grace suddenly felt the desire to call him) instructed her to unbutton her pants, pull them down below her waist, and lift up her shirt. He pulled the ultrascope's glass viewing screen over his eyes, squeezed out a wide ring of cold jelly onto Grace's abdomen, then pressed the probe into it and swirled. Grace watched Dr. Ben's gaze focus on the screen being projected on the glass covering his eyes. He moved the scope around, presumably to view her insides at as many angles as possible.

"Would you like to see the baby?"

Grace's breath almost stopped. It was something her dad had not taken the time to offer for fear of being caught. "Could I?"

"Of course. Too early to tell at this point if it's a boy or a girl, but you can definitely see the face and fingers and toes." He slipped the eyepiece off his head and put it over Grace's face. And there it was, there *he* or *she* was, focused with three-dimensional, lifelike precision on the electronic visor. "There, see the face?" Dr. Ben shifted the probe up and twisted it, and there it was, her child's face.

Incredible. A miracle.

The tiny hands were already forming, held together up near its nose and minuscule eyes. There was a leg, a knee, a shin, a foot, and tiny little nubs for toes. The baby's head still looked huge compared to the rest of the body, and Grace's imagination twinkled at the thought of what thoughts that tiny brain might someday produce, if it would ever have the chance. Grace took a moment for herself to hope. This beautiful thing was her responsibility now, her gift to a darkening world. She looked closely at the ultrascope's screen and saw ears on the baby's head. *Ears! At not even twelve weeks!*

Somehow, the baby's miniscule hand curved into a fist. Grace gasped.

Awe. She was in awe.

"There, see? Is it moving? Looks healthy, from what I can tell without blood tests, even though Sheila said you had bleeding early on, like a lot of Bozarth's other women," Dr. Ben said. "You'll get all the proper tests up at the Cliff House, but suffice it to say I'll clear you for departure. We're on a tight timeframe here. Oh, and the baby's already kicking and swimming like crazy, but you won't start feeling it for another month or two. It'll happen when you least expect it."

Grace continued staring at her child, who was floating around in peace, oblivious to the dangers already threatening it. Seeing this new life up close, Grace realized how impossible it had been before for her to understand what pregnancy truly was, what it meant: the creation of a soul.

My oh my, she thought. *If only Dex had stuck around to see this. He would have stayed.*

"It's lucky ultrascopes are so portable now," Dr. Ben was saying. "This is an old model, obviously, but it used to be that ultrasounds ran off massive machines doctors had to wheel around their examination rooms. It would have been impossible to be incognito with prenatal screenings back then. You're fortunate everything medical uses ultrascopes now, in a matter of speak—"

A low rumble sounded from somewhere above them. The ultrascope's visor, holding the image of Grace's child, vibrated in front of her eyes.

Then, from a distance, came the unmistakable wail of sonic guns.

CHAPTER 22 ✳ (HIM)

YOU PATHETIC FOOL. LOOK WHAT YOU'VE BECOME.

Dex sat in Blitz's holding room, which was actually nothing more than an office near the end of a long hallway, the dark one he had seen veering left beyond the main chamber as Sheila escorted them in. Judging by its size and the electrical outlet holes still in the brick wall, he guessed the room had once been a crowded studio living space of some sort, when this place had been a terror shelter during the Bio Wars. Just before Blitz shoved him into the room, Dex had noticed the blinking security lights of another airtight door even farther down the hallway. He could only assume it led out another exit. After ten minutes of silence, Dex addressed the immense bouncer.

"Am I under some sort of Opposition arrest?"

Blitz was standing with nonchalant posture by the door, chewing on sunflower seeds. "Well, sort of," he said. "Only until we figure you for a coward and not some sort of mole. Dr. Trojan'll debrief Ms. Willy on whether the woman you came with is actually pregnant, and then we'll ask the necessary questions. If she ain't got a baby in her, it looks like you both might be in some trouble. We don't like to harm folks, but if someone gets in the way of our operation, there ain't much we can do. Me? I'm guessing you're just scared, like I was. I ran, too. My girl, they got her after that. Got the baby, too."

"She's at the Sanctuary?"

Blitz shrugged. "Don't know. That would be a blessing. From what I've been hearing, though, they've been taking women to harvesting camps for the past year or so, where their eggs'll be taken as needed, once they build the new engineering facilities. I think that's what they did with my Stacy."

"How come they didn't catch you?"

"Like I said, I ran," Blitz replied. "Just like you."

"I made the wrong choice."

Blitz leaned forward now, his lips stretching into an alarming grin. "But there's something else to all this, man. I'm low on the totem pole here, so I don't really know, but it's got to do with the Sanctuary. The NRO ain't taking women there no more, which means they sure wouldn't be taking failsafes either. I've heard rumors that the Opposition—"

Somewhere above them, a thundering boom shook the bunker.

A detonation.

The door, Dex thought.

"What the *fuck* was that?" Blitz yelled, pulling a gun off his belt. It was the illegal kind with metal bullets, the type that could not distinguish between damage or death. Blitz spun his massive body around and pulled Dex toward his center of gravity. "Did you rat us out? *Did you show them where we were?*"

"No!" Dex choked. "I have no idea who else was up there! I came with Fletch Novotny!"

Suddenly, the shriek of an alarm echoed through the bunker.

"Fletch Novotny, the little panty waste who fashions himself a terrorist?"

What? Terrorist?

"God, everyone he knows is under investigation by the police! He was planning to bomb an engineering facility before Sheila set him straight a few months ago, and his name got out! I thought Ms. Willy fucked him into line, but it looks like she fucked that too!"

Dex's mind raced, retraced every step of the day. It could not be a coincidence that the facility was being raided just minutes after he and Grace had arrived.

Then came his answer: it was the man who had flashed him a glimpse of lustful eye contact in the bathroom hallway, the same one who had been stirring a martini at the Fallopian. He was an undercover fag, and they had led him straight to the Opposition.

CHAPTER 23 ✸ (HER)

"THAT'S A BREACH," Dr. Ben said, carefully but swiftly pulling the ultrascope off Grace's head. "We need to get you downstairs. Those are NRO weapons." For a moment, Grace only stared at him without an aim in the world. It was her and Dex, it had to be. How else could the police have found the Opposition at the exact same time? But they had been careful going to the bar, purposefully eating dinner in a restaurant that had two exits, and leaving through the back. . . .

"Ms. Jarvis, come on! We need to get you out!" Dr. Ben yelled. He was already dialing his com. A second later, he was speaking, looking anxiously toward the entrance. "Yes, Mr. Redmond. This is Minneapolis. We've had a breach. Eight women were scheduled for tonight with escort Sheila Anne Willy, TruthChip number 743-2934-82. I wanted to confirm, in case they can get out—"

Sheila was just running up to Grace's examination partition as the man drew back the blue curtain. Her words came out between gasps. "Something happened. They must have found Fletch upstairs. I tried to buzz Barry, but his com went straight to voice message!"

"They might've found the rear entrance too," Dr. Ben told Sheila, holding the com away from his mouth. "Christ, there are seven other women. Can you wait?"

"Is it smart?"

Dr. Ben shook his head. "You're right. Go. I'll lead them out. You take Ms. Jarvis here. You know how to get to the tunnels." He glanced past Sheila, at the other women filtering out of their respective partitions. "Look, there're three more now. I'll tell them to follow you!" He ran, yelling into his com again, leaving Sheila and Grace amid the clamor of panicking dissenters.

"Come on," Sheila said, grabbing Grace's wrist. The woman pulled her down a hallway she had not noticed when they first entered the medical chamber. It was lit but empty, and closed metal doors sailed past as they ran. Suddenly, footsteps sounded to their right. Grace looked up. It was a stairway, filled with more people moving down from some higher floor—Opposition members who all seemed to be yelling at each other, as if such panic could somehow save them. They continued down the stairway, past Grace's floor, into darkness.

"We have to find Dex!" Grace screamed over the clamor. "I can't leave him!"

"He left you!" Sheila yelled back. "We have to get out! He should have stayed with you!"

"But he's my baby's *father*!"

Then, another explosion shook the bunker, this one much closer. Turning around now would be impossible. Grace could barely feel her feet as they carried her with the wave of people, deep into the black.

CHAPTER 24 ❋ (HIM)

"WE MIGHT BE IN SOME BAD SHIT," Blitz said before pushing Dex to the back of the room. "Wait here."

But Dex followed him into the hallway. They ran down the darkened corridor and toward the light, leaving the empty waiting room behind. In a matter of seconds, they were back in the main chamber with the hospital curtains and cubicles. The room was in chaos. Three women, who looked just as new to the bunker as he was, stood in the middle hallway with pale faces and terrified eyes, yelling names of those who had presumably brought them underground. "Dr. Trojan!" one woman was crying over and over. People in cubicles were either sitting with bouncing fingertips at their desk coms, waiting for data to finish deleting, or ripping out the coms' cloud chips outright. A group of nearly twenty people swept out from a hallway Dex had not even noticed, one lined with closed doors, and they ran past him, in the direction of the holding cell.

The other air-locked door, Dex thought. *It's the only way out.* He hoped he was wrong.

Blitz turned around to see Dex standing behind him. "Are you some sort of idiot? Get back to the other door! Follow them out the back!" Blitz disappeared into the fray of scurrying rebels, gun drawn, running straight toward the entrance. He lumbered past the woman screaming for Dr. Trojan, who swung around in tandem with the bouncer as he rushed by, as if he and his weapons might somehow help her. But she froze in her tracks, centering in Dex's field of vision. Dex ran forward, toward the blue curtained examination rooms, to direct the panicked woman toward the back. If he could help her, perhaps it would undo just an ounce of what he had done to Grace. But through the scattering people, he saw purple-clad figures swarming on the other side of the glass quarantine door. The Bio Police.

Grace. I have to find Grace.

He turned to the screaming woman. "Go! Go that way! There's another door!"

But just as he said it, a screaming crowd poured back out of the darkened hallway, the same one Dex's holding room was in. "They're at the back door too!" a man screamed. "No-go on the back door! Get out through the cave! Down the stairs!" Those who could find a sense of order ran down the hallway with the closed doors. Others milled about like ants caught between stomping feet.

"If there's another way out, they'll know it! Follow them!" Dex yelled at the woman before jumping to the curtain on his left and ripping it open. Inside, another ashen woman, just as confused as the other, was standing erect but motionless with wide eyes. "Go!" Dex said, ushering her out. "The NRO's here! Go! Follow that crowd!"

Dex ran from curtain to curtain, ripping them open, horrified to see that the rest of the medical partitions were empty. There was no sign of Grace, and with that emptiness came the crushing truth.

You left her to die, and now you've lost her for good.

Behind him, the quarantine door exploded, and the sound of police boots and pointed sonic guns filled the room. Dex felt the skin on the side of his face burst as brick shrapnel tore into him, and then came the piercing beat of a gun pulse, hitting him directly on the side of his head. Suddenly, his body seized, and his stomach jumped upward, into his chest. Nausea took Dex, and he fell.

PART TWO:

THE STORM HAS COME

"PEACE BY PERSUASION HAS A PLEASANT
SOUND, BUT I THINK WE SHOULD NOT BE ABLE
TO WORK IT. WE SHOULD HAVE TO TAME THE
HUMAN RACE FIRST, AND HISTORY SEEMS TO
SHOW THAT THAT CANNOT BE DONE."

—Mark Twain

CHAPTER 25 ✳ (HER)

THERE WAS A TUNNEL underneath the Sterile Me Susan's facility, leading through Sheiks Cave and under the Mississippi River. When Grace and Sheila finally emerged into the frigid night, Grace called her dad's pocket com right away, telling him only the necessary details: something had gone wrong, and she and Sheila needed an inconspicuous way to travel north, to Duluth, preferably without having to scan their TruthChips for any purchases or rentals. No, he could not come with them; no, Dex Wheelock was not coming either. Stuart refrained from prying further and complied within the hour. He booked them a hotel room in a fringe suburb of Minneapolis, bought them two grocery bags of food, and rented a car they could keep for four weeks. He made no mention of how he might get the car back on time, and Grace offered no ideas. She could be anywhere in four weeks. Sheila had made no claim that Frederik Carnevale's Cliff House would be their last stop.

"I'll be in touch when I can," Grace said, hugging her dad goodbye in the hotel parking lot. *I might never be back*, she wanted to say but could not. He already knew.

Stuart hugged the air right out of her. "I love you, Pix. More than you'll ever know. I hope I was good enough."

"You've been the best dad in the world." It was impossible to hold back tears. "And can you tell Linda that I didn't know it would end this way? I would have said goodbye."

"I'll tell her."

"And even Father. And Abraham and Lars. Tell them, if there's ever a good time."

Stuart held Grace until Sheila tugged on her sleeve and said, "We should get a move on."

They parted ways. The two women settled into their hotel room and collapsed into bed within minutes. Sheila slept the night, but Grace's sleep came in fragments. Every time a police siren passed on the streets below, she awoke, sure they had been found out. But each one continued on its way, fading into the night. It seemed, at least for a time, that they were safe.

THEY LEFT THE TWIN CITIES AT THREE O'CLOCK the following afternoon, hoping the rental car would keep them inconspicuous on their trip up I-35. As the buildings disappeared behind them, dried-up and harvested cornfields, each dotted in distant spots with year-round greenhouses, flew past them on either side. Patches of yellowed corn stalks left for wildlife to use as winter refuge shone with incongruous warmth against the purple winter sky.

"I hope we beat the heavy snow," Sheila said, hunching forward and peeling her eyes at the thickening clouds. In front of them, white flurries were already racing at the car's windshield, flying into oblivion when they hit. It was just their luck that by nightfall the snow would begin accumulating. "We've got another two hours before we get up to the North Shore, but if the snow gets worse, it's going to be a pain in the ass," Sheila said. "The Cliff House is . . . well . . . on a cliff. Which means this little car will have to make it up the hill. And they don't salt that driveway, as a rule, except in emergencies. Better for it to look untouched."

That Grace was about to enter the home of one of the New Rainbow Order's most lauded representatives still seemed both improbable and imbecilic, a trap beyond obvious. But Sheila had insisted when they first climbed into the rental car, "No, no, no. Carnevale inherited this house from his fathers, who were also involved in the Opposition. This goes back to even before the Queen rose to power, hon. Trust me on that."

"But how do you know all this?" Grace asked. "What makes you so sure it isn't all just another way to get rid of people like us?"

"I'm still breathing. That's what makes me sure."

"It doesn't mean they're trustworthy."

Sheila sighed. "Do you want to escape or not?"

"I don't want my baby to die."

"And you want to be part of the Opposition?"

"I already am."

"So, then, trust them. I've been a recruiter for Bozarth's girls for just under two years now, and I've visited the Cliff House. Got turned on to it when I was just like you. Totally naïve to everything going on in the shadows, you know? I met a chick in Sandstone Prison. Another of Bozarth's, just like us. I was clueless about everything when I got pregnant, but this woman was not. Betty Stevens was her name. She told me in jail that she had been on her way to a safe place to have her baby when the Bio Police caught her. Betty didn't behave very well, and I got out of jail before she did. But right before I left, she turned me on to a contact she had with some 'rebel group' operating out of a mansion north of Duluth."

And the rest was history. Sheila explained everything as the sky thickened and the flurries turned into full-on snow. Betty Stevens's bio crimes had been no more severe than those of Sheila or Grace, but she had an attitude, and her punishment had involved almost constant torture. The Bio Police visited daily to interrogate her about where she had been heading when they caught her. Betty had been careful to erase all incriminating information from her com, but the police still captured a suitcase packed not just with daily essentials but also with obvious keepsakes: holopanels, jewelry, love letters—the mementos of a woman disappearing forever.

Betty had toyed with the Bio Police, mocking them, claiming the New Rainbow Order's effort to dominate society would eventually crumble. But she would never tell them how or why, not on her life. Nor would she breathe a word to them about the Cliff House or the informant who had told her about it, because the joke was on them: she would die before revealing secrets of the Opposition.

On the day before Sheila's release from Sandstone Prison, Betty had spilled everything to her over lunch, all in whispers, as the prison guards stood at the cafeteria doors, watching them both. Sheila had learned about the Cliff House and the com number to call to meet people who could lead her there. "Use my name when you talk to the man who answers the com," Betty had instructed Sheila. "Tell him what I told you and that you want in. I know your type, and I know you hate the NRO as much as I do. The Opposition needs people like you."

Sheila had sat tight for nearly a year after her release. The police were still monitoring her, not because she was a biological threat but because her anger could inspire rash behavior that might expose the Opposition. They knew Sheila had become chummy with Betty Stevens, and they suspected she had also become privy to the information they so coveted.

"But finally, one day, I was alone in a bar where I worked, cleaning up for the night. There was a public com there, one anyone could use, where it was easy to call any random address without being traced. So, I called the one Betty made me memorize."

It was surprisingly simple after that. The man who answered the com had run a background check on her, seen her crimes against the government, seen their resulting punishments, and inducted her into the Opposition in a matter of days. It was necessary that new recruits with previous criminal records be treated as near-strangers, only to be given assignments with objectives vague enough not to warrant unwanted attention. Her assignment was to monitor a selection of Theodore Bozarth's secret female weapons.

"But I fell in love with the man who met with me," Sheila told Grace. "He took me to the Cliff House. Just for two days, to help with some new intakes. The police had finally started leaving me alone by then, so for all they knew it might have just been a simple holiday on Lake Superior. Nothing their prejudiced little minds couldn't wrap around."

The Cliff House was over four hundred years old, she explained, and it sat just northwest of an equally ancient traffic tunnel on Highway 61. It was elevated, secluded, and the road to it was hidden in the old-fashioned way wealthy people often preferred, so that any approach by snooping strangers would prove difficult, if they were inspired to seek it out at all. Rumor even had it an old Hollywood movie star had once owned the house. The glamour involved in that era of art history had always fascinated Grace, and this would be like touching part of it, like being in one of the old movies herself.

But she had questions: "Am I going to have my baby at the Cliff House? Does it have . . . medical equipment?" The inquiries came out sounding juvenile.

"Women are examined and monitored here, that much I know for sure. Again, I've been there only once for those two days. I'm on a need-to-know basis, and there are certain things I haven't needed to know. This will be a first, me being an escort."

Sheila had indirectly avoided giving a solid answer, so Grace pressed further, trying a roundabout approach. "Dr. Ben called there during the raid."

"Yeah, he would have. And to answer your second question: yes, they have ample medical facilities at the Cliff House. The mansion is a normal mansion, and the Opposition facilities are below, hidden inside the cliff. Tunnels, more or less. Carved out even before the Bio Wars, from what I gathered."

They drove in silence for a few minutes. Then, another question occurred to Grace. "What happened to the guy you fell in love with? Does he still work up there?"

"He's gone."

It was a succinct answer. Noticing Sheila's tightly closed lips, Grace asked no more.

THEY CONTINUED NORTH. As the interstate's flatness gave way to the craggy hills surrounding Duluth, Grace watched the day disappear. It still struck her as surreal that she was living the nightmare scenario driven into every heterosterile during childhood. Yet she had survived the night, and here she was, alive. It was already counting for something.

Duluth was one of the few cities still removed from the spread of civilization between Minneapolis and Chicago, resting along a stretch of hillside on the western tip of Lake Superior. Once a simple, middle-class city contained in its own economic bubble, it had transformed into a hidden refuge during the Bio Wars as disease and fire had disintegrated the larger world. It was a sparsely populated and self-sufficient city with a limitless supply of water, so land values had surged as the terrified wealthy of the Midwest flocked there in droves, bringing the population (then dwindling due to sterilization trends) to a new equilibrium of around fifty thousand. As genetic engineering overtook heterosexual reproduction, Duluth continued to attract entrepreneurs, politicians, artists, and those who could afford an alternative residence during summer months.

Today, one of those residents was Frederik Carnevale. Or, as Dex had put it, one of the New Rainbow Order's "premiere-fucking-fags."

Now, bright dots of light greeted them as they came over the last hill and wound down the slippery interstate into the city. Most of

Duluth's buildings were old, well over a hundred years, and there were many spanning back further still, to the age before population control and the Bio Wars. The mishmash of structures rushed by in the dark. Newer buildings rose as high as sixty stories, and older ones bowed beneath them, like slaves in deference to the glitters of modernity. The freeway ran through a series of aged tunnels before ending just a few hundred feet from Lake Superior's shoreline. Tonight, with the snow, there was no moon reflection to spark life into the stretch of black water beyond.

Thirty minutes later, city lights were scarce. Trees lined Grace and Sheila's left side; Lake Superior lined their right. The passage of Highway 61 was narrow and crumbled, and north of a small town called Two Harbors, antiquated metal road signs brightened momentarily in the car's headlights to mark towns that no longer existed. It was as if people in the north, even the nitpicky homosexuals who now populated it, had simply forgotten to update this section of the world. Grace doubted it had changed much since the Bio Wars.

Suddenly, Sheila slowed the car and turned left.

Loop Road, Grace read on a faded green street sign.

After about one and a half miles, they turned right and began ascending a hill that had been obscured in the darkness. Through the trees, however, a single light was visible and growing closer. When Sheila switched the car off, she turned to Grace and grinned. "We're here."

CHAPTER 26 ❄ (HIM)

ANOTHER FIST, ANOTHER SPLATTER OF BLOOD on the floor beneath his chair.

"*What else do you know about that facility?*"

Dex's questioner, Detective Lance Riley, was massive and muscular in his skintight purple uniform. The man was standing over him in an interrogation room at the Bio Police detention center in South Minneapolis, where the walls were white, the LED lights blinding, and the metal table and chair ungodly cold against Dex's naked body. Two officers were standing next to the door with their zippers undone, their pants unbuckled, and their bodies ready to punish him if he did not answer the questions. And he did not.

"Okay, you asked for it," Detective Riley lisped.

It was not so bad at first. The two officers only gagged him between words. It was all Dex could do to resist the urge to latch onto their erections with his teeth.

"I don't know anything," he repeated when breathing was possible again. Yes, he could tell them about Fletch Novotny, Sheila Willy, and Frederik Carnevale, then about Grace Jarvis and the baby he had just abandoned. But he had been cowardly enough for one night. These awful homosexuals could use their sex to abuse him all they wanted. He would stand his ground, perhaps even laugh at them.

Dex gagged when the guards forced themselves into his mouth once again. He wondered how they punished their own kind. Women? Nude grandmothers sitting on their faces?

Two minutes passed before the officers pulled out for a second time.

"At least you guards are attractive, as far as fags go," Dex choked.

Detective Riley leaned forward, toward Dex, rubbing his own crotch. "You want to see attractive?" He grabbed a bottle of lube that was sitting at the center of the table.

Thank heavens Dex's middle school teacher Mr. Jacobson had given every male in the class a dildo on their first day of seventh grade, because otherwise this sensation would have been completely new. Dex had experimented with the dildo simply because it was considered a social standard, and it actually had been quite pleasant. Today, that experience paid off. It hurt this time, but he was still able to retain his last shred of dignity. He focused, held it close, tried to forget what was happening.

"*Who else is involved in this? Who brought you there tonight?*"

With each question came a harder thrust. They came faster and faster.

"*Were you there with Fletcher Novotny? What were you planning? Who else knows about this? HOW DID YOU FIND OUT?* Oh, God—!" Officer Riley collapsed backward, into the chair Dex had been sitting in, suddenly looking bored with his interrogation. He waved a hand at the other officers.

They dragged Dex down a hallway and threw him in an isolated jail cell lined on all surfaces with painted-white steel and lit round the clock by those same blinding LEDs. It would be his home for the foreseeable future, they said. Every hour, a new guard came to poke fun at him. Torture in any form was strictly prohibited under New Rainbow Order law, but the Queen had signed an amendment four years ago giving Bio Police clearance to interrogate "biologically." Fight to destroy the world again with reckless heterosexuality, and the homosexuals would catch you, punish you, and use their own alternative to make you see reason.

It didn't take them long to realize that sexual torture was not the key to Dex's secrets. But they kept his clothes, which made the blood trickling down his thighs feel extra sticky and extra cold. It dried against the frigid steel floor, tearing at his skin whenever he moved.

Isolation. It was a perfect way to think.

This is what I get for walking away from Grace. For being a coward. It serves me right.

It was an honest judgment. Dex had always despised cowardice, but when courage had become the moral option, he failed the test.

In the night, shivering, he cried.

THE BIO POLICE GAVE HIM CLOTHING the next day. Detective Riley seemed to have had his fun and left Dex alone, and now the younger homosexual minions were left to watch over him. There was more questioning, more verbal abuse, but no more bodily harm. One jail guard, a young man who approached Dex with unexpected gentleness, attempted to claim they weren't out to hurt him badly, but the words wobbled out with shaky uncertainty. He was young and blonde, and Dex saw something familiar in his face: an irresolute sway toward cowardice, knowledge that his actions were wrong but also tethered to the paralysis of fear.

Dex had always known this section of the government was an entity entirely separate from general law enforcement, but he had never seen up close and personal the anarchistic disorganization that could only be the brainchild of a government terrorized by possibilities. Bio Police had no rules for investigation, because protection for potential enemies would defeat the purpose. Therefore, detectives like Lance Riley were free to do anything.

What happens when population can no longer keep up with a socially and economically balanced society? Dex thought. *What'll you do then, Detective Riley? Do you really think three thousand engineering facilities can populate an entire civilization?*

Maybe the entire plan was for homosexuality to kill off humanity once and for all. Let Earth reclaim itself, free of human greed, destruction, and shortsightedness.

Dex chuckled. If that was their vision, it would almost be noble.

He knew some things for sure. The Opposition facility beneath Sterile Me Susan's had been shut down for good. Its discovery and containment (probably his and Grace's fault) had been a grand victory for the Bio Police, yet it was thus far proving to be insignificant. That morning, when two guards had brought his clothes and shoes back to the freezing cell, Dex heard them talking in the hallway. Yes, most of the people in the hideout had escaped through a tunnel in Sheiks Cave, but no, the Bio Police had not learned of any other significant locations for Opposition activity. Opposition emergency procedures had been quick and efficient. Its members had erased all links to external com data servers, run self-destruct programs on each local system, and then fled. The Bio Police had uncovered medical facilities that suggested illegal reproductive activity, but they had not captured any pregnant women.

Dex visibly breathed his relief for Grace at hearing this, and the guard handing over his clothing noticed.

"What, did you know one of them?" he asked, bringing his face to Dex's level. "Were you trying to breed with a woman, little man?"

Dex grinned. "You're no Detective Riley," he said. "You might want to practice being an asshole before you try and act like one."

This earned him a punch in the face, but he got to keep his clothes. And, of course, they gleaned no useful information from him.

I hope you made it out of there, Grace Jarvis, Dex thought. *If I ever get out of here, I'll find you.*

But the promise died as it hit his mind. Yes, Sheila had mentioned some sort of Cliff House on Lake Superior, but she had also mentioned that the time frame for them to get there was tight, which implied something more: wherever this Cliff House was, it was not Grace's final destination. It would not be her safe haven for long.

Which rendered Dex as ignorant as the Bio Police. Perhaps for the best.

In his cell, he waited, wondering every so often what the time was. It was all a jailed criminal without a window could do. And the lights. Those goddamned LEDs. So bright at all hours of the day that he found no sleep, no refuge.

A MEMORY ✳ (HER)

GRACE IS SITTING IN HER GRANDPA JARVIS'S STUDY on *Easter morning*, tired of all the fuss over Jesus and tired of the snow outside, which should have finished melting weeks ago. She is playing the game she used to play as a little girl: spinning Grandpa Jarvis's antique globe with closed eyes and a pointing finger. The globe has all the world's old boundaries marked on it, from before the Bio Wars, when most of Earth's people died. Now that she is almost thirteen, it is sobering to play this game. As a child, she had never appreciated this old world's country borders, what their absence nowadays really meant. It is exciting to imagine a world that was divided in more ways than just the continents.

I'm going here! *she thinks as the spinning globe stops under her fingertip.*

Srinagar. Northern India. Funny! It actually is a place that still is fixed up and civilized, because it's near some of India's best fresh water sources.

Playing this game makes Grace sad, because she has a dream to see the world. Both her father and dad are like most other people here: afraid to travel, afraid to step out of the safe bounds that the government has set for them. Oh, people travel, and she might be able to sneak some money for a plane ticket someday, but all in all, the risk of a terrorist attack happening is just too great. Her fathers have never been off the continent, and they prefer to keep it that way. What if one of the remaining sects of God's Army were to strike again, and they got stuck somewhere?

Grace sighs, then allows herself to feel what she is really feeling: sadness and fear.

Grandpa Jarvis—her one remaining grandfather—is about to die. Everyone knows it, but nobody wants to talk about it. He has a cough that hasn't gone away in a year, and this winter, it's gotten a lot worse. "It's our last year with him, I think," her dad has been saying when her father isn't around to hear it. James Jarvis doesn't like the idea of death, even though his two fathers engineered him very late in their lives. They could have died when James was much younger, and it would not have been unusual.

Irresponsible of them to have had kids when they were so old, Grace thinks, even though she loves Grandpa Jarvis.

But people can always die. So many crazy things are happening in the world, so Grace thinks maybe Grandpa Jarvis is lucky. People are screaming and protesting on the news every night, because they say there won't be any freedom anymore. The new Secretary General, Vincent Metzer, is a drag queen who never shows his real face, and he is as sexually conservative as they come. Grace barely knows what this means, but she knows it isn't good for heterosteriles like herself. Not once but three times, her parents have begun discussions about Metzer that ended in outright screaming matches and separate bedrooms for the night. Her father is excited about Metzer, and her dad is absolutely terrified. Something about how Metzer got into office and about the General Assembly that voted him in being "a conservative majority."

Because her dad is the nicer parent, Grace trusts him and is nervous, too, even though (and she would never admit this) most of the politics don't make sense to her.

She spins the globe again, realizing that nowhere her finger lands could ever be her escape if everything her dad worries about comes true. It settles on her own continent, near Pittsburgh, Pennsylvania, which is now part of the Unrecoverable Territories. She is disappointed and thinks: At the very least, Globe, send me over an ocean.

Grace worries they have cancelled dessert, because she is getting what her father calls "chubby." Nobody comes to fetch her, so she continues to spin the globe, over and over. Here in her dying Grandpa Jarvis's study, lands beyond the North American continent are hers to experience, if only—and forever—in the caverns of her imagination.

CHAPTER 27 ✳ (HER)

THAT PEOPLE SPOKE OF THE CLIFF HOUSE in context of being just one of many Opposition stations spread around the planet left Grace with the stunning realization that perhaps she would, after a lifetime of burning desire, see the wider world. The Cliff House itself, a classically decorated mansion on its three aboveground floors, was simply a façade for what its caretakers claimed was the largest Opposition facility in North America and the third largest on Earth. It was nothing unusual for politicians to have summer mansions on the Great Lakes, especially if they were engineered and raised on the continent. Lake Superior was still considered a haven for those who could afford homes on it, as it had both the largest and the least populated shores of all the five lakes. This was due partially to the extreme development restrictions placed on its North Shore by none other than Frederik Carnevale's great grandfather, who, Grace learned, had also been an underground government dissenter and third-generation owner of the Cliff House.

Albert Redmond was the base's unofficial director of operations. A tall and chiseled male with eyelashes so dark and thick they mimicked mascara, Redmond had the looks, wardrobe, and persnickety attitude to pass as a perfect homosexual male.

"But he's not a fag," Sheila whispered as he ushered them out of the cold night into the seemingly empty mansion. "Trust me on that. I've visited with him in Minneapolis a few times."

Grace did not ask for details, and the only explanation Sheila offered was a wink and a grin.

Albert Redmond did not smile once at Grace and appeared to mean only business. After collecting and deactivating her pocket com, scanning her TruthChip, and reading her public record, he led them directly to a hidden door in the basement's wood-paneled wall. Through it was a gallery-like hallway decorated with at least forty paintings, three of which Grace recognized.

"Sheila! Look! Are those wheat fields Van Gogh originals?"

"Beats me," Sheila said.

But as Redmond approached what appeared to be a security system control panel on the far end of the hallway and began punching in a code, he said, "Yes, they're originals. Salvaged from the Bio Wars, obviously. Frederik *really* likes art."

Frederik. Albert Redmond was on a first-name basis with one of the most powerful movers and shakers on the planet. This was the first time Grace really sensed the new reality of her life, that she had accepted a one-way ticket toward an extremely vulnerable chance at living out a new ideal.

The blinking red light on the security panel turned green, and a white door seemed to appear out of nowhere. Its rectangular panel moved into the wall at least twelve inches, exposing a breadth of solid metal gears that mechanized the door. It slid left to reveal a spiral staircase carved out of the cliff's igneous rock, leading downward. At its base, the cliff rock met with steel walls and another blast door. It reminded Grace of the facility at Sterile Me Susan's, only this place already felt cleaner, stronger, and safer.

Through the blast door, Grace met her new life.

What they called "the first floor" turned out to be the highest of the underground levels. It housed what Redmond called the communications room, a glassed-in mini-office covered top to bottom with wall and desk coms. Below, on the second floor, were the medical stations. Comprising the third and fourth floors farther down were individual living spaces; these were closest to the cliff's base in case of an emergency evacuation. The third floor was for visitors like Grace, and the fourth was reserved for regular Cliff House personnel. The spaces on both of these levels were not much more than furnished bedrooms with a bathroom for every four.

What appeared to be glistening night views of Lake Superior on the hallway walls were revealed in the morning to be holopanels. Today, through these false windows, it was summer, sunny and warm. In the distance, Grace saw a lone sailboat moving out onto the grand lake.

"Almost makes you forget where you are, doesn't it?" Sheila said as she accompanied Grace to breakfast. As the fifty-room capacity for visitors was nowhere near filled, Albert Redmond had invited Sheila to remain a guest until they figured out her best option. At this, they had both exchanged glances that made it obvious there was more to the decision than Grace would be privy to.

What aren't you telling me? she wondered at them but could not bring herself to ask. She was at the Opposition's mercy now, and she would learn its secrets in due time, perhaps at her first doctor appointment, which was scheduled for the third of January. The Cliff House's resident medical professional, Dr. Sylar Kovak, was out on business of some sort and would not return until then.

There were eighteen other pregnant women at the Cliff House, only seven of whom were accompanied by the failsafes who had impregnated them. Four more, however, were accompanied by current failsafe partners who, Grace learned through Sheila's gossip, were not the babies' real fathers.

Where there were social barriers, Grace was on the outside. Sheila Willy tried to serve as a buffer over those first few days, occasionally making unwelcome rounds in the kitchen and cafeteria during meal times. Some of the women regarded her with skepticism, eyeing her frizzy red hair and peculiar outfit, which was the same celestial-like ensemble she had worn to Sterile Me Susan's. It was clear by the residents' few words and body language that they had already settled into a routine at the Cliff House, and they had enough other people around to brighten their lives. They did not invite friendship, though one woman, a bouncy blonde named Hilda, did make the effort to introduce herself to Grace in the cafeteria food line. "Pretty crazy what's about to happen, huh?" she said, piling salad on her plate. Before Grace could respond, one of Hilda's friends interrupted them and ushered the young woman off to their usual table.

It seemed Hilda knew something about their future that Grace did not, which made her even more nervous. Sheila seemed purposefully to be avoiding the subject, much to Grace's frustration. "Just let yourself acclimate to all this. Relax for a few days. Dr. Kovak will let you know everything once he examines you and everything is good to go with you and your baby."

So there it was: her value to the Opposition was the baby growing inside her and nothing more. It could be assumed, then, that if the baby was not healthy, her involvement would be cut short, perhaps cast aside completely. Of course, she knew too much now, and they could not simply release her back into society, under the eyes of the Bio Police.

The hypothetical alternatives kept Grace awake at night.

She found herself craving solitude in the tiny bedroom, where she could soak in how alone she really was. Everything she had ever known was stripped away forever, all because some rebel scientist had decided her life would not have been important enough were she to be a normal heterosterile. And there was grief at the thought of never seeing her fathers, brother, nephew, and friends again. Yes, half her family would have turned her in to the Bio Police, but could she not have spent just one last day, one last minute, appreciating them as the people who had always meant the most to her?

And there was Dex. Always Dex, in the back of her mind.

I could have loved him, Grace thought. *And if I'd had more time, I could have convinced him to stay.*

Now, he had been captured by the Bio Police. Reports of the raid had finally surfaced on Twin Cities Com. "Minneapolis Raid on God's Army Facility Exposes Dozens of Insurgents," read the headlines. They had put the "God's Army" spin on the story, fueling rage among civilian homosexuals, many of whom, when interviewed, expressed a desire just to exist peacefully, without heterosexuals threatening their families, government, and lives. Twice, she saw Dex's mug shot on the news, along with about twenty others. It frightened Grace how similar they all looked.

I hope they don't keep him alive in misery, she thought. *It'd be better for him to die so he doesn't have to suffer.*

But Dex was water under her bridge. She had a baby to worry about now, and there were seven other women without partners at the Cliff House for her to befriend. One of them in particular, a seventeen-year-old girl named Marvel Suture, formed an instant bond with Grace. She was sitting alone at an empty cafeteria table on Grace's fourth evening at the Cliff House. Still being maddeningly evasive, Sheila had slipped upstairs that afternoon to "visit" with Albert Redmond, so Grace went to dinner alone for the first time.

"Is anyone sitting here?" she asked Marvel, who, according to snippets of female chatter Grace had overheard, was the closest thing to an outcast the Cliff House had.

"No! No, not at all," Marvel said, looking up with a violent flip of her jet-black curls. "Say, you're the new chick."

"I think I'm too old to be called a chick," Grace said. "Lord knows I'm about to lose my body anyway."

"You're Grace, right? I remember from yesterday. Too old? What are you, like, twenty-three?"

"Try twenty-eight," Grace corrected with a grin.

Marvel took a bite of her taco salad but spoke through it. "You've been hiding out all week. I saw you the other day when you first got here. You looked like a nice person, you know. One of those *real* people."

Grace flushed. "Well, thank you. I'm glad you think so."

Marvel's entire upper torso rose in a shrug. Her curls bounced. "I'm new here, too. Got here about a week before you. Did you menstruate much before getting pregnant?"

"I think, maybe, but not a lot," Grace replied, fighting the urge to reserve herself in front of the blunt young woman. It was clear enough she was simply looking for a friend. "Seems weird, but I guess that's just how it worked. Theodore Bozarth sure knew how to hide the truth about his specimens, didn't he?"

"I didn't know who he was until I got here," Marvel said. "My Moms had me, but I was dictated, I guess. They didn't have a choice."

"My dad was always a straight rights activist, and he made me a heterosterile on purpose, before the NRO took away people's option to choose," Grace said. "I don't think my father ever forgave him for it."

It turned out this was Marvel's second pregnancy. She had sought out an underground abortion the first time, which, in her words, "was a drama worthy of old Hollywood." This amused Grace, as it turned out she and Marvel shared an affinity for classic motion picture art from the days before the Bio Wars. The girl had been only fifteen during her first pregnancy, and she had nearly passed the five-month point by the time her search for a legitimate underground abortion facility turned up any leads. She had always been quite round, and the developing baby bump had disappeared well under baggy clothes. Few in her friend circle had been liberal enough to be of help, and it was a random woman from Cock & Vaj Alliance who had recognized Marvel's symptoms and pointed her toward an abortion clinic masquerading as a tea house. Marvel had signed up at the straight rights group as a volunteer in one last attempt to expose herself to help. It worked.

"I didn't hate myself after the abortion or anything like that,"

Marvel said. "But I was scared, you know? Thank God my moms unlocked my TruthChip and linked it to a bank account that year, or I'd have had to come clean to them to get money to pay for it. They *still* don't know. And now I've disappeared. I tried to warn them when I realized I was pregnant again, but I don't think they would have had the mental ability to face the truth anyway. It's better this way. I'm just glad the Opposition found me early this time. Turns out they had a file on my last pregnancy, but I had fallen through the cracks before they could get to me."

Grace stopped at this for a moment, and then remembered: Theodore Bozarth had equipped his later girls with mechanized TruthChips that would alert the Opposition to new pregnancies. These younger specimens had it so easy.

"So, are you excited about the *trip*?" Marvel said next.

"Trip? What trip?"

Marvel gasped. "You mean nobody *told* you yet?"

OVER THE NEXT TWENTY-FOUR HOURS, Grace learned enough to know she would never see her fathers, brother, nephew, or Linda Glass ever again.

"You're being taken to our Mount Tasman station in New Zealand on the twenty-ninth of January," the flighty Dr. Kovak told her the following morning, as he allowed her to shut her legs after his hands-on inspection. "It's the largest Opposition facility in existence, right there in the Southern Alps. You have a choice, of course, whether you go. But suffice it to say that you are all *very* special women, Ms. Jarvis, and Theodore Bozarth gifted you with a very noble responsibility. I should hope you won't choose death, when you are a woman who can give *life*."

If there was one thing Grace had learned with pregnancy, it was that she did not enjoy having strange men examining her private regions. And now the doctor was examining her abdomen with an ultrascope.

It made the news difficult to digest.

"Why New Zealand?" she asked. "What's Mount Tasman?"

Dr. Kovak flipped the ultrascope visor up. "Mount Tasman is the second tallest mountain in that territory. The facility inside it was built in secret by a private party with the undisclosed consent of New Zealand's government, twenty years before they succumbed to the NRO's rule. Sherman Boyens was the prime minister at the time, when they were still sovereign. And his friend with the money was an ancestor of Frederik Carnevale, who just so happens to be the gay politician who is saving your life."

Yet Grace's pulse had quickened. "Okay. But New Zealand? Isn't that where they ship people off to the Sanctuary from?"

Dr. Kovak approached her with a needle and blood tube. He pulled her arm to stretch it, then searched for an easy vein to pierce. "This won't hurt a bit. Just running a blood analysis to gauge your hormone levels, check for any irregularities, and the like. And the facility is in New Zealand because it's far removed and, as you said, in close proximity to Antarctica. It's about as unlikely a headquarters for a grand scale resistance effort as there can be. Not to mention that the Mount Tasman refuge has existed in secret for over fifty years. I'm only privy to certain pieces of information, but as far as I know, it's where you and all the other resistors will wait until the final phase of our counterstrike is carried out."

Counterstrike?

Grace pulled her arm back from Dr. Kovak. "What do you mean, counterstrike? What is it going to involve?"

Dr. Kovak held up his hands, as if to assure her he was beyond reproach. "Don't ask me about the details, Miss Jarvis. I know general secrets, but I make a point not to know the details. Do you get my drift? When people who know too many details get caught, they *die*. Or worse."

Grace suddenly felt claustrophobic and struggled to keep still as Dr. Kovak took her arm again and inserted the needle. Blood began filling his tube. The man's explanation perturbed her, and she shook her head. "But don't you people realize you are stringing nobodies like me along through your process, so that by the end we *will* know all the details? Don't we put you at risk if we get cold feet and . . . decide to leave?"

"If you would rather die, be my guest," Dr. Kovak said. "The Cliff House is not a facility to perform abortions, Miss Jarvis, as that is against our cause. So, unless you want to beg Albert Redmond to let you back into your normal life so you can either find an underground way to kill your unborn child *or* simply wait until somebody notices your growing uterus and reports you to the Bio Police, I highly suggest you listen to what I have to say."

The sprite of a man paused, seemingly waiting for her acquiescence. After looking him head to toe, wondering whether he was homosexual or heterosexual and realizing she did not care, Grace nodded.

"Thank you," Dr. Kovak continued. "I know you're trustworthy, because you made it this far, and even if you were to escape and expose our operation, nobody would touch us up here, because nobody would dare investigate Frederik Carnevale. He's *that* important in NRO circles, not to mention he heads up the Order's Department of Biological Defense and, thus, the Bio Police. Thus far, they don't even have a hint of where his true allegiance lies. Now, what you must understand is that the NRO has finally realized that an underground resistance like ours does exist and that it's probably getting stronger. This is what inspired the NRO to use Mandate 43 as a cover-up to distract people until they stage an attack they're calling Operation 69, which will enable them to declare martial law, publicly round up heterosexuals and dissenters, and ship them off to camps. We have it on good authority that the attack is coming *soon*. Within four weeks. Which means we are getting as many fertile people as we can down to New Zealand before martial law makes travel all but impossible, at least for a while. Make sense?"

Sheila Willy had alluded to Mandate 43 simply being pavement for martial law, but it still begged a question.

"What kind of staged attack are we talking about?" Grace asked. "This is going to be *before* an Opposition counterstrike?"

Dr. Kovak withdrew the needle from her arm. "Of the NRO's staged attack, I've heard only the rumors. It will be significant enough to scare people into surrendering power completely, which is why our counterstrike is being planned. Again, I'm not privy to the details, but I know the general idea." He pasted a bandage over Grace's vein. "If our operation goes as planned, humanity will be starting over. With people like *you*."

Starting over?

"You mean illegal breeders will be hiding out in New Zealand until it's safe for us to repopulate? Isn't that a bit drastic?"

"Don't you think the NRO is a bit drastic? Not just its actions but the very concept? Our Opposition is drastic because it's long term. We have humanity's future on our shoulders. It's bigger than any one of us."

Dr. Kovak snapped off his latex gloves and set Grace's blood sample on the counter.

"Now, we just have to hope nobody caught in the Minneapolis raid will talk. Human weakness is the only way the Opposition will crumble."

A MEMORY ✳ (HIM)

SABRINA CANTOR'S BODY IS EXQUISITE, *maybe because she is a junior in high school and Dex is still a sophomore. Dex has her sitting on the solid oak kitchen table, facing him, with her legs spread apart and wrapped around his lower back. He is standing up, thrusting into her, making her scream his name over and over. It is the third time he has had hetero sex, and it is intoxicating. Nothing matters but the blonde strand of hair caught in Sabrina's lips, the glimmer of sweat between her breasts, and that warm (but so dirty, so unnatural, so wrong) hole between her legs. He kisses her in the middle of an awkward, tandem grunt and thrust, but she swallows the kiss with a grunt of her own, her mouth begging for more.*

It is a day off of school, and they have been planning this sexual escapade all week in a series of text and holomessages between their pocket coms. Nobody is home, they have all afternoon, and Dex is vaguely aware that this is the table both his mothers will later eat dinner on. Sabrina says she has already had an orgasm, and Dex takes her knees, one in each hand, and spreads them, so he can see himself plunging in and out of her.

"Oh, God, oh God, Dex, do it. Do me. Fuck me. Oh God—"

He is not a talker during sex, but Sabrina doesn't mind. She is one of five heterosteriles in their entire high school, and she managed to notice Dex staring at her during study hour four weeks ago. They made eye contact, and suddenly, his secret was out: he was attracted to her. He has known for many years now that he is different from most of the other boys, and why his mothers have failed to mention his status as a failsafe is beyond him, even though he remembers vague conversations here and there from childhood about his mothers "keeping him a surprise." It angers him, and it fuels his every thrust into Sabrina, makes him want to throw this animalistic proclivity for females into his mothers' faces.

"Oh, Dexy, baby, do it harder! Let's show those faggots we mean business! I'm getting close again, oh God—"

The crashing of glass on the kitchen floor makes him slip right out of Sabrina.

His mother is standing in the doorway over a fallen bag of groceries, agape.

Sabrina has already jumped off the table, but she cannot gather her clothes, because they are in the living room. The kitchen was just one of many rooms in which Dex had planned to fuck her.

"Get out of my house," Karen hisses at Sabrina. "You goddamned heterosterile whore. Get out of my house!"

Sabrina rushes past Karen to gather her clothes as Dex, stark naked, stares his mother down. Thirty seconds later, their front storm door slams, and he can hear Sabrina's sandals clicking down the sidewalk.

"This is how you desecrate our home?" Karen whispers.

Dex says nothing. Now, he is looking at the broken jars of pickles and tomatoes on the floor. Their juices creep right around his mother's loafered feet.

"I thought you had to work," he says.

She almost spits her response back. "I decided to take the afternoon off and make an anniversary dinner for your mom and me! And now I can never eat on that table again!"

"I saw you and Mom fingering each other on the table once."

"But that was real!" Karen trills. "That wasn't abominable, dis-

gusting, unnatural heterosexual fucking!" She has never used the word "fuck" in front of him. She purses her lips so tightly that, for the first time in his life, Dex sees in her an old woman.

"Well, you knew you created a failsafe!" he screams. "You had to have known!"

Karen shakes her head. "Your mother volunteered us for a surprise. But obviously the engineer had to fill his quota. I always knew that, but your mom remains blissfully ignorant about how the world really works. I always knew you'd turn out this way. Someday . . . someday, it's going to get you hurt." His mother has never cried in front of him, but she puts a crumpled hand to her lips and averts her gaze from his.

"Pardon me for being a natural human male," he says, knowing the argument won't do him any good. If the old way of reproducing had been a good thing, overpopulation would not have been so harmful to the world back before the Bio Wars. But he knows there is more to his mother's concern than just this.

"Get dressed," Karen orders.

"Are you going to tell Mom?"

"I don't know."

"Well, you better."

"Get dressed."

Covering his genitals, still smelling Sabrina on his skin, Dex walks around his mother and into the living room to find his clothes.

CHAPTER 28 ✳ (HIM)

SYSTEMATIC GANG BANGS were literally almost backbreaking, but Dex had to commend any homosexual who actually found the receiving end of such a thing erotic. A man had to be tough. Dex apparently was not, but he was surprised at his body's ability to recoup. He had hoped the sexual punishment was over after they left him alone during the period of solitary confinement, but when Detective Riley ordered his relocation to the main cell block on the detention center's fifth floor, there were new guards, each ravenous to have their way with him. Despite his short height, Dex was attractive for a male. It made life difficult.

But a coward who sacrifices his dignity doesn't deserve much more than this, he thought during one of his torture sessions, glad at least that his withdrawn cellmate was not suffering the same wrath.

"You just gotta let yourself go," the man whispered one morning, after Dex had spent the night being defiled. It was the first time Dex had heard his voice. "Stop doing pushups every day. They love pecs. Can't control themselves when they see 'em. Let your chest get flat."

But letting his muscles atrophy could take weeks of disuse, unless he were to starve. If unattractive pectoral muscles were the key to keeping the guards genitally flaccid, it seemed his only option for the time being was to hope they would grow bored.

It was Dex's luck that they did. The reprieve came after he was so exhausted that he simply began submitting to their every whim. First one day passed without torture, then two. It seemed his putting up a fight had been the thing keeping them interested.

The main cell block was on constant glow from white LEDs. The cell doors faced each other down the long row and were all magnetically sealed, and each had an eight-inch square window through which to see out into the hallway. Unlike the isolated cell, which had been an empty square room, Dex and his cellmate's chamber was equipped with a set of bunk beds on one end and a toilet, drain, and shower head on the other. The cold shower turned on once every day for four minutes, followed by a blast of warm air that jetted from a vent in the wall. No soap, no towels, and Dex and his cellmate had to share the space and time. They received a minute's notice via an intercom in the ceiling so they could both get undressed. Sometimes, the guards watched through the square window, laughing and making sexual hand gestures.

The cellmate had remained silent during their first few days together, up until his suggestion against doing pushups. He had acknowledged Dex each morning with a masculine nod and nothing more, yet he had also been kind enough to show by example how to make the best of shower time. His brown hair was thick and hanging over his ears, and he wore horn-rimmed glasses—an old-fashioned habit, as the need for corrective lenses was so easily fixable. He reminded Dex of Grace's dad, Stuart.

On the fifth of January (if Dex's internal calendar was correct), the man introduced himself as Exander Baker while they were eating their miniscule allotment of breakfast. Like showers and nature calls, this happened in their cell. The detention center was no communal lockdown with common areas for prisoners to mill about; it was a holding pen. What might happen when they were let out was a question Dex tried not to think about.

"What are you in for?" Exander grunted after they were finished eating.

"Being a coward," Dex answered. A second later, he added, "Caught in a raid."

Exander nodded, then resigned himself once again to his own company.

He did not speak again until the next morning.

"Why do you say you were being a coward?"

"Because I'm a natural father who abandoned the woman carrying his kid. I was scared of what they'd do to me. Coward, see?"

"She was a genetic mistake?"

"No, something different."

Another day passed without words between them. All day and all night, the cell lights reflected so brightly off the white walls that Dex developed an interminable headache. There was no peace here.

On their third day of communication, Exander asked two more questions, one in the morning, one in the evening. He whispered both times, gesturing at a speaker in the ceiling that Dex could only assume was also a microphone used to monitor their conversation.

"What did you mean 'something different' than a genetic mistake?"

"Meaning the woman I got pregnant wasn't a heterosterile, like she thought. The guy who engineered her was a homosexual working against the NRO. He figured out a way to cause activation of the ovaries' Lrh1 genes later in life, or something."

"By planting zinc fingers? Delaying them somehow?"

"I've no idea," Dex replied.

More hours of silence. And finally, even after Grace's face crept through his mind's eye, some sleep. Exander slept without trouble.

He took a seat on Dex's bottom bunk the next time they were both awake. "I'm not in here for anything. I might have heard a few things here and there, but they took me without any kind of due cause.

I was studying genetics at the university, and they arrested me right out of the lab one night."

What was this, an attempt at trust? A gesture of friendship?

"They don't need a reason anymore," Dex whispered back. "My guess is they're just prepping to make it easier to ship us all off to those new camps."

Exander shook his head. "It isn't camps, man. I heard they're dumping the failsafes somewhere else. A huge pit, down in Tennessee. Five hundred feet deep. The NRO is planning a staged attack that will look like God's Army all over again, then martial law. Then they'll send us down to the pit on trains."

Neither Sheila Willy nor Blitz the bouncer had mentioned such a rumor. "I heard the same thing about martial law," Dex said. "But where did you hear about the dumping pit?"

"One of the guards," Exander replied. "A few of them took me to the interrogation room . . . to do their thing . . . but there were a few others in the hallway when I passed by. They were talking about how funny it was that the failsafes thought they were going to survive Mandate 43. That it was all a joke to begin with. One of them mentioned the trains, and the other mentioned the pit."

Dex grimaced. "I had a chance to escape and join the Opposition. But I didn't."

At this, Exander shook his head. "Dude, don't buy it. Don't buy any of it."

"Buy what?"

"The Opposition, man! It's a farce! It's all a farce!" The volume of Exander's voice was rising. Dex shot him a warning glance, gesturing with his eyes to the ceiling's intercom. The man continued shaking his head, but his whispers returned to normal. "No, man. Don't join up with that. I bet you a million bucks it's all part of the NRO's plan."

"Trust me on this, man," Dex said under his breath. "It's real, and it's big."

"What do you actually know?"

Dex examined the white wall on the other side of the cell to search for blemishes on it, as had become his new hobby. It gave him time to think. Perhaps he had been too hasty in sharing information with Exander. They knew nothing about each other except for the bits and pieces already shared, and the intelligent choice would be to cease this conversation immediately. Still, would the Bio Police really go to such lengths to glean information from him? Throw one of their own into this atrocious white cell, make him shower naked under cold water with Dex, then wait for him to weasel out a scrap of trust? Dex no longer trusted his intelligence, just his gut. His gut told him Exander was a good man. Yet he had to think about Grace and his child. If they had escaped, their survival could now depend on whether the Opposition continued to thrive. If Exander was a plant from the Bio Police, he would already know the Opposition was real.

"I don't know you or trust you," Dex said. "Until we're on those trains, riding to our deaths, I'm not going to give you any details."

"Fair enough," Exander replied. "I was thinking the same thing about you, when they first threw you in. It would be easy enough for you to fake getting gang banged if you were one of them, you know? I mean, you'd have done it before. But then I realized I had no information they wanted, so they probably wouldn't have planted you here to spy on me. So, I'll trust you, and you can decide how trustworthy I am whenever you want."

So, Dex learned about Exander. A student of genetics at the University of Minnesota, he was an academic at heart, working toward his fourth degree with loaned funds from Prism Bank, which catered to heterosterile and failsafe students whose education by law could no longer be funded by the government. His interest in genetics was a smokescreen of sorts, and he had only just started a new round of schooling in September as a way to defer his loan payback for the first three degrees. He had been in the university system with ambiguous aspirations to "become somebody" for so long that reality had actually hidden itself in his mind: he was a failsafe, and not a well-connected one. Finding a job that would remunerate enough for him to repay the hundred and twenty thousand dollars he owed Prism Bank would be next to impossible. Just one big break was what he wanted. One degree that could open the door to a more fruitful existence. He knew deep down it was wishful thinking, he told Dex, but what did it matter? When rumors had surfaced that failsafes were on their way out of society in some way or another, he had waited for the bank to catch up and force him to pay for his previous schooling. Up until four weeks ago, it still had not happened.

"So, now I'm in jail," he said. "Probably on my way to that dumping pit, and I don't have to care anymore."

And there had been a woman in his life. Nina, her name had been. She was a bombshell redhead with a big heart, perfect material for motherhood, if the world had been a different place. Exander and Nina had been living together in a small apartment on the university campus, in one of the old buildings built before the Bio Wars. They had been nearing their fourth anniversary when a head-on automobile collision on Washington Avenue took Nina's life. The other driver had been high on hard methamphetamines, and the coincidence of it was that he had been one of Exander's professors, off for the weekend and taking a break from grading assignments.

"Professor Rudy Howard. Genetic Re-Engineering and Social Change 1. He actually was a pretty balanced teacher, for a fag. Objective, and all that." Nina had now been dead for eight months, and there was an emptiness in Exander's expression that made it clear he was still broken over it. When he continued, tears filled his eyes. "And you want to hear the worst thing? My whole life was turned upside down when Nina died, and nobody really cared. There was nothing legal or familial about our relationship, you know? One of the guys in my class had a husband die around the same time, and people made him dinners every night for two weeks. To help him grieve, or whatever. I even made him a veggie lasagna. He was the only one who did that for me after Nina died, oddly enough. The rest of the people couldn't really get themselves to care, because she was a woman. What we had wasn't real to them. You know how it is."

"I'm sorry," Dex said, honestly feeling it. He had experienced similar reactions when Diana disappeared.

"How about you? Did you love the woman who was having your kid?"

Dex rested a hand on his knee and examined his skin. After a week of imprisonment and hunger, it looked sallow and loose. Old, even.

"I could have. I think. But it doesn't matter anymore, unless I somehow get out of here."

"I don't know about you, but if I could get out, I'd light on out to the Unrecoverable Territories. Search for a place to live off the land. Mexico, maybe. Somewhere warm. Somewhere the obstructer bombs didn't wipe out completely, where there'd be fresh soil to plant food and stuff. There's so much empty space in the world now, just waiting to be repopulated, if they can ever clean up. Places like New York, though? I think a meteor would have to wipe us out to ever make a dent in those ruins." Exander chuckled, then turned to Dex. "Where would you go?"

Dex thought back to Sheila Willy's monologue during their venture underneath Sterile Me Susan's, about the Cliff House owned by Frederik Carnevale. The nagging possibility that Exander was a plant by the Bio Police was dwindling in his mind, but even so, mentioning the Cliff House now could lead to its ruin, if it truly existed. If Grace had made it there, he did not want to risk it.

"I'd find her," was all he could say.

"If she's with the Opposition, I'd be worried, man. They're sour.

It's a gut feeling, and I've never had a gut feeling that was wrong. I just don't think they could keep under the radar if they weren't somehow part of the NRO's plan. It'd be the perfect ruse. Like a funnel to weed out all the serious dissenters."

Against Dex's will, Exander's logic crawled under his skin. He looked back to the white wall and searched for imperfections, hoping his cellmate's paranoia was a mere symptom of anger, grief, or madness.

CHAPTER 29 ✳ (HER)

NONE OF THE WOMEN AT THE CLIFF HOUSE were yet so pregnant that hiding it would be impossible during their trip to New Zealand. In the second week of January, they suffered the final step in preparation for the journey: new TruthChips in their wrists, which would provide and register the women and any accompanying failsafes with new homosexual identities in the TruthChip Corporation's database. The company, operating under the New Rainbow Order's Department of Identification, was responsible for the manufacturing and implementation of identification chips worldwide. Grace's new name was to be Claire Elizabeth Austen. One of the nurses explained to her that TruthChip provided empty chips in bulk to every engineering facility on the planet, and each came with an activation code to create a new record in the automated database.

"It won't be foolproof, in the off chance their digital trackers pick up on odd registration patterns of new individuals," the nurse told Grace. "That said, we haven't had a problem with chip replacement yet. It's a big database, something the NRO takes for granted. They're still too busy recovering from the Bio Wars and planning for the future to monitor vestigial technology like TruthChips."

It was a minor surgery that would require not just removal of the old chip and placement of the new one but also expedited flesh rejuvenation. The latter was an hour-long process involving micro-electroshock therapy in the skin cells surrounding the slit at the new chip's insertion point. This would ignite accelerated cell renewal and healing, but the therapy had to be precise, which required near-artistic skill on the part of the operator so the wound would not over-heal with obvious scarring. Any sign of unnatural dermal growth around the chip site would be an immediate signal that a person's TruthChip had been replaced—a key characteristic of anybody who did not want to be found and a red flag for the police. Passing as regular homosexuals would, at the very least, allow them to travel, unless for some reason the government's staged attack happened sooner than Albert Redmond was expecting.

"I HAVE IT ON GOOD AUTHORITY that Operation 69 is still on schedule," Redmond told the Cliff House populous during a meeting in the cafeteria on the thirteenth of January. "It will take place on February fourth in multiple locations: Chicago, Sydney, Salzburg, Minneapolis, and possibly more. We have precious little time. Now, part of the NRO's plan is to empty all the jails just prior to or during the attack, so that it goes completely unnoticed by the panicked citizens. They have built a brand-new infrastructure of magnetic levitation trains beneath all major North American cities, which are connected to the cities' respective Bio Police detention centers far underground. The trains run east, into the Unrecoverable Territories, to locations already constructed by the NRO. During the attack, they'll usher out all the current prisoners to make room for later, when they'll call all heterosteriles, failsafes, and carriers in for the social assessments. The social assessments will lead to detainment, then removal. It will happen similarly on all populated continents."

Whispers fluttered throughout the cafeteria.

"Now quiet, people, quiet," Redmond continued. "I don't have a lot of time here tonight, so let me finish quickly: I think we've gathered all the Bozarth specimens we can. Thus far, of the eight thousand women Bozarth engineered to be fertile, 7,647 are still alive. Of those, 2,803 of them have achieved pregnancy, and 2,156 of them have been identified and recruited to New Zealand, some of them with their male companions. The Opposition has also been fortunate enough to recruit a number of other fertile couples from territories around the globe. We have enough heterosexual women and men to rebuild the *world*. On January twenty-ninth, you forty-three individuals will be the last to join them."

The thought tingled on the back of Grace's neck. She glanced around to look for Sheila, who seemed to have skipped the meeting. Indeed, the woman was nowhere to be seen.

In the two and a half weeks they had been at the Cliff House, thirteen more pregnant women and four accompanying failsafes had arrived for relocation to New Zealand. As Marvel put it during dinner following Redmond's speech, "There are enough people here for us to say 'fuck the Opposition' and do it ourselves!"

Except Marvel's free-spirited nature led to a problem, which Grace heard about two days later. While sneaking around and exploring during a bout of sleeplessness the night after the meeting, the girl had witnessed something alarming: Sheila Willy, in the communications room, discussing the Opposition's counterstrike with a mohawked man on one of the desk coms. They had been using blatant phrases like "nuclear," "wipe out society," and "reclaiming the fucking planet," and from what Marvel gathered, the man had been speaking from the Mount Tasman facility in New Zealand. Sheila had not seen her, but the man on the com had, through the camera. "Someone's behind you," he said, causing Marvel to spin around and run to the stairs, back toward the bedrooms.

Shaking, she relayed the story to Grace during breakfast. Grace tried to remain calm, but the thought of such a widespread attack left her feeling numb.

She spent the next two days brooding. If the counterstrike

Dr. Kovak had mentioned was to be nuclear, on a grand scale, everyone she knew would die. People she loved, regardless of their sexual orientation. Even the fringe acquaintances who had colored the tapestry of Grace's life, like Mr. Dietrich at his grocery store sample station, screamed in her imagination, all dying in an unfathomable inferno. If Grace was to be part of this Opposition, if she chose to save both her life and the life of her child, their blood would be on her hands forever—if not directly, then by association and a blind eye. What was the moral slant then, really? Who better to save, herself and her unborn child, or the rest of her family? Would she even have a chance to save anyone?

Everyone but Dad, Linda, and the heteros would have turned me in to the NRO, eventually, she thought.

But the innocents? It was not in Grace's nature to become complacent with a situation and absolve herself from doing everything possible to ensure justice. Yet society had tipped the scales too far to regain its ethics without drastic intervention. The bigger picture had now rendered true justice ambiguous. She could try warning her dad and Linda, but they might then try to save their own loved ones, potentially exposing the Opposition and overturning its attempt to save humanity. Then, everyone would lose.

On the seventeenth of January, eighteen days before the government's supposed staged attack was set to occur, Sheila Willy left the Cliff House to return the rental car to Stuart. It was a meeting she had arranged without telling Grace. Sheila had become far more reclusive as the days passed, and Grace was surprised when the woman sought her out to say goodbye. She was leaving to meet Stuart in Duluth, she said. There, he would exchange the rental car with his own, so Sheila could return to the Cliff House. When Grace asked her about the counterstrike, the woman simply wrapped her in a hug. "I don't know, honey. I just don't know. And I also don't know why you of all people have my heart tied up in a knot, but you do. Maybe because you're so goddamned innocent. But we'll talk about it all later. When I get back."

At this, Sheila sniffed, and Grace realized she was crying. She broke the hug. "You have my dad's com number, right?"

"Yep, I got it. I'll let him know you're safe. Tootles, girl." The lightheartedness in Sheila's tone did not match her teary eyes.

After she left for Duluth, she did not return.

Grace crossed paths with Dr. Kovak the next morning and asked if he knew where Sheila was. He replied with a shrug, saying he had not seen her. Panic began to squirm in Grace's chest. Something was wrong.

When Sheila failed to return that afternoon, Grace decided it was time to make a trip to the communications room and try contacting her dad. So be it if he learned secrets of the Opposition. If he had met with Sheila, he might know where she was. If he had not, it would mean Grace had befriended Sheila under false pretext. She could not shrug off the feeling that it had all been a trap, and she had been stupid enough to take the bait.

During dinner, Marvel informed Grace that the doors between floors inside the cliff remained unlocked. "It's not like this place is a prison," she said. Even so, the girl did not know how strictly the coms were monitored, and she urged Grace to make any possible calls on voice mode to avoid showing anybody where she was. It was worth a try, so Grace went upstairs at 1:00 a.m. If she knew her dad, he would be sleeping next to his com, waiting in agony for a call.

The communications room was empty, but as she had feared, access to the message coms was password protected.

But luck intervened.

Just as she was about to give up guessing possible eight-digit key codes, somebody knocked on the glass from outside. Almost falling out of her seat in shock, Grace turned around, sure her face was flaming with guilt.

Standing in the hallway was the flighty Dr. Kovak. He sauntered into the communications room with an intoxicated wobble, accompanied by the smell of rum. Grace supposed even Opposition doctors needed to kick back and relax once in a while.

"Ms. Jarvis, isn't it?" he slurred. "What are you doing up here?"

"Just trying to call my dad on a scrambled address," she replied. Then, in an attempt to mislead him without lying outright, she said, "Mr. Redmond didn't tell me you had to have a key code."

Dr. Kovak frowned for a moment, looking confused, then shrugged. "It's a precaution, but if Al said you could do it, here you go." The man leaned over and punched in a code. Grace tried to memorize it, but his fingers moved in a blur. "Just be careful what you say," he said with a cough, which finished with half a burp. "I've got to go to bed."

He toddled out of the room.

She wasted no time, and her dad picked up on the second ring.

"This is Stuart."

Hearing his voice was like sun hitting a shadow. He sounded alert but unrested, as if he had indeed been waiting up with hopes for a call. It was a shame Grace had so little time. "Dad, it's me," she started, trying to fend off tears. "I don't think I'm supposed to be calling you."

"*Pix?* Where are you? Are you okay?"

"I'm okay, but listen, I need to ask you something. If you're sleeping in the same room as father, get out of there now so we can talk in private."

"He's at the bathhouse," Stuart replied. "But honey, wait—"

"No, I don't have much time. Now, did Sheila Willy ever meet you in Duluth two days ago for the car exchange?"

"Car exchange?" he asked, sounding groggy. "You mean the rental? I got a receipt of return sent to my com yesterday. She must have returned it."

Damn it.

"Then something's wrong, and I don't know what. Maybe she

got cold feet. But listen to me. Something's about to happen. Attacks. First a small one by the NRO. They're going to make it look like God's Army did it."

She could hear him rustling in his bed covers, probably sitting up to help focus his concentration. "What do you mean, Pix?"

"Go somewhere out of the way," she whispered into the com, wary of any other Cliff House dweller who might frown on her decision to share Opposition intelligence with an outsider. "Go somewhere in the mountains, where they wouldn't think to attack. And stay there as long as you can. Or . . . go where I'm going."

Too much.

But she couldn't help herself.

"Where, honey? Where are you going?"

"New Zealand."

Too much! Someone might be listening!

"New Zealand? Why in God's name are you going there?"

"There's a place there for me, but I can't say anything else. Find a way down there. Either now, or go hide somewhere closer for a few weeks, and try to get down there after the NRO declares martial law. I don't know how easy it'll be to travel after that, even if you're a homo—"

"Wait, what? *Martial law?*"

"Tell Father you're going away. There's going to be a counterstrike, a big one—"

Footsteps echoed in the hallway somewhere behind Grace.

"Dad, someone's coming. I don't know if I'll be able to call you again. I'm going to try to call Linda Glass, but if I don't, tell her to take Celine and Rita and get out of Minneapolis! Any of the major cities!"

"Honey, wait—"

"Daddy, I love you. Father and Abraham and Lars, too."

Stuart sniffed back tears on the other end of the call. "I'll have my com, honey! Wherever I go, I'll have it!"

"I love you, Daddy. So much."

"I love you, too, Pix. You're my little girl!"

Grace pressed the screen to end the call and shuddered. There was a chance she would never hear that voice again. It felt as though the last vestiges of love were falling from her grip forever.

She turned around slowly, only to jump out of her chair when she noticed a black-clad figure standing in the hallway. It was Albert Redmond. He was watching and waiting with his dark, vigilant eyes. For a moment, they stared at each other through the glass, like animal and prey. Then, he walked down to the doorway and into the room. When he spoke, he remained quiet and collected.

"You're crying," he said.

She wiped her eyes. "I just made a call."

"And how, pray tell?"

"It doesn't matter."

"It sounded as if you were warning somebody to evacuate."

Shit.

Redmond's gaze wandered down Grace's body, but not in a lustful way, from what she could tell. In his own peculiar fashion, he was taking her in, considering every inch of her. "You know, Ms. . . ."

"Jarvis."

". . . Jarvis. This is a scrambled com connection, but that doesn't mean it's totally safe. Furthermore, do you realize what a risk it would be to disseminate rumors among the general population? To inspire mass panic and public revolt, which could bring on martial law early and prevent us from moving you to a safe location?"

Grace's defense fizzled in her throat. "I . . . I couldn't go without warning my dad."

"What did you tell him?"

It took every ounce of gumption she had to keep her eyes focused on Redmond. "Only what I've heard."

"Heard from whom, pray tell?"

"I don't remember," Grace lied. She would not tell him about

Marvel having overheard Sheila's conversation. Grace realized now that while Marvel had been perfectly aware of the situation's seriousness, they both may have been too naïve to realize that resisting the Opposition might put them in an entirely new sort of danger.

"It's not your place to know more than you need to know," Redmond said. The gentleness in his voice had a razor edge.

"Excuse me, Mr. Redmond, but it *is* my place," Grace replied, shaking with nerves. "I have family and friends who could lose their lives if the Opposition's counterstrike is going to be drastic. That *is* my business!"

Redmond stomped his heavy boot against the cement floor and raised his voice. "And if we took into account every civilian life that isn't directly working for or supportive of the world's current political monster, what then, Ms. Jarvis? Let the NRO take you, kill the child inside you, and ship you off to an egg-harvesting camp with all the other females? Because *that* is what's coming to you if we don't act!"

"It doesn't excuse killing innocent people," Grace retorted.

"None of this is excusable!" Redmond seethed. "*None of it.* But what I must ask from you, Ms. Jarvis, is a higher level of moral consideration here. You aren't just saving yourself by saving your baby's and your lives. You're saving the very ideal of *humanity*. What they are doing—" Redmond whipped out his finger and pointed it into oblivion, "—is destroying humanity, bringing us back to day one, and walking backward in social, evolutionary, and ethical progress! If humanity was at its peak before the Bio Wars, it's now on its way out. You choose, Ms. Jarvis. But just know that you're too far in now to get out."

"Meaning what?"

"Meaning if you try to leave this compound, your life might just accidentally slip out from under you."

"Are you threatening to kill me if I opt out, Mr. Redmond?"

"You'd bring it upon yourself. Goodnight, Ms. Jarvis. Or, what is the name on your new TruthChip? You'd best memorize and start using it. And consider what I've said."

Before Grace could ask about Sheila Willy, Mr. Redmond marched out of the room and disappeared down the hallway, toward the passageway upstairs. For whatever reason, he was wearing a trench coat, and it sailed behind him as he hurried away. And there Grace was, looking after him, numbed by the fresh reality of her life as a mutineer against the New Rainbow Order. Yes, there was a price to all of this. Fear had opened her arms to the Opposition, but now it threatened to force allegiance upon her in the same fashion as the government. She knew too much to run, and she would end up with blood on her hands if she stayed.

That night, as the hours ticked away, Grace weighed her options. Finally, as she imagined the sun outside might finally be rising, she erred on the side of motherhood, of fierce protection for the life growing inside her.

You are the only innocent one in all this, she thought at her child. *You and all the other babies the Opposition is trying to protect.*

In the end, that glimmer of innocence sealed Grace's decision. When she arrived in New Zealand to have her baby, guilt would not consume her. It simply would not.

CHAPTER 30 ❄ (HIM)

LIGHTS OFF, in the middle of the night.

Time had adapted Dex, and he was fast asleep when the world went dark through his eyelids. It was the wee hours of morning on January, the twenty-seventh.

"Up, up, up!"

An alarm of some sort, low pitched, wailed over and over through the speakers in the jail cell. Above him, Exander's bunk squeaked, and the man's single blanket shifted as he sat up. The cell door's mechanical lock unlatched, and police boots galloped into the cell.

"Up, up, up!"

"Huh—?" Exander stammered, making no move at first. Dex remained in his bed as well, out of pure incredulity.

This is a dream. It's all a dream.

Boots, racing toward Dex's ear. Something jabbing his side, and hard. The butt end of a gun. Another jab, then a squeaking sound and crash as Exander jumped off his bunk.

"Up, up, up!"

"Why are the lights off—?" Dex stammered.

"No questions, just *move!*" It was one of the younger guards, Officer Maleck, who had taken particular joy in torturing him when

Detective Riley had transferred him to the main cell block. He jabbed Dex again. "Get up, Wheelock! NRO orders!"

Dex pushed his blanket back and heaved his body off the bed. When his bare feet hit the cold floor, his eyes focused. The main lights were off, but there were other lights now, emergency ones glowing a dull red in the corridor outside. And there were echoes of other boots, other screams of "Up, up, up!" and a steady clamor of footsteps.

"What's going on?" Dex asked.

"Get up! No questions!"

Exander was already on the floor, scurrying toward their shoes in the corner. He threw two of them to Dex before the guard came and beat him over the head with the butt of his sonic rifle. "No time for that, you slimy fuck! Get up!" It was impossible to see the shoes in detail, but both he and Exander managed to slip them on—Dex with two left-fitting shoes, Exander with two right ones—before the guard dragged them out. Dex could only think over and over how smart it was of Exander to go for the shoes, because who knew what was going to happen to them now? They were rushing down the glowing red hallway at gunpoint with all the other detainees, moving toward the far end Dex had seen only once, when being brought to his cell.

"Down the stairs, down the stairs, down the stairs!" one of the guards was screaming, directing the confused men through a door with his rifle.

Don't question it, Dex thought. *Just go. You brought this upon yourself.*

From somewhere far below, Dex heard what sounded like a light wind blowing through a tunnel. It was a familiar sound, and he raked his mind, knowing he was dancing around the obvious answer. The noise lowered to silence, and Dex suddenly placed it. *It's a maglev train coming into a station, just like all the commuter rails. Only this one . . .*

This one was built underneath the Minneapolis Bio Police Detention Center.

Murmurs among the men grew louder and louder with each round of the staircase. Finally, after at least ten stories, Dex looked over the railing and saw men flowing off the stairs, onto a floor that was nearly invisible under the dusky crimson lights.

"There's a train down here!" a prisoner's scream echoed up the stairwell. "Where are you taking us?"

Whispers ascended in a spiral, breathing like a cold whirlwind from person to person. A train? To where? Why would there be a train under the Bio Police detention center?

"To the dumping pit!" somebody screamed behind Dex. Then there was the sound of a man falling under a blunt impact. One of the guards' guns or clubs, no doubt. Then came raging screams from a number of inmates, and then bodies, tripping and tumbling downward, into the crowded mess of people. And, finally, high-pitched sonic pulses.

"Dex, go faster!" Exander yelled. "They're using their guns!"

How did the world come to this? Dex wondered, hopping down the stairs, fighting with each step not to tumble onto the men in front of him. They were farm cattle, racing into the butcher's pen.

They reached the bottom of the stairway. The air was cold, and Dex clung to his own torso, shivering, as a guard ushered him into a hallway. It was still lit by pulsing red lights, but Dex could see normal LED illumination at the end of it, breaking through the bobbling prisoner heads outlined against it. In this horrible confusion of night, they were all running blindly toward that light, as if there was no other choice. *Grab one of the guards' guns, grab one of the guards' guns, grab one of the guards' guns!* Dex thought in a repetitive chain, horrified that his footsteps were simply falling in line with all the others, following without any attempt to make sense of the eerie silence braiding between them.

As they broke out into the light, it became pandemonium. Prisoners were scurrying to nowhere, screaming, "Go back, go back!" but to no avail. There was no exit. They were in an enclosed atrium glowing under standard blue LED bulbs, and there it was, sitting on a pair of gleaming new tracks: a high-speed magnetic levitation train, in the depths of South Minneapolis. It was gray, unmarked, and had only doors for openings, no windows. Only a section of it was visible on the short platform, and it disappeared into a black tunnel on either side. While some of the prisoners were screaming about dumping pits, others were screaming about camps and Mandate 43 and government conspiracies. But there they went, tripping up the steps of the one train car with an open door, because their only other option was to face the Bio Police's weapons.

"Exander!" Dex screamed, craning his neck to see the man who had become his friend. But they had lost one another in the madness. Was it possible Exander had stayed back, that he really had been a plant from the Bio Police to garner information from Dex? It didn't matter now. The flow of panicked prisoners had swept Dex to the side of the train.

"Get on it! Move!" a guard next to the door screamed, pointing his gun in Dex's face. Its pulse generator glittered yellow deep inside the barrel. A yellow generator meant death, not stun.

Goodbye, Grace.

Dex jumped onto the car, and in a matter of moments, he was rushing through the caged blackness, moving down the length of the train, from one seatless car to another, mostly by the feels and pushes of other prisoners and twice by guards patrolling the small passages where the cars connected. By the time they were beyond the point of no return, lost in the dark, the screams and murmurs had disappeared into hopelessness. Only the dampened sound of caged breathing escorted them now.

"Exander!" Dex yelled, hoping the quiet might reveal his cellmate's response, so they could fish each other out of the fray. Men were tromping over Dex's feet, pushing him to the front of the car. "Exander, are you in here?"

"Dex!"

"Exander!"

"No, Dex! Is that you? Dex Wheelock? It's Fletch!"

Fletch.

"What? Where?"

"Off to the right, up in the front! In the corner!"

"I'm coming!"

The other men piped up now as Dex pushed his way through their sweating, gasping bodies. Finally, he reached what appeared to be the front. A hand closed around his head and felt its way across his short hair, and then its owner grabbed Dex's hands and brought them into a separate, more tangled mop.

"Fletch!"

"Dex! I didn't know you were in here, man! I thought you might have made it out with Grace!"

"No," Dex said, out of breath, suddenly realizing that oxygen might get scarce in here very soon, unless the train's engineers had been kind enough to provide vents. The thought alone made him almost mad with claustrophobia. "No, I didn't make it out with Grace. I thought they'd killed you! We all heard explosions from upstairs during the raid."

"They stunned me! Doesn't matter! It all doesn't matter anymore, Dex. We're fucked. Totally fucking *fucked*!"

"Did you hear about the dumping pit?"

"That's where they're taking us," Fletch said. "I didn't want to scare you before, so I didn't tell you. I'm sorry, man. But I saw *pictures*, Dex. *Pictures*. It's a massive pit in old Tennessee! They'll stop the train on a really thin bridge that spans the thing and then just unload us! We've got to find a way out!"

Dex's scattered wits were settling in his mind, and horror coiled in his gut. "Didn't you see those doors? Totally air sealed. And it's a maglev train. We'll be moving fast."

Suddenly, their lack of momentum pushed them backward, and an airy burst rushed under their feet. The train was moving. *Think*,

Dex told himself. *Just think about any and all possibilities.* If it was true about the dumping pit, time was flushing away with every second. The train was surely fitted with remote conducting technology, which meant the only humans aboard were those designated for the pit. Their conductor would be a puppeteer in some distant control room, piloting the machine by holocamera. If they somehow managed to escape the air-tight tube, it would still be impossible to stop the train and gain control of it. Without somebody tampering with the train from the outside, they would die. But these trains were still secret. Nobody but the highest government decision makers and the builders would know of them, or at least of their purpose.

Except there was Fletch's Opposition. Might they know about the trains and have some sort of plan? Was it even possible? If not, this jungle of packed bodies was about to become the last memory of Dex's life.

CHAPTER 31 ❄ (HER)

IT WAS BLACK IN GRACE'S ROOM when she awoke. Another dream about her child, running in a joyful fit. This time, there had been a mountain in front of her, a towering, snow-capped peak, as if straight out of a myth, but it was all in the middle of a sandy desert. Her child, a little girl, was dashing about with pigtails bouncing behind her, through the sand, pointing and laughing at the gleaming, rocky summit.

New Zealand isn't a desert, Grace thought, just before looking at the clock.

5:08 a.m.

And there was activity outside her room, in the halls. Footsteps, voices. Then a loud knock on her door, and a latch opening.

"Everybody up, everybody up!" echoed the voice of Albert Redmond. "There's been an emergency change of plans, everyone, and we need to get you all to New Zealand as soon as possible. Up, up, up!"

Just as Grace registered this, she felt a tiny flutter in her belly. Movement. *A kick? The first!*

But there was no time for elation. Redmond repeated his message as he moved from door to door, waking the men and women in residence. Soon, Grace stood in the hallway with a crowd of confused, pajama-clad people. It took a few swallows of her dry mouth to realize she was thirsty, that Sheila was gone, that her only friend in this crowd would be Marvel, the seventeen-year-old. And there she was, fifteen feet away, with those curls bobbing up and down, even after being flattened against a pillow for six hours.

"Cafeteria, everyone, cafeteria!" It was Redmond's voice again, reverberating from the next floor down.

Five minutes later, he was addressing them under the cafeteria's smooth white lights. On the holopanels this early morning were night views of Lake Superior. A bright moon shimmered on the water.

"We've received intelligence from affiliates in Minneapolis, Des Moines, Green Bay, the Chicago area, and the Kansas City area that the NRO has activated their attack strategy a week early. Our friends monitoring power grids in those cities have reported that the NRO's new trains began running early this morning. Whether they're full of people at this point, we have no idea, but sources have confirmed that each train has begun passing through its allotted lineup of Bio Police jails, starting in Minneapolis just an hour ago. We have reports of the Minneapolis train moving south. It has stopped at the first of three detention centers across Iowa, on its way toward more in Kansas City, where it will cut over and cross through Missouri, toward the Unrecoverable Territories. Same thing goes for the Chicago train, which will cut down through Illinois, toward Kentucky. Now, we believe this is the real deal, and they are at the very least removing detained failsafes toward a massive dumping pit on the eastern edge of old Tennessee."

Gasps fluttered through the crowd. "*Dumping pit?*" people whispered to each other in horror. Grace stood stock still, watching Redmond but seeing something far away: Dex, at the Sterile Me Susan's facility, hating himself as he said goodbye.

I hope to God you got out, Grace thought at him, wherever he was. An unexpected surge of grief wrenched her chest as she envisioned

Dex diving out of a train car to his death. He had been a good man. Better than most others she had known, despite his flaws.

Redmond was very succinct: They would be leaving for New Zealand within the hour. According to the intelligence, bio-detainee removal was the first step in the New Rainbow Order's staged terrorist attack. The Opposition expected mass pandemonium once the attack happened, enough for the train operations to go unnoticed. Detainment and removal of all heterosteriles, carriers, and failsafes would follow in a matter of days, once propaganda made it publicly accepted that heterosexuals were behind the attacks.

"It's likely the NRO will have infiltrated a true group of God's Army rebels so that nobody but those doing the infiltrating will realize the entire conflict is staged," Redmond said. "It will look on all counts like a terrorist effort, but we are expecting something far more drastic than the isolated attacks we've seen since the Queen rose to power. This will be a coordinated, worldwide effort, and it will spark a rush of mass heterosexual genocide."

"What the hell happened to the Sanctuary? Why aren't they using it anymore?" asked Ruth, a woman of Middle Eastern descent who had arrived at the Cliff House just four days prior.

"Suffice it to say that the rumors you may have heard are true," Redmond said. "The NRO has ceased to operate the Sanctuary in exchange for a more straightforward means of extermination."

Ruth shook her head. "And we're supposed to get to New Zealand before all this happens, without anyone noticing? Are you fucking stupid?"

Redmond glared at Ruth, then took out his pocket com and used his fingers to pull up information. "At six o'clock this morning, central time—that's in just under an hour—one of Representative Carnevale's private chartered jets will leave its hangar at Chicago Midway and fly to Duluth Intercontinental," he said. "This is nothing unusual, nor is it unusual for Carnevale to book travel for an entourage, even if it is forty-three people. He orders chartered flights for friends at least twice a month, partially so that it won't be unusual when he helps shuttle Opposition members to New Zealand. None of you are showing too prominently yet, but it's cold today, so jackets are in order. They'll help cover you in case anybody is overly perceptive. As it is a chartered NRO flight ordered straight from the top, security will be lax. With your new homosexual names attached to Frederik Carnevale, you *are* security. And remember, none of you are pregnant, none of you are heterosexuals, and only same-sex people can show each other any type of flirtation or otherwise sexual affection. You already know who your new legal partners are based on your new TruthChips, so you will pair up accordingly as you travel. Put on an act. Females with females, males with males. Failsafes, when you are in public, it will help if you are extremely touchy with each other, and not just the ones you are pretending to be married to. Failure to do this will make your homosexual act extremely unconvincing. You should already have your phony wedding bands to accompany your new identities, save for you three men, who are a single threesome. . . ." Redmond pointed at three failsafes—Steve, Alan, and Jackman, if Grace remembered correctly—and then shrugged. "Questions?"

Grace raised her hand. "Yes, Mr. Redmond."

"Are you getting cold feet, Ms. Jarvis?" he said before she could ask her question.

"No, sir. I'm only wondering how long of a flight it is to New Zealand."

"From here, eight and a half hours."

Even for a liquid hydrogen jet, that was fast.

"Of course, if they aren't ready to receive us on the New Zealand end, it could complicate things. We'll know once we're in the air."

"*Once we're in the air?*" Grace asked. "What's that supposed to mean?"

"It means I have to tell you yet again, Ms. Jarvis, that this situation is bigger than just you," Redmond sniffed. "Our Mount Tasman facility is extremely secret and extremely particular in the way it can be entered, and too much activity in the area would alert the NRO to our presence there. I can't foresee a reason you will not be in New Zealand by nightfall, but it's what happens after you land in Christchurch that we have yet to receive confirmation about."

Marvel's voice rose from the crowd. "Aren't you coming with us?"

Redmond pursed his lips and kept them tight for a moment, then spoke. "No. You'll be accompanied by three other Opposition members, plus the hydro plane crew."

"Can we trust them?" Alan the failsafe asked.

"If you can trust me, you can trust them," was Redmond's response.

And there it was, in Grace's heart: a flutter of doubt.

CHAPTER 32 ❅ (HIM)

THIS IS WHAT DEX did not know:

The gray maglev train was racing at 260 miles per hour through the cornfields of Kansas, the culmination of much speculation and even more shoulder shrugs of the region's farmers. Three years ago, they watched construction of the tracks and saw test trains running late in the night, but since then, the tracks had remained abandoned. Some saw this first gray train pass in those wee hours of the morning, but as it was winter, any farmer doing his work was either inside a solar greenhouse or prepping his morning coffee that would accompany him through the day. Four hundred miles to the southeast, however, in another cornfield on the edge of Missouri, a small group of Opposition affiliates waiting patiently for this day (but surprised anyhow at receiving their call to action) had explosives ready under a section of track five hundred feet long. The explosives had been set for nearly three months, ever since the New Rainbow Order's plan had become not just apparent but definite. Blowing the tracks early would have brought undue attention to the Opposition and offered the government a chance to rebuild. Instead, striking on the first day of operation would catch them in the act. Stop them in their tracks, so to speak.

It was not just in Missouri. Each of the seven track lines leading to the Tennessee dumping pit had an unknown explosive hinge point set in the middle of nowhere. Nearby shadow people were watching and waiting with their pocket coms ready, displaying the codes to detonate.

Abel Johns of Kansas knew how to hack into the wireless controls of the train, and he knew how long it would take to gain access with the hack. He also knew the train cars—surprise surprise—had a fail-safe option in case the trains were held up for any reason. Not only were the cars capable of heat and chemical release that would eventually push the failsafes to jump out the doors into the pit of death, but they were also capable of simple incineration and had little to distinguish themselves from mobile crematories. True, they did not burn instantly with fire, but they could heat and kill within thirty minutes, char in an hour, and completely render men dust in two. Vent releases in the cars' bases could then dispose of the dust in one fell swoop, powdering the countryside in death. *Then why have the dumping pit at all?* Abel Johns wondered. *Why not just char the men and run the train in circles to release the ashes?*

Perhaps such an easy and prudent mode of extermination would be too boring. Everyone knew homosexuals liked to be extravagant and that they had been planning their takeover of the planet for centuries. Maybe they wanted to savor their victory by watching the heterosexuals jump to their deaths. It would be poetic.

As the train passed through Kansas, Dex sat in pitch blackness. No windows, no last view of the sun—at least until he was flying downward, into the supposed dumping pit. The men around him were silent, packed together like canned fish. Their groans of desperation had ceased. Oxygen filtered through vents along the top of the car, keeping them alive just enough to dive out when they finally reached the pit.

"Dex, do you feel that?" It was Fletch Novotny speaking. Dex had managed to crouch with him in the corner of the crowded car. Amazing, the luck of finding his friend. They did not have to die alone, at least. But he wondered about Exander.

"Feel what?"

"Holes in the floor. They're small. Feel it."

"I felt them already."

"There's heat coming from them."

Dex had noticed this as well. "Maybe they just want to be careful we don't get cold. It's January."

Neither he nor Fletch laughed.

But there was time to think now, as the train took them on their way. What had sparked the sudden evacuation of the prisoners? Why so early this morning, of all times? The train had been perfectly situated under the detention center in South Minneapolis, ready to speed toward Tennessee. They had stopped seven more times and heard more shouting and more screams. Dex wondered if his detention center had been only one of many along the track. Was it just men on the trains? Failsafes being removed from society? The detainees had been divided by gender at the detention center, and Dex had not seen or heard any women in the ruckus on the train platform, so he guessed this was the case. Failsafes to the dumping pits, heterosteriles and carriers to the egg harvesting camps. It seemed the rumors about the Antarctic Sanctuary's original purpose having been abandoned were true.

All Dex could hear was the steady whooshing sound as the maglev raced with almost-imperceptible speed over the track. At this rate, he would be dead by noon.

"Dex?"

"Yeah?"

"Do you think it's the attack everyone talked about? That they're going to round up all the heteros?"

"Probably," Dex said, but caring was beyond him now. He had always been a short guy acting tough and rugged to compensate, and now he was just a sardine on the ride of his life, proven a coward and dying one, too.

AN HOUR AND A HALF LATER, in the middle of a dried-up cornfield on the edge of Missouri, the train tracks flew out of their bolts, into the air, carried by a five-hundred-foot-long sheet of fire. It was 8:13 a.m. The faces in charge of setting off the explosives, to remain nameless, were late to implement the operation due to a disconnected fuse that needed repairing at the last minute. They were lucky the steely gray cargo train had not already passed. The prisoners on the train, however, were not so lucky: they were flying at over two hundred miles an hour toward a gap in the track, only ten miles ahead.

It took the train's remote conductor, a flighty fag who was sitting in front of a control screen in Chicago, nearly a minute to realize smoke was rising somewhere ahead and nearly another to realize it was smack-dab in the middle of his set course. By that time, it was impossible to stop the train before it hit the obliterated stretch.

But this frightful trajectory was insignificant compared to the atrocities that had just begun to unravel in eleven of the world's most influential cities. In Minneapolis, Chicago, Sydney, Wellington, Srinagar, Cape Town, Salzburg, Nice, Stockholm, Chengdu, and Irkutsk, buildings full of innocent, blind-eyed civilians plunged into rubble in a matter of seconds. Where it was daytime, sonic bombs destroyed office buildings and shopping centers. Where night, they destroyed hotels and high-rise apartment complexes. It happened in controlled demolitions "inflicted by an enemy," or so the New Rainbow Order was going to say—acts of war at a level of destruction unseen for a hundred years.

From that hour onward, the homosexual regime had its intercontinental martial law and complete control of the world.

CHAPTER 33 ✳ (HER)

GRACE LOOKED OUT AT THE ATMOSPHERE, which hovered between brilliant blue and the blackness of space beyond. Just as her thoughts were delving into that vastness, into the humorous reality that her personal predicaments were thoroughly confined to the globe beneath her, the hydro plane's wing flaps moved slightly. The engines' airy roars lowered with a groan.

They were slowing down, and much too early.

The captain and every attendant on the plane, Albert Redmond had assured them, were friends of the Opposition. Yet nothing prepared Grace for what came next over the video intercom: a virile male face turned downward in a grave expression, awash in tears.

"Passengers, this is your captain speaking," the man lisped. "I had no idea it would be this big, but the NRO has staged its attack, and the results are . . . horrific. Absolutely horrific. Multiple buildings in eleven different cities around the globe, including Chicago and Minneapolis on our own continent, have collapsed in massive demolitions. The NRO has sent orders to ground air traffic immediately on the closest possible runways. We've just reached fifty thousand feet, but we're still flying over the Unrecoverable Territories. The old state of California, to be exact. We've received clearance to land at an NRO base at what used to be Los Angeles International Airport."

Grace's anxiety froze in her chest: *Los Angeles. The City of the Dead.*

It was a legendary city, the "City of Angels," as it had been known before becoming the first major city to be destroyed by obstructer bombs in the final years of the Bio Wars. No civilian nowadays ever dreamed of visiting such ruins. Grace had learned of the government's base there when the General Assembly disclosed the details of Mandate 43, and the news had come as a shock. The very idea of humanity making a dent in the world's Unrecoverable Territories had always seemed laughable, an impossible goal. But here Grace was, about to fly into an inhabited military base in Los Angeles. At once terrified for the Cliff House refugees' prospects and unduly elated that she was unexpectedly going to see this renowned place with her own eyes, Grace watched the captain outline their scheme.

"From what I understand, there are a number of you on this aircraft who are nearing four months pregnant. Until we get the lay of the land, I'll ask that you all stay on the plane after landing until you receive further instructions. If anyone does recognize you're pregnant, we'll pass you off as active carriers from before Mandate 43 went into effect. It'll be my call, once I feel out the situation. As always, it won't be beneficial for us to pretend this is a jet filled with individuals banished to the Antarctic Sanctuary, because it would mean our plane would be flagged for an immediate and particular protocol upon arrival in New Zealand, which these days we can assume means you would be taken and dumped somewhere."

Grace and Marvel exchanged apprehensive looks. This raised the stakes.

As they descended over a range of snowcapped mountains, Grace craned her neck to look out the window. The mountains were mostly rocky and desert-like, dotted with green here and there. The snow dusting their higher ridges glowed in the sun, and the sky crowning the mountains was crystal clear. As they flew west, however, the morning became hazy in a way Grace had never seen before.

From the ocean!

Goosebumps tingled along her arms.

And then she saw them: ruins, tall shadows in the haze, looming in the distance. The shapes were familiar; she had seen them outlined in countless motion pictures from the cinematic golden age. Behind them, barely visible through the dazzling brume, was the outline of another long mountain range.

That's downtown Los Angeles, Grace thought. *Still standing after all these years. Incredible.*

The buildings were still far enough away to appear vague, but she could swear some of them were letting through light, as if their structures had remained intact while entire walls were blown out.

Three billion people had died of disease during the Bio Wars, and the United Nations had exterminated another two billion on top of them to keep the plagues from spreading. Southern California had been the first major American zone to suffer this fate, followed within three months by the rest of North America's West Coast. To see it now was an astounding yet sobering experience. *Millions died here*, Grace thought. *Victims of those who were fighting on the same side as I am now.*

Greenery teemed through the rubble of streets and buildings below, and it passed faster and faster as the plane lowered. Suddenly, they were over a concrete runway, and the reverse thrusters pushed Grace forward in her seat.

Touchdown.

CHAPTER 34 (HIM)

THE TRAIN SLOWED WITH A SUDDEN, volatile jerk, sending Dex and Fletch flying into the car's front wall. A shooting pain tore into Dex's shoulder on impact, but a low-pitched moan from under the train swallowed the ache and spat back something much worse:

Terror.

We can't be in Tennessee yet, Dex had time to think before the bass whine of the car's electromagnets disappeared into the deafening grind of the train running off its course. Bodies tumbled forward, crushing Fletch against him and the wall, tighter and tighter and tighter. Men screamed, grappling at nothing as the momentum sent them into a struggling cluster. Dex fell to his knees, shielding his head. He pressed himself into the corner as an avalanche of men piled onto him. The corner provided an odd sort of protection, but Dex's head was pressing hard into his arm, which in turn felt as though it was breaking against the hard metal barrier. The men's body heat stuffed up the air at the bottom of the pile, and in his collapsed state, Dex struggled to fill his lungs.

This is how it ends. This is where my fear brought me.

The train car overturned with a violent, downward lunge. From outside the shroud of bodies came the muffled sound of feet, heads, and hands bracing against the rotation. Only exclamations poured from the men's mouths, no words of sense.

Suddenly, Dex was on top. The world moved beneath him; men who were now crushed against the train's upturned ceiling wiggled for all they were worth. But the angles were all wrong. Most of them were sprawled on their backs, tangled with one another, hopeless victims of gravity. Dex stood up to move but found he was balancing on top of screaming men's faces, chests, and hands. Their squirms almost brought him down into the fray, but he maintained his balance. If he could get off the pile of men and find a bit of free space, perhaps they could right themselves.

"Fletch!"

"Dex!"

"Where are you?"

"I can't see anything, man! I'm here, I'm here!"

A flailing arm smacked Dex upside the head, and he grabbed it. "Fletch! Is it you?"

"It's me! What the fuck is happening?"

"Derailed!"

"Holy Christ—"

Screeching against the ground outside, the train car bounced Dex forward. He dragged Fletch with him, and they tumbled toward the back of the body pile. Their darkened world jerked to a sudden stop. The men who were buried in the unlucky position Dex had just escaped shrieked under the force of it, but the nightmare was completely invisible in the car's pitch darkness.

For a moment, everything was silent.

The air pressure suddenly shifted in Dex's ears. He looked up. Behind what used to be the car's base but was now serving as its ceiling, something was glowing red. He could see it through the tiny holes he and Fletch had felt earlier. They could not be more than a centimeter in diameter, but thousands of them now dotted the entire overturned floor with red light. It looked as though there was another ventilation system at work. A warm breeze was blowing out of the holes. Dex's eyes began to burn.

The other men on top of the pile and closer to the glowing vents voiced it first, initially letting out shocked yelps, then clawing at their eyes under the devilish light with tortured bawls. Dex squeezed his eyes shut, but whatever was causing the ghastly sensation found its way through his nostrils, into his lungs. The agony was immediate, almost enough to distract him from the rising temperature in the car. He dared to open his eyes and find his way forward. Behind the ventilation holes, the car's glowing innards were now a fiery orange. They were getting warmer. Hotter.

The car is an oven.

"Fletch!"

Through his searing tears, Dex could see his friend in the dull light. Fletch was holding his eyes shut and screaming, shaking his head at the pain, clambering over stretching, waving limbs, toward the door at the back of the car. Though they had been commanded onto the train and then stuffed down through the chain of compartments, the door was identical to that of their entry car.

Of course, it was air sealed, and the air was now burning up.

Fletch screamed, jumping off the heap of men piled at the far end of the car. He landed on the ceiling and approached the upside down door, which was merely a metal outline. No handle, no windows. And it was getting hot.

Following three other failsafes, Dex climbed across the fumbling bodies toward Fletch and the door, avoiding heads, being as careful as possible to step on the most robust-looking limbs he could find. But seeing through his tears and sweat was almost impossible. He jumped off the pile and landed next to Fletch, then doubled over. His eyes, throat, and lungs were on fire, overpowered by the sour, industrial pungency of some synthetic chemical. The hellish sting burrowed into his skin and his insides, feeling as though it were undoing the flesh in its path, dissolving it in a wash of burning agony.

It was the first time Dex had ever heard himself truly scream. A real scream, the kind he could not control, the primal human response to a corporeal nightmare.

"It's sealed shut!" Fletch screamed back, choking over his words. "I can't find any sort of emergency release—!"

"There's not supposed to be an emergency release, you fucking idiot!" one of the other men yelled. "It's gotta be the backup plan in case of an accident!"

Fletch heaved himself against the metal door. Rationality was disappearing. Dex guessed the door was a sliding door, and even if it was not heavy duty and air tight, his friend would never get it open.

Here you are, one of the many, came a voice fully within Dex and, dually, fully without him. It was a voice made less of language than of light; his knowledge of this was potent, immediate.

He smelled the singe of hair, then felt the top of his scalp bubble under the heat.

Was there a God? Was there anything to be gained from dying, having been a coward but at least now facing the repercussions head-on?

Stop screaming, the light said. *Stop screaming, and you won't feel the pain. You're a gift, as is everyone, and you've always had a purpose. You have nothing to fear.*

The failsafes in the tumbled pile were righting themselves one by one and rushing to the door. Now, Dex found himself once again being pressed between the metal walls and a tumult of desperate souls. Only now, the metal burned.

Are they hearing the voice too? Dex wondered, losing himself. *Are they hearing the voice of God?*

CHAPTER 35 ✳ (HER)

GRACE PEERED OUT THE WINDOW, through the morning haze. The plane taxied slowly over the cracked, overgrown runway of Los Angeles' forsaken airport, and soon her window revealed three other hydro planes parked near the remnants of what could only be an old terminal.

Just like the ones in Minneapolis, Grace thought. *Only here, the shelf life was cut a bit short.*

Once the plane came to a stop, a motorized stairway wheeled toward them. Controlling it from the top step was a middle-aged government soldier, complete with a rainbow band around his bulging, uniformed arm.

"Remember, passengers, you are homosexuals on a funded holiday to New Zealand," the captain said across the video com once more. "I don't think we'll run into any problems. From what I hear, the team at this station is somewhat . . . lax."

"Hopefully these faggots'll be too interested in getting with that hot captain to notice us," Marvel whispered to Grace.

The pilot exited the plane, kissed the soldier on both cheeks, then walked down the steps, onto the ancient runway. They stood and talked for ten minutes before walking toward a large collapsible bunker near the old terminal.

Grace turned to Marvel and shrugged. "I guess we wait," she said.

"Yeah, but I don't like it. Like, if this is some kind of military base now, won't they totally know what's going on?"

"I think it'll depend on Frederik Carnevale and what kind of story he spins to make an excuse for us," Grace replied. "If he even has to answer to them. At least we have his status on our side."

Grace looked past Marvel, out the opposite window. There were hills in the distance, and they were mostly green. It looked positively inviting, as if nature had finally found its edge in reclaiming this expanse of shattered civilization. Closer, across a field of cement, the deteriorating remains of structures were visible: a control tower, hangars, and what must have once been office buildings or hotels. If the obstructer bombs had not fully demolished the surrounding area, it was safe to assume there might still be houses standing. Grace wondered if there were human remains in them. At most, they would be skeletons now.

"What if we run?" Marvel whispered. "Escape this place if they find us out, and just go make our way into the wild?"

"Fences," Grace whispered. "I saw some when we were flying in."

"Yeah, but I'm sure they're broken in spots. I'm sure we could get through."

Grace regarded Marvel with as much earnestness as she could muster, and her surprise came at the serious expression on the girl's face. She was even more pale than usual, with shaky hands clasped in her lap, as if she were holding onto herself for dear life. Marvel meant it, her idea of escape. If their stop in the City of the Dead went sour, they could cut and run. Try to have their babies the old-fashioned way. Live off the land.

Maybe she's the smart one for thinking of a backup plan.

Five minutes later, the captain returned.

"Off the plane," he told them. "It looks as if we might be here a few days."

The anxious passengers, Grace included, did not move. *Explanation, please*, she thought.

"There's a hangar on the north side of the old terminal, and they're bringing out trucks to drive you there. I told them the situation, that you're an entourage planning to meet Frederik Carnevale in New Zealand. They followed up on the plane's registration and flight path, and the story checked out. If Carnevale was the actual one to charter this flight, he covered his bases. Now, failsafes: we need one of you in each truck load, if possible. Flirt like hell with the drivers. Instigate handjobs. You need to keep them as uninterested in these women as possible. If there's one thing that can distract any man from reality, it's sex. So play your parts!"

As Grace stepped off the plane, a salty, warm breeze hit her face. Somewhere close, hoards of exuberant sea birds were greeting the new morning. Even in the mess of broken, overgrown cement surrounding the intact runway, Grace could see the appeal of Los Angeles as it must have been once, long ago. The green cropping up from the ruins signaled a paradise in the process of rebirth. She had always imagined the Unrecoverable Territories as hot beds of filthy, smoking destruction, horrors frozen in time by stories of the Bio Wars, the ones that colored every facet of the New Rainbow Order's checkered history. But no, this place was not dead. Far from it, in fact.

Because the universe rights itself.

Inside her, the baby suddenly kicked. Grace smiled.

CHAPTER 36 ✳ (HIM)

AND THEN THERE REALLY WAS LIGHT, not just a voice. Blinding, dazzling, beautiful, a breath of hope.

It's the light you always hear about from people who have died and come back, Dex sensed more than thought. *The light from the other side.* But there was air, too. Ice cold, whooshing into the train car, bathing the dying failsafes with life. Like fish to water, they took to it, following their instincts more than intellects. Dex was lucky to be one of the first men out, scrambling across a smoking ditch of earth and twisted metal.

Train tracks. Somebody bombed the train tracks!

Again, there were many things he would never know: that Abel Johns, sitting at his encrypted desk com 250 miles to the west, had experienced more difficulty than he had hoped in hacking the train's remote-control system; that, in the end, the man had found his way into the Department of Transportation's digital infrastructure and located the override to open the doors and shut off the ovens; that those Opposition members who had exploded the track were now running for their lives, fleeing the Bio Police and their hover jets, due to a tip-off from a rat within their trust circle; and that Grace, at this very moment, was experiencing a kick hello from their growing child.

As the stacks of blasted ground and mangled tracks flew under Dex's feet, he risked a glance backward. The surviving prisoners were scattering out of the open train doors like ants from a hill under attack, dispersing over the wreckage in flowing tangents. And the train was much longer than Dex had realized. Twenty cars at least. Now, it made sense why they had stopped six times, why there had been more train than platform space for their boarding in South Minneapolis. The Queen had devised his jailing system to coincide with methodical extermination.

Dex's rage fueled his navigation out of the burning crater. *Right under our noses*, he thought. *They planned this right under our fucking noses!*

"Dex!"

It was Fletch's voice, yelling.

"Dex! They did it! Somebody fucking did it! They must have hacked in and done something! Who the fuck knows?" His friend was whooping with joy, dancing his way out of the trench left by whatever explosion had taken out the track.

As soon as they were clear of the damage, Dex turned around to survey the derailed monster. Men were still emerging from the smoke, some struggling to move, others stopping like Dex to look at the wreckage, to breathe in their pure luck.

Then, Dex saw Exander. He was fighting his way out of the ditch, struggling to find air in the plumes of smoke. Moving, but only in a struggle. He was stuck. Dex jumped back into the mess to help his cellmate. Closer, he saw what was trapping Exander. It was not a lack of oxygen or an injury; it was a foot stuck somewhere between a pair of twisted steel beams—not crushed, by the look of it, just fallen into an awkward spot.

"Come on, let me help!" Dex screamed. "Move so I can get your foot loose!"

"Dex!"

"Move over and let me down so I can see how it's stuck!"

"Dex, your Opposition! It had to be your Opposition that got us out of this!"

"Still doubting them now?" Dex yelled, fighting tears from the smoke but laughing just the same.

Exander doubled over in a fit of coughing. His foot was lodged at an odd angle between the blown pieces of railroad track and two large boulders. Dex heaved one of the boulders off the ankle. "Pull it out! Go!" Exander yanked his leg up, cracked his knee on one of the steel lines, and swore.

"I'm okay, I'm okay, I'm going!" he bellowed.

And once they were free of the rubble, surrounded by a dome of pristine blue sky and miles of harvested winter cornfields, Exander kept moving. He passed Dex and Fletch without a second glance.

"Dude, Dex just saved your fucking *life!*" Fletch said, still gasping in the clean air. His eyes, Dex noticed now, were red. When Exander turned in response, Dex saw that his too looked the same, as if all the blood vessels were broken. Surely, his own were no different.

"Better me than somebody who's going to stand around and wait for the NRO's cleanup crew to fly in and pick up this mess!"

Dex jumped into a run after Exander. "Hey, wait! Wait up! Where will you go?"

"You know where I'm going!" his cellmate hollered. "Unrecoverable Territories! Somewhere warm! I'm getting out of this hellhole and living out my life where these faggots don't have control!"

"Wait! Think about it for a second. How are you going to—"

"Don't think, Dex, just *act.* Go with your gut, like you didn't do last time. Come with me!"

No. I can't.

"What are you, a coward?" Exander said, still walking backward over the winterized cornfield. He was shaking his head with an incredulous smile. *Haven't you learned your lesson yet?* the smile implied.

"No, not anymore," Dex said.

"What, then?"

Grace. He was going to find Grace. "I have someone who's waiting for me," he said. And now it was blooming inside him, pure and unscathed: courage, untainted. Perhaps it was the type of valor one could feel only after fear was finally frightened into nothingness.

Exander smiled, knowing. "Then good luck, Dex. I hope you find her."

"You too, friend. Be careful."

Dex watched Exander bolt into the vast, snow-dusted field. Soon he was a bobbing dot against the sky. Beyond him, less than a mile away, was a grove of trees. Part of Dex's broken heart mended at the site of Exander escaping, daring to hope.

And now you go and do the same thing. Do what you couldn't do before.

Was this the voice from the train? Dex could not know. Perhaps it had been his own all along. He leaned over, hands on his knees, and hung his head. Neither the yells nor the metallic groans from the derailed train could take away the sweet peace enveloping his heart. In that moment, clarity found him. He closed his eyes and breathed in the odor of smoke mingling with raw, cold air.

But in the distance rose the low hum of hydro rotary engines. As the seconds passed, it grew louder and separated into multiple drones. Hover jets. Exander had been right.

For God's sake, run!

The other men who had stopped to bask in their freedom were turning their eyes to the sky. Expressions of joy turned to horror as they registered and recognized the noise. Louder and louder the bass vibration became, and Fletch was screaming. "Run, Dex! We gotta get out of here! That dickhead was right!"

They ran.

We can't have escaped just to die, Dex told himself over and over, willing his feet to carry him over the broken, harvested corn stalks toward the trees Exander had disappeared into. An icy wind pushed them north, across the field. Two hundred other men were running the same trajectory in a line the length of the train.

Three hover jets, each bearing the government's rainbow insignia, appeared in the sky over the smoking train like monstrous dragonflies. Streams of bullets, the old-fashioned metal kind, ripped up the ground first behind Dex, then in front of him, leaving him no time to think. But three hundred feet ahead was something he had not been able to see from the wreckage: a long patch of yellowed corn stalks, left uncut. *For the winter animals*, Dex thought. *Food and refuge.*

It would provide a moment's cover but nothing more. It was the only obvious hiding spot before the trees and, thus, would be a prime target for the hover jet gunners. He and Fletch were the first to reach the frozen shoots, which scratched across their faces as they disappeared into them.

"Stop, Dex, stop!" Fletch screamed over the whipping sounds of other prisoners dashing through the rows of dead corn.

"No, keep going!" Dex screamed.

"We can't! They'll see us on the other side!"

"Then we're fucked either way! This is a bull's eye for them!"

No other options. No time to think. Do it.

Dex slowed, waited for Fletch, then grabbed his arm. One of the hover jets grew louder, nearer. Its engines rumbled in Dex's chest. The dried corn stalks bent under their generated wind, exposing all the fleeing bodies like roaches surprised by light.

More bullets, more screams. Men were falling.

And then Dex and Fletch were free of the corn patch, tumbling on confused feet into the field, toward the looming grove of trees. Behind them, the shower of bullets was getting closer.

"Fall, Dex! Pretend you've been shot! Count of three! One, two—"

"Three!" Dex screamed, forcing lifelessness into his legs and plummeting to the ground. He felt a sharp corn stalk puncture his leg, and he rolled three times, letting the frozen earth cut into his face. He could hear bullets raining to the ground around them, past them. Survival would be a gift of pure luck, if it continued at all.

Don't move. Don't breathe. Be dead to the world.

Dex was not much for classic television from the cinematic golden age, but once, he had seen an old program about plane crash survivors on a mysterious island. On it, a doctor character had described a botched surgery and how he had overcome the incapacitating terror his own mistake roused in him. He counted to five, letting the fear in, then willfully flushed it out when the count finished. At the time, Dex had seen little value in the arts and complained when his friend Milla forced him to watch the fictional series. Today, however, it offered him some unforeseen value. Today, he remembered that doctor.

One, Dex counted to himself.

More bullets.

Two.

The hydro engines were the angels of death, approaching Dex for the second time that day.

Three.

The spray of bullets had ceased, but—

Four.

The hover jet was flying away. Back toward the train.

Five.

Dex dared to open an eye, and the first thing he saw was Fletch's foot, only inches from his face. They had not even touched each other while toppling onto the field, and their near-adjacent positions now were almost comical.

"Fletch. They're leaving. It worked!"

No response came. Dex called for Fletch again but knew after that first silence that the man was dead. When Fletch Novotny was alive, he was talking. Dex waited five minutes, until he was sure the hover jet pilots had finished their immediate effort in the cornfield.

Finally, he gathered the courage to move. He propped himself up, peered over the ruffles in Fletch's dry, dirty clothes—the same clothes he had worn to Sterile Me Susan's the night of the raid—and saw a blackish-red exit wound in the man's face.

Play dead. Right.

An unexpected burst of tears followed the thought. "It was a good idea, buddy," Dex said aloud. He touched Fletch's leg, wishing his dead friend still had eyes to close, as they had always done on those old programs. But time was falling away. Dex took a moment to remember Fletch as he was, then set out across the field, sobbing, hoping he was far enough away from the hover jets to become a mirage.

A MEMORY ✳ (HER)

*P*ULLING GRASS UNDER HER DAD'S CRABAPPLE TREE, *reading* The Reserves *by Alwyn Templeton, eating toasted pita strips and guacamole, all while paying little attention to any of it: that is what Grace is doing. It is lonely, and she is torn between being thankful for her life and wishing her dad had not forced her father to volunteer her to be a heterosterile. Had they engineered a child differently, the other one she might have been would have had a normal life, have been a normal person.*

The long threads of grass tickle between Grace's fingers, and she tosses them into the still summer air, then picks more, repeats. She has been reading the same page of words on her com for the past ten minutes. All she can think about is Linda after the movie, when they were balled up in her bedroom and watching the scene with the naked woman lying in the roses. Linda had been very vocal about how sexual she felt during that scene, and Grace could only shrug with an ill feeling. She was nowhere near as skinny as Linda or the girl in the movie, and all she could think about during that was the layer of fat building on her own stomach. It wasn't normal for a fifteen-year-old girl to have fat, because everyone exercised. But then Linda asked Grace how she could know she was a heterosterile if she had never tried kissing a girl, and Grace hadn't had an answer, because she just knew it to be so, and then suddenly Linda was leaning in for a kiss, and a lifetime's lack of confidence and self-worth made Grace kiss back, because surely the fact that she liked boys could change, if she really wanted it to. But it was like kissing cardboard. Linda had pulled back, looking hurt and disappointed, and run from the room. They have not spoken since.

So here she is in the middle of summer with no friends, reading the only novel she has memorized enough to read without actually paying attention. It makes for a good way to look busy while really just wallowing in misery.

"Grace, what did I tell you?" comes her father's harsh voice (still and always a snake, even though she loves him) from the patio. "No snacks between four and six o'clock! Do you really want to make us the family with the fatty? You know how that looks, especially nowadays!"

The Queen has been in office for only two years, but he has already spoken out against people with more than 20 percent body fat.

Grace misses Linda. Nothing is good.

The seconds drag by as hot embarrassment rises in her face, and she looks stubbornly ahead, toward the empty guest house, as she hears her father shuffling across the yard to confiscate her afternoon snack. He does, and she refuses to look at him or say a word. Not once has he asked why Linda Glass doesn't come over anymore.

And then comes a coincidence Grace will never forget: her pocket com rings with a call. It is Linda, for the first time in over four months. Relief, disbelief, and humor flood Grace's senses, and just as potently as she was moments ago hopeless, she is light as air and answers her best friend's call. Perhaps there is goodness in her future after all.

CHAPTER 37 ✳ (HER)

THERE WERE TWO COMBATING FACTIONS here in Los Angeles: the New Rainbow Order's armed forces, and the people they called "the natives." As of late, the former were losing their claim of the land. The remains of LAX (as the airport had once been called, Grace learned) made up the area's only operating military base. It was little more than an old airplane hangar that was, miraculously, still in working condition.

The settlement was only seven years old, but contrary to what Mandate 43 had implied, soldiers here claimed the government had no plans to rebuild over Southern California's sprawl of deterioration. This was a hunting base, because unlike most other areas of the Unrecoverable Territories, the natives of Los Angeles were becoming a threat. It was the only Unrecoverable Territory where the population appeared to be growing, despite the government's best extermination efforts. The natives, descendants of natural procreators who had survived the Bio Wars, had weapons from the olden days: bombs, guns, gases, and chemicals. They were unafraid to use them.

Sergeant Blake Linder, who led the ground crew at the dilapidated airport, was a particularly muscular homosexual. Shirtless and dressed only in tight rainbow faux-camouflage exercise shorts, he exuded potent masculinity as he led Grace and her cohorts to the hangar and described the military's situation.

"They're leftover breeders whose ancestors survived the plagues and obstructer bombs back when this territory went up in smoke. We still know next to nothing about them, only that they have a better claim over the land than we do, and their old weapons have wiped out our automotive equipment more times than I care to admit. And they're good at hiding. But we have our orders from the Queen: stay here until the job is done."

Luke the failsafe, acting perfectly homosexual, approached Sergeant Linder and put a hand on the man's buttock. "So, what do you boys do here in your spare time?"

Linder's eyes flitted over Luke, and he smiled. "We hunt natives when things are going well, swim in the ocean when we're hot, and fuck when we're feeling horny. Can't think of a better way to spend my time, can you?"

The soldiers on site were too preoccupied with the new collection of men to care about the truckloads of pregnant, irritable women invading their hangar. Not only were the failsafes effective at playing gay and luring the soldiers' attention, but everyone was buzzing about the morning's terrorist attacks. Three other hydro planes, all of which belonged to general civilian airlines servicing New Rainbow Order territories between the Americas and Oceania, had also been grounded at LAX. Unlike Grace and the other Cliff House refugees, these planes' 204 passengers were leisure travelers heading to Sydney, Perth, and Fiji.

A crowd had gathered around the strip of wall coms lining the far end of the hangar, in what amounted to a mess hall. The pictures streaming over the coms were like videos from the old wars. Pillars of black smoke were rising over cities around the globe. There was Srinagar, one of the only western Asian cities still flourishing, one

Grace had always dreamed of visiting. An entire complex of public housing was burning in the night; behind the blaze, the Himalayas stood outlined against the last of their day's light. Even the soldiers were staring at the catastrophe with helpless expressions. WorldCom flashed again to video from Minneapolis, the home Grace would never see again. The IDS Center, the oldest remaining skyscraper in the city and the most recent to receive rainbow sun reflectors, was gone.

A pile of rubble, Grace thought. *Just like that. Just like here.*

She fingered the replacement com in her pocket. It was part of the Opposition's effort to pass them off as civilians, as it was highly unusual for anybody not to be carrying one. The com was real, but it could only receive messages. Grace wanted nothing more than to call her dad, only now, she could not. Her anxiety had been on a high since that final goodbye from the Cliff House's communications room. Had he listened to her warnings? Had he left the Minneapolis area? If not, surely these attacks would inspire him to act. Judging by their past behavior, her father, Abraham, and Lars would jump on the bandwagon of blaming remnants of God's Army. Still, if her dad left them to die in the larger retaliation effort Albert Redmond had hinted at, what would that make him?

It would make him smart. Yet Grace was unsure how to reconcile that thought with the image of her father, brother, and nephew perishing in a nuclear attack.

Destruction unfolded on the com screens. Each one showed a different live video feed, and one, at the far right end of the mess hall, was showing a news hover jet's view of a demolished stretch of winter cornfield. The camera was panning over a massive smoking pile of metal that looked to Grace like a derailed train. She stepped closer and stopped behind three soldiers, one of whom appeared to be in his mid-forties. By the way he spoke, it was clear he was of a higher rank than the other two. Apart from Grace, they were the only three people paying attention to this last wall com.

"They shouldn't be showing this," the oldest soldier muttered.

"Sure seems like a good way to raise a bunch more rebels, don't you think, Major?" one of the younger ones replied.

"If civilians find out about the trains, we could have a legitimate uprising on our hands. Makes me glad we're stuck out here."

"So they got all of them?" the third soldier asked in a hushed voice.

The oldest one adjusted his crotch. "Every fucking track."

The com screen suddenly cut away from the cornfield image, back to a confused-looking news anchor. He wore a blank expression and was looking off camera, as if listening to some order through his earpiece. Then, the screen cut to images of Chicago, which had suffered the worst destruction. Seven skyscrapers had dropped like children's building blocks, leaving a cloud of smoke and dust strung along the city's skyline.

The oldest soldier turned and saw Grace staring at the screen, which gave him a moment's pause. With a quick glance at her breasts, which even homosexual men sometimes admired, he stepped around her. The other two guards followed.

Every fucking track," he had said. Did that mean the Opposition had succeeded? That the trains heading for the dumping pit had been impeded?

Grace jumped when a hand gripped her elbow.

"Just me, honey," Marvel said, playing lesbian. She kissed Grace on the cheek, then hugged her, torn by the drama unfolding on the coms. The girl was crying. "My moms live four blocks away from the IDS Center. I'm so fucking scared, Grace."

Grace clasped Marvel's hand and squeezed it, wishing she could take the girl's worry away. "We're all in this together, hon," she said. "You've got me."

"Man, you really *are* starting to sound like a dyke," the girl sniffed.

DESPITE OUTSIDE AFFAIRS, the soldiers seemed to be excited about their visitors. Most of the visitors were men, which meant new sexual conquests, but at a deeper level, they simply seemed enthusiastic to play host for people from the outside world. Over the next two days, they shuttled the new arrivals to and from the Pacific Ocean in two long buses, both of which were antique, pre-Bio War machines that ran on solar power. The soldiers were thrilled to act as tour guides. There appeared to be little else for them to do on the LAX base, as they had all been called in from hunting natives since the attacks. True to their pilot's request, the pregnant women were always accompanied by the failsafes, all of whom were doing remarkable jobs of distracting the soldiers. As prominent as some of the developing baby bumps became when the daytime heat made it conspicuous for the women to wear multiple layers of clothing, nobody seemed to notice. The soldiers were too busy being human. It was a relief.

Grace's first step into an ocean's surf was like living a dream.

The same stretch of water that touches Asia, she thought, in awe. It was funny to think that the waves in front of her hadn't once stopped, ever. No matter what happened in the world, nature continued on its course. Watching the bright, glittering bubbles wash over her bare ankles, Grace wondered if humans could be considered part of that cyclical, constant universe. Or were they some anomaly that rubbed against the grain? Life would provide no answer for that, she was sure. It was simply her responsibility to go on and see where the days took her. She would make the best of it. She had to.

The Queen's declaration of martial law was immediate, and the length of resulting military rule was indefinite. The com screens in the mess hall remained on at all hours, and when backaches or the cot Grace slept on left her uncomfortable, she often walked back to the coms to watch the world tangling itself further, toward all the supposed answers. The Rainbow Charter had officially been suspended. The military patrolled the streets now, and all people were being scrutinized, especially those trying to travel. Commercial airlines were to remain halted for at least thirty days, in accordance with the global emergency lockdown. It was a measure to ensure the Rainbow Intelligence Agency a better chance of cornering those responsible for the attacks. Restricted travel would make it difficult for any of the terrorists to escape. But it would not last forever.

"This is a time when fear could make us bow to the heterosexuals who did this," came the Queen's speech over the com, late on Grace's third night in Los Angeles. She was sitting awake in the mess hall under the blue LED lights' dim midnight glow. The Queen's press conference had been running on loop for two days, and for the first time ever, his sequined dress, eye shadow, and lipstick were all a matching blood-red. "Peaceful society succumbing to fear is exactly what these heterosexual terrorists want," he declared next. "Spreading discord is what they have done since the dawn of man, and it now has to stop. We *will* prevail. We *will* show them the errors of their ways. The colors of the rainbow will *show them we are strong!*"

His audience, a group of journalists made up mostly of fags, stood and cheered. Some of them were crying, hugging, and kissing each other, and the cameras captured it all. The Queen, with his makeup awash in camera flashes and praise, dazzled the world with a triumphant smile.

Of course, there was no mention of the New Rainbow Order being behind the attacks. This had nagged at Grace since her arrival at LAX. The horrific images gleaming out of the com screens made her realize that the chances of these attacks being masterminded by the government were just as strong as the possibility that they were orchestrated by legitimate remnants of God's Army. Grace was hanging her very life on the words of people who had known about the attacks before they had happened—known about them, and blamed the government. But what proof was there? If the Queen's spies had infiltrated God's Army to instigate an assault against society and turn heterosexuals further into scapegoats for everything wrong in the world, how would anyone ever know? How could Grace know if Albert Redmond and other members of the Opposition had been telling the truth? What if, instead, the Opposition was creating a giant scapegoat out of the New Rainbow Order to instill fear in Theodore Bozarth's specimens and further its own agenda? It was possible.

But I'm still alive, Grace thought. *Pregnant, sitting in a mess hall in the Unrecoverable Territories with a bunch of NRO soldiers, and still alive.*

It had to count for something.

But Marvel was sneaking around again. While making her way from the empty mess hall to the temporary airline passenger quarters, Grace saw and smelled a cloud of cigarette smoke rising from behind one of the makeshift walls near the hangar's entrance. It was Marvel. She was standing across from a set of collapsible barracks, where most of the soldiers on site would now be. There were guards on duty, of course, but not to watch over the grounded airline passengers; they were stationed outside with infrared thermal imaging systems that could detect body heat as far away as fifteen miles. Natives were the threat here, not civilians.

The hangar door was open enough to provide a five-foot doorway to the taxiway, and the cool night air blowing through it smelled of ocean.

Marvel turned her head as Grace approached. "Care for a smoke? I swiped a pack from one of the tables."

"I thought smoking was bad when you're—"

Marvel's curls bounced as she held up a hand to shush Grace, who snapped her mouth shut so hard that it sent a cold pain into her teeth. She had forgotten how easily voices carried during the night.

"I mean . . . no, I'm fine. Thanks though."

"I made friends with a couple of the night guards," Marvel said.

"They were actually sort of nice. Probably because they're just so bored out here. They're waiting for natives to attack. Sounds like a blast, huh?"

Grace gave her a sarcastic nod. "Are you going to the beach tomorrow?"

"Probably. Except . . ." Marvel, who was courteous enough to blow the cigarette smoke out the door, stepped closer to Grace and lowered her voice. "Except I'm starting to feel like they can't possibly *not* realize we're all . . . you know. Nobody is totally obvious yet, but I'm getting there. If we're really stuck here for another month . . ." Marvel's gaze drifted out of the hangar, into the black night. Shadowy bags weighed down her eyes. She flipped a quarter inch of ash from her cigarette, then whispered, "I just don't think we're going to get out of this."

Grace had no good response to offer, so she stood with Marvel and stared into the night. The strip of sky made visible through the opening of the hangar's massive door was alight with stars in a way Grace had rarely witnessed. A few distant lights lined the edge of the airport's perimeter, but the moonless night brought an awesome display of stars so bright and so countless that it seemed to make the ground sink away. Grace felt as if the world was about to tip forward and thrust her off, into that vastness. It was so close, so clear. If there was one good thing about the fallen civilization under their feet, it was this: the calm of the stars, the galaxy haze spreading through them, and the other worlds that must exist somewhere, out there, in peace.

"I'm never going to see my moms again," Marvel said.

Grace put an arm around her shoulder. "You're on a new adventure now. We all are."

"How many natives do you think are out there?"

"I don't know. It seemed like a lot, from what they said."

"D'you think it's possible to hide from the NRO's body heat sensors? At least until the squads are sent back out to hunt?"

"I'm not sure. The natives seem to be doing it."

More silence, more stars. Somewhere inside the hangar, a man grunted to sexual climax before his sounds disappeared into the darkness.

"I think I will go to the beach tomorrow," Marvel said.

It was the last thing Grace ever heard the girl say.

THE NEXT MORNING, AFTER BREAKFAST, the soldiers started the electric bus and announced a beach run. Marvel was one of the first to stand up. They had been sitting together at a mess hall table, eating breakfast in silence. Grace felt Marvel's hand drag over the top of her head in what seemed like a peculiar and fleeting display of love. Not their fake lesbian love, but something real. Grace asked Marvel to wait up, but the girl barely turned her head to acknowledge it. As the bus bounced west along the fractured road leading out to the old highway, Marvel showed Grace only the back of her head, which remained turned toward the window. But they were holding hands, still playing lesbian. When the bus stopped, Marvel squeezed extra hard, then turned to Grace. Tears were falling down her eyes. Marvel smiled, and the reason for her disassociation became too obvious to doubt.

She's leaving.

They stood in the surf, holding hands like two lovers. The waves in front of them crashed, washed up, enraptured their feet, then pulled back. It was peaceful, a fitting goodbye. Behind them, the guards were playing naked volleyball with some of the stranded men, including three failsafes, who actually seemed to be having fun. Strewn along the beach were at least thirty more people enjoying the bright, blue reprieve from the airport hangar. Sea birds sang around them. For those few minutes, it was like heaven.

Marvel let go of Grace's hand. It took Grace five minutes to build the courage to look after her. When she did, the girl was far down the beach, disappearing into the sparkling morning haze. If the soldiers were keeping tabs on her, they probably thought she was simply walking, like so many of the others.

The haze swallowed her. She did not come back.

The soldiers were nowhere near organized enough to do a headcount of the passengers, and nobody but Grace missed Marvel when they returned later that afternoon. As far as the soldiers or other passengers were concerned, everyone who had journeyed to the beach that morning made the return trip. Grace knew better than to go after Marvel; the girl's resolve had been clear enough. If she wanted to come back, she knew the way. As air travel would be restricted for at least another month, Marvel would have time to rethink her decision.

Only she did not. First one day, then two, then three. Marvel had gone to find the natives. She had chosen to become one of the hunted, a human breeder trying to survive in the City of the Dead.

CHAPTER 38 ✳ (HIM)

Dex walked. He did not know where he was, though he assumed it was somewhere in Kansas or Missouri. Four days had passed since whatever force running the universe spared his life, and with each breath and passing step, he praised it with gratitude and humility. He would never try to take the easy way out again. From now on, he would live to serve what he knew in his heart to be right and true. Dex's experience on the train had unlocked something in him, a unique—perhaps universal—awareness of something bigger, an acknowledgement that actively doing good was far superior to simply behaving in a neutral, passive manner. His mistake in leaving Grace at Sterile Me Susan's had to be remedied, if only by these simple steps that were now bringing him across Missouri.

The two left-fitting shoes Exander had thrown to Dex during the evacuation became a godsend. They made walking a bit painful, but it was preferable to the alternative of bare feet. On that first day, he had made a successful escape across the field, to the trees. Deflated when he failed to catch up with his cellmate, Dex continued running until he was sure it was safe to rest. The trees were not the grove he had assumed they would be; they were a true stretch of forest, providing enough safety and security for him to ponder what he had just lived through. The military had not sent dogs to chase down its prisoners, nor had they sent hover jets to scour the area with thermal imaging systems. Perhaps the necessity of cleaning up train wreckage that was not yet supposed to exist and avoiding any looming questions had rendered the possibility of a few escaped prisoners harmless. Bigger fish would fry for this accident, and Dex was determined not to get caught again in the crosshairs.

There was nobody to talk to on this walk, and he welcomed the silence. Judging by the position of the sunrise, he was moving west. Dex used the time less to think than to meditate, and each minute passed like some brilliant, hypnotic gift. He had rested easily that first night, despite the cold, and the second. Only on the third, after tree cover had disappeared and he was exposed to potential threats, did Dex allow the unease brought on by common sense to direct him. He walked by night when the weather was coldest in order to stay warm, then napped under the sun by day. Winter in Missouri was not the snowy mess that Minneapolis was, but it was still dangerous enough to risk freezing without thicker clothes. He could barely feel his feet, but at least they were dry.

There was the problem of food. All he had eaten since his jail cell were wild winter berries and one tough corn stalk, which had been nearly impossible to chew. He was still tramping the open fields, avoiding roads, and he had yet to see another section of uncut corn left for the winter animals. Dex was one of those animals now, and he dreamed of finding an actual corn cob buried in a frozen husk, somehow left unseen by scrounging deer. The reverie kept his feet moving, even though the fields ahead of him were barren. The morning was cold enough for Dex to see his breath, but it was not freezing. A low fog hung around him, but the rising sun made it shimmer: first pink, then yellow, then white, before it cleared.

Later, the growl of a hydro truck engine and the crunching of tires racing over gravel woke him from his daytime sleep.

It was closer than Dex thought possible. He was huddled in a fetal position, facing the noise, and the sun was startling in its warmth. As the truck grew closer, Dex dared to open his eyes.

Three hundred feet away, a rusted utility truck roared by, as if through the muddy field itself. It took Dex a full ten seconds to realize he had been walking along the edge of this particular section of farmland. The ground rose at a slight incline, and as he had heard only the sounds of nature for the past two days, Dex had assumed it was simply a roll that descended back onto another stretch of cropless winter soil. But no, there was a road. The truck was high enough for its driver's side window to be visible, which meant the driver could see him. Dex hoped he or she would not decide to glance left.

The truck passed, but not before the driver tossed something yellow out the window.

A banana peel.

When Dex was sure the road was clear, he jumped onto his feet and dashed toward the fallen bit of food, which was already browning. There was a bite left of the banana at its base, and the peel itself would at least fill his stomach for a short while. The peel had a muted, chalky taste on the outside, and sweetness on the inside. Dex ate it in seconds and experienced a gloomy sense of emptiness when the experience was over. He would need more food and water, and soon. The snow that had dusted the fields four days prior was gone now, and he had come across only five streams with water clear enough to risk drinking.

Suffering a stomach ache after eating the banana peel, Dex tried to fall back asleep, wondering just how publicized the derailed train had been. If farmers in the area knew to suspect bio fugitives of crossing through their lands, he could have little time left as a free man. Even so, he was lucky with the warm weather. It could turn back to a freeze at any time, rendering the issue of starvation moot.

You need to keep walking. Follow that truck.

Whether its destination was a home or a town, Dex had no way of knowing. Following the road was his best bet, but was it worth the risk? He could always run again, if the wrong person found him out. And there was always that last question: How many people knew about that train, and how many people now knew what it was built to do? If there was any good left in the world (and despite his exhausted state, Dex was now sure there was), there would be people who did not support the government's genocidal intentions. He simply had to find them before the weather turned. At the very least, he needed heavier clothing and some solid food.

And a new TruthChip, he thought. *One scan of my wrist, and it'll alert the police.*

As it turned out, luck was not finished with Dex.

From the field, he followed the road all day, lying flat whenever an automobile passed. By nightfall, there were lights in the distance—a farmhouse, he saw after growing closer. The road led to its long gravel driveway, at the end of which was a red and white yard sign reading "Support Unity!"

Support Unity. It was a slogan supporting heterosexual reintegration.

The lure of food and warmth took his feet toward the wraparound front porch. The house was very large and extremely old, a boxy Midwestern farmhouse built under a triangular roof. Dormers adorned the highest floor on all visible sides.

Come on the right night, and I bet you'd see a ghost standing in one of those windows. It was an unusual thought for Dex but also characteristic of who he had become since escaping the oven train: a man thinking more and more in terms of the metaphysical. Or, perhaps, he was simply more hungry and fatigued than he realized. A long shoe rug under the porch's awning caught his eye. In what seemed like a perfect decision, Dex picked it up, shook out the dirt, and sank to the wooden floor, using the rug as a blanket. He was a small man, and it covered him head to toe. Thoughts of warmth and a friendly world lulled him into a deep sleep. At multiple times during the night, between his dreams, he woke, then slipped away again, to the sound of distant hover jets.

NOT EVEN THE COOL SEA AIR mixed with blistering-hot sun could cheer Grace. Thoughts of her immediate family, memories of lost friends, and her sense of dislocation and isolation had pulled a shade over her world.

And there was another problem.

One of the soldiers, a man with a dirty-blonde crew cut who looked no older than twenty-five, had begun staring at her. Grace noticed it the afternoon Marvel left, and it continued into the next day. He was paler and thinner than most of the other soldiers, still muscled but lanky enough that his stature looked more awkward than powerful. Something about him struck Grace as different; he carried himself with an air of reservation and artificial confidence. It was possible he was just shy, and seeing as he did not strut with the same sexual swagger as most of the other soldiers, it could have been that his leggy body left him feeling out of place. On the day Marvel disappeared into the mist, this soldier had been playing volleyball on the beach. Grace thought nothing of him then, but later that evening, she caught him staring at her from across the mess hall.

The following morning, when Grace stepped out of the hangar to greet the hot sun, he was sitting on a lawn chair to her right, in rainbow faux-camouflage pants and a white T-shirt. He was reading something on his pocket com. On her other side, three soldiers were kicking a small beanbag around, guffawing in their fun.

In her peripheral vision, she saw the whites of his eyes shift toward her. On instinct, she slouched forward so that her lower abdomen's profile would not give away her condition. She moved as if to turn her head toward the soldier, and his gaze darted back to the com. Grace finished her motion by glancing upward at the fresh blue sky, but her attempt to look relaxed felt phony and forced.

He knows something is up. Get away from him.

Grace returned to the hangar and lay down for the remainder of the day, but her nerves remained heightened. That evening, she walked to dinner late to avoid the crowd of hungry, stranded passengers. A cargo plane of fresh produce and poultry had arrived that day, and dinner was to be a feast. Grace thought she would be lucky to get even a chicken leg, but as it turned out, the scraps were enough to feed another army. Grace loaded her plate with a chicken breast, steaming vegetables, a salad, two rolls, and a bowl of strawberries for dessert. For a moment, it brought a flashback to her early adulthood, when food had been a crutch so frowned upon by her family.

Let me be an Obesaland fatty, she thought, digging into her meal. *I've got a baby to feed and feelings to purge.*

The food was palatable, far better than the cardboard military rations they had been forced to eat over the past five days. Grace had no idea when her next normal meal would be, so she went back for seconds. And thirds. Each bite made the confusion, doubt, and loneliness burrow deeper inside her chest. They were funny things, feelings. Even though the brain produced them, they seemed to bloom or hurt or shatter in the heart. People sometimes put hands to their hearts when verbally communicating a feeling. Tonight, Grace would have done that had there been anybody to confide in. Most of the Cliff House women kept to their two- or three-person friend circles, none of which included Grace. Only one, the young woman Hilda, had approached Grace since Marvel's departure. "Is everything all right?" she asked. Grace had simply nodded and smiled, ashamed at her inability to welcome Hilda's friendliness. All she wanted was to get out of this dead city and take the next step toward something—anything. Comfort, family, and love were things of the past, and accepting that fact would be the least burdensome modus for facing new days.

She ate another strawberry. With it came the warmth of a recent memory: Dex Wheelock, feeding the fruit to her in the bath.

"I won't blame you if you decide to save yourself and run," she had told him that night. *"Just give me the word, and I'll figure it out myself."*

Is that what she was doing now? Figuring it out herself? Hardly.

"What happened to your wife?" a voice asked from across the table.

Grace jumped out of her mind, shocked, and looked up from her bowl of strawberries. The lanky soldier was sitting directly across from her, resting his folded, square arms on the table. Up close, the idiosyncrasies of his face were more apparent. His wide-set eyes were an unnerving green, and his prominent nose and inset lower jaw lent him a falcon-like shape that made his expression look like one of perpetual distaste. It seemed almost pompous. Staring straight at Grace, he reached across the table and ate one of her strawberries.

"Don't worry, we have more."

Am I being interrogated? "It's okay. Take what you need."

He leaned forward, his gaze still boring into Grace. "So, what happened to your wife? Or was she your girlfriend?"

"Marvel?"

"Short, almost stocky. Dark, curly hair. You know who I'm talking about, because she was holding your hand on the beach the other day. She didn't come back on the bus."

Red, inky heat rushed into Grace's face. She looked down at the last two strawberries, then pushed the bowl toward the soldier. "Here, have these. I'm done." Making to get up, she stopped when the soldier held up a hand.

"Wait, wait. I'm not trying to scare you." He flipped his wrist downward, toward the strawberries. It was a classic homosexual mannerism, but on him, it looked unnatural. Grace sat straight up on the bench, itching to turn away but deciding to give this man a chance. He glanced around and, seeing that they were alone, said, "I'm Clarence Helio. *Lieutenant* Clarence Helio, rather."

"Nice to meet you, Lieutenant. I was just going back to my cot."

"I've been noticing you. And the woman with the curls. And some of the others."

"Noticing us? Okay." Grace's attempt at indifference tumbled forth in a bundle of nerves, and she knew Lieutenant Helio was not buying it. Trying to channel the tension into curiosity, she added, "Is there a problem?"

"I know you're pregnant."

Grace's chest did a double flip, and it took only a second for sweat to break out on her exposed arms and hands. She glanced down at them to see their color draining away. In a sad attempt to appear blasé, she scratched the top of her leg.

This is it. I'm dead. Everything I left for, all for nothing.

"I'm a carrier. We both were." It was a hasty, unconvincing lie.

"And all the other women?"

"I don't know anything about that. We were on our way to New Zealand to visit our friend's resort."

Clarence shrugged, then nodded. "Fair enough. But if you want to know what I think, here it is: you're pregnant, and for whatever reason, you're trying to get the hell out of Dodge. I can't say I blame you. Now, will you listen to what I have to say? Because I think all your lives depend on it."

Grace's hands were shaking now, and she clasped them together. It was gesture enough for Lieutenant Helio to continue.

"Thank you." He leaned back in a more relaxed manner, but his gaze was still darting in all directions. "I need for you to continue to act as if we're strangers, and I'm simply here keeping you company. Frankly, nobody has really taken to suspecting you passengers of anything, especially the ones from your plane. People from your plane are here because of Frederik Carnevale, and that's all anybody cares to know for now. We don't question orders from that high up."

"So what's your point?"

"My point is that, in a month, you're going to be too obvious. Most of the men here haven't even looked at you chicks, because they're too focused on getting laid by all the new dick. It's not going to last, once you start getting bigger. If air travel remains restricted, it's going to present a problem. My problem is that I did notice, and I want to get you on your way. I'm not part of this army because I had a choice, and if I had, I'd be working on your side."

"I don't know if I'm on any *side*," Grace said.

"*I'm* on the side that doesn't want to kill people," Lieutenant Helio continued. "I'm lucky you decided to come late to dinner. Now, you and that woman with the curls were not really married. If you were, you wouldn't both be legal carriers, and both of you were pregnant. I can tell the difference between a pregnant woman and a fatty. It's rare I get to see one, and when I do . . ." His gaze wandered down Grace's neck, over her breasts, and down.

Her defenses blurred as she realized there was something comforting in the lieutenant's youthful display of indulgence. "What, are you hetero or something?" she whispered, reaching for the last strawberry.

"Don't ask, don't tell," he replied.

"And you're in the military? They let you in?"

"My father ranks high, and let's just say I was an accident." He pushed Grace's empty bowl off to the side and leaned closer again. "You know genetic mistakes? Well, they aren't limited just to females.

As far as my TruthChip is concerned, I'm as gay as you are. I could tell you and that woman weren't lovers."

Grace was trapped, and the lieutenant had forced this conversation on her so suddenly. They were too deep into it now for her to turn and run. And perhaps he was trying to prevent that. She had heard of the possibility of male genetic mistakes, but she had never met one in person.

"How far along are you?" he asked.

"Just past four months."

"Jesus Christ," Lieutenant Helio whispered. "You're walking a tight rope, you know that? You're already becoming obvious, and wearing big clothes won't help you a month from now."

"You don't have to tell me that," Grace said. "I'm just taking it a day at a time."

"Doing that will get you killed. We need to get you on your way, which is why I'm talking to you. Can we take a ride? If anyone asks, we can say you dropped your com on the beach today."

Grace barely affirmed his suggestion, but within five minutes, they were in a hydro truck, driving down the taxiway toward the fenced gate to World Way West, the broken road leading toward the ocean. The sun had just set, and the sky was a deep, cool purple. The first of the night's stars, her last link to Marvel, were peeking through it. Now, yet another random life was crossing her own, changing her from the inside out. Grace no longer cared for the coincidence, the luck, the strangeness of it all. She simply longed to be safe, at peace.

"Now, do you want to know why you can trust me?" Lieutenant Helio said.

Grace nodded, and the lieutenant explained:

He was going to blow up one of the four landed hydro planes, blame it on the natives, and inspire the Queen to lift air travel restrictions from the LAX base.

"The Queen has no love for civilians, but I don't think he and his military are ready to strand two hundred of them in the Unrecoverable Territories, in a place being attacked by natives. It would give people reason to question his motives, and word about his true agenda could get out too early, which is why I think they'll lift the restriction. One of my fathers is General Tom Helio, and I can get him to set you civilians free."

Grace almost hissed out her next breath. *I knew this guy's name sounded familiar.* General Helio was the Queen's combative arm, and his name was a quasi-permanent fixture in the movement to forcefully relegate heterosexuality to a dying evolutionary track. Never was he seen without his peroxide-blonde hair, a rainbow band around his arm, and a bulging crotch. It was rumored he stuffed his pants with a sock to convey a sense of power.

Lieutenant Helio drove Grace to the beach, where they sat in the parked truck surrounded by the darkening sea and its salty, organic aroma. There, he explained who he was, how he came to be stationed in Los Angeles, and why he was now an enemy of the dictatorship symbolized by his very uniform. A career outside the military had never once been an option for Lieutenant Clarence Helio. His other father, while not a prominent public figure like Tom Helio, was still a high-ranking commander in the Recovered Europe branch of the New Rainbow Air Force. Both his parents had unofficial but secretly lauded instances of anti-heterosexual violence decorating their reputations, and being forced into the military (and by extension, sexual activity with other males) had been the least of the Lieutenant's worries.

"There were probably five Christmases when all of us were together under the same roof," he told Grace. "On one of them, we had a steak dinner delivered from the Bull's Ball, and the delivery guy was obviously hetero. Hung his eyes on the ground when talking to my dads . . . you know. Wasn't checking them out and obviously wanted to get out of there. They asked him flat out if he was a failsafe, and he answered yes. You want to know what they did to him?"

Grace neither nodded nor shook her head. Outside, the purple waves crashed, one after the other, in a constant rage.

"My father the Air Force commander held him while my father the general ripped his clothes and shoes off, kicked his penis and testicles until they were a bloody mess, and sent him back to his car. I was fourteen. The next week, I started hanging holopanels of naked men on my bedroom wall so I could hide the fact that I'd been jerking off to thoughts of naked heterosteriles for the previous three years."

Lieutenant Helio had a habit of blinking when he did not need to, Grace noticed. It was a nervous tick, perhaps his version of being emotive. He continued telling Grace about being filtered into Sean Cody Military Academy, graduating with top honors and his insidious secret still intact, and joining the military ranks in the Los Angeles Unrecoverable Effort. The general had pushed for early promotions for his son, escalating him to Lieutenant in just four years.

"Now, here's the clincher, and this is why I want to get you out of Los Angeles before you're found out by anyone else. Trust me, if they were looking, they'd notice. The NRO put a silent hold on legal carrying almost a year ago."

This was news to Grace. Nobody affiliated with the Opposition had mentioned this. Not even the pilot had known. If Albert Redmond had made the Cliff House visitors privy to this information, he had done so when Grace was not present. Did that mean Frederik Carnevale, a supposed premiere-fucking-fag of the New Rainbow Order, did not know either? Or—and this would be far more menacing—had he kept the hushed ban on carriers a secret from the Opposition?

"But . . ." Grace was about to express her concerns before she stopped herself for fear of exposing Carnevale.

Lieutenant Helio had already connected the dots. "If your plane was truly chartered by Frederik Carnevale, it means something big is going on, and I want in. I can't do my job here without somehow doing my part to save humanity as well."

Save humanity. He sounds like Albert Redmond.

There was a truth beating under the surface here, something Grace had not yet learned enough about to put her finger on. Lieutenant Helio was hinting at some missing, ever-important piece to the puzzle.

"What do you mean, 'save humanity'?"

The lieutenant took a deep breath. "I mean there are those of us in the military who are aware of what the New Rainbow Order thinks of as its noble cause. They're not just trying to do away with human procreation. They're trying to give our planet a second chance by doing away with *the human species.*"

Grace searched the lieutenant's eyes for any glint of humor, but under the day's dying light, his stony countenance made it obvious he believed his words. Two of them had been very indicative: *noble cause.* The homosexuals had risen to power under the guise of being the collective underdog with all the answers to humanity's struggles. Human population, which had been their planet's most serious hazard, had since decreased to a mere fraction of what it had once been. Now, Lieutenant Helio explained, they were pushing that agenda to the very end. According to his fathers, the clinics promised by Mandate 43 were a joke, and the Queen had a high and mighty vision of humanity dying out and nature reclaiming the earth.

"The Queen thinks it's his spiritual duty to rid the world not just of the breeders but of *everyone.* According to him and the men working under him, we're all nothing but a stain on this beautiful planet."

There it was: the numbing truth. Grace's hands were bunched into cold, white fists. Her throat was dry when she continued. "But what about the Queen and all the other homos? Why don't they just nuke us all? Make it quick?"

"Because their interest is an earth without humanity. Not a destroyed earth. They want peace, and they don't see peace in humanity's future. Their answer of genetic engineering for human reproduction was never supposed to be a fool-proof way of preserving humanity with total control. It was just a way to set the parameters for human extinction. The Queen thinks he is doing God's work, and the secretary generals after him will further that work. Mandate 43 has effectively ended human engineering, and once all the heterosexuals are gone, including all those ones we're hunting out there . . ." Lieutenant Helio waved a hand, gesturing down the beach. "The remaining homosexuals will die off naturally, one by one, ultimately leaving the earth peacefully, and in peace."

"But killing off humanity isn't peace!"

"Isn't it? The Queen and his executives count themselves as part of the human threat, albeit a part that has the ultimate answer. The rainbow. God's promise of faithfulness toward all living things. They simply want to remove us from that group, because we're the only living things who can't stop hating each other and destroying everything around us. The only ones who laugh at God's rainbow. Why shouldn't we die off?"

The lieutenant was being the devil's advocate, but Grace chuckled now at the grand sense in it. Everything was falling into place. And here she was, a victim of coincidence, sitting on the edge of one of the lost oceans with a perfect stranger who just happened to have all the answers. Yet she had heard it from Sheila Willy as well. Mandate 43 was just cover for something bigger. Sheila, however, seemed to have been blissfully unaware of how drastic the Queen's plan really was. That it was, as the lieutenant said, *noble*.

"Is that why they stopped sending people to the Sanctuary?" Grace asked.

For the first time that night, she saw a shred of uncertainty in Lieutenant Helio's eyes.

He shook his head. "That's something I've been wondering about. Rumors are flying everywhere, but even my fathers are tight-lipped about it. All I've gathered is that something happened down there, and the NRO doesn't want anybody to know about it."

"Why do you suppose?"

"My guess? They're scared. Whatever happened down there, it changed their grip on the future." Lieutenant Helio let his right arm fall from the hydro truck's steering wheel onto the cab's empty center seat. For a moment, they sat listening to the waves, feeling the wind's constant urgency flutter through the open windows.

And then he wrapped Grace's hand in his own. At first it was a shock, and Grace's initial reaction was to recoil. But then she realized she had nothing to lose, that there was no reason to deflect this sudden display of affinity. She was all alone in this Unrecoverable Territory, and here was a man trying to save her life, to share a gesture likely sparked by a lifetime of loneliness, grief, and desire to expose the affection so skillfully hidden in his heart.

"I've never been this intimate with a woman before," he said, turning his face to Grace with a sheepish grin. "I think you're the most beautiful one I've ever met, and I don't want to see what would happen if you're found out. I also think you and this Carnevale crew are somehow part of what happened in Antarctica, which means I have no idea if blowing up this plane will actually help you or somehow make it worse. All I know is that if you women don't get out of here soon, you won't get out of here at all."

Grace surprised herself by squeezing the lieutenant's hand, holding it tight. There were chances to be taken here, some big, some small. They were alone; nobody was watching. They could run right now, abandon everyone back at the base, and seek a life among Marvel and the natives. They could make love, take this fleeting opportunity to forge a connection that would cure their distress, if only for a night. Or, they could sit here on the beach until the sky grew black, dreaming of all other possible futures, but only dreaming. Lieutenant Helio was a good man, perhaps the best kind. But she could not forget Dex Wheelock. She could not forget the miracle they had created, the miracle growing between her and the lieutenant now.

"Blow up the plane," she whispered. "Let's get me and these other breeders the fuck out of here."

A MEMORY ✳ (HIM)

*D*EX AND BOBBY SALINGER OFTEN SPEND *their after-school hours behind the gym, hanging out on the small knoll where all the smokers spend their break times. Three weeks ago, Dex started smoking, much to Bobby's disgust, but it's okay. He and Bobby complement each other well: Dex is becoming a cynic; Bobby, a star-crossed idealist, even at age sixteen.*

"Straight Alliance is for goody-goodies," Dex says, taking a drag off his marijuana cigarette. These days he feels angry most of the time. "Besides, it's no use if they're going to shut it down anyway. You heard about Mr. Cormick filing a complaint, right?"

Bobby balls his fists. "Yeah. But I still think we need to join. We've got to meet more people like us, man."

"Staying invisible is the best bet in this dump. God, I hope I can get into a college."

"Come to police school with me. My dad will get you in. He really wants to get the police force integrated, and he knows chiefs all over. Bio and normal police," Bobby replies. "I'm totally going to do it."

Dex laughs, then shakes his head. "No thanks. No way I'd go work with all those fags and risk getting raped every day. You can't get a badge without scanning your wrist and all them knowing you're a failsafe. What then?"

"Not going to stop me. Attitudes like that are what make it okay for the NRO to let discrimination happen all over the place. I want to stop that kind of shit."

Bobby's desire to go to police school makes little sense to Dex, as law enforcement is the very embodiment of the discrimination he is talking about. There are still laws to protect heterosteriles and failsafes from violence, but to Dex, they have become little more than smokescreens for the scary things happening every day. All one has to do is consider Delilah Jacoby, a heterosterile who was recently raped with a cucumber by a group of fags. She was in Dex's art class until it happened but hasn't been to school since. All five fags are remaining hush-hush, and the police have made no arrests.

North American departments are also pushing to reimplement TruthChip tracking, an anti-privacy measure that was abolished with the Spatial Freedom Act after four decades of martial law following the Bio Wars. Now, the recent terrorist attacks in Australia, which the secretary general is attributing to a resurgence of God's Army, are bringing the issue to the forefront once again. Dex mentions this, but Bobby shakes his head.

"No, man. It would take twenty years at least to go through the legislation for that, because nobody would stand for it. People would rip their chips out and revolt on a mass level."

"That's what your dad says."

"If they made you replace your chip with one that would track your every move, would you keep it in?"

"I'd rip it out and go to jail."

"Okay, so imagine if all five hundred million citizens of the NRO did that. The government wouldn't have enough jail space, and they'd lose the fight."

"Not if they just killed everyone," Dex says, then takes a hit off his cigarette, which he doesn't even like. He is floating now, flying, keenly aware that he believes the New Rainbow Order could someday sink that low. "Give it time," he says. "Humanity is fucked."

Bobby, always hopeful, scoffs. Again, he says, "Nobody would stand for it."

The track team, heading out for a run on the trails behind school, shuffles past them. Every single boy stares at them as they run by, and some laugh. One boy, Casey Simonson, even mimes a cunnilingus action by spreading his hands and diving between them with a wagging tongue. At this, the entire team erupts in laughter.

"Failsafe fucks!" Casey yells.

Dex gives him the finger.

Casey yells back, "I'd love to, baby. You just let me know when you're ready!"

Will it always be this way? Is there hope at all for his life to mean something? Already Dex feels as if his one chance to make something of himself has come and gone, simply because of who he is, and it isn't worth dreaming about a second. Chances come on the shoulders of goodness, which seems impossible to come by.

"Mary in *heaven*, he's probably *starving*!"

"Desperate is more like it, if he's curled up on *our* front porch."

"Do you think he's related to that train derailing? His head is all blistered! If those queens on WorldCom would just give us a hint about what that was about, maybe I could make an honest assessment!"

Dex opened his eyes to the sound of gay male chatter. Two men, one with hair graying from black and the other with hair graying from strawberry blonde, were staring down at him. Both had leathery skin and about fifty years apiece on their faces. The brawnier one was standing tall with hands on his hips, shaking his head and making a snapping sound with his tongue over a gritty expression. His darker hair was matted, and he was dressed in a bathrobe, shivering. The lanky one with a more vibrant flare in his eyes was on his haunches, closer to Dex, holding a mug of steaming coffee and dressed in a T-shirt and boxer shorts. His lighter hair was still sporting yesterday's style, only slightly mussed from his night's sleep. Both men's breath was visible in the frosty morning air.

Suddenly remembering he had curled up on the front porch of a farmhouse, Dex turned his face to see the yard, only to get a face full of the squatting man's wrinkled penis. He was perfectly positioned so that the slit in his boxer shorts was exposing it. Dex could not help but chuckle.

"Rainbow and stripes, he's alive," the man attached to the penis said. "Moses, honey, go add a few more eggs to the pan. Wait, bring out a banana so he can have something right away!"

Dex looked back up, saw the standing one, Moses, give his husband a skeptical shake of the head, then step back into the house.

The more excitable one stood up but continued to look down at Dex. "Honey, you're not going to kill us, are you?" he asked.

"No, I'm not." Dex realized he was shivering when the words quivered on their way out. He took the remaining man's hand and stood up, letting the rug fall to the porch. It was freezing outside, far colder than it had been on any of the previous four days. Dex glanced at the driveway, where he saw the hydro utility truck from which yesterday's banana peel had been thrown. Its license plate was bent, rusted, and covered with mud.

Country fags, Dex thought. *They're either going to lynch me or save me.*

Then the yard sign he had nearly stumbled over the night before winked in his memory. "Support Unity!" it had read.

"Look at you!" the man in the boxer shorts exclaimed. "You're thin as a rail! When's the last time you had anything to eat?" He ushered Dex into the house and slammed the door shut behind them. "Heavens, I haven't even introduced myself. I'm Sam Archer. There in the kitchen is my husband Moses. Don't mind his attitude. He's always a bitch in the morning."

The farmhouse was indeed antiquated, cluttered with the accumulated stuff of years shared by two people: shabby jackets, muddy shoes and boots, holopanels lining the walls (a few of which seemed to have lost power), unmatched furniture, and random knickknacks that seemed as out of place as they did perfectly agreeable. Sitting along the hallway's left baseboard was a family of ceramic lawn gnomes grinning at the opposite wall. On that wall was a printed painting of an old Hollywood actress whose face Dex recognized but whose name he did not know. At the far corner of the room into which the hallway opened (a living room, by the look of it) stood an antique clock even taller than Dex, the type he had only seen pictures of. The hardwood floors were dull and worn with use, and the hallway creaked under his feet.

From the kitchen wafted the heavenly smell of breakfast. Never before had Dex so appreciated the possibility of food. The warm aroma of sizzling onions, peppers, fresh fruit, and biscuits enveloped him as the hallway broke on the left to reveal Moses Archer cracking eggs over a sizzling skillet.

"Here, take this," Sam said, shoving a banana in Dex's face. Dex accepted it, ripping it open with such desperate speed that Sam shrank backward and let out a relieved gasp. "When did you last eat?"

"Yesterday. A banana peel one of you two threw out of that truck out front."

Sam turned to scowl at his husband. "Moses, I told you to *stop littering*."

"Well, it gave this boy a snack, so stop making such a deal of it," Moses growled. He turned back to the skillet, then spoke with words obviously directed at Dex. "Now look, we've got knives and clubs and a million other things to hurt you with, should you decide to attack us. Lucky for you, my queen of a husband there is such a softy that—"

"Moses! We already made sure he didn't have any weapons on him."

"Well, look at his clothes."

"What about them?"

"Come on, Sam. He's not from around here."

"Really, Moses, sometimes you just aren't even human." Sam swung back to Dex and approached him with open arms. He ran his hands down the stubble on Dex's cheek. "Look at this face. Could it *be* any more attractive?" The man settled a hand conspicuously on Dex's left pectoral muscle. "Honey, tell my husband here that you're not going to kill us."

Dex swallowed the lump of banana in his throat, then turned to Moses, humored at the hand still holding his chest. "I'm not going to kill you."

Moses did not look convinced. "Well, then, tell us who you are."

As Sam ushered him to a bar stool at the kitchen counter, Dex began his story backward, from seeing the yard sign, to the train, to the raid at Sterile Me Susan's, and finally to his being the natural father of an unborn child. He was too dazed by his good fortune in this kitchen to lie. Within five minutes, the two men knew more about him than his own mothers did. Dex was risking his life by telling the truth, but he was too hungry and thankful to be apprehensive. He disclosed his plan to get back to Minneapolis and track down Grace and their baby.

Moses stood listening with a fist on his hip, and Sam's eyes glistened with tears. The former finally looked convinced. He dished up a steaming plate of food and thrust it under Dex's nose.

"We're officially friends," Moses said. Sam gave his husband an "I told you so" look, and a minute later, they were all digging into breakfast.

Sam and Moses were the type of aging couple to finish each other's sentences without second thoughts, snapping at each other one minute, then reverting to gentle acknowledgment and mutual respect the next. Their devotion to each other comprised what Dex thought any couple's should: patience, caring, and selflessness—the elements of love. The way Moses automatically refilled Sam's coffee complemented the way Sam waited without interruption for Moses to form his thoughts before speaking.

Their discussion lasted well into the morning, and Sam made a point to congratulate his husband on being able to set work aside for the sake of their new visitor. Moses scoffed, but as he turned around to fix another pot of coffee, a grin colored his face. They owned and operated a ten-thousand-acre spread of corn, beets, and tropical fruit, including the bananas Sam had so readily shoved at Dex. The corn and beets were seasonal, outdoor crops, and the bananas, pineapples, papayas, and mangos grew in four solar greenhouses that stretched north, a half-mile apiece, from the farmhouse's back yard. Sam and Moses's crops supplied grocery stores, restaurants, and food manufacturers as far west as Omaha and as far north as Chicago. It seemed reasonable to assume they had far more money than their creaky, drafty house might suggest. They had been married for thirty-three years, since Sam was eighteen and Moses was twenty.

"Fell in love just like that," Sam told Dex, snapping his fingers. "I don't know why in God's name Moses appealed to me, because all he ever did was gripe, but that's how the carrot crunches, I guess."

"And Sam is *still* into the drag revival scene," Moses said, showing Dex his second smile. "He's begging me to join him at the Queens of the Midwest convention in Kansas City next weekend, but he won't ever live to see *me* in a dress."

"Don't ask why we *ever* survived this long together," Sam said. "Just go with it!"

Dex did. Like many people in the agriculture and food business, which relied on a sustained population, Sam and Moses Archer were sexually liberal. But there were deeper reasons for their animosity toward the government's stringent laws, about which Dex soon learned.

Sam and Moses had engineered a son, Efron, who was a failsafe.

"Yes, *was*," Sam reiterated. "He was on a call in Kansas City one day, and he stopped in a breeder bar for a drink. From what witnesses said, he left with three lipstick dykes who were flirting with him, pretending to be heterosteriles. I guess they were known around Missouri for messing with failsafes. We found Efron tied to our barbed-wire fence out front the next morning."

"Beaten to death, then strung up like a pig," Moses added. "Those cunts drove all the way back here just so we'd be the ones to find him."

And the rest was history. The murderers got off with seven month's rainbow probation, three months of tolerance education, and not even a day of prison time after one of the women's fathers posted their combined bail totaling six hundred dollars. Sam claimed the police had tampered with evidence in favor of the three lesbians, and the municipal judge in charge of hearing the case had an intense prejudice against heterosexuals. His sentence on the women was a slap on the wrist, and to this day, it enraged the two farmers. As far as they were concerned, Efron, whose digital life-cycle portrait hung above a dusty piano in the living room, had been a casualty of the New Rainbow Order's disintegrating ethics.

"Didn't matter to the judge that Efron's orientation was dictated by the government to begin with," Moses said. "Still thought of him as disposable. And now those dykes walk free."

Efron had a striking resemblance to both his fathers in different ways. Dex watched the small boy mature into a young man as the holopanel completed, then repeated, its cycle. A wave of sadness crushed his heart as he imagined Sam and Moses subjecting themselves to this portrait every day, each time suffering the memory of their son's life coming to a grinding halt. They did not deserve such grief. "He was a beautiful kid," Dex said, at a loss for better words.

"That he was," Moses responded.

Sam sent Dex to a large upstairs bathroom to shower. They would figure out what to do later, he said, and first, a good cleanup was in order. Sam sized Dex up after throwing a set of fluffy white towels into his arms. "You're almost a good foot shorter than both of us, but I'll find you something to wear. You don't mind *drag*, do you?" Sam's grin fluttered into the realm of suggestiveness before he spun away, down the hall. Smiling, Dex stepped into the bathroom and shut the door, sure since hearing about their son Efron that neither of these two men would try to jump him while he showered. Even so, after his experience at the detention center in Minneapolis, Dex wanted security. He pushed the lock.

When he looked in the bathroom mirror, he was shocked to see bright red scars on his forehead where his skin had begun to swelter inside the baking train car. Miraculously, his eyes were not red, as Fletch's and Exander's had been. His left shoulder was bruised purple, however, and his legs had shallow gashes where the chopped corn stalks had punctured them. The pain had been so constant during the last five days that it had slipped out of his consciousness.

The shower stung everything at first. Dex cooled the water to wash his head, then turned it hot again for the rest of his body, which had not been close enough to the train car's oven vents to burn. The constant stream of pressure tingled on his skin, washing the scarring remnants of the week off him. The horror dripped away, and in the glass chamber of water and steam, Dex prayed to the voice he had heard in the train car.

Whoever you are, I'm getting the message. I promise I'll make the best out of this second chance.

No voice answered, but the new sense of peace continued to comfort him just the same. For the time being, he would trust it.

AN HOUR LATER, he was in the kitchen, eating a second breakfast, when Moses rumbled through in a pair of dirty overalls, off to start his day's work. He stepped out the back door, muttering vague words about the military and the inevitability of their being found out and questioned. When the door slammed, Dex turned to Sam with a confused look.

"Why would the military have anything to do with this?"

The bubblier farmer frowned, then asked, "How much do you know about what happened?" Dex just shrugged, looking perplexed.

"Stars in heaven, he has no idea," Sam said to himself. He brought Dex to the living room couch and sat him down, in front of the wall com. He switched it on, then glanced back at Dex. "I didn't even think about the fact that you wouldn't be aware of any of this. Take a look. It's been all over the news for days."

The devastation in the eleven attacked cities left Dex dumbstruck. The world had just changed forever, and he had been too busy riding on a death train and escaping to know it. His thoughts jumped first to his mothers, who so rarely left their distant suburb that it was doubtful they would have been caught in the attack. Even so, his first inclination was to call them and make sure they were alive. He was about to ask Sam for the nearest com when the heartbreaking truth made him hesitate. He was now a fugitive of the Bio Police, which meant anybody related to him would be under surveillance. Not only would calling them now put himself and the Archers in danger, but it could also frame his mothers as resistors, which would lead to their arrest—possibly even their detainment and execution, if his recent experience on the train was anything to judge by. He had already said goodbye to them once. Was it worth putting them at risk to do it again, before setting out to find Grace?

Grace. Dex wondered if she had made it to Frederik Carnevale's Cliff House, the one Sheila Willy had mentioned. It was maddening to know nothing and almost impossible to accept that his last glimpse of her had been at the Opposition facility under Sterile Me Susan's, where he had left her alone before their survival strategy went up in flames. Watching the piles of rubble still sending billows of smoke into the air, Dex relayed to Sam the other bit that Sheila Willy had shared with them: the Queen had been planning a staged attack, followed by a period of martial law. But the farmer seemed apprehensive.

"I don't know. He's saying this was a resurgence of God's Army."

"It's the NRO," Dex insisted. "I'm sure of it."

And then he saw his own face on the WorldCom report. He

froze. It was the photo the Bio Police had taken upon his incarceration after the raid on Sterile Me Susan's; Dex recognized the wounds on the side of his forehead. Aghast, he turned to Sam. "Did you just see that?"

"Ugh, same faces they've been flashing all week. Escaped prisoners, or something."

"*I* was on there!" Dex exclaimed, gawking at the screen. "Could you turn up the volume?"

Sam did, but not before Dex saw him tense slightly. The man's breathing quickened, and after turning the sound up, he began drumming the surface of the couch with his fingers.

A flighty reporter was standing in downtown Minneapolis. ". . . insurgents were caught in a massive raid on a rebel facility in Minneapolis three weeks ago. Bio Police authorities say these men escaped during transfer to a more secure facility and that they may have had help from the inside. Questions abound now as Bio Police squads are calling all failsafes, carriers, heterosteriles, and known heterosexual supporters in for questioning, as part of the Mandate 43 social assessments. All the prisoners were associated with the aforementioned social groups, but some protestors fear such questioning will soon filter down into the general population itself. The Queen insists that security—sometimes at the price of freedom—is the only way society will survive in peace. Citizens with any information regarding the men shown on this screen are encouraged to call 82.70.100.100 and report it. Under the NRO's new martial law, suspicion of one's failure to do so may now result in his or her immediate incarceration."

The footage cut back to images of Chicago, where military vehicles bearing the dictatorship's rainbow insignia patrolled the streets. Armed soldiers were holding back a crowd of rioters demonstrating in front of North America's Rainbow Headquarters. The reporter continued. "We bring you live to Chicago now, where protestors have gathered to demonstrate against the newly instigated martial law, which effectively prohibits the very right of citizens to hold such demonstrations. . . ."

Sam switched the com off. They sat in silence for almost two minutes. Finally, the farmer spoke. "I'm one of those people who likes to believe the best about others, even though it's *completely* silly in this day and age. I do believe your story, even though I have little reason to."

"I appreciate that, Sam. Thank you."

"But if you're right, and the NRO really is orchestrating all this to forward its social agenda . . . then I don't think there's much hope. For any of us."

In the corner, the antique clock ticked.

Sam Archer struck Dex as an optimistic man, more so than his husband Moses. But a crushed, colorless aura emanated from him now. Dex recognized the feeling as one he himself had experienced. It was despair, the anguish caused by a sense of utter helplessness against the machine of power. It begged a hundred questions, the most important of which was: What was the value of life if one had to live it without freedom, under an ever-looming penalty of death? But Dex had seen the answer on the train.

Structure surrounds every society, whether it's peaceful or not, and everybody dies.

"What matters is what you *do*," Dex said aloud. "And maybe you have to create hope. For the people who come later, I mean. Even if it will never be perfect."

Sam chuckled, but his lips were curled in a grimace. "Oh, listen to *you*, Mr. Fabulous Philosopher." But the spark in his eyes had reignited, just a little.

OVER A DINNER OF ROASTED CHICKEN, beets, and green beans under a mango sauce, the Archers discussed their options regarding Dex. They were gracious enough to include him in the conversation, though they made him repeat a good chunk of his story again. This time, they focused more on the parts Dex did not know about for sure: the Queen's conspiracy and the Opposition's possible routes of retaliation. They worked through the logic behind each possible theory. Ultimately, there was no way they could know for sure who had orchestrated last Sunday's attacks, but they did know that the story conveyed by the government had obvious gaps. First, if they could assume Dex was being truthful, the prisoners whose faces WorldCom was flashing around the world, the ones caught in the Sterile Me Susan's raid in Minneapolis, could not be associated with the attacks, because they had been on a train to the supposed dumping pit that morning. Second, they had seen nothing on the news about a train derailment in Missouri, nor had there been any public explanation for the train's construction. Whatever torment Dex had suffered, the Queen was keeping it under wraps, which suggested there was truth in the story about the dumping pit. If that was the case, the world's only legal authority had bowed to the simple, terrible answer of genocide to forward its agenda. This left every living soul on earth at risk.

After finishing his food, Moses leaned forward on the table, holding both sides of his head. "We more or less became rebels by taking you in, didn't we?"

Sam inhaled, loading an arsenal of words to reprimand his husband, but stopped when Dex nodded and said, "Yeah, you pretty much did."

Moses sighed. "Well, that could be a problem."

"What about St. Louis?" Dex asked. "How close are we to there?"

"Two hours."

"Do you know of any places that could replace my TruthChip?"

"I told you, we weren't rebels before tonight."

Sam waved a fork at Moses. "Don't you act like you regret taking this poor boy in, Moses Aaron Archer. Efron wouldn't have it any other way, not with what the NRO has become."

"But where does it leave us?" Moses asked.

"In a major fucking pickle. But we'll hide him in the old bio shelter if necessary. And in the meantime, we'll feed this lucky man and treat him like we'd treat our own boy. But where in Dorothy's name do we find someone to replace his chip?"

Moses rolled his eyes at Dex and, referring to his husband, said, "This is how she is. Think first, act later, and then think again in circles." But as he licked a bit of mango sauce off his knife, he grinned.

FOR THREE DAYS, Dex recovered. Sam was like a mother goose caring for a lost chick, fluttering about him at all hours of the day, making sure he was comfortable and well fed. Moses, on the other hand, was more fatherly in nature. On their fourth night together, he and Dex stayed up late into the darkness, musing about and guessing at the secrets of the New Rainbow Order and the secrets of the Opposition. Moses smoked a pipe, just as Dex's grandfather had. Its warm smell in the quiet evening filled the comforting silences between them long after Sam had retired to bed.

"You're fighting a tough battle, dear," Moses said at one point. In the corner, the clock ticked away.

"Yes I am," Dex replied.

"Do you think it's worth the effort?"

After a pause of consideration, Dex said, "It must be, because I'm getting a second chance to do it. Maybe that's all that matters."

Moses's pipe burned out. Outside, a crescent moon grinned over them.

CHAPTER 41 ✳ (HER)

THE MOON AGAIN. Grace watched the eclipsed ball rise to its spot of nightly authority. Back home, her fathers would be able to see it, too. And, somewhere, Dex as well, if he was still alive.

Tonight was the night.

The grounded Cher Airlines Flight 212 hydro plane was about to disintegrate into a ball of fire and smoke. In relation to the other three airliners, it lay around the corner of the old terminal, which, according to Lieutenant Helio, would block the explosion from causing any severe damage to the other planes and the hangar's main section. "Now, don't act any differently tonight," he had told her before disappearing. "Do what you always do, but after it happens, round up the women from your flight."

Grace waited. One hour, two. The hangar door where she liked to watch the night sky became uncomfortable against her back, so she walked back to her cot among the other stranded passengers. Most were sleeping, but a few were up late, whispering. The failsafes on Grace's flight had done a good job of acting homosexual; they had indeed abandoned their women by all appearances, and two were even in the early stages of an orgy with a small group of civilian male travelers on the far left side of the partition. When it came to survival, people would do anything, it seemed, even change themselves.

Grace tried to drift into sleep. That way, when the blast happened, it would shock her awake with everyone else, and any suspicion that she had somehow known about it could be lost in the fray.

But anticipation kept her awake. When would it be? What was the lieutenant going to do? He had mentioned a store of weapons the army had confiscated from the natives; in it, he said, there was an old-fashioned rocket launcher. He was on night guard duty tonight on that side of the base, and nobody would immediately suspect him of taking it. Fire would mix with the plane's liquid hydrogen fuel, and mayhem would follow. Then panic. Then the evacuation of the non-military personnel who were relying on the remaining planes.

Survival was mingling with prospects of failure, however, and anything could go wrong. Somewhere in that horrible thought, Grace found sleep.

IT WAS HAPPENING AGAIN—a dream about her child. As always, it was a girl, but this time they were running down a dark alley, toward a mountain lit by giant spotlights. Behind them was a wall of water, chasing them through the narrow brick tunnel.

"Run!" Grace tried to scream at her daughter, but it was no use. She couldn't speak, and her strides were impossibly slow, as if she were stuck in glue.

And the little girl was slipping behind her.

Cold water was just sprinkling on her neck when the mountain in front of her exploded in a ball of white light.

What—?

Grace woke to the sounds of the hangar's rumbling metal ceiling and people shrieking in panic.

"Oh my God, oh my God, oh my God," one of the fags on a nearby cot was repeating. Grace took only a moment to orient herself to the sounds of booted soldiers running down the hangar's makeshift hallways, screaming at each other to move, move, move! This was it.

Lieutenant Helio had done it, and now it was time to keep her group of breeding passengers together. It turned out to be an easy job, as all the civilians on the premises were already being escorted to their night quarters if they were not there already. The lights came on, and Grace stood up to make a quick count of all the passengers from Frederik Carnevale's flight.

Forty-two.

There were supposed to be forty-three.

But I counted everyone! She thought, counting again. Nearly all the women from her plane had congregated in the back right corner of the open chamber, and she recognized every face. All but four of the failsafes were there as well, but those missing had made friends with other passengers near the front, and they were all accounted for.

Then she remembered.

Marvel. She's the one who's missing.

Now, the only thing Grace could do was wait. Speculation and terror rippled through the crowd. Was the explosion one of the four civilian carriers, they wondered? Had the natives somehow known the military at LAX had visitors? Did they somehow have coms, or at least the technology to intercept news about the worldwide attacks? Nobody suspected outright that it had been caused by one of the soldiers.

Ten minutes later, Grace heard Lieutenant Helio's voice, screaming in what now served as the hangar's main foyer. She moved away from her crowd, closer to the makeshift wall that separated the civilian sleeping area. "It came out of nowhere!" he was telling a group of soldiers. "I had the area on a constant scan, and it didn't pick up a thing until the last second! Jesus, it was close!"

"Which direction did the missile come from?" one of the men asked him. Grace recognized his voice. It was the major who had become incensed when WorldCom had accidentally aired footage of that derailed train the morning of the attacks.

"From the southeast," Lieutenant Helio, said, still gasping, even making sure to apply a slight lisp to his words. "Lit up the infrared sensor, but it was too fast. One of their rockets, you think?"

"It would make sense," the older man said. "Squads Three and Four to the plane! We need to get that fire out, or the whole terminal'll go up! Move! One and Two are already combing the perimeters. Private Salin, take Johnson and run a check on the weapons bunker. Make sure they're not making a try for the ones we've confiscated."

Lieutenant Helio had planned to steal one of the natives' confiscated rocket launchers. If these two privates were privy to the exact number of weapons the bunker had in store, there would be questions. The general's son was already aware of this, and he was prepared to take the fall should it come to an investigation. His primary goal was to get the pregnant women back in the air.

Now, he was standing no more than forty feet away from Grace. A long, red shrapnel wound and glistening sweat tarnished his sharp, terror-stricken face. The act was impressive, complete, save for his shifting eyes. Their gaze found Grace for a split second, and their shared secret sang in the empty space between them, dancing in the light from the fire outside.

Then, he turned to join his rainbow brethren in the fight.

CHAPTER 42 ❋ (HIM)

THE CHIMES OF SAM AND MOSES ARCHER'S DOORBELL broke the night's stillness. Dex was still on the couch and fast asleep, but the living room lamp was off. Moses was unconscious in his lounge chair with his mouth hanging open, and snores choked the back of his throat, sounding like a broken hydro motor. Through windows to the back yard, the nighttime security light perched atop the first greenhouse washed the room in a cool glow and inky shadows.

The doorbell chimed again.

The feather-light steps of Sam creaking down the stairs brought Dex back into this witching hour's reality. Moses, too, opened his eyes at the sound of his husband's footsteps. He glanced around the room in confusion, as if wondering where he was.

"Must have fallen asleep."

"Maybe your husband turned off the light," Dex said.

But Sam's whisper cut through the darkness. "Quiet, both of you! There's a military truck out front!"

Moses came to alertness, then stood up from the chair. "How many soldiers?"

"I don't know! But Dex, you've got to sneak out the back! Run for the first greenhouse, in the space between it and the garage. I kept the third door down the length of it unlocked in case we needed to hide you. If you hear the soldiers coming into the house, *go*. But check the back yard first! Make sure they're not waiting for you! Shoes by the back door. Moses keeps his tied so he can slip them on easily. When I open the front door, be ready at the back. If you hear me flirting with the guards and inviting them inside, *run*."

Moses nodded in agreement. "Harder to hear you make any noise if Sam is talking."

Dex didn't think; he followed Sam's directions at once, shaking off his sleep. As the two farmers shuffled toward their front door, Dex peeked out the window to the back. The yard was clear. The light from the greenhouse was shining toward the back porch, so Dex's shadow would fall in that same line if he had to run. The house would block it from the view of any soldiers out front. Its rear exit was made of thick sliding glass, and he eased it open, then stepped onto the back deck. It was made of newer wood than the front deck, and it remained silent under his feet.

With his head still stuck into the house, Dex heard the front door open and Sam say, "Can we help you?" Whoever spoke back to him had a voice too low to carry, so Dex was at the mercy of his new friend's uncanny ability to make himself heard from anywhere. "Well, sugar, I don't quite understand how having a *yard sign* would make us harbor any fugitives, but be my guest," Sam said with a forced yawn. "But mind this hallway . . . there's some clutter. Wouldn't want you falling down and showing us that *fine* little tush, now, would we?" More muttering, then the sound of boots on hard wood.

Dex slid out the door, pulled it shut, and ran down the deck's wooden steps. The frost on the grass glistened under the large security light. Dex ran straight for it, fighting the urge to slow down and check if Sam and Moses had led the soldiers into the living room. It took him only ten seconds to clear the yard, and when he passed into the narrow corridor formed between the garage's left side and the greenhouse's glass wall, shadows engulfed him. The garish light disappeared from his eyes, and the cold clarity of night took its place.

Behind him, from beyond the house, came the whirring of a motor. The truck was still there. That it was still running suggested the soldiers were making a cursory pass across the Archer farm. Yet Sam had mentioned his yard sign, which implied some sort of suspicion.

Not to mention that they showed up in the middle of the night to catch the Archers off guard, Dex thought.

The greenhouse stretched as far as Dex's eyes could make out, but he found the third side door three hundred feet in and pulled up on its horizontal handle. It loosened as the air pressure changed, and the glass door swung open. Dex stepped into the greenhouse's intermediate entry and closed the door behind him. A small number pad blinked red, urging him to activate the lock, but he did not know the code. He would have to test his luck. Ahead of him, the small chamber led to another door, which opened automatically. Humidity dampened his face, and he entered a jungle of papaya trees.

The greenhouse looked larger from the inside. Its width spanned at least a hundred feet, and the clear, arched ceiling reached at least four stories upward. The stringy tree limbs hung on either side of Dex as he ran along the path that trailed inward from the door. The smell of plants and soil teased his winterized nose, clashing with the February chill he had just experienced outside.

Dex turned right at the first aisle and moved deeper into the greenhouse.

He chose a random row of papaya trees to hide under. Their trunks were thin, and all their leaves ran together. There were enough trees to confuse anyone looking through them; if he remained still and covered by darkness, he would be almost invisible.

Dex waited. Moonlight filtered through the glass roof and broke against the canopy of papaya tree leaves, offering just enough illumination for the thin trunks below to imitate a crowd of emaciated captives. Somehow, his imagination pasted faces on them, and the effect sent a cold finger up his spine. He thought of the screaming men on the train.

They're trees. Just trees.

But those faces haunted him through the night, accentuating the artificial jungle's eerie silence. He leaned up against one of the narrow tree trunks to chase sleep, but he never caught it. It was a nicer hell than the train car, but in this darkness, with those gaunt trunks awake and climbing out of the ground around him, Dex recognized a shred of his old fear. It whispered in the leaves above him, rapped on the glass ceiling, settled like a cold wind next to him as he waited to hear an army of soldiers storm the greenhouse. But none came.

THE SHREDS OF SKY VISIBLE through the papaya tree canopy had just begun to glow a warm pink when Dex heard one of the greenhouse's outer doors decompress, then open. The whoosh of the second door followed.

"Dex?"

It was Moses.

"Dex, my boy, are you in here? They're gone! We had to make sure before we came and got you!"

Dex heard his joints creak as he got to his feet and began fighting his way through the papaya trees, which were now just trunks and leaves and fruit, faceless. Moses was walking down the first aisle when Dex emerged from the jungle.

"They found Sam's drag outfits and made him give them a show," Moses said. "His performance was one for the ages, actually." He smiled, then shook it out of his wrinkled face. "You think they actually had a clue you were here, or d'you think their visit was just routine?"

"I don't think we should wait to find out. I need to get out of here. Get my chip replaced."

"Well, Poplar Bluff is the closest town with any size to it," Moses said. "We can get out of here on the back roads. I'll have Sam run a com search on chip replacement, and so be it if they're somehow snooping in on that, too."

"Why did they show up? What was their excuse?"

"They knew we were heterosexual rights activists by our yard sign, apparently. They said soldiers were making rounds over the entire territory for the escaped prisoners they say were behind the attacks."

"They were talking about *me*, then."

Moses grimaced. They walked back to the house, shivering as their feet crunched over the dead, frosty grass.

It was Sam who came up with the solution to get Dex off the farm, unnoticed. "Honey, if your face has been pasted all over the news, we're not risking taking you into town, just to have somebody recognize you and call the police. But that's where I come in. Tell me, have you ever been to the Queens of the Midwest drag convention?"

THAT MORNING, Dex stepped into a dress for the first time in his life. Sam's drag wardrobe was vast and took up an entire room on their third floor. He was a collector on top of being just a wearer, and there were dresses, feather boas, fake breasts, and wigs of all shapes and sizes. Sam first made Dex shave his chest, arms, and legs, then covered his wounds with makeup. Next, he adorned Dex with a royal blue sheath dress. It was a bit large and fell down his front, but Sam used pins to keep it in place. "The convention doesn't start until Saturday, but it's more or less a weeklong party," he assured Dex while painting his eyes with gaudy blue eye shadow. "It's been five years since I've gone, mostly because I lost a lot of my drag friends after Efron died. They tended to be traditionalists, and if it wasn't related to homosexuality, they wanted nothing to do with it. Well, my baby boy wasn't a homosexual, and when he died, they didn't even pretend to care."

"Will they recognize you?"

"Honey, we're not actually *going* to the convention. We just need a viable disguise to get you to Kansas City."

"What's in Kansas City?"

Sam rolled his eyes. "Dexter, it's the fourth most populated city on the continent, and you need a chip replaced. All we need to do is find the hetero part of town and ask around. Then, we'll buy you a com and get you safe and sound back to Minneapolis, if we can get you past the military travel wardens. I saw on the news that they're making people scan their chips for public ground travel like trains, but roadways in and out of the big cities are only being monitored visually. Too many people to stop and check every car." Sam hunched down and brought his eyes within five inches of Dex's face in a careful attempt to apply a shimmering gold lining to his eyelids. "Don't worry. We're not going to give you up without a fight."

"Sam, hurry up!" came Moses's voice from downstairs.

But Sam scoffed. "My husband has *no* appreciation for the art of drag. If you're going to pass for a real drag queen, we've got to do it right."

Dex chuckled, then said, "Either way, I thought of some people who might be able to help us research a good place to find a chip replace—" He was about to elaborate on his idea of contacting Sheila Willy or Linda Glass when Sam gave his face a light slap.

"Makeup now, planning later! Let me finish my work!"

BY EIGHT O'CLOCK they were in Moses's truck, bumping down a narrow dirt road that lined the men's property. It would be a six-and-a-half-hour drive from the farm to Kansas City. Both men had left their pocket coms at home as a precaution against being tracked, but Dex had looked for three com addresses in the Public Address Database before their departure. Stuart Jarvis was not listed, but Sheila Willy and Linda Glass were. Dex had no idea if Sheila had survived the Sterile Me Susan's raid with Grace, but if she had, there was a chance they were together. If Sheila was a dead end, Linda Glass would be able to put him in touch with Stuart, who might know something. Dex had decided to forego completely any attempt to contact his mothers. Keeping them oblivious to his survival would help them stay safe. The notion of returning to Minnesota and making no effort to see them one last time was unthinkable, but there was no better option; Dex wanted them to finish their lives in peace. If ever there came a chance, he would let them know—perhaps anonymously, if necessary—that he was alive and still loved them.

Sheila and Linda's connections to him were more obscure. He jotted down their addresses on a note pad and tried to put the slip of paper into a pocket, only to remember he was wearing a dress. He shoved it down the front, between his bra and silicone breasts. It was a particularly original sensation. Sam had transformed him completely. As if the dress, makeup, and auburn bob wig weren't enough, Dex could barely balance in the high heels. He had a change of clothes packed in a duffel bag, of course, but he would have to be a new man under this costume for at least a day. He wondered how many eyes would follow him when he got out of the truck to try calling the two women. With any luck, there would be a public com that had a private booth, so he could default to his true personality while speaking.

Moses turned onto Old Route 60 just past the town of Essex, and twenty minutes later, he stopped in Poplar Bluff. "Snacks," the man said, pointing to a Target Express on their left. "Also, I think there's a public com booth just up ahead, next to the Prism Bank." He pointed up the main street, and Dex saw the bank's rundown sign. Below it was indeed a row of booths, each one a closed alcove with an open back. They would be private enough, and they were free for the first five minutes, meaning he would not have to scan his TruthChip.

Sam gripped Dex's shoulder. "Honey, remember: balance, and one foot in front of the other when you walk. If anyone talks to you, channel *me*, and you should be fine!"

Dex could not help but grin. "Thanks, Sam."

He balanced his way down the uneven sidewalk. His confidence was meager at best, and there was no way he would pass for an authentic drag revival enthusiast if his strut wasn't convincing. Two fags around his age were approaching, holding hands. Dex imagined Sam's buoyancy inflating him, and suddenly, balance came more easily. He mustered as colossal a sense of fun as he could.

Test yourself out. Act the part.

"Good morning, handsome and handsome!" he said, tipping his heart-shaped sunglasses as the fags approached. He made his gaze flit down their muscular, country-fed bodies, then back to their eyes.

"Morning honey," one of them said with a polite smile. Dex noticed that both men were focused on the bicep connecting his hand to the sunglasses. He flexed.

"You off to Kansas City for the convention?" the other fag said.

"You know it," Dex replied. He puckered his lips and smooched the air toward them and continued walking. Neither fag seemed to think twice at Dex's costume as he walked by. But just when he thought he was in the clear, the first one called after him. "Hey, what's your name, sister?"

Dex froze. Sam had not helped him pick out a drag name.

Play the part, he thought. *Don't let them see you hesitate.*

Dex stopped, turned, and sauntered back. He leaned in toward the first fag and touched his pointer finger to the man's lips. As he did so, the answer appeared in his mind.

"Papaya Fruitcake is my name. And don't you forget it, sugar buns."

He swung himself around, suddenly feeling worthy of the high heels, and strutted down the sidewalk, toward the com booth. A rush of adrenaline charged his walk. The shoes clacked against the cement, piercing the small Missouri town's morning peace. If there was one thing Dex had never imagined for himself, it was this. He smiled, hoping Sheila Willy and Linda Glass had survived the attack in Minneapolis. If either one answered her com when Dex called, it would be the miracle he needed to get back into life's game and track down the woman who had made him a man.

She'd be laughing if she could see me now, Dex thought with a grin, standing there in his dress. He reached for the public com's handset and punched in Sheila Willy's address.

GRACE HAD BEEN WAITING for four hours in the airport hangar, under the smell of smoke and the continuous wail of the station's emergency alarm, when Sergeant Linder entered the provisional sleeping bay to address the stranded civilians. Flanking him were the four commercial hydro plane pilots. Grace recognized hers on the farthest left. Once again, the sergeant was dressed only in rainbow faux-camouflage army shorts, but tonight, he looked sweaty and tired.

"May I have your attention please!" He spoke it as an order, even though nobody was talking. "Thank you. As you may have figured, we've just suffered an attack by the natives. One of your planes. Cher Airlines Flight 212, bound for Sydney. I've received clearance from General Thomas Helio himself to start evacuating you from this base within the hour. However, ninety-eight of you are now without a jet. I've spoken with your pilots, and we are going to divvy up open space on the three remaining airliners. The remaining two commercial jets have a total of sixty-eight open seats, and Representative Carnevale's chartered jet has another thirty. Each plane will continue on its planned course, and those still stranded in the wrong city upon landing will be provided accommodations until the restrictions on air travel are officially lifted. Please gather your belongings, and those of you whose planes are still intact, your pilots will be waiting outside.

Those from Cher 212, your pilot will direct you onto your new plane. All your identities will be processed upon landing at your final destinations. Questions?"

Nobody spoke.

"Good. It's been a pleasure having you in Los Angeles, and may the colors be with you as you journey onward."

Sergeant Linder scratched his chest, then turned, leaving the pilots to gather their respective passengers. Grace stood alone as people began organizing themselves. She offered hopeful smiles to some of the Cliff House women, and they smiled back, but they had other friends to deliberate with. If any of them noticed Marvel's absence, none cared enough to say anything. In the silence of the ruins, the girl, wherever she was, would hear their plane depart forever, perhaps even see its lights disappearing over the Pacific. The startling truth was that now there really was no turning back for any of them. Despite having told herself this every day for the past month, Grace saw the precipice of her future clearly now and accepted what was imminent: that final leap into a world unknown. The next time her feet touched land, she would be across the ocean, at the bottom of the world.

CHAPTER 44 ✳ (HIM)

Dex's call to Sheila's com address rang only once before someone answered. Relief jumped in his chest, then disappointment crushed it.

"I'm sorry, but the com address 29.323.22.10 has been disconnected," a mechanized voice told him. "If you would like to try another address, please cancel this call and enter it now."

Goddamnit.

Dex entered Linda's address. It rang four times before he heard a click, a rustle, and then a woman's voice.

"This is Linda."

His heart leapt with joy and gratitude. He had five minutes to speak before the com would require a chip scan for payment.

"Linda Glass?"

"Yes, that's me."

"Linda, it's Dex. Grace's Dex. I'm calling from a public com, and I don't want to put you in any danger in case your calls are being monitored, but I need help."

"Dex!" Linda exclaimed. "Where are you? Where is Grace?"

With guilt weighing on his chest, he gave Linda as many details as he safely could in the fastest manner possible, including his plan to find a way to replace his TruthChip. Also being very careful not to mention too many details, Linda gave Dex a rundown of events on her side, including the fact that Grace was alive, and she had called her dad from some secure location. Dex wanted to twirl on his high heels with excitement, but the call clock was ticking, and he jumped to the point.

"We can talk more when it's safer, but right now, I need your help. I have to see Stuart Jarvis once I get back. Can you arrange a meeting for us? I don't think I can go to his house, because last time I was there, it was being watched."

"I can do that. No problem. He's been shacking himself up in a hotel to get away from Grace's father. Apparently the attacks sent James into a bloody fervor against the heteros, and he and her brother have joined something called the Civilian Defense Squad. They're marching all over the Twin Cities, holding demonstrations and public executions. Even Lars and his Gay Youth are taking part in it. It's *horrible*, Dex! Stuart said Grace wanted him to warn me to get the family out of here, but I don't know where to go!"

By the com's clock, Dex had only twenty-two seconds left on the free call. "Linda, my call is running out, but I'll call you when I get a new chip and a new com. Keep an ear out, and I'll get there as fast as I can. Tell Stuart I'm alive, and that Grace was going somewhere safe. That's all I know."

"But Dex, she told Stuart—"

"Tell me when I get there. The clock is out—"

And the call ended. Dex hung up the handset. He swung out of the com booth, his shoulders back and his head held high, and put on the best drag queen performance he could. One foot in front of the other with complete confidence, just the way Sam had told him. He was too exuberant to feel embarrassed, too thankful Grace was alive to care if he was convincing. When he arrived back at the car, Sam had his wig on and was touching up his makeup using the truck's visor mirror. Dex told him about the conversation with Linda Glass, and he beamed.

"God's looking down on you, honey, you know that?"

Dex nodded. "Something's keeping me lucky, that's for sure. Let's just hope it lasts."

SIX HOURS LATER, they were approaching Kansas City on I-70. The newer skyscrapers were glass, much like those of Minneapolis, but not all of them were coated with the same reflective material that would emit a rainbow under the sun. The metro area here was smaller than that of the Twin Cities, but over the past two hundred years it had become the epicenter of farming and agriculture for North America. Rife with fountains and green space, it was the crown of their vast heartland—a wider open and less murky version of Minneapolis and Chicago.

Moses was driving near the middle of the six-lane highway as they approached, which left them more or less out of reach when they came to a military checkpoint. As they slowed for the cars to be observed and then waved through, Dex noticed that the sky was abuzz with hover jets. In the city, soldiers patrolled street corners, and he noticed in one downtown park that there was some sort of rally going on with people wearing rainbow arm bands. He thought back to what Linda said about the Civilian Defense Squad and public executions.

It's happening here, too. Terror crept into him at the thought, and he had to make a conscious effort not to let it threaten his newfound hope. All he could do was his best, and fear had no place in that.

Sam had booked a hotel room that morning, just four blocks from the city's newly rebuilt convention center, publicized on World-Com as "The Fountain." It was the site for the Queens of the Midwest convention, so both Dex and Sam would blend in with the rest of the attendees who were staying the week. Moses would simply look like a dragged-along husband ("Pun intended!" Sam had wisecracked as they discussed their plan), if anybody happened to pay close attention to them.

Hotel check-in was not for another hour. Sam suggested they search out the hetero bars to begin their quest to find an underground chip replacement specialist. It was not particularly easy for upstanding citizens to burrow their way into illegal activities, but they had to start somewhere. Sam was holding a pad of paper, where it appeared he had jotted down a set of directions before leaving his pocket com at the house.

"Moses, baby, you're not going to like this, but I've got an idea of where we could start."

Moses simply glanced at his husband and waited for the answer.

"I think we should go to the Jayhawker."

Dex noticed Moses's knuckles turn white on the steering wheel. "What's the Jayhawker?" he dared to ask.

Sam sighed, then looked into the back seat. Through his curly blonde wig, pink eye shadow, and red lipstick came a twitch of grief, followed by a shake of his head that ruffled into a look of emboldened purpose. He blinked twice, then said with a heavy voice, "The Jayhawker is the hetero bar where our Efron was murdered."

PART THREE:

LIGHT WITHOUT DAWN

"I HAVE SET MY RAINBOW IN THE CLOUDS,
AND IT WILL BE A SIGN OF THE COVENANT
BETWEEN ME AND THE EARTH."

—Genesis 9:13

A MEMORY ✳ (HER)

*K*EN, THE COOK AT THE SOUP KITCHEN, *is crashing around with the pots, pans, and utensils, and Grace knows it is because of the God's Army attacks in Kansas City and Melbourne. It isn't just because all those people died but also because it's just another excuse for the Queen to stay in office another term. This, in turn, is going to make it difficult for him to keep the soup kitchen open.*

"This fucking cucumber just won't *fucking cut!" Ken screams, throwing the vegetable onto the ground. It is the second to last one in his pile.*

Grace is twenty-one and volunteering, as she always has on Saturdays since starting at the University of Minnesota. The soup kitchen smells like years of burned food, and it's dank and cold, just like everything in Obesaland this October.

Ken shakes his head, then grabs the last cucumber. This time, the slicer works again, and the phallic green shaft unravels into spirals. It is strange that the salad he is making has become one of Grace's favorite recipes. "You know," Ken says, "you're fucking stupid to be volunteering at a place like this."

Everything he says stings; that's just how it is. Grace lets the thread of truth in it hurt, then roll off her back. She is preparing a platter of a hundred chicken breasts with spices. They don't look half bad. Healthy food for the fatties. They always come, but they always seem to get food elsewhere, because so many of them remain fat and never get on their feet.

"We're living in scary times," Ken says. "Mark my words."

"I still think the world can change," Grace replies, glad that confidence in the statement's truth fills her veins. The world is constantly shapeable; she refuses to believe society is set on a single path.

"You're talking like the little rich girl who volunteers and never had to work for a damned thing in her life," Ken says. "Trust me, you'll learn otherwise. The world is fucking cruel, and we're sitting in front-row seats."

She has had to work for things, but they aren't things Ken would respect. Self-confidence has been one thing; belief that she can make a difference has been another. Both are rare traits for a heterosterile. Yet she has to admit she is lucky the Bureau of Genetic Regulation has not called on her to become a carrier against her will. Some women—lesbians or heterosteriles, as neither orientation is a delineating factor anymore— jump at the chance to carry, even though it means surrendering all freedom and sexual privacy to the New Rainbow Order. The Queen has made it so, but Grace is sure it won't get worse, as Ken is saying it will.

"You just have to be more optimistic," she tells him.

Ken tosses peanuts into the cucumber salad. "Optimism is the nectar of the delusional."

A trickle of agreement makes Grace shiver for a moment, but again, she lets Ken's words roll off her. There is always room in the world for optimism, and she knows it, and nothing will ever prove that otherwise. Even in the worst cases, people can do their best.

"Best efforts are the nectar of hope," Grace wants to say but does not, because she isn't quite sure the statement makes sense, and she doesn't like to look stupid. In any case, an idea like that would be wasted on Ken the cook.

CHAPTER 45 ✳ (HER)

T HE PACIFIC OCEAN WAS UNFATHOMABLY VAST, and New Zealand appeared suddenly. Grace was sitting on the right side of the plane, staring out the window, when a green expanse under a string of white cloud emerged like a gentle creature from the water. It was far below and distant, but the morning outside was sharp, and the pink sunrise was just beginning to turn gold, carving the ropey cloud out against the soft green of the island. It was not long before a large lake interrupted what appeared from the sky to be rolling hills, and on one side of it, two large mountains jutted upward. Grace recognized their conic shape.

Volcanoes.

"We're nearing Wellington," came the pilot's voice over the intercom fifteen minutes later. "The government buildings there were leveled in the attacks. Looks like they still haven't doused the fires yet."

The sky outside was indeed hazy. A stem of dark smoke rose from Wellington, which was built on a circular inlet of water. Nobody on the plane had witnessed any aftermath of the attacks until now; their layover in the City of the Dead had preserved in them a serene degree of ignorance. Passengers seated near windows watched the city elapse as quickly as it had appeared, and those without a view who could only imagine it fell into a cascade of mournful whispers.

New Zealand was comprised of a North Island and a South Island that were differentiated by their natural and political environments. The North Island, home to political conservatives, was both temperate and tropical in spots, while the more liberal South Island was a staggering blend of rainforest, jagged mountains, farmland, and mystical fiords. A running joke about the territory was that topography had followed politics, not vice versa, even though the small civil war between the two islands had happened just over a hundred years ago. The Treaty of Colors had ended the war and ushered the separatist country under the umbrella of the New Rainbow Order, much to the disgrace of those living in the south.

The more liberal island was already visible through the window. Cloud cover was heavier along its coastline, but protruding through the cotton-like puffs were jagged mountain tips, some dusted with snow. The range seemed too small to be the headquarters of the Opposition, because within minutes, the terrain became green and farmable once again, and the pilot announced their descent into Christchurch Intercontinental Airport.

And then the sky broke in a dramatic shift. The clouds reached their swift end at a front, clashing with open sky as if it were an opposing army, and the boundary formed by the front line steered Grace's gaze downward, to the western horizon.

She gasped.

The Southern Alps—spiked, majestic, and dwarfing the closer mountain range they passed earlier—formed a wall that lined the entire island. Peak after peak of praying rock reached toward the heavens, like cathedrals built to exalt some invisible creator.

My new home, Grace thought.

Would it be any better than Antarctica? She had no way of knowing, but the idea of mountains—of beauty—she could bear, as long as her child survived. Without that, New Zealand would simply become a moral prison in which she would pull her weight to save humanity.

They landed. Until it was safe for the captain to direct them further, Grace and her party were aimless. Nobody on Frederik Carnevale's flight had uttered a word about Mount Tasman or the Opposition, because the thirty passengers transferred from Cher Airlines 212 had necessitated flawless role-playing from the refugees. Grace tried to suppress the tension gathering in her clenched fingers by looking past two fussing Cher 212 passengers, out the opposite window. The plane taxied past what appeared to be the main blue-and-yellow terminal before turning left, showing her a fleeting glimpse of a mechanized stairway wheeling to meet them. This seemed normal enough.

She glanced out her own window. At first, what met her eyes made perfect structural sense, and she almost ignored it. Then, revulsion pummeled her gut.

Less than three hundred feet away was a tangle of heavy chain-link passageways—a fenced-in queuing area—following a main gate displaying the purple arc logo of the Bio Police. It ended on the right side with a large open space, almost a common of sorts. Painted on the ground was a giant **H** to mark a hover jet landing pad.

Goosebumps formed on Grace's neck.

That's the gateway to Antarctica. Where they funnel through the bio prisoners to fly them away.

Ever since her childhood, it had been the subject of regular WorldCom images that stirred fear and created nightmares—but the passages had always been full of people shuffling toward that ultimate consequence of broken biological law. Today, the queuing area was conspicuously empty. *Unless we're the people about to shuffle through it*, Grace thought.

She could barely move. Had it all been a joke? Had the plan since the beginning been for the pregnant women and their partners to be shipped off to Antarctica? She noticed now that the visible points of the airport's perimeter were dotted with high security towers, identical to those of a large prison yard.

The plane stopped, and Grace forced movement into her limbs as the captain led her and the other passengers down the portable stairway, into an escort of armed soldiers and airport ground staff. She braced herself for an onslaught of violence.

But the use of this empty taxiway section seemed only to be some sort of makeshift security procedure. The soldiers receiving them, despite their sonic guns, were quite polite. They ignored the females, mostly. The transferred passengers from Cher 212 were all civilian males, and their natural flirtations with the soldiers began in a matter of seconds.

Frederik Carnevale's chartered plane was the first to fly over the territory in eight days. Because of this, Lieutenant Helio's plan turned out to be a blessing; instead of being curious about Carnevale's peculiar entourage, the ground staff seemed to be more interested in the events at LAX.

Grace heard murmurs of awe from some of the uniformed men. *"Los Angeles! They got to visit the Unrecoverable Territories!"* said one man. *"I heard there was a bomb! Almost blew them all up!"* said another.

Grace imagined Marvel back there, in the wild ruins, doomed to a life of running and hiding. If the girl had survived, she was gaining firsthand experience with a corner of Earth seen by few living people. Grace's fleeting friend had taken a gamble. Perhaps she would win. And then there was Lieutenant Helio, sworn by his profession to hunt people like Marvel down, perhaps now inspired to make greater rebellious gambles of his own. Like so many people in Grace's life as of late, they had walked in and out, leaving footprints on her heart and nothing more.

I hope they find peace, whatever that might be now.

"Excuse me, Miss, could I have your name?"

A military officer wearing a rainbow arm band was staring her in the face.

Grace shook herself back into the moment. "I'm sorry?"

"Name please," the guard said. "Can I please see your wrist? We're not running security through normal routes this morning, considering the circumstances. We're checking everybody here, outside."

Hoping her status as one of Frederik Carnevale's passengers would preclude her from presumed politeness, she held out her wrist to the officer in an off-hand manner. It was a moment of truth: Would the new TruthChip work?

The man scanned it with his pocket com. Like those of the soldiers in Los Angeles, his device was military-grade.

"Thank you, Miss Austen." He read the com's identification results. "You were one of the original passengers for this flight?"

"Yes," Grace replied, remaining as detached and aloof as possible.

"Must be nice to have friends in high places," the soldier continued, offering her a genuine (if not slightly jealous) smile.

Grace wanted to be polite, but she kept her expression cool, then turned to face the conspicuous gray holding pen in front of the plane. Walking, she could reach it in less than a minute; it was that close. She suppressed a shudder as images of the Antarctic Sanctuary swam through her mind. Something had happened there, but what? Lieutenant Helio had suspected his father and other government officials were scared. This could imply any number of things, but if the lieutenant was correct in his assumption that whatever happened was somehow related to the Opposition, there existed the absurd possibility that the Sanctuary was now in the Opposition's hands. This, in turn, brought with it an uneasy prospect: What if her initial fear at seeing these fences really wasn't a false alarm? What if Mount Tasman, like the Cliff House, actually wasn't the last stop, and Carnevale was using the Sanctuary to house breeders until their counterstrike was complete?

Stop jumping to conclusions, Grace thought. *Lieutenant Helio was only assuming it had to do with the Opposition.*

She had no way of knowing the truth. The government might simply have slaughtered everyone there. Perhaps now they were hoping that any lingering, influential liberals of the civilian world would remain oblivious to the genocide until their operation was past the point of no return. Grace looked at the steel gate again. If the rumors were true and the people at the Sanctuary really were dead, the fenced square in front of her was nothing less than a portal to death. Her stomach churned at the thought.

The soldiers directed Frederik Carnevale's party to a reception in the main terminal, for which they provided a speedy hydro shuttle. There was food of all sorts: fresh produce, roasted meats, and an array of appetizers. The airport's government lounge staff served Carnevale's guests with as much graciousness as they could muster.

"Second entourage in two months," one of the servers griped quietly to another as they had their backs to Grace. His accent sounded like that of the Australian Territory representatives Grace often saw on the news, only the inflection was more contained, quicker to the point. The other server, a woman who was either a lipstick lesbian like Linda Glass or a pretty heterosterile, shrugged and turned away from the first server with a worried expression.

The young man turned with a tray of appetizers and saw Grace. He pasted on the phoniest smile she had ever seen. "Shrimp on kumara?" he asked, holding out the tray. Grace took one, and he walked away in a huff. She bit into the cracker, which was topped with a sweet potato puree and a wedge of honey-glazed shrimp.

Carnevale isn't the most popular guy around here, she thought. *If only these people knew the truth about who they were helping, maybe they'd be nicer.*

Limousines came next, six of them, each one bearing a government-issued, rainbow-colored license plate on its rear. The security team led the Cliff House refugees to a private pick-up zone at the rear of the airport, where the black vehicles were lined up in a row, gleaming in the morning light. Grace climbed into the last one with six other women, including the friendly blonde Hilda and the brown-skinned pack leader Ruth. They marveled at the automobile's plush interior while Grace sank into her seat with a stoic expression. All she could think of was the world they were about to leave behind. As the limousine began to roll away from the airport, she turned her face toward the window, hoping to hide any tears that might come.

THEY RACED WEST ACROSS THE CANTERBURY PLAINS, toward the looming wall of mountains. They were to access Mount Tasman from the west coast, their driver explained, which meant they had to journey across the island and over the Southern Alps at Arthur's Pass, the middle of only three highways crossing what he called "the West Divide." Sheep dotted the fields left and right as the mountains grew closer, and soon, the limousines were passing a spread of rolling hills scattered with peculiar rock formations. From a distance, they looked like herds of petrified beasts tumbled into place by some giant wave.

Ruth's booming voice overtook the limousine. "This is incredible, isn't it, ladies? I've never seen anything like it!" Ruth was the big girl on the playground, and all the other women, even Hilda, gasped in agreement.

It was true, of course; the vista was unlike anything Grace had ever seen back home. As they progressed into the mountains, the strange rock formations gave way to tall alpine ridges and rocky gray summits. The highway sloped upward, weaving through a curvy tunnel of trees. Their mysterious, cool-green color ascended the banks of the valleys, stopping in spots to make way for sparkling waterfalls washing down from the crags above. Soon, the trees broke to offer a view again: wildflowers lining the roadside bush and descending into a vast river basin. The river shimmered in the sun, winding downward in shallow lines from the valley's far end, where the mountain peaks closing it were high enough to have summer snow.

Grace had not outwardly agreed with Ruth's enthusiasm over the beauty, and when her gaze meandered back into the car, the woman was eyeing her in a manner that seemed both curious and vindictive: a momentary, silent showdown.

Are you angry because I don't submit to you? Grace thought, surrendering to a gust of bitterness over Ruth's commanding and unflinchingly optimistic leadership. *Do you think it's smart to get these women excited for a future that might be thrown back in their faces, if whatever happened in Antarctica really does somehow affect us?*

Cynicism was a new experience for Grace, and over the next four hours, sour at the irony, she tried like mad to keep her eyes dry and lose herself in the scenery Ruth so loved. Up ahead, creeping between the rolling mountain peaks, was a strand of gray rain cloud. Its top glowed white under the afternoon sky, but underneath, it was a dark gray shadow, consuming their path. It grew larger and larger as the limousine curled across the mountain pass, and when they entered it, the sun disappeared. Rain came quickly, hiding the picturesque surroundings in its fury. They bumped over a long cement bridge that was crumbling along the edges; underneath it, through the haze, was another shallow river snaking across a bed of rocks.

Soon, the road descended, and the cloud grew lighter, bright enough for the lush greenery lining either side to glisten as it emerged from the ghostly fog. When the clouds broke, there was sky, and only minutes later, the sea: a brilliant, turquoise vista glittering under the sun, which just moments ago had seemed so far away.

Maybe Ruth is doing the right thing, Grace thought, begrudging the woman for feeling so enthusiastic. *I'll be positive for the baby's sake.*

The highway stretched south, and apart from an unusually solid-looking strip of fog falling out of the mountains to the east, the day remained crystal clear for the duration of the journey—a rarity, said the driver. At one point, the road wound eastward briefly. Dense forest lined either side of the highway. Some stretches of it bordered farmland, and others tumbled up the steep foothills, hiding what lay farther down the coast.

And then it came, a fleeting glimpse through the trees that sank like a dead weight in Grace's stomach: two mountains, higher than any others, so far away that they were almost lost in the blue sky, save for peaks that dazzled white. They dwarfed her even from a distance.

One of those is Mount Tasman, she thought. *It has to be.*

But the mountains disappeared behind a closer ridge of rainforest, and the limousine turned again, so Grace was looking at a tangle of abundant foliage. Through the occasional spots where the trees broke, she saw more sheep dotting open fields and birds galloping through the sky in diving flocks.

"How about you, Jarvis? What do you think?"

Grace had to refocus her attention on the other women at the mention of her name. How did Ruth even know it?

"Excuse me?"

"I said, what do you think?"

"About what?"

"Jesus, she hasn't even been following the conversation," Ruth said, and her followers giggled. "We're talking about Mount Tasman. How big do you think it is? Did anyone tell you?"

Be cordial.

Grace shook her head. "All I know is it's supposedly the main headquarters for the Opposition, so it has to be pretty big."

"I wonder what the rooms are like," Ruth exclaimed, turning to her friends with a wide grin. "I mean, if they're keeping a few thousand people there, the place has to be *massive*, but also pretty nice. I mean, how else do they expect us to survive for however long it takes?"

Hilda dared to share an original opinion, one closer to Grace's. "Well, it sounds kind of like the Sanctuary to me," she said. "I'm guessing it's pretty crowded."

"It's *nothing* like the Sanctuary," Ruth hissed. "We're going there to *save the world*, not *rot and die*."

Grace offered a fleeting smile to Hilda, who simply gave her a matter-of-fact shrug in return. The young woman was clearly capable of thinking for herself.

The conversation continued in circles all the way to a town called Franz Josef. Just west of the Southern Alps, it looked like a ghost town, complete with a dilapidated sign that seemed more a warning to stay out than an invitation to come in. The buildings that remained standing were faded and rundown, and many of them had broken windows and unused refuse of the old world piled up next to them.

Hilda squeezed her face into a nervous wince as she peered out the window. "Some town," she said.

They passed a fuel station where a lone car was refilling its hydrogen cell. There were people in Franz Josef after all, then. Judging by its size, the town could never have been larger than a few hundred people at most, unless buildings had been torn down and trees had taken their place.

The intercom in the back of the limousine sprang to life, and the driver spoke to them.

"Ladies, we're in Franz Josef. Gateway to the Mount Tasman facility. The Carnevale family bought this place, more or less, about seventy years ago. Since they were all hoity-toity in the NRO, they also bought up all the businesses here and shut them down. Used to be a huge tourist hub. Scenic hover jet rides, and the like. Now, everyone here is working for the Opposition. We keep the fuel station and dairy open for travelers, but for all they know, it's a dead town. People know the Carnevales have had a house down here for decades, but it's just cover. We're at the end of the world, and nobody's going to suspect our big mountain is full of pregnant women now, ay?"

He turned left and drove up a paved road, which was straight at first before turning to dirt and winding into the forest. They came to a faded red gate. A rusted sign dangled from it, reading **NO TRESSPASSERS**. The gate opened automatically. Grace wondered who monitored it, and from where. From the mountain, or somewhere closer?

The dirt road twirled upward, into the foothills. The trees were unlike any Grace had ever seen. They looked coniferous at first glance, but when the limousine slowed for a curve, she saw through the tinted glass that tiny leaves dotted their tangled branches. Where the light broke through them from behind, it lent the forest a sparkling quality before falling like dust onto rolls of green moss covering the ground.

After thirty minutes, the canopy broke, and the vehicle bumped off the dirt road, onto a long spread of pavement. Resting on it were three hover jets. The limousine shook from the vibration of their rotary engines.

This is it, Grace thought. *I'm really going.*

Instead of exhilaration, doubt rang like mad bells in her heart. The worm of despair that had burrowed into her since Los Angeles had a firm hold now, and not even the thought of giving birth excited her. What remained of her life was a volatile wager against the probable. At any moment, the Opposition could become a casualty of some weak link brought to a snap, some unfortunate instance leading to exposure. What of Mount Tasman then? Might the Queen's military storm it and exterminate the dissenters? Even if the wager paid off, what would she have to show for it, other than a child whose life was bound to be sunless and miserable? Grace longed for her dad, her father, her brother, Linda, Dex—anything or anyone to bring her back to the illusory peace she had enjoyed before the Opposition consumed her.

"Come on, ladies, let's go!" Ruth exclaimed, opening the limousine door and jumping out. The driver had parked next to three other limousines; Grace saw a number of Cliff House women and failsafes already gathered on the landing pad. Ruth and her cluster of friends climbed out of the limousine first, leaving Grace for last. When she stepped out, the fresh mountain air barreled into her, for a moment washing out her feelings of regret and loss. There it was again, however brief: her sense of adventure.

Suddenly, a green bird was floating in the air, in front of her face, flapping its wings.

"Oh my—" she started, and her driver turned and laughed.

"They're cute, kea birds, ay? Pesky buggers, but bloody smart. They know this is a spot where humans visit. And where humans visit, so does food."

The bird was grayish green on the outside, but a brilliant orange lined with black-and-yellow stripes colored the underside of its wings when they opened. It fought the hover jet wind current and landed at Grace's feet, bobbing toward her in an inquisitive manner. She grinned and knelt down, breaking off a bit of the protein bar she had swiped from the limousine's snack buffet. The bird ate it out of her hand, then cried for more. Grace broke off a larger chunk, and this time, the feathery friend clamped his black beak around it and swished into the air, nearly catching her forehead with its wingtip. Laughing, Grace spun around to watch the bird.

She gasped when she saw its path.

It was heading straight for a colossal snowcapped mountain that towered in the distance, between the valley's diagonal slopes. There was no doubt: it was one of the two icy peaks she had seen from a distance, on the coastal highway.

"There she is," the driver said, grinning. "The birthplace of a new humanity."

Snow, impossibly bright and impossibly high, blew in a ribbon off the mountain's summit, trailing into nature's oblivion.

"Mount Tasman," Grace said.

The words caught in her throat as the kea bird became a mere dot bobbing in the sky.

This was my choice.

Grace fell into line with the rest of the Cliff House refugees, and within ten minutes, she had a seat on a hover jet bearing the government's rainbow emblem. There was adrenaline in her; there was fear; there was, however insignificant, a glimmer of hope. The hover jet lifted off the ground, and the afternoon light blazed on Tasman through the windshield. Tears fell down Grace's round cheeks now. With hands clamped over her belly, she shut her eyes, hoping to imagine a life far, far away from here. But there it still was, burned into her closed lids: the mountain, growing closer and closer.

CHAPTER 46 ✳ (HIM)

The Jayhawker's owner, a dried-out fag covered in tattoos symbolizing sexual and reproductive equality, knew Sam and Moses Archer by their faces.

"Saw you on Kansas City Com after it happened, but only on that one report," he told them, reaching above the bar and bringing down three glasses. He dumped ice into them. Dex looked around the establishment. There were only two other people in it: a man and a woman, in the corner, enjoying drinks. "I never forget a face, and I'll never forget your boy," the owner said. He mixed three vodka tonics and slid them over the bar. "On the house. They'll be shutting me down anyway, within the month, I'm betting. They're putting out all the straight rights supporters they can. I heard the Queen on WorldCom yesterday . . . he said anybody who supports heterosexuality can now be considered a member of God's Army."

The bar owner never introduced himself. After Sam explained the reason for their visit, however, he gave Dex a once over, then said, "You'll want to see Canvas Ojala. He owns another bar down on Armour'n Harrison. Three blocks east, then left on Harrison. You'll run into it on the corner. Meatheads, it's called. Ojala knows his way underground. I myself've been stoppin' short of illegal, whatever the case, so I can't help you much more'n that. Just be careful when you're there. They've set up an execution stage right across the street."

Sam, Moses, and Dex were all in the process of sipping their drinks, but they stopped at this.

Moses's hand was shaking. "An execution stage?"

Sure enough, a black paneled tavern sporting a tattered green sign reading "Meatheads" stood just a ten-minute walk away. It was one of two structures standing amid a dissipating crowd of people. The other was the stage the Jayhawker's bartender spoke of, erected in a vacant lot opposite the bar. By the look of it, the scattering people had been watching an event there that had driven some of them into a fervor. An orgy of men was in progress on the lot's dirt ground, and some of those involved had red streaks crossing their chests and faces. For a moment, Dex wondered what it was. Then, he looked at the stage.

Its white base dazzled with blood.

Sam put a hand to the small of Moses's back, and they gaped at the red display. "Did they kill somebody up there?" Sam whispered.

The blood on the stage was still wet, and the men from the mob, bucking and fucking and painted with gore, appeared to be celebrating the carnage. Dex watched Sam and Moses stare at the empty stage. They wore hollow expressions. The shared memory of their murdered son Efron draped their faces like a ghost, rendering their heartbreak transmissible. Whoever had just suffered a grisly death on that stage had been loved at some point, one could guess, just like Efron. Now, the person had been deconstructed into dirty crimson smears.

A red-haired boy was dancing through the crowd, toward Dex, Sam, and Moses.

"*Kill the breeders, kill the breeders!*" he was screaming, pointing a finger like a gun and stopping to shoot, and then weaving again through the dwindling mob. The boy passed them in a flutter, then stopped to point his finger straight at Dex.

"*Kill the breeders!*"

Pow.

He shot his imaginary gun and ran off, up Harrison Avenue. Moses had gone pale, and Sam's mascara had mixed with tears and was beginning to fall down his cheek. Dex wiped a finger over the man's face to catch his running makeup.

"We should get moving," he whispered.

SEEKING OUT A CHIP REPLACEMENT turned into an expensive and dangerous game of connecting the dots. Meatheads was packed with people, most of whom had stopped for a drink following the execution. It was a perfect lion's den, and Dex wondered how on earth they were going to find a lead on anti-government activity in this party of bloodlust. The muscular bartender, however, disappeared into a back hallway after Sam asked for Canvas Ojala. He returned a minute later with confirmation of a meeting, then ushered them back to wait next to a closed door with a red handle. Moses settled against the wall with his arms folded in on one another. Dex felt silly striking the same pose in high heels and a dress, so he followed Sam's lead and stood with a hand on his hip. They waited twenty minutes before Moses looked at his watch and shook his head in frustration. After another twenty, he bounced free from the wall and rapped on the locked door. It opened two seconds later, and a balding fat man dressed in sagging white underwear and a gold necklace glared at them. Behind him, sitting naked on a desk, was a pale, thin boy who looked no older than fourteen.

"Excuse me?" the man said, exasperated. "Can't you see I'm busy?"

"Yeah, well, we were told you'd meet us back here, and that was almost an hour ago," Moses said in a low voice. "A bartender from the Jayhawker sent us. We're looking for a chip replacement."

"Two thousand gets you a referral."

"*Two thousand dollars?*" Moses asked, looking incredulous.

"No, blowjobs, you fuckwit! Of *course* two thousand dollars. No money, no referral, and I forget I met you."

He was about to close the door when Sam held up his wrist. His silver bracelets tinkled against each other. He turned to Moses, who looked livid, and said, "Honey, we've got the money." He then turned to Ojala and thrust his wrist forward. "Here."

The sweaty beast of a man turned around and grabbed a credit reader off his desk. He set the price, then scanned Sam's wrist.

"Kal Mauer. 413 East Thirty-Third Street. Tell him I'm still waiting for my commission."

"And where is Thirty-Third Street exactly—?"

But Ojala slammed the door in their faces, and they heard the deadbolt roll into place. Sam gave the door a miffed look, as if he had been expecting a shred of common courtesy. Moses pulled him back toward the bar.

"We'll ask the bartender."

Kal Mauer turned out to be another greasy-haired lead, and he too asked for money—this time three thousand dollars—before scanning Dex's barcode and running it through what he explained was an illegal mirror of TruthChip's identity database. Dex seized with horror as he realized Mauer could easily be an undercover member of the Bio Police, and his current chip would immediately expose his criminal status. But it was his criminal status, on top of his being a failsafe, that bought Mauer's trust. Only after the man gave them the com address for somebody named Flevin did Dex notice the sonic gun attached to his hip. If he had been an undercover police officer, there was a good chance all three of them would already be dead. But the gun stayed in its holster. Mauer typed Dex's name into a separate com database and sent the three men away.

Sam tried calling the mysterious Flevin from a nearby fuel station's public com, but there was no answer. After Moses drove them back to the hotel, Sam called again from the com in the room—once before dinner and once after. Still no answer.

Calling, waiting, and hanging up became routine over the next three days. Between attempts to make contact, Dex spent most of his time in the hotel room in order to avoid wearing the drag costume. When he needed to move his legs, he walked the hotel hallways, avoiding maids and guests whenever possible. The Archers, however, took to the streets. After growing frustrated with the Flevin possibility, they began hopping around different hetero-friendly bars to see if they could uncover new options. While they were out, Dex continued to call Flevin's com address. On that third day, just as he was about to give up for good, somebody answered.

It was a gruff-sounding woman.

"Hello?"

Dex was so shocked that somebody actually picked up that he almost forgot the reason he was calling. "Um—hello—I'm looking for Flevin," he said, cringing at his amateurish intonation. But the woman replied in the same brusque voice.

"This is Flevin."

A tangle in Dex's gut almost froze him up.

Talk, idiot, talk!

"Oh, hi. My name is . . . Actually, I should probably tell you I was referred to you by a man named Kal Mauer. I'm looking to get a chip replacement."

"Full name?"

"Dexter Michael Wheelock."

"Call me back in twenty minutes."

Flevin ended the call, leaving Dex in silence. He waited twenty minutes, then redialed her com address, as instructed. Kal Mauer had typed his name into what had probably been a shared database, and Dex guessed Flevin was checking to make sure he was real. Sure enough, when Flevin answered and he identified himself, she launched immediately into business. It was clear her words were a memorized speech for potential customers.

"It will be twenty thousand dollars up front, and you don't leave my presence until the replacement is finished. We will destroy your current chip upon its removal, and your record with TruthChip Corporation will show you to be officially deceased, marked as such by the proper authorities. By all appearances, you will disappear from the NRO's radar forever under your current name. As you know, the NRO's Department of Identification owns all branches of TruthChip Corporation, but I have an affiliate working at the Kansas City branch, and he has created a live, updateable mirror of the database that we can merge with his own at any time, which lends us a 100 percent success rate for chip replacement services, though I have no way to prove that to you. For all future registration purposes, you will be catalogued by your new identity. The twenty-thousand-dollar cost includes everything you need to disappear and integrate back into society: the new chip, the attached fabricated history in TruthChip's official Identity Database of Individuals, a new dollar account containing five thousand dollars to get you started, and accelerated skin renewal over the new chip's insertion point. By the end of the day, you will be a new human being. You will meet me at the corner of West Tenth and Baltimore at ten o'clock tomorrow evening, from where I will escort you to our next stop. I am of Asian descent and will be wearing a black jacket. Do you need me to repeat any of this?"

"Uh, no. West Tenth and Baltimore. Sounds good. I'll most likely be . . . in a dress. I'm pretending to be part of the drag—"

"I've already seen your photo, but I'll keep the dress in mind. Good day, Mr. Wheelock."

Flevin's com went silent once again.

Now, all that remained was letting Sam and Moses know the cost, which was astronomical. It was the first time in his adult life that Dex had been financially dependent on anybody. It would be unfair for him to expect anything from the two farmers, but he had faith they would agree to give him the money, if they had it. Whether he would be able to pay it back was the question. Dex needed only to consider his situation to face the obvious answer.

When Sam and Moses returned to the hotel room later that evening, they were slightly drunk and seemed to be in an extremely reckless mood.

"We're *totally* breaking the law, and we're *totally* standing up for what's right!" Sam slurred, hugging Dex around the shoulder. His hands wandered down Dex's biceps, and Dex allowed him the indulgence. It was the least he could do. Moses was a calmer drunk, but he nodded at each word that came from Sam's mouth. "For the first time in *forever*, we actually feel as if we're paying tribute to our son in a *real way*. And you, Dex, are to thank!"

"Well, I've got something else you can thank me for," Dex said, wincing as the story about Flevin and her twenty-thousand-dollar fee came out. It hit the two men like a freight truck. For a moment, they simply stared at Dex with their jaws dropped. Then Sam began shuffling around the room.

"Okay, okay, we can manage that. It's okay, Dex. No, *really*. We just . . . we need to figure out how . . ."

"Twenty fucking *thousand*?" Moses growled. "How the hell do those criminals make their living when other criminals are their only customers? Where does anybody pull up that kind of money?"

Sam spun around and held a flat hand up to his husband. "Moses, dear, don't even start. We'll figure a way." He turned to Dex. "We have the money, hon, so don't you worry. It's just . . . it's been a slow year, as even more people have turned lately toward neighborhood greenhousing, and it's taken its toll, particularly on the banana market. But we have a retirement fund, and we have Efron's life insurance."

"Yeah, there's that," Moses concurred.

Dex's face was red with humiliation. The worst part was that the Archers were clearly not as wealthy as he thought they might have been, based on what they had spent on his behalf over the past four days.

As much money as the chip replacement required, neither man for a moment appeared in favor of leaving Dex to fend for himself. Moses used the hotel's com to transfer money from their "untouchable" retirement savings account. Gratitude and love pierced Dex's heart as he watched the transaction, and what accompanied it was fleeting but unmistakable: a sudden awareness that hope was a living, breathing, constant facet of humanity. As long as human beings existed, so would goodness, despite all evils.

You've gotten me this far, Dex said to the voice from the train. *Now, watch over these men. They deserve to have my luck when all this is through.*

THE FOLLOWING EVENING, Sam and Moses accompanied him to the intersection of West Tenth Street and Baltimore Avenue. The streets were neither empty nor particularly bustling with nightlife, but Dex and Sam were inconspicuous in their drag queen apparel. As the convention center was only a few short blocks away, those visiting for Queens of the Midwest had congregated in the neighborhood for the week. It was a Monday night, and most of the people walking the streets seemed to be out for fun. Moses was the person who stuck out most, as his hands were buried deep in his pockets, and he walked with the nervous and stiff stature of a man emasculated by his surroundings.

True to her word, Flevin was standing on the southwest corner of the intersection, kitty-corner from the one they were waiting at. She stood against an antique stone building with one high-heeled boot pressed against the wall. She was tiny, with sharp black hair and narrow eyes. Her black jacket was made of expensive leather that glimmered under the street light but was unzipped to expose a startling red party dress beneath it. Dex waved, and Flevin waved back, as if they were old friends. There were no approaching cars, so Dex, Sam, and Moses crossed diagonally through the intersection.

Up close, Flevin almost passed for a transvestite, if not a drag queen. The makeup on her face was one step past gaudy, and her legs were wide set, so she walked toward them with a slightly masculine gait.

"Hey, how *are* you?" she said enthusiastically, hugging Dex. Then, she whispered. "Follow me. Act as if we're all drag friends. We don't have far to walk." Then, she leaned back and looked at Sam and Moses, adopting once again her socialite persona.

"Are these your friends?"

"Yes. They're buying everything tonight," Dex said, turning to them, trying to smile. "Aren't you, boys?"

Sam leaned in to kiss Flevin's cheek. "Honey, you can bet on *that*. If I have one too many drinks, my husband here will show you where to scan."

Moses was still angry at Flevin for the cost of helping them, but he shook her hand nonetheless with a crisp nod. From there, they walked east six blocks to a retail center on the first floor of a high-rise condominium complex. They entered a bustling shop called Sex Me Sideways. Sexual paraphernalia of all types lined the shelves, but Dex barely had time to look, because Flevin was leading them straight to the back, toward an aisle of live males, who were all standing over hefty price tags on podiums upholstered in plush red fabric. Just like every other sex shop Dex had ever been in, the models smiled and tried to entice the customers who walked past. One in particular, a thin blonde teenager, was in the process of wooing a man who looked no younger than seventy.

"No no no, Bruce," he chirped to the old man, who was trying to grab his legs. "A hundred dollars, and you get me for an entire hour, just like last week. But you have to pay Flevin first!"

Flevin grinned at the young blonde as they passed. "Send him to Aiden. He'll scan the guy's chip."

"Sounds good, boss," the boy said, smiling. His gaze intersected with Dex's for a second, and Dex saw in it a flicker of desperation. Even for a young homosexual male, being a sex worker was not particularly glamorous, even if there was good money in it. It was doubtful the boy was happy having to service wrinkled old men. Dex smiled at him before the podium disappeared behind another aisle of merchandise.

At the rear of the store were six doors lining the wall, all of which were closed. Sitting at a nearby desk and reading something on his com was a muscular black man wearing a tight orange tank top. He looked up as Flevin approached with the man and two drag queens in tow.

"This one with the bobbed hair is here for a private show with Chaos," she said in her sharp business voice, and then she pointed to Moses. "This one's paying."

The man gestured with his finger for Moses to come closer. With a lackadaisical lift of his arm, he brought up a credit reader, set the price, and held it out to Moses's wrist. Moses took a deep breath as the reader scanned the chip, and he pursed his lips at Sam with raised eyebrows.

Flevin nodded at Moses, then turned to the man at the desk. "Thanks, Bart. If anyone calls for me, I think Chaos should be done with him in about two hours." She turned to Sam and Moses. "Feel free to wander the store while your friend is getting his private show. All items are half off for people who buy shows with Chaos."

She said it with such a straight face that Dex wondered whether the man at the desk had any clue what was going on here. He had already turned back to his com and was flipping through the digital pages of what looked like a fitness magazine.

Flevin snapped at Dex. "Chaos has a busy schedule tonight. Come on."

She led him to the closed door that was farthest to the right, then scanned her wrist against the lock reader. After pulling the door open and ushering Dex through, Flevin followed and shut the door. They were in a small room containing a round bed, red velvet draperies hanging from purple walls, and a mirrored ceiling. The small woman led Dex straight through it and knocked on the far wall. After a moment of silence, it opened to reveal a hidden chamber replete with medical supplies, desk coms, and even what appeared to be living quarters consisting of a bed, shower, and small kitchen.

"This is Chaos," she said, pointing into the room.

There sat a man so fat that Dex blinked twice to make sure there were not two. Chaos looked more like a triangular mound than a human being, by typical social standards. He was sitting in what had to be an office chair, but only the chair's wheels were visible; his midriff, thighs, and rear had all sagged to hide the seat. The man's chin drooped in a five-inch wattle that shook when he turned around to greet them with a dreary smile.

"Hello," he said.

Dex wondered how the man was able to move, but he did; he lifted an arm and gestured for Dex to sit in a chair opposite his own, across a small stainless steel table. Not only was Chaos frightfully obese, but he was also paler than any human being Dex had ever seen, as if he had not left this windowless room in years.

That might explain why he looks so sad, Dex thought, feeling sorry for the man. When he spoke, however, the pity dwindled.

"Another fucking failsafe?"

Flevin nodded. "You saw the record Mauer sent over. He paid, so switch him up."

Chaos seemed already to have prepared Dex's new chip, which lay in a covered Petri dish in what Dex hoped was a sterilizing solution. The man was wiping an alcohol swab along the shaft of a long needle connected to a full syringe.

"Hold out your hand," he told Dex, and Dex complied. "Local anesthetic. Your chip is farther into your skin than it was when you were a baby, but a quick ultrasound will show me exactly where it is, so it won't be difficult to make a slit on the side of your wrist and retrieve it. That is, unless for some reason it's deeper than usual."

Chaos inserted the needle into three different points on Dex's wrist, then opened the Petri dish to make the new chip accessible. He scanned the chip with a reader that was connected to a desk com at the end of the table. A database identical to Kal Mauer's mirror of the TruthChip database was already open, and a new record popped up.

"When we're done inserting the empty chip, we'll finish building your new record with a new identification photo, a new financial account with our affiliated bank, and a random sampling of data typical for a man your age, and we'll make the database software think you were born thirty-something years ago. Easy enough. You will be able to close your new bank account and transfer to a bank of your choice at any time, just as you would if you were legal. Would you like to make any changes to your appearance? Say, a head shave, at the very least?"

"Is that included in the cost?"

Chaos glared at him, then turned to Flevin. "Is he serious?"

"He'll go for the head shave," Flevin said.

Dex did not object. Hair grew back, and it could only help him on his return to Minneapolis to look different. He was already much thinner than he was three weeks ago. But he had another question. "What's my new name going to be?"

"Based on the decade of your birth and popular names of the time, I came up with Marcus Hepburn Flint. Do you object?"

"I guess not."

"Then stop asking questions. Let me get this done. If you're this twitchy when I do the micro-electroshock, you're going to have a shitty-looking insertion line, and it'll give you away to any smart cop. You dig?"

Go eat a sailor, Dex wanted to tell Chaos, but he resisted. He sat back and let the gargantuan man do his work.

CHAPTER 47 ✳ (HER)

G RACE WAS DARING TO HOPE.

The mechanics of Mount Tasman astounded her: the amount of work that had been necessary to blow out the mountain's interior, the construction inside of a shell large enough to house a small city's worth of buildings, the ventilation made possible by carefully mined tunnels—it all left Grace feeling tiny, insignificant. She had heard of facilities built within mountains before, but erecting a headquarters for the Opposition in a place as remote, as beautiful, and as conspicuously close to Antarctica as this had been ingenious. Frederik Carnevale's family had laid the foundation for humankind's salvation—no easy task—and it seemed to be thriving.

Grace's party had entered the mountain through a gray blast door at least three stories high. Their "refugee liaison," a kind-looking man with a black mohawk, drove them through the massive tunnel that followed, explaining during the ride that any working members of the Opposition not yet inside Mount Tasman would hopefully arrive by May, before winter really kicked in and blocked the access point. Ice and snow could be unpredictable between June and September, and due to the Opposition's plans for the future—the counterstrike, Grace knew but did not say aloud—they would not be reopening the mountain.

It took five minutes to reach a loading dock preceding a second steel blast door. The mohawk man parked the transport next to three others along the far right wall, where a fifth one was just pulling out. Its driver waved at them.

Going to pick up more people, Grace thought, pulling her suitcase—everything she had left of her life—off the carriage. The blast door opened, and ten people, seven men and three women, entered the chamber. They welcomed the new arrivals with gracious smiles and gathered their bags. The failsafes carried what they had, but pregnant women were exempt from labor here; the refugee liaisons insisted on carting their luggage. Grace did not object. The last twenty-four hours had sapped all her energy, and it was almost impossible to fathom that just a day ago, she had been anticipating the explosion of Lieutenant Helio's bomb in those empty, isolated ruins of Los Angeles. When she considered the last five months in their entirety, who she was before and who she was now, it was like looking in a broken mirror. Her life had cracked in so many ways that only the bits seen through the shards were recognizable.

"Now that we can all hear each other over the vents, *welcome*," the mohawked carriage driver said as they crossed from the loading dock into a hallway with dull metal walls. It stretched almost as far as Grace could see, but doors interrupted it on either side about a hundred feet down. "We are nearly a kilometer into the mountain, and our four-hundred-thousand-square-meter facility is spread throughout an excavated space surrounded by an ungodly amount of mostly greywacke rock. The main spine of the Southern Alps is made up mostly of greywacke, which is a kind of super-hard sandstone. Anyway, I'm doubting any of you care about geology as much as I do. I'm pretty much the only one here who thinks it's amazing." He smiled, and so did Grace. Their eyes met momentarily. For a moment, the mohawk man seemed to look at her as if she were familiar, and his gleeful expression flickered with melancholy.

Did I just imagine that? Grace wondered, suddenly feeling

self-conscious. But none of the other women seemed to have noticed. Ruth was walking along beside her, yawning but still trying to maintain an authoritative, attentive gait.

"In any case, we are going to check you in based on our communications from Frederik Carnevale's Cliff House in the American Territory. I myself used to work there, and I've been the one organizing your transportation, along with Albert Redmond."

That would explain his American accent, Grace thought. Suddenly, something else felt familiar about the man, but she could not immediately place it. It was not his soft blue eyes, which were reminiscent of Dex Wheelock, nor his thin body, which reminded Grace of her father. As it turned out, she did not have to pick her brain very far to make the connection; he did it for her while registering the new recruits in a large receiving lobby through one of the hallway's left doors. Grace was third to last in line. Most of the women had already disappeared down a hallway decorated with holopanels showing sky views of New Zealand's Southern Alps.

"Claire Austen, or Grace Emilia Jarvis?"

"I guess we can use our real names again, right?" Grace said with a tired grin.

But the man was looking at her with a pensive gaze.

"I thought it might be you, for some reason. It says here you were recruited by Sheila Willy. The only one out of this bunch. That true?"

Grace's heart leapt with excitement. "Yes! I was. Do you know Sheila?"

The man nodded. Suddenly, Grace remembered: Marvel had mentioned spying on Sheila in the Cliff House communications room. She had been discussing the counterstrike with a man who had a mohawk.

"Yeah, I know Sheila well. Very well. She's . . ." The man's words trailed off, but a smile lingered on his lips.

This is the man she fell in love with, Grace thought. The realization made her forget all sense of propriety, and a rush of questions poured out before she could control herself.

"Are you still in touch with her? Do you know what happened? She just left the Cliff House one day and didn't come back! She was supposed to contact my dad—"

The man nodded, then looked around the lobby with a surreptitious expression.

"We'll talk about it later," he said. "I'll find you. We need to get everyone checked in and scheduled for medical examinations—"

But Grace was barely registering the woman and failsafe still waiting behind her. This was it, her one chance to salvage a shard of her old life. The urge to grab hold of it was overpowering. If Sheila had survived the attacks, she might even be able to put Grace in touch with her dad. "Is Sheila coming here, like she planned? Can you tell her to call my dad? The coms they gave us at the Cliff House can only receive calls, so I can't tell him where I am!"

"Grace, I—"

"Please? I just . . ." Her words drifted into the wake of reality. Excitement was futile. The chances of this man being able or willing to contact her dad were remote at best.

As if to confirm this, he grimaced, then sighed. "I'll find you later. Okay? I really have to get everyone checked in."

Grace regained her posture, but adrenaline left her feeling electric, untamed. "I'm sorry," she sputtered. "I just . . . I liked Sheila. It was confusing when she left. I was all alone."

"I'll do what I can to relay your message," the man said. "Now, if you could follow the rest of the women into that corridor, you'll be escorted to the maternity dorm, where we'll set up your appointment with Dr. Thrace."

Maternity dorm? Dr. Thrace? There were too many damned doctors.

"Yes. Okay. Thank you. . . ."

He extended a hand. "I'm Orion Skelby. Sheila mentioned you, and I really will see to it she gets your message, if I can. We'll talk later. I promise."

Grace shook Orion's hand. She offered him a weak grin as he turned away to continue his work.

In the days that followed, however, Grace saw Orion only in passing, and it appeared as though he meant to keep it that way. As a refugee liaison, he was always on the run, dealing with the inevitable day-to-day problems involved with integrating forty-three new people into a dorm already housing over three hundred. The rooms were indeed dorm-like—small, three women apiece—and there were no artificial windows, as there had been at the Cliff House. The rooms, common areas, and cafeterias were equipped with the bare essentials: things to eat, places to sit, and ceilings with exposed ventilation and piping. Holopanels were sparsely placed and failed to lend the cave a sense of openness. It was downright industrial, a gritty center of operations for an intercontinental resistance effort much larger than any one person living there. Most mountain staff members had separate living quarters in another part of the mountain, so when they were not helping the new recruits, they were busy with their own lives. The depressing truth was that Grace and her intent to contact Sheila Willy were not Orion's first priority, nor could they be.

Four days passed without so much as a head nod from Orion, and she found herself falling into a self-constructed psychological cloister, devoid of any human spirit but her own. During the night before her first appointment with the obstetrician Dr. Thrace, however, the baby inside her was dancing in summersaults, as if to remind her that no, she was not alone, that she had been accompanied through this upheaval of her life all along, lest she forget. It was true. Grace had almost forgotten. Save for the back aches, the kicks, and the growing levels of exhaustion, the fact she was pregnant—truly and humanly *pregnant*—had become a neglected truth juxtaposed with her effort to avert the Bio Police. Now, she was in a safe place until the baby came.

"Would you like to know the sex?" Dr. Thrace asked the next morning, during her medical checkup. She was a beautiful woman, blonde and rough around the edges but also enthusiastic over Grace's pregnancy.

Her question inspired an unexpected burst of joy between them. For the first time that day, Grace smiled. "Tell me."

Dr. Thrace handed her the ultrascope visor. "You're having a girl. A beautiful baby girl."

A MEMORY ✳ (HIM)

*T*HESE ARE THE FORMATIVE MOMENTS, *the ones a man, even a worthless failsafe, will never forget. There are few people left in Dex's world now, and he shuns the heterosexual community, because he is growing afraid of building associations that could be misconstrued by the government as threatening.*

"He was a good boy," his mother Roberta says, standing next to him, watching as Bobby Salinger's father opens the urn. Bobby's ashes fall into the Rum River. He was raped and murdered by three police officers on the fifth day of his job at the South Minneapolis detention center. Rumor had it he had not partaken in the initiation orgy for new recruits, the rest of whom were normal homosexuals who had embraced the tradition.

"I told him he was stupid to try to be a cop," Dex replies. "The only hetero cop in a building full of faggot pigs."

He has to whisper; Bobby's father is less than twenty feet away, with the rest of the family. Officer Salinger has been met by cold stares from his own department; nobody is taking responsibility for his son's death.

"But he was right to hope," Roberta says. "He was working for an ideal."

"Same ideal you worked for by not telling me I was a failsafe," Dex replies. "There are just certain realities you can't ignore, Mom." Next to the river, guttural sobs rise from Bobby's father, who is on his knees in the dirt, holding the empty urn.

Tears are falling down Roberta's face. "I didn't want my child to be told what or who to be, because that's what brings about these mindless atrocities!" she tells Dex with gritted teeth. "I was doing it because I needed to be the light I wanted to see in the world. That's what your friend Bobby was doing as well."

"And look at the price he paid."

"Yes, look at it. What will you remember him for? Being scared and hiding, or being brave and hoping?" Roberta turns out of Dex's embrace. He knows she loves him too much to be angry, and their argument about his engineering and upbringing is one beaten to death. He sees her point, but today, he is watching his best friend become river mud and wondering what could possibly spark a person to be so idealistic, so brave. Was it something in oneself? Was it God? Was it all some sort of cosmic joke? These are not new questions, either for him or for human history.

But they remain unanswered.

Dex turns to follow his mother away from the funeral. He wants to say goodbye to Officer Salinger, wish him a happy life, and tell him they won't be seeing each other again, but he does not. Salinger has been like a father to him, if that is what fathers are like, but it is his fault Bobby is dead. He encouraged his son, and now they are here, next to the river, watching the young man's ashes disappear downstream. The gap left in Dex's path by Bobby's death is a black sinkhole he must learn to step around, impossible as it seems. But there is only more coming—more death, more pain. Where in that is the light his mother spoke of?

CHAPTER 48 ❄ (HIM)

Dex Wheelock, known to the world now as Marcus Flint and dead forever to the mothers who had raised him, could barely endure the low hum of the maglev train from Kansas City to Minneapolis. But there were windows on this train, and seats. No holes, no heat, no chemicals to burn his eyes. When the Mississippi River finally appeared in the low fog outside the train's right side, Dex felt a rush of serenity about the decisions he had made. After thirteen days in Kansas City, he was going home, and he had already called Linda Glass to set up a meeting with Stuart Jarvis for that evening. Sam had insisted Dex remain in Kansas City until his burns and gashes healed enough to be inconspicuous. They switched hotels three times after the Queens of the Midwest convention ended, and they refused to let Dex pay with money from his new account for fear that the TruthChip replacement had been a scam. On the eighteenth of February, however, Dex scanned his wrist to buy a jar of peanut butter, and the identification and payment worked perfectly.

Moses had examined Dex in their hotel room later that morning. "Can't even tell they put a new chip in you. Those burns up top aren't too obvious anymore either. Worst-case scenario, you can wear a hat and cover most of them up."

Sam paced back and forth. "But if anyone *does* notice them, they might recognize you from the WorldCom reports." The two men had fretted over Dex and discussed every possible downfall he might face if he took the train to Minneapolis, but finally, they had to let him go. Both men attempted to hold back tears outside the train station's military checkpoint. It was the huskier of the two who failed.

"You be careful," Moses told Dex, kissing his forehead. He wiped his eyes quickly. "I know it's only been a few weeks, but you've given me reason to feel good again."

Dex held the man close. "You too, Moses. Thank you."

And Sam, squeezing Dex in a hug, whispered, "Thank you for sleeping on our front porch! You've been a light in our world, I hope you know. Your mothers were lucky to have you. We'll try to get in touch with them as soon as it seems safe."

"I'm going to make it up to you if I can," Dex said. "I'll wire a fund transfer pass to one of your coms, if I can ever find the money."

"You'll do no such thing," Moses commanded, sniffing and wiping his tears.

"Yes, I *will*. If I find a way. You both saved my life."

They had purchased Dex a new pocket com and entered all of their contact information, so it was now up to him to stay in touch. Yet the underlying threat to their goodbye tore at Dex's gut. There was still a chance the Bio Police had tracked him to their house, and if that was indeed the case, they would have to face questions and possible detainment. Both Moses and Sam had downplayed the possibility in front of Dex, but he could see under their bittersweet goodbye that a return to their old life would mean facing the potential consequences of everything they had done for him.

"If all goes to hell, say hi to Efron for us," Moses said with a grin.

"Let us know when you get there safe," Sam said. "We love you, Dexy. Oh, and remember . . . look *all* those guards in the eyes, and give them a 'fuck me' look. They won't bat an eyelash."

True to Sam's prediction, he passed the military checkpoint with flying colors. The soldiers patrolling public areas were dressed in dazzling rainbow faux-camouflage, their standard non-combat attire. Dex locked eyes with the soldier who scanned his new bar code and patted him down for hidden explosives. The man spent an extra second feeling Dex's crotch, which, seeing as it had been weeks since his last orgasm, complied by being more firm than usual.

His new TruthChip performed with admirable normality, and nobody appeared to recognize his face. Flevin and Chaos had done an exceptional job in establishing a new identity for him, and if he survived the trip long enough to see Linda Glass and Stuart Jarvis, it would be worth the financial pain he had caused Sam and Moses Archer. He had not mentioned it to them for fear the plan would not work, but Dex had resolved not only to seek Stuart Jarvis's forgiveness for leaving Grace but also to set his needs bare and ask the man for money to repay Sam and Moses. It was the only possible way for the two farmers to regain their loss. They were not expecting it, but money was money, and if Stuart would give without caring and the Archers could replenish their savings, it would rectify at least a small percentage of Dex's mistakes. The obstacle was, of course, Stuart. Whether he could ever forgive Dex for having abandoned his pregnant, frightened daughter was the question hanging in the rafters.

The trip to Minneapolis took less than three hours. During the ride, a uniformed soldier carrying a sonic rifle took a seat across from Dex. He had dark hair, a protruding jaw, and a gentle smile. Channeling Sam, Dex looked him in the eye, nodded, then checked out his physique. The man did the same to Dex.

"You're pretty brave to be traveling, huh?" he said.

"Been stuck in Kansas City since the attacks," Dex replied.

"Man, I hear you. Nice that they opened the trains back up, anyway."

The soldier grinned, and his eyes lingered on Dex.

Best to keep making conversation and keep up the flirting. He can't expect me to hook up when he's on patrol.

"So, where are you stationed?" Dex asked.

"A hotel in downtown Minneapolis. I'm on a volunteer basis. I went through basic training back in the day, but I'm actually an accountant. My office in Minneapolis *and* my condo were damaged during the bombings, so now I'm out of work and a house for the time being. Military volunteering is my best option right now." After a slight lull in their conversation, the soldier said, "I'm off duty tonight. You interested in getting together? I'm a top."

Damn it.

"I'm a top too," Dex replied, faking a regretful shrug.

"Aw, fuck," the soldier said. He stood up. "I'll find somebody else. Have a good night, man. I'll be hanging out at Rapture if they're back open yet, in case you change your mind. People need to get their rocks off, even if the world is shot to shit. See you if I see you."

"Maybe you will."

The soldier offered Dex a friendly salute. "Peace, brother." He turned to resume his security rounds.

Peace. It was a dead possibility as long as humanity survived. He almost felt sorry for the man, who seemed kind enough apart from the orders his uniform forced him to live by. Under the government's new standards, he and Dex were complete opposites, enemies to the death. Stripped of such labels and ideals, however, they were just two men making friendly conversation on a train ride to Minneapolis.

All intercity trains arrived at the Warehouse Station Depot, where passengers had to scan their TruthChips at an exit checkpoint. Dex had used his new chip at least a dozen times since leaving the hotel in Kansas City, but he could not yet present it without experiencing a dither of terror. For some reason, it always brought him back to the train car: scrambling, burning, screaming to get out—the consequence of being caught. Minneapolis was the type of city where it was easy to cross paths with someone familiar. It was a risk to be coming back. Dex took a deep breath and approached the soldier he had visited with earlier. They smiled at each other as he held out his wrist and scanned it.

"Stay safe," the soldier said.

As Dex ascended Warehouse Station's escalators to Washington Avenue, he heard the systematized clamor of marching feet and the raised voices of children. The majority sounded as though they belonged to young boys, chanting the same two phrases over and over.

"Support the Colors, wipe out the Others! Support the Colors, wipe out the Others!"

The Gay Youth.

As Dex's eye line rose with the stairs to street level, he saw a flowing wall of children dressed in purple uniforms, sporting rainbow striped bands around their right arms. Some had hats to fend off the snow, which had replaced the rain that was falling farther south, and some had their heads exposed to the elements. They were parading down Washington Avenue in front of Colors Park, holding candles and surrounding a flatbed hydro truck doubling as a stage on wheels. Three older boys were standing on it holding spiked metal clubs. As one of them moved to reveal the center of the stage, Dex realized what he had stepped into.

It was an execution. This time, it was still in progress.

Three men, presumably failsafes, were naked and chained to a single wooden column in the middle of the stage. Their genitals had been cut off. Lit by blinding LED lights mounted on the truck's cab, they were screaming, trying to hide their bodies, and being met only by cheers and jeers as the chanting dwindled.

Horror caught in Dex's throat as one of the teenage boys on stage raised his club.

"Do you know what these men are?" he screamed. He must have been wearing a microphone, because his voice boomed into the cold, cloudy night.

"*Breeders!*" the crowd of children replied. The teenager brought the club down in a terrible arc and bludgeoned the nearest man, then circled the pillar and battered the two others. The spikes ripped into their heads, then pulled out bits of flesh upon their withdrawal. Two of the men fell, swinging on their chains around the column. The third had survived and was using his chain to swing away.

The young man with the club raised it again. "Caught this morning trying to buy their way out of their social assessments! Trying to hide from their crimes!" Down came the club again, and the third man, soaked red, went limp and dangled with the others. The crowd cheered, then resumed its chant.

In a panic, Dex walked southeast on Washington, toward the city center. He needed to find a cab out to the suburbs. As the blocks passed under his feet, however, all he could see were the three men being bludgeoned, over and over, knowing it could be him if he took the slightest misstep. When he finally looked up, Dex noticed military patrols on every corner. Save for a few bystanders hopping in line with the Gay Youth, he was the only person walking, and it was against the flow of children.

He was making himself conspicuous.

There was no way he could help those ill-fated men on the stage. Forcing composure on himself, Dex stopped for a red traffic light, even though the streets were blocked for the marching children and there were no cars. Candlelight dotted the visible stretch of Washington Avenue, and try as he might to see the end of it, more children, hundreds yet, were coming. In the mass of it was a bright spot, moving closer: a second execution stage.

Jesus Christ. Get out of here!

He turned back around to face the direction of Warehouse Station. The parade turned left a block past Colors Park, up Sixth Avenue, which meant the streets might be open for him to hail a cab on Seventh.

Dex began walking back the way he had come, along the parade's periphery. He passed Colors Park and broke off from the group as they turned left. The children's chanting of "Support the Colors, wipe out the Others!" grew more subdued as he left the parade behind.

Except there was one voice behind him, chanting. It did not dwindle with the others, and footsteps followed it.

Dex turned his neck, and under the bobbing glow of a handheld candle thirty feet behind him was the pale, bony face of Lars Jarvis.

"Support the Colors, wipe out the *Others*!" he screamed one final time, then grew silent.

By pure happenstance, Dex's luck had just run out. He could only play dumb and hope this was happening for a reason. Turning back on his way, he offered the boy a confused chuckle as he hid his face and began walking. But Lars screamed after him.

"Where did you take my aunt Grace?"

Dex froze. He turned around again, hoping his act could hold up against the perceptive boy. "Excuse me?"

"*I know who you are*," Lars hissed. "You and Grace disappeared, and then I saw your face on the news! You think you look different with a shaved head and a trench coat? I saw you come out of the train station!"

"I'm not sure what you're talking about," Dex said. "Do I know you?"

"Do you think I'm *stupid*? You're Dexter Michael Wheelock, age thirty-seven, height five-foot-three, birthday on September nineteenth, 2347. Failsafe, and prisoner of the NRO. I had Daryl look you up on his friend's database after we saw you on WorldCom!"

"My named is Marc," Dex said, at a loss, his heart pounding.

But Lars shook his head. "No, you ate at my grandparents' dinner table. You got my aunt Grace *pregnant*. You two are *breeders*!"

It was pointless to refute the boy; there was no fooling him. Behind him, the Gay Youth were moving on, marching and chanting as the failsafes on the second stage screamed for mercy. Lars stared into Dex's eyes, and for a moment, they stood head to head in an intimate battle of the wills. It was the boy's ruthlessness that dared Dex to run, and Dex's utter sorrow that dared the boy to remain silent. Less than a hundred yards behind him was a pair of uniformed soldiers, casually strutting toward them.

Dex had one chance, and he had to act fast. He began walking slowly toward Lars. Despite the boy's perfectly sculpted adherence to this culture of hate, he possessed a potential vulnerability. Dex had witnessed it at dinner the night they met: Lars had been attracted to him, intimidated. For whatever reason, Dex had broken through his tack-sharp personality and exposed a thread of insecurity.

"If you come any closer, I'll scream," Lars said. His voice had broken under a mixture of hoarseness and fear, and Dex saw him shudder. Closer, what had appeared to be the boy's ruthlessness was clearer: the look in Lars's wide eyes was frantic, unpredictable. The atrocities he had witnessed since their last meeting, the reality of hate, seemed to have unraveled him.

"You would have turned me in already," Dex replied. His heart was pounding, and to show his fear would be his undoing. The soldiers were getting closer; each wore a loaded gun belt. Lars stood his ground, but his pale face, flirting with darkness over the fluttering candlelight, was quivering with terror.

Dex reached him in ten steps. "You came after me because you hoped I could give you some comfort."

The boy's whole body was shaking now. He said nothing.

"Do you know your aunt Grace loved you, Lars? Even though you were a quiet and menacing kid, she loved you. She wanted the best for you." Dex touched Lars's shoulder, and the boy blinked, appearing for a moment to succumb to the gesture. "Now it seems to me that part of you cares if your aunt Grace is alive. Cares whether or not she's been torn to shreds like the men on those stages. Otherwise, you wouldn't have had the courage to come after me just now. I know you find me attractive. You're at the age where you'd do anything to satisfy your curiosities about my body if given the chance."

Lars shuddered, and his gaze fell to the slushy sidewalk. The snow had begun to pick up, and the flakes were sticking to his black hair like specks of dust.

"You'll have to make some adult choices now. You'll have to choose whether you think your aunt Grace deserved to die, just like those men up on the platform, or whether she deserved to live. How come you never turned her into the Bio Police after you saw her bleed? You knew she was pregnant, didn't you?"

There it was, a slight nod. Dex pitied the boy for the paranoid life he was bound to lead from here on out.

He leaned closer and whispered.

"Don't you realize they'll kill you if they find out you kept the truth from the Bio Police? You're just as guilty as those men being executed."

The boy's nod was more prominent now. The bottoms of his eyes glistened with tears. The soldiers, thumping with their heavy boots, were getting closer. Dex looked up. It was the soldier from the train, the volunteer who was really an accountant, walking with another man toward Seventh Street. Grinning, he checked out Dex again and extended a hand. Dex took his own from Lars's shoulder and shook it.

"So, we meet again!" the soldier said. "I thought I saw you head off this way. We're stopping at my hotel room for a while before heading out." He exchanged a sexually charged glance with his friend, and then both of them eyed Dex. It was an invitation.

Lars jerked his head toward the soldier's feet. If he was going to turn Dex in, it would happen now. Dex took him by the shoulder again and grinned at both men, then gestured at Lars.

"I'd love to join you guys, but I'm in the process of trying to tell this one he's too young to be flirting with me. I'm a friend of his dad's, and he always used to check me out after my showers at their house. Saw me here today and came after me, but I told him to wait until he's fifteen. Then I'd consider."

The soldiers laughed and patted Lars on the back. The boy just stood there like a mannequin waiting to be moved.

"A few more years, kid," the soldier from the train said. "You'll make a cute fuck."

"If I can get to Rapture tonight, I'll try to find you," Dex said. "Otherwise, another time."

Both of the soldiers began walking again. The accountant waved. "Another time, man."

Lars remained motionless as the two men disappeared up Seventh Street. Relief rang through Dex.

"Support the Colors, wipe out the Others!"

The mantra was fading up Sixth Avenue now. The parade had passed.

"Better get back to your crowd, Lars," Dex said. "Think about what you're doing. The future depends on boys like you. On if you'll have courage to make the right choices." He pivoted to follow the soldiers up Seventh Street.

"Wait," Grace's nephew said. He raised his pale face into the street light once again.

The snow was getting aggressive now, and a wind had kicked up.

Dex turned. "Yeah, kid?"

"Is my aunt Grace alive?"

"She is," Dex said. "Remember her before you decide to stay loyal to the NRO." Lars stood in silence as a cluster of snowflakes snuffed out his candle. Dex shook his head at the boy, then turned and walked up Seventh Avenue. He did not look back.

CHAPTER 49 ✳ (HER)

DIANA KRING HAD DISAPPEARED, and here was her name and a short message, scribbled on what residents of Mount Tasman called the Wall of the Future:

*Diana and Michael Kring—Love to all we
left behind, January 16, 2385.*

The new women from the Cliff House and the 306 others residing in the maternity dorms lived in awe of the wall. It was on the side of the underground dormitory complex opposite the entrance Orion Skelby had checked them in through. Modeled to look like smooth rock, the wall lay on the dormitory's top floor in a long, empty hallway, at the end of which was yet another steel blast door. There were hundreds and hundreds of names scribbled and scratched on it, and Grace found Diana's name on her eleventh day inside the mountain. Her reticence had left her oblivious to the wall, but when she finally made the effort to join the other women for dinner one night, the table was abuzz with discussion and speculation.

Diana's name was written near the end of the tunnel three feet from the floor. The only reason it stood out to Grace was because it was written in a soft orange, different from the reds, blues, and blacks of most other names.

Here's the answer to your mystery, Dex, Grace thought. *And it looks like you had another child. A son. Michael.*

It was Dex's middle name. A good name. Grace longed to meet Diana here, face to face, to befriend somebody and become common links for one another, but the regulations were strict. Only those who had given birth were allowed down the tunnel and through the door. That was when the biological refugees wrote their names on the Wall of the Future. Right before they took that last step.

So, why did they keep the pregnant women separate? Why wait until they gave birth to move them again? Lieutenant Helio's confusion about the hushed government panic over the closed Sanctuary weighed on Grace, but she purposefully avoided contributing to the rumor mill that churned with new ingredients every day.

"I heard it's because the living conditions are *horrible*, even worse than the liaisons are telling us," some of the women were saying, contradicting the optimism Ruth had displayed on their drive to Franz Josef. "I mean, five thousand people living in a *mountain*? It's going to be a *rats' nest*!" But there were whispers from others that were more sinister. "Some people think it's all a joke. That people just go through there to a bunch of gas chambers, to their *deaths*."

Nobody who worked in Mount Tasman—not doctors, not maintenance crew, not refugee liaisons like Orion Skelby—gave credence to the rumors, and they maintained constant assurance that the door led to the part of the mountain where the refugees who had already given birth lived, and it was slightly more cramped than the maternity dorm, which they reserved to keep the pregnant ones comfortable during their confusing and possibly frightening life transition. Yet Orion avoided Grace for nearly two weeks, until she cornered him one morning in the cafeteria. Thirteen days had passed. Not only was Grace growing restless, but she was also rabid for any news from Sheila Willy or her father, which Orion had promised to help her get. Trying to find patience and solace inside the mountain had been difficult.

When Grace cornered Orion that Tuesday morning, he was grabbing an apple from the food line. She approached him with confidence, but it fractured into bits of desperation as the words came out.

"You never came to find me."

Orion recognized Grace and sank back. He threw the apple into the air, then caught it, as if trying to hide his guilt over having ignored her. "You got me."

Grace's anticipation sank. "Do you really know Sheila Willy? Is she really okay?"

"I do." Orion seemed perfectly aware that his answer did not help Grace at all, and he conceded with a shrug. "Okay, I know I'm not much help. But to be honest, I haven't had the chance to talk with Sheila. She hasn't answered her com in almost a month now. But I did leave her a message after I met you."

"Were you the one she knew from the Cliff House in Minnesota? The one she fell in love with?"

Orion nodded. "Sheila and I were close. But then I took the opportunity to get to New Zealand. We hadn't yet received intelligence about when the NRO was going to stage their attack, and I wanted to get down here before it happened. Sheila didn't. At the time, Carnevale thought the attack might be coming within a week, but it turned out to be almost a year later. I've been stuck here since then."

"What do you mean, 'stuck'?" Grace asked.

"Stuck. Meaning, once you get here, you're stuck. You have only one option."

"Which is?"

"To stay with the Opposition. Until everything is over. It might not even be in our lifetimes."

"'Everything' meaning the counterstrike."

"To restart the world."

Grace swallowed the urge to let loose her tears. "So you mean you're here until you go through that door upstairs? Why don't they just let everyone through at once?"

Orion was avoiding Grace's eyes now. "Because once you go through, you don't come back. That part of the mountain is depressing, to say the least. But it's the only option humanity has. The mothers, failsafes, and babies who've gone through there . . . you've seen their names on the wall . . . they make a commitment to that part of the mountain. We want to keep people here until after their babies are born, because it doesn't help our women to finish out their pregnancies in a place that's less than comfortable. We like to keep you as relaxed as possible. Have you been to the deck yet?"

Deck?

Grace's silence made her confusion obvious.

"So, none of you newbies have figured it out yet, huh? Well. I'm going to show you."

She allowed the change of subject, because it was pointless to continue theorizing about the rest of the mountain, especially when the staff's answers never changed. The deck, however, was a section Grace wished she had known about from the beginning. She had not even noticed a glass door at the far left side of the first floor's cavernous common room, having been there only twice for icebreaking games during her first week in the mountain. Yet it became obvious once Orion pointed it out.

"I find it helps to bring something to read," he said. "Helps sell the illusion."

The door slid open as might one onto any ordinary house deck, but beyond it was a ten-foot passage leading to another door, which was solid. Orion opened the door, and Grace gasped.

She was outside, on the ridge of the mountain, overlooking the stunning vista of New Zealand's Southern Alps. It was cool but not cold, breezy but not windy, and even humid but not damp: an impossibly perfect day in the middle of the most stunning view she had ever seen.

"I should have kept my eyes open on the hover jet," were her first words.

Grace did not even see Orion close the door, which seemed to have vanished into the clean, invigorating air. He walked her forward, over an open, rocky platform.

"Look over there," he said, pointing toward a mountain peak that looked even more colossal than Mount Tasman. "That's Mount Cook, the tallest mountain in the territory. A bit taller than Tasman. They make a nice pair, don't you think?" He pointed slightly left of Mount Cook to where a valley led out of the mountains, toward a long strip of light blue. "Lake Pukaki. You can see it from here, but barely. An unnerving color blue, isn't it? Funny to think how old all this is, what it's been through. The world, I mean. Not this holosphere."

Grace nodded, and her face scrunched against an onslaught of tears. *Damn these pregnancy hormones*, she thought.

Yet all this was incredibly sad: the room was not real, she was still stuck inside a mountain, and she might never again breathe fresh air. On top of everything, she was alone.

"But this really helps," she whispered aloud, surrendering her consciousness to the near-perfect illusion.

"Excuse me?" Orion said.

Grace blushed and smiled with embarrassment. "Nothing. I mean . . . I'm totally alone here. I have nobody. Being stuck inside a mountain is the most depressing thing to ever come my way, and this deck . . . this will make it a lot more tolerable. I hope."

"Virtual reality of the most advanced sort," he said. "Of course, it's almost thirty years old, so I'm sure they've actually learned to *create* new realities by now. But for what they're worth, holospheres like this get the job done."

For a moment, Orion stood with her in silence.

Then, Grace said, "You can't help me, can you?"

"By talking to Sheila, you mean?"

"By getting her to bring my dad down here."

"I'm not sure. I'm just a refugee liaison. They're strict about letting homosexuals in. Did you have a failsafe?"

"He's gone. Arrested, but he might have escaped. I saw his face on WorldCom. We were both at Sterile Me Susan's in Minneapolis when the Bio Police came. I think we might have led them there, actually."

Orion dug his boot heel into a small pile of loose rock. "The only reason I think I can get Sheila here is because she had a spot reserved before. And she could still work for us, even though the NRO stole her uterus. Did she tell you that?" Tears had formed in Orion's eyes. He turned away and gazed over the mountains. "She had a chance to come here, but she didn't," he continued. "It could still work out, though, and if she gets my messages and contacts your father, I *might* be able to pull some strings and get him in too. But he'd have to commit to leaving society forever."

"The NRO is going to wipe out humanity anyway," Grace said. "That's their whole plan. To save the world by getting rid of its most destructive species."

When the words didn't quite sink in with Orion, she told him about her discussion with Lieutenant Helio in Los Angeles. He took the news first with an incredulous expression, then an uneasy one.

"I'll keep calling Sheila," he said. "She has a new com that Albert Redmond gave her at the Cliff House. Unless she's somehow dead, I know she's checking it." He turned to leave, then stopped. "Oh, just so you know, the door out of here is through the holosphere, right where the kea bird is sitting." He pointed to a craggy rock behind Grace. Sure enough, somewhere just past the platform of mountain rock that served as the deck, a landed kea bird—an illusion, of course—was bobbing in circles.

Grace still had so many questions, but Orion left her in this holosphere of make-believe magnificence. She sat for hours, staring into the crisp blue sky, basking in the artificial mountain breeze.

Sometimes, she saw a kea bird flying in the distance, over the ridge of Mount Cook. If she no longer had freedom, this was the next best thing. The homosexuals had succeeded only so far in their fight against heterosexuality, and her very presence here was one step closer toward delivering them a memo of futility: *Sorry, but your efforts have failed. Humanity will go on.*

In the two weeks since leaving Los Angeles, her belly had grown so much that it would have been impossible to hide the pregnancy, even from fags who would otherwise pay women little attention. Her body shape had changed steadily over three months in mild weight gains, but since she crossed the four month mark, the changes had increased with exponential fervor. Her hips were wider, her rear end was now more cushioned, and the bump on her stomach was rolling outward with the unmistakable mark of a carrier.

This is what we're fighting for, little girl, she thought, gazing over the mountains. *If we don't help keep people around, who's going to appreciate the world? Who's going to look at these mountains and love them for their beauty?*

Grace and the rest of humanity—they were all just animals, of course, like every other species in nature. They could create life from nothing; they did not need engineering labs. Controlling human proliferation had its place, but to do so by force and, worse, by murder, was what separated the human species from the others. Murder was a moral conflict, and morality was a human trait, a glimpse through the keyhole separating light and dark. It had existed since the dawn of mankind, that keyhole, and every person on earth found it sooner or later. As she soaked in the beauty around her, knowing these mountains existed in reality somewhere above this frightful cave she now called home, Grace realized she was on the side of light.

This is where I'm supposed to be. And I'm not alone.

Inside the mountain were hundreds of other women just like her. Some were in the maternity dorms, and the others, Diana Kring included, had passed through that final door, into the part of the mountain nobody would come out of until the end, that holding zone for humanity's future.

I can be content with this, if I let myself.

Grace looked inward and saw her lonesomeness for what it really was: self-pity. She had lost her family, her friends, and the failsafe who had helped pave this road to begin with, only to lose focus on the opportunities for life, love, and the happiness still surrounding her. Marvel, dear annoying Marvel, had seen an opportunity and seized it. Lieutenant Helio had done the same in his own small way, reaching out to her that night on the beach. Grace could follow suit with what she still had, here and now, if she truly wanted to. Perhaps with some resolve, it could happen without her having to forget everyone she had ever loved.

CHAPTER 50 ✻ (HIM)

Dex could barely look Stuart Jarvis in the eyes, yet the man wrapped him in a hug and held him as if he were his own son, despite their being near strangers bound solely by circumstance. Dex found himself crying into the embrace, letting the flush of shame sink out of his heart. Flickers from the past rained out of his eyes: Grace looking up at winter's first snowflakes the night she found him at the bar, the smile she had worn as he fed her strawberries in the bathtub, her fallen expression underneath Sterile Me Susan's when his cowardice had finally crawled between them—all these things had turned Dex from an impassive man into a feeling one. In his old life, he would have been embarrassed.

"I don't blame you," Stuart whispered. "You let her go, and she survived. And so did you."

"I almost didn't," Dex said.

"You'll tell me all about it," Stuart assured him. "From now on, you stay with me."

They were standing next to a frozen lake, under light from the moon, far west enough of Minneapolis to be secluded. Linda Glass was watching them, crying herself. Despite putting herself and her family at risk, she had arranged the meeting.

"We're living in times that will make or break the world," Stuart said. "We've all had moments of confusion. I myself almost killed my own husband when he threatened to turn Grace in for banishment to Antarctica. Now *that's* saying something."

The reunion was a discussion of choices. Stuart told Dex what he knew about Grace: she had survived the Sterile Me Susan's raid, and he had set her up with a hotel and a rental car that very night. She had departed the next morning with Sheila Willy, and they were heading to a place the red-haired woman claimed was safe. Here, Dex filled Stuart in on what he knew about Frederik Carnevale and the Cliff House. But Grace had called her dad from there on a scrambled com and told him something that curled Dex's heart into a knot: they were transferring her and the other pregnant women all the way across the Pacific Ocean, to New Zealand. That territory was secluded and politically divided, and it would be pleasingly obscure if not for the fact that it was also the gateway to the Antarctica Sanctuary. Grace had given Stuart no further hints about what waited for her in New Zealand, but she had mentioned an Opposition counterstrike.

"Sheila Willy said something about that when she took us under Sterile Me Susan's," Dex said.

Stuart shrugged. "Yeah, well, Grace seemed to know more about it this time. It's supposed to be *big*. The attacks a few weeks ago? Grace said they would happen. That they were staged by the NRO, so they could declare martial law."

"And start the process of rounding up heterosexuals," Dex said.

"But there's something bigger coming. Grace told me to go to New Zealand, or somewhere else far removed from the NRO's main cities. She said the Opposition is going to wipe out humanity. That might mean a nuclear strike. I just don't know."

Dex turned to Linda. "Did you know this?"

The sumptuous blonde licked the tears off her lips. "Stuart told me."

"Why haven't you left?"

"I have a life here," Linda said. "If I were to leave now, it would just look suspicious. Besides, the NRO is patrolling every major travel route. I don't know what to do. Celine and Rita have no idea what's going on. I don't know what to tell them."

"Tell them you're saving their *lives*," Stuart told her. But Linda, looking downcast, only shrugged.

There, in the empty park, the three devised a plan. Dex would remain with Stuart at his resort hotel on Lake Washington. It would not help them if the Opposition decided to launch nuclear weapons at the Minnesota region before the government lifted its ban on air travel, but hiding out at the resort would keep them away from police radar. Stuart explained how the Bio Police had seemingly left him alone after the raid on Sterile Me Susan's, which he guessed meant their vehicles stationed outside his Wayzata mansion had strictly been investigating Dex back in December. Stuart had noticed police hanging around for a week following Dex's arrest and his daughter's flight, but then they disappeared entirely. Better things to investigate? Most likely. Stuart had since sought out an illegal com untracer, which scrambled the data running in and out of his address, should anybody be listening in.

"Five thousand dollars," he told Dex in the car, after they had parted ways with Linda for the night. "You'd think the price of something as simple as a com scramble would be slightly more reasonable."

It was a perfect time for Dex to ask Stuart the question he dreaded.

"Speaking of price," he started, trying to quell the guilt swelling in his chest. "Are you and your husband as . . . I mean, I guess I should say . . . are you as well to do as you appear?"

Stuart took the question in fair stride and nodded. "You could say that," he said. "James's dad was the founder of DoMe Clinic, and he left us with more than I'll ever know what to do with. I have a fair bit in my personal account. Why?"

"I'm wondering if I could work off a debt," Dex continued. He explained how Sam and Moses Archer had spent almost thirty thousand dollars to help him lose his previous identity and continue life as a fugitive. "They had no reason to help me, other than to honor the memory of their son Efron. I put them out of a lot of their savings, and I have no way to pay it back."

"Consider the repayment done," Stuart said. "We'll sort it out this week. If I can return goodness with some goodness, I can die a happy man when all this is all over."

"Have you no flaws?" Dex asked in a joking tone, shaking his head in disbelief. "I've done nothing worth gaining your trust or friendship. If there is any way I can repay you—"

Stuart jammed on his brakes suddenly. Dex looked at him, then out the windshield, where the headlights had stopped a monstrous deer in its tracks. "Jesus, Mary, 'n' Gaga!" Stuart screamed. "Heavens to Betsy, that came out of nowhere!" The hydro car screeched to a stop, and the deer darted off, across the country highway.

"That was a buck," Dex said.

Stuart was shaking in his front seat, gripping the steering wheel more tightly than necessary. They sat on the road in silence, watching the cement disappear out of the headlights' reach, into darkness.

"There is something you can do," Stuart said as his gasping ebbed. He slowly accelerated the car again.

"What?"

"About the repayment."

"Oh!" Dex exclaimed. "Anything."

"You follow my daughter to the very end, to the best of your ability. If you find her and my little granddaughter or grandson, promise me you'll stay with them."

"I promise." This time, there were no doubts in his mind, no lingering trickles of hesitation. Fear would never leave him completely, but now, he was no longer capable of letting selfishness make his decisions. If Grace was still alive, and if he could find her, they would journey together toward whatever life held in store.

Stuart had checked himself into a suite at Lake Washington Lodge. It was an upscale resort, but his unit was one of the modest ones. There were two queen-sized beds in the bedroom, and Dex took the unused one. They ate a quick room service meal of chicken parmesan and steamed green beans before retiring for the night.

After jumping into the deep end of bravery undone by cowardice, death counteracted by serendipity, and a rebirth coaxed into existence by charity, here Dex was, lying on a bed in the same hotel room as Grace Jarvis's benevolent dad. They shared a common purpose now. Both had abandoned their lives; Stuart had left James for good, Dex learned, because the man had shown more unflinching reverence to the Queen and his agenda after Grace's disappearance than concern for their daughter herself. Like everyone else in the world, James had seen Dex's face among all the others arrested in the Sterile Me Susan's raid. The man had correctly assumed that Grace was with Dex that night, and he had dismissed her as his daughter, deciding instead she was a wanton fool who had fallen into biological depravity.

James had known without doubt Grace was pregnant, Stuart explained, but he refrained from turning her in. When she disappeared without a trace, James had shown no sensitivity to the possibility that their daughter might be on her way to Antarctica, or worse (if the rumors were true), on her way to die. Stuart had left James the very night Grace had found a way to call him. He had packed his bags five days prior, itching for an excuse to leave, and then taken the opportunity to slip out when James was off at his favorite bathhouse. He had not returned any of James's calls since, as much as it broke his heart. The man was no longer a true husband; the New Rainbow Order's evil had thoroughly warped his spirit.

All Stuart had left behind was a note asking James not to call.

"He was the one who elected to have separate bank accounts," Stuart said as they lay in the dark hotel room, "so there's no way he can track where I am unless he chooses to involve the police. But I know James. He'll just let me go. He isn't malicious . . . just apathetic. And sometimes cruel."

DAYS PASSED. Dex and Stuart waited, hiking around Lake Washington, eating fabulous meals in the resort's restaurant, and bonding as might a father and son. They could do nothing but hope for the government to lift air travel restrictions, and according to WorldCom, the General Assembly was still debating the date to reopen travel routes. "It's a shame North America has no shipping ports off the Pacific coast," Stuart said. "I'd even take a boat to New Zealand if it wasn't for the fucking Unrecoverable Territories. You'd think they'd have at least rebuilt the sea ports!" Dex refrained from telling Stuart how useless ships would be in the age of hydro jets. The man was restless, intent on making sense of their helplessness.

The Friday after their reunion, Stuart arranged a fund transfer to Sam and Moses Archer in the amount of forty thousand dollars. The two men were thrilled to hear that Dex had made it safely to Minneapolis, but at first, they refused to accept the repayment. It was Stuart who finally spoke to Sam over the com and convinced him to accept the money.

"Dex took out a loan from me, and he's repaying you for all your help whether you like it or not. Don't deny him that privilege!"

In the end, they agreed to accept the fund transfer, which made it easier for Dex to talk to them about other things.

"*New Zealand?*" Sam exclaimed. "But how do you know your woman is there?"

"I don't," Dex said. "Not for sure. All I know is that she called Stuart and told him to go there whenever he could. She also said there's going to be a massive Opposition counterstrike. It sounded like an attempt for heterosexuals to reclaim the planet, which means you and Moses might want to steer clear of any of the major cities. Maybe you could use the money to get down to New Zealand, too. Abandon your farm and start a new life, if you can."

Sam took the news with solemn silence. It was Moses who, when Sam handed him the com, said, "This really is it, isn't it? A time of reckoning." When Dex said goodbye to the Archers for the second time, they agreed not to make a fuss of it. It was goodbye for a little while, they all decided. A little while, nothing more. It was an effective way to invoke comfort. Yet it was obvious Sam and Moses knew as well as Dex did that, if he disappeared to New Zealand and found Grace, they would never see each other again.

A MEMORY ✳ (HER)

*H*ERE IS LITTLE RITA, *perfectly new and perfectly innocent, just brought home from the engineering clinic in Minnetonka where Celine gave birth. Linda is cradling her, humming the melody to "Open My Mind" by the Cock Knockers. Celine is lying on the couch, asleep, holding a beer, which she avoided all pregnancy long, at Linda and the doctor's orders. They will feed little Rita with the regular baby formula, even though carriers produce natural milk. Linda has just finished feeding her. Grace watches the joy on her best friend's face and is disgusted at the traces of jealousy snaking through her body, settling in her lower abdomen, which today, for the first time in her life, feels immutably empty, immutably pointless, immutably useless. She will never be able to engineer a child, never have anything that is hers. For homosexuals, lesbians get the short end of the social stick, but compared to heterosteriles, they live lives of utter privilege, because they still have an accepted place in society. At the same time, Grace knows she has no right to complain. She has grown up with two parents, as much money as she could ever need, and creature comforts that would make the vast majority of people alive today quite jealous. Yet her very existence is about to become a vestige of the past. Heterosteriles are not going to be necessary for much longer; of that she is certain. Bioengineers have already finalized at least two models of artificial wombs for human* *gestation. But this is here, this is now, and she should do everything possible to discard those shreds of pessimism, instilled so furtively into her during those years of volunteering, college, and now working her job with the city, which she would not have if her dad hadn't pulled strings with a few of his prestigious friends.*

"Look at her little fingers!" Linda says, stepping closer to Grace. She is thrilled to be a mother. Who wouldn't be? It has been ten years since anybody could freely plan to have a family with any real certainty; the government dictates everything now.

"She's beautiful," Grace replies. She holds a finger out to Rita, who makes the slightest curl of a tiny fist to grab it.

"You've had practice with kids taking care of little Lars," Linda continues. "Any suggestions? We seriously have no idea what we're doing."

Lars. Grace still cannot believe Abraham has a son. Her brother is one of the most insecure and immature people she knows, and not just because his horrible husband Scott spent the first three years of their marriage beating him up and stomping his confidence into the ground. Abraham passed on to Lars his thin, bony genes. That much is already clear. She loves the boy and always will, but she worries about what will become of him.

"Abraham still has no idea what he's doing," Grace tells Linda, hoping the resentment she should not be feeling is transparent. She's almost sure it isn't. She shakes her head, steps back from Linda and Rita, and puts her hands on her hips. Here come tears, embarrassment, shame.

Grace knows what needs to be said. She wastes no more time.

"Linda, I'm jealous. I just want you to know it, because then maybe I can get over it. I'm jealous that you can have a baby. I love you so much, which is why I'm telling you. There, I said it."

Linda's face is unreadable, and she simply stares at Grace for a moment, continuing to rock Rita.

"Rita is beautiful," Grace continues. "Absolutely beautiful. I wish I

could have a baby too, so they could grow up together and be just like us. But it's not going to happen that way, is it?"

They are both crying now. Linda forgives her; of course she does. Grace approaches them again and kisses Rita on the forehead, feeling her velvet-soft skin warm her lips. She takes Rita from Linda's hands and cradles her close, feeling every moment of it, because holding a baby has been and always will be a rare occurrence for her. The Bureau of Genetic Regulation has allotted Linda and Celine only one child. This one is it.

Linda smiles, and the tears on her face shimmer in the afternoon light. "She's just as much your family as I am, Gracie. I wish you could have one, too. God, I really do."

"It'd be a one-way ticket to Antarctica."

They laugh now until they can't stop, and Grace has to sit so she doesn't drop Rita. At this, they laugh even harder. This is friendship; this is love; this is life. It won't last forever.

Grace is relieved. For the moment, her pain, her jealousy, and her sense of worthlessness have lifted.

CHAPTER 51 ✳ (HER)

Ruth, the Cliff House's "single-girl group leader" (as Grace had come to think of her), had befriended an eight-month-pregnant woman named Chloe Zeffarelli, nicknamed "Sister Chloe." By early April, Ruth had joined in leading with Sister Chloe what they called worship socials, congregations that welcomed all women and men in the maternity dorm. In the past two weeks, Grace had attempted to integrate herself with the mountain's other inhabitants, actively seeking them out for conversation, games, and possibly even friendship to pass the time. The effort had not been in vain; at least ten people now knew her name. She was still skeptical of the worship socials, but it was something to do. Chloe had been inside Mount Tasman for five months now, watching her belly grow almost to the point of bursting, and from what Grace gathered during her sermons in the first floor common lounge, she had recently lost a friend through the final hallway, the secret door. Ruth, then, seemed to be a replacement. Chloe, whose jet-black hair and pale face made Grace think of Lars, was a large woman by default. The pregnant belly (twins, a woman named Syl had whispered excitedly to Grace during one of the services) lent the woman an authoritative presence that held many of the women and men of Mount Tasman rapt.

"Soon, I'll be gone," she said with a shudder of ecstasy, on the tenth of April. Both she and Ruth were standing before a congregation of at least two hundred people. The common lounge was overflowing. "Soon, I'll move on to the next section of the mountain where the families live. And am I *scared*?"

"No," Ruth answered for her. The microphone crackled.

Grace was sitting near the front, next to Hilda from the Cliff House. Hilda had been the one woman to warm immediately to Grace's rekindled effort to make friends; the rest of the women she had shared the limousine with still spoke to her with a cold edge. Since they were both alone, Grace and Hilda had become partners for the birthing and mothering classes, which they took together on Wednesdays. There, they learned about different techniques for birthing, how to breastfeed, and how generally to care for infants. Chloe and Ruth were also in the class, where they carried themselves with the same sense of superiority they exuded now.

"And where do I go from here?" Chloe asked the congregation. "Where does my spirit find peace?"

Ruth raised a hand in exaltation. "In God's plan."

The larger woman nodded. "*In God's plan*. This mountain—this final, beautiful resting place for our future—is a fortress of the human spirit. Here, God's secret workers slaving inside the depths of Satan's homosexual regime have created for us a temple of procreation. Of life force. Of the very thing homosexuals sought to snuff out from the beginning!"

Gosh, if only they knew the rest of it, Grace thought to herself. She thought of a world without human beings. It would be peaceful, all right. Empty and peaceful.

Chloe rearranged her feet, a motion which, on her, looked strenuous. "We've all taken baby steps to get to where we are. Jumped off small cliffs, blindfolded, trusting in faith, only to be shown the next jump once there was no way back up again. We've walked by faith, and now we're finally there. Won over by hope. A team, at its core, completely humanitarian. God led us here, and soon, I will write my name on the Wall of the Future and move deeper inside our new mountain dwelling. Our home at the end of the NRO's filthy rainbow."

"Amen," Ruth said. She lowered her hands and bowed her head in solemn reverence to Chloe's words.

"Which means, of course, that I, like Sister Felicity and Brother James before me, will be passing along the torch of worship. This time, it will go to Sister Ruth. From what I have gathered in my five months here, worship socials have been a tradition for newcomers to the mountain since the first group of refugees arrived here eight years ago. Eight years' worth of women, men, and children, growing into a new society to ensure human survival!"

Many in the congregation cheered. Grace glanced over her left shoulder. She had seen somebody come into the room and stand against the wall, near the door. It was Orion Skelby. He stood with his arms folded, looking with a skeptical expression at Sister Ruth. Then, his gaze scanned the crowd and rested on Grace. He gave her a subtle wave. Was she mistaken, or had his skepticism just arched into a grimace?

He gave Grace a nod, then walked out.

SINCE BECOMING FRIENDS IN FEBRUARY, Grace and Hilda had developed a tradition of making weekly trips to the deck early on Friday mornings to watch the sun rise over the mountains. It was early enough that there were rarely any others enjoying the holosphere, and they had privacy. As they had grown bigger, they puffed their ways down to the deck and eased themselves onto the real mountain rock that formed the ground. Most often, they talked about the lives they had left behind. Hilda's background could not have been more different from Grace's. Before finding her way to the Cliff House, she had worked as a drug runner and occasional prostitute in downtown Minneapolis. Both her fathers had succumbed to purposeful overdoses (they had even left a note) and left Hilda, an only child of fourteen, with nothing. That was eight years ago, just after Mandate 39 had prohibited public social and medical benefits to heterosteriles and failsafes, regardless of age. The bank had repossessed their home, and the teenage girl had been kicked out, onto the street. For being a woman colored by such misfortune, she had a remarkably gentle demeanor. Now, she was five months pregnant, a month behind Grace.

It was the Friday after Sister Chloe had christened Ruth the new leader of the worship socials, and Grace and Hilda were awake before everyone else, watching their weekly sunrise on the deck.

"It's hard to believe we've been here for over two months," Hilda was saying, digging her fingers into some of the loose rock on the mountaintop. To their left, the kea bird marking the holosphere's exit shook off its virtual feathers, which glowed in the golden morning light.

"Almost ready for our little girls to open their eyes on the world," Grace said. "You know, I wish we could give birth in here. At least they'd see something pretty when they come out."

Hilda grinned. "I don't think they can see much right after they hatch. Dr. Thrace says it takes a while."

Grace quivered in disgust at this use of the word "hatch," and her friend giggled. It was a common phrase to exit Hilda's mouth, especially around all the pregnant women.

Suddenly, Hilda's grin disappeared into a confused expression. "Ouch! What is . . .?" Her arm stiffened as she felt something in the loose rocks. Her fingers fumbled with the ground for a moment, and then she pulled up something metal. It was one of the cafeteria forks. "Ha. Looks like someone ate their dinner here. Litterbugs."

"They obviously had no regard for nature," Grace joked.

From somewhere in the distance came the rumbling echo of an avalanche. Grace looked from the fork to the face of Mount Cook. Sure enough, a river of snow was tumbling from one of its ridges.

"Hey, there's something written on it." Hilda held the fork closer and examined its handle. Her face contorted in confusion, then fear. "Look." She handed it to Grace.

There they were, written in black permanent ink, three tiny phrases that pummeled Grace in the gut and shattered all shreds of hope she had managed to piece together since arriving in New Zealand. The ink covered both sides of the fork's handle:

> *There is no dorm past the Wall. They send you to the*
> *Sanctuary anyway. I should have let my baby die.*
> *—EAV*

CHAPTER 52 ❄ (HIM)

O N THE TWELFTH OF APRIL, two things of significance happened: First, and it came as an announcement on WorldCom's morning news by General Thomas Helio, the New Rainbow Order opened skies to commercial airlines once again. Piggybacking on it was a new but expected development: as there were still terror suspects at large, only homosexuals could travel, and each would have to undergo a background check by scanning his or her TruthChip upon arrival at the airport. It would be no different from train travel, so Dex was confident his new identity would allow him through.

Second, just seventeen minutes after General Helio's announcement ended, Stuart's pocket com buzzed on the dresser. He picked it up and held it out to Dex, looking both anxious and excited.

"Unverifiable address!" he said. Over the past week, Stuart had missed three untraceable calls, each time because he had been too slow to answer his com.

Dex almost choked on the glob of yogurt he had just eaten. "Hurry this time! It could be Grace!"

Stuart fumbled for his com, then answered. His exclamatory expression froze. As he listened to the person speak, his hope turned sour.

"So, it's *you* who has been trying to call," Stuart said. "You're about three months late. You never returned my messages about the rental car."

Oh my God.

Dex jumped off the bed and into Stuart's face. "Is that *Sheila Willy*?"

Stuart nodded. "Miss Willy, I'm listening, but before you go any further, there's someone here who would like to say hello." He handed the com to Dex, who brought it to his ear so quickly that he hit the side of his head.

"Oh shit...Sheila? It's Dex! Dex Wheelock!"

"You're shitting me," came the scarecrow woman's voice after a long pause.

"I'm afraid not," Dex replied, grinning.

Sheila mixed a gasp with a chuckle. "So you got your second chance after all. I must admit, I'm shocked. Glad and shocked. I saw your face on the news after the raid."

"And what about you? I heard you left Grace, too. Did you get her to the Cliff House?"

"I did my part," Sheila said, sounding resolute.

Dex shook his head, struggling not to show his frustration. "So why call now? We've been calling your com every day for weeks, and it's gone straight to voice message."

"Like it or not, Dex, I'm a human being too, and let's just say I've been brooding over a particularly crappy decision. I ditched that com, because I'm a new person now. I'm a lesbian named Wanda Tykes, born January the sixteenth, 2355. Chip and com replacement at the Cliff House. Grace got the same thing, but her com can only receive calls. Of course, nobody has the address. The Opposition didn't want any of their girls to accidentally slip and let loose sensitive information."

"Well, you're a bundle of sensitive information," Dex said. "How come they gave you a normal com?"

"Because I demanded it, and I threatened to tell the refugees at the Cliff House what I knew. By the way, any audio, video, and hologram data sent from my com is scrambled, so whatever I say is safe. Safe as coms can be, anyway."

The men had more questions, and Sheila had answers. Dex switched Stuart's com to holo-mode, and Sheila's orange hair sprang to life. It seemed the woman had loosened her pride about the Opposition since the night of the raid; now, there was a trace of bitterness in her tone when she spoke of it. Yes, she had left the Cliff House, and no, she had not told Grace about her plan to desert it. After driving the rental car Stuart had provided back to the Minneapolis area, she had rented another car and disappeared to her great aunt's cabin outside of La Crosse. She had known about the agenda set for Grace and the other pregnant women, and a man named Albert Redmond, who ran Carnevale's Cliff House, had given her the option to follow.

"It's a funny thing," Sheila said. "I fell in love once, and only once, and it was with the man who first brought me to the Cliff House. He decided to follow the Opposition to a place they wouldn't let me go to. He was afraid of the future, and I became a casualty of that. When I was at the Cliff House with Grace, I had a chance to speak with him over a com there. He arranged it that I could finally come and join him, only then, I was the one who was too afraid. That's why I left. Now, I heard from him again, and he says they're giving me another chance. If I go, it really is the end of everything I know. Assuming my new chip works to let me travel, I still have a choice to follow Grace, and that's the clincher."

Stuart leaned in toward the small com hologram. "To New Zealand, you mean? Is she really there?"

"Which is half the reason I'm *calling*," Sheila continued. "She met my man. His name's Orion, and he saw on her registration that I was the one who recruited her to the Opposition."

"Well, Fletch helped," Dex said. The recollection of his friend's torn-up body lying dead in the cornfield came as a shock. It always did.

"Oh, dear Fletch!" Sheila exclaimed. "How is our favorite little prejaculator doing?"

"He's dead."

Sheila's gimmicky sarcasm fizzled, and her expression became serious. "Oh," she said. Her gaze wandered to some point outside the hologram's capture field. "I didn't know."

Stuart jumped back in. "But Grace? You know she's alive? Can we get to her?"

"Quite frankly, I don't think so," Sheila said. "But I'm the best hope you have to get in. If you're going to New Zealand, you're going to need me there. The thing is, I haven't had the money for a flight since Orion cleared me to join him, and I chickened out when I had the option to go with Grace's group."

"Just where *is* this facility?" Stuart asked.

Sheila told them, and the very idea came like a cold whisper on the back of Dex's neck.

Grace and our baby are inside a mountain.

The woman described what she had been told about the facility, chuckling half the time for some reason Dex could not infer. He found nothing funny about a sunless mountain reserve supposedly filled with thousands of pregnant women, children, and failsafes. How could they ever have planned for enough space? Wouldn't it become cramped? Wouldn't they run out of artificial greenhouse space, eventually? Dex was about to ask these obvious questions when Sheila's words froze the breath in his chest.

"But it's all a hoax."

Keep talking. . . .

"What do you mean 'a hoax'?" Stuart demanded.

"Meaning all those pregnant women down there aren't *staying* in the mountain. They're going to Antarctica."

"*God almighty damn it to hell!*" Stuart screamed, and he slammed his fists onto the desk.

Dex's com-holding hand had broken a sweat and was shaking. "Do they know?" he whispered.

"Orion says they'll find out after they give birth. It's part of the Opposition's strategy for a lot of reasons, I guess. Mostly because they wouldn't *have* an Opposition if Bozarth and company's pregnant women knew what it would mean to take a stand against the NRO. Most of the women who don't want to risk illegal abortions are so scared they'll do anything else to avoid banishment to Antarctica. They seek out help. They find it. They see an opportunity to hope, and they go to Mount Tasman so they can carry their pregnancies to term. They're made to think it's the last stop, but really it isn't. Once they have a baby to take care of and their only option is to let the Opposition relocate them to Antarctica, they can't object."

"*Jesus Christ,*" Stuart seethed. "Who told you all this?"

"Orion. He told me when I spoke to him from the Cliff House in January."

Dex was numb. The news was so horrible, so unthinkable. The God he thought had whispered to him on the train might as well have been a devil. "So it was all for nothing," he said.

"Oh, no, it isn't for nothing," Sheila said.

She's smiling, Dex thought, looking at the woman's holographic face. *She's actually smiling.*

"Frederik Carnevale's Opposition has passed a tipping point of influence against the NRO, and it's winning," she continued. "What NRO officials haven't told us and WorldCom and even its own military is that the Opposition has infiltrated the Sanctuary. It's ours. And we have nuclear missiles, sonic ray bombs, and every other type of weapon under the sun ready to mount a strike on all populated NRO territories. The Opposition is collecting fertile heterosexuals in Antarctica, and they have the NRO at a stalemate. When they collect enough to maintain humanity at the Sanctuary long enough to outlive the destruction they plan to unleash, they're going to blow the populated world sky high."

The Opposition was broader in scope than Dex ever imagined. The New Rainbow Order, for all its clout, had been losing its battle in silence.

"So, *that's* the reason I left the Cliff House without telling Grace why," Sheila said. "I couldn't bear to tell her the truth."

Stuart buried his head in his hands. "And now she's down there. Oblivious. Just waiting to be shipped off to that God-awful place."

"Desperate times call for desperate measures," Sheila said. "Haven't you heard about the trains the fags have been emptying out all the heterosexuals on? They're bringing every registered hetero-sexual in for social assessment and questioning, detaining them, then sending them off on trains. We've finally come to a head. It's happening all over the world."

Through his disgust, Dex chuckled. "Yeah, I know all about that. Remind me to tell you sometime."

"So, you still want to go to New Zealand, Dex? Be part of the Opposition that you were too afraid to join the first time? I promise I'll do everything to have Orion get you in. And you can meet your baby."

There was no choice, really. Not anymore. But it was Stuart who voiced it.

"Ms. Willy, you better make your way to Minneapolis. When you're here, I'm booking us all flights to New Zealand. In return, you do everything you can to help Dex and me see my daughter again."

THE AIR TRAVEL RESTRICTIONS WERE PHASED OUT SLOWLY. As stranded passengers had first dibs on all flights, the earliest tickets to New Zealand Stuart could book were for the twentieth of April. Sheila agreed to meet him and Dex at Twin Cities Intercontinental Airport the evening their flight departed.

Dex and Stuart stopped by Linda Glass's house on their way

there to say goodbye. Linda crushed Stuart's neck in her arms. "This is one of those forever goodbyes, isn't it?" Stuart nodded. Both their faces glistened with tears. Stuart had already signed an electronic fund transfer to Linda for two million dollars and sent it to her com. Now, in their embrace, Stuart was whispering, begging her to use the money to keep her family safe. In a burst of sobs, she finally nodded, and Stuart squeezed her extra tight. When Linda pulled back from the hug, she held a hand up. "I know you have to go, but give me two seconds. I want you to give something to Grace, if you ever find her." She rushed into her bedroom. Dex heard a drawer open and close, then silence. When Linda returned, she was wearing red lipstick. Handing Stuart a small brown envelope, she sniffed and wiped her tears. "Don't forget." On the envelope was a bright red kiss mark from Linda's voluptuous lips. She hugged Stuart again, then Dex.

"Leave as soon as you can," Dex whispered. A minute later, they were off.

By nightfall, they were cruising on Cher Airlines to Auckland, New Zealand's main air hub. From there, they would catch a flight to Christchurch on the South Island, just six hours' drive from the Mount Tasman facility where Grace was supposedly hiding. Stuart, Dex, and Sheila all sat together. Sheila settled into her seat and fell asleep. Stuart drummed his fingertips on his knees while waiting for departure, then closed his eyes and grabbed the arm rests as the hydro plane took off. Dex himself had never flown before. Apart from it being expensive, there was nowhere in the continental territory worth traveling to. Only brave people traveled overseas, and until recently, he had never been one of those. Today, they had been lucky; none of their TruthChips were flagged in the identity database. They were in the air, free.

The hydro plane cruised toward the ozone, and Dex was awed when he looked out the window during sunset and saw mountains far, far below. *The Unrecoverable Territories*, he thought. *I wonder if Exander ever made it.*

They arrived into Auckland at 9:55 in the evening on April twenty-first. Two hours later, they were in Christchurch, in a taxi, on their way to a hotel for the evening. Dex had seen nothing of the territory on the way in, and now, the city was nothing but passing lights. Off to the west were mountains, the taxi driver told them. He was a stout, bald man who seemed particularly proud of his homeland. The town they needed to get to was called Franz Josef, Sheila had said, but when Stuart accidentally mentioned it in passing, the driver turned his head backward, in confusion.

"Franz Josef? Nothing there but a fuel station, mate. What's your interest in that place?"

"I just heard of it once," Stuart replied. Nobody spoke until they reached the hotel, where he paid the driver with a quick scan of his TruthChip.

Sheila made a call and left a message for her friend Orion, letting him know they had arrived in Christchurch. Last they heard, Orion had not yet cleared Dex and Stuart for transfer to Mount Tasman. Sheila, however, had put in a good word for both men. They would be driving to Franz Josef in the morning to await further instruction. If Orion could pull the right strings, they would all be inside the mountain by tomorrow evening. Grace was due in just over two months, which meant their secret transfer to Antarctica would come faster than Dex wanted to imagine. This was his age of bravery, however, and the crumbling world around him somehow made this future seem adequate.

"Now, we wait," Sheila said, hanging up her com. She dug inside the hotel's mini-refrigerator and pulled out three small bottles of whiskey. "To the future!" she said, throwing one each to Dex and Stuart.

They drank themselves into a healthy oblivion, laughing all the way, celebrating the lives they had led and being content that, at least for a time, they had been lucky enough to experience the world at all.

CHAPTER 53 ✳ (HER)

G RACE HAD BEEN BURSTING with a mixture of anger, excitement, and terror for the past ten days. On the twelfth of April, the day Hilda had nearly been punctured by the prophetic fork, they had returned to the halls of the maternity dorm in a shell-shocked state of contemplation. They ate breakfast in silence, then ascended to the facility's top level to sit under the Wall of the Future, where they spent the entire day deliberating over the fork's meaning. Who had written it? Could it be real? Were the Cliff House and this mountain asylum really the ultimate con she had feared? They looked at the hundreds of names and messages scribbled onto the wall. Could it really be possible all these people had been sent to Antarctica? When Grace roamed into the cafeteria that evening, it was as if she were on the outside, looking in.

"Do we tell people?" Hilda whispered.

Grace spotted their usual group of women at a table far across the cafeteria. They were all convulsing with laugher. "I don't think we should," she replied. "At least not until I can talk to Orion."

"Even so, do you think it'd be right? To dash everyone's hope?"

It was a valid argument. Selfless, too. It was not the first time since joining the Opposition that Grace had to face a moral dilemma: Expose an untruth, or keep a secret for the greater good? What gave her hope were those nefarious bits of information Lieutenant Helio had left her with, and she shared them with Hilda now. The Queen and his government were afraid due to whatever had happened in Antarctica. If this was so and if the words on the fork were true, it seemed as though her original instincts had been correct: the Opposition was using the Sanctuary to serve its own agenda. It was the same horrible end she had always feared, but it was now a means for something altogether hopeful.

Even so, anxiety held her in a vise grip. Wilkes Land was the region of Antarctic coastline south of the Indian and Southern Oceans, just west of Victoria Land. Until 2248 when the New Rainbow Order overtook the continent and banned all scientific research there, Wilkes Land had been claimed by what remained of civilized Australia and France. Grace knew only what she had learned through the government's public education system, but it was enough to give her an idea: the Wilkes Land Sanctuary stood atop thousands of feet of ice, which lay above ground that had not seen the light of day for millions of years. Built on ungodly strong metal stilts that ran five hundred feet down, the Sanctuary was a series of conjoined artificial biospheres covering a radius of over five miles. It was considered one of the Nine Wonders of the World, a feat of human engineering genius yet to be matched. It had solar and nuclear power centers, neighborhoods, farms, irrigation systems, water recycling facilities, animal reproduction centers for meat, and anything else one might need to survive in the frozen, lifeless desert.

Grace's life had come to a place where she could no longer predict the future with any real faith. The truth of this was terrifying, but the reality of knowing life might become her most reviled nightmare was even worse. To her surprise, Orion had approached her in the hallway after breakfast, the morning following Hilda's discovery of the fork. Grace was about to unleash her worries on him, but he spoke first.

"I have news."

She put a hand on the hallway wall to brace herself. "News? What news?"

Orion's messages to Sheila Willy had paid off. The carrot-haired woman had finally called him back, and with information that was about to make Grace's day: her dad, her failsafe Dex, and Sheila herself were all still alive and would soon be traveling to New Zealand in hopes of reconvening with the Opposition. It took a moment for Grace to register Orion's words. Then, an amalgamation of shock, relief, and joy seemed to lift her clear off the floor. For all the uncertainties plaguing her, here was a spark of elation strong enough to counter them. As had become habit, she looked down at her growing belly. "Did you *hear* that?" she exclaimed to her daughter. "They're coming! Your daddy and grandpa are *coming!*"

Orion grinned. "I'm doing everything I can to get them all here. But there might be a problem. I *think* I can get your failsafe to come in with Sheila Willy. Technically, he should be allowed in without much question, though Sheila tells me he's had a chip replacement outside of Opposition circles, so he will register as a homosexual. I'll beg the administration to let Sheila vouch for him, and we'll bring you in if necessary. The problem is with your father."

"My dad," Grace corrected.

"Homosexuals are less likely to get clearance to the mountain. They'll consume unnecessary resources."

"But it won't matter," Grace said, the gears of rationality grinding in her head. "Antarctica is self-sufficient, isn't it? Won't there be enough food?"

Orion's face went pale, and Grace realized what had slipped out of her mouth. For a moment, they stared at each other, sizing up the truths they were both holding back. Three women passed between them. They waddled down the hall, giggling, blissful and ignorant.

Orion gritted his teeth. "What do you mean by that?"

Grace told him about the fork. He listened with a pensive

expression, which became almost dolent as he tried to formulate a response.

"I had no idea anybody figured it out," he whispered. "People are usually told once they pass through the door, on their ride to the rear hover jet platform. We give them insulated jackets to keep warm for when they land in the Sanctuary's main entry. By that point it's all pretty obvious, I think."

"But you're duping them," Grace said, feeling broken.

Orion looked to the ground, and for a few seconds, he simply breathed. When he looked up, there were tears in his eyes. "I hate myself every day for having to lie. It's all I can do not to seek out Carnevale himself and beg that he be honest with everyone. But word would get out to the public, and there'd be a mass panic. Because there's something else. . . ."

He told Grace about the Sanctuary, how the Opposition had overtaken it. They had an imminent counterstrike in place that was keeping the New Rainbow Order in a deadlock. For the first time in two hundred years, the world government had a legitimate revolution on its hands, and it had no solution.

"Have you seen the Sanctuary?" Grace asked. "Do you know it's true?"

Orion nodded. "Yes, I've seen it. Pictures, anyway. Frederik Carnevale goes down there about three times a year to check on everyone's progress. I've seen pictures of families. *Natural* families, standing with Carnevale. Everyone is smiling, because . . . they know what they are."

"The future."

If her dad or Dex could accompany her to the Sanctuary, she would still have a life, just as those smiling people had. Love and family made for happiness, did it not? The only truly horrible thing would be if the dumping ground rumors were true, but she now doubted them. If the government had secretly lost the Sanctuary to enemy hands, what better way to continue generating fear in the general public than by pretending nothing was wrong? Disseminating vague rumors was a perfect way to cause confusion.

"Did you tell anyone about this?" Orion asked.

"No," Grace replied. "Hilda Leopke is the only other one who knows. She didn't want to tell anybody else."

"It would cause an uproar."

"So it's really true? That's where they take us after we go through that blast door?"

"You'll have a week in the mountain's hospital wing after you give birth, unless there are complications with you or the baby that require more time. But then, yes, you'll be transferred. But Grace . . ." Orion shook his head in worry. "You can't tell a soul. Do you think anybody would have joined the Opposition if they'd known we'd overtaken the Sanctuary? Without this lie, we wouldn't *have* an Opposition. Going to Antarctica has been everyone's nightmare for the past seventy years. I didn't know the truth myself until I elected to be transferred down here. We're interested in saving as many lives as possible before the counterstrike, and I saw it as the only way out. At the time, Sheila did not."

"But now, she does."

"Now, she does. The counterstrike will happen very soon."

The next nine days passed so slowly that all Grace wanted to do in her waking hours was sit on the deck and talk to her little girl, the baby who would soon be seeing the world. On the night Stuart, Dex, and Sheila arrived in New Zealand, Orion updated Grace. He had spoken to Sheila and directed all three of them to drive to the fuel station in Franz Josef, and while Dex had been cleared for transfer to Mount Tasman, her dad had not. For Grace's sake, Orion had scheduled a meeting for the next morning with the mountain's administrative offices to make one last case for Stuart.

"It's not looking good," he whispered on his way out.

But at the very least, my little girl will have a father.

The dichotomy that formed in Grace—fear and elation frolicking together, or perhaps it was the simple miracle of pregnancy—had built so steadily over the week that her appetite, her ability to sleep, and even her bathroom habits had stopped working with any sort of synchronicity. Sheila, Dex, and her dad's looming arrival in New Zealand had been enough to drive her wild with speculation. She had scores of questions, but it was Dex she was most curious about—that man who so fleetingly seemed as if he might devote himself to their child. She had seen his face pasted on WorldCom first among those caught in the Sterile Me Susan's raid, then along with the supposed escaped God's Army prisoners the Queen claimed were responsible for the attacks. Surely he had spent time in jail, but how had he escaped? How had he managed to get back together with her dad? Furthermore, there existed potential for familial concerns in the near future. Dex had another child, a son from Diana Kring named Michael, if the Wall of the Future was to be believed. They would also be in Antarctica. Would he eventually find Diana there and have to make a choice between his two families? Did the concept of family even matter at the Sanctuary?

Time will tell, she told herself. *Just relax, and hope for the best.*

Hilda waited in the cafeteria with her the next day, and they discussed Grace's worries until there was nothing left to say. It was Hilda who had the last good word.

"You're lucky you're getting your failsafe back." She took a scoop of Grace's untouched frozen yogurt. "I wish all of us could have that."

It was almost four o'clock when, finally, Orion appeared in the doorway to the cafeteria. It was impossible to tell by his cryptic expression whether he had been successful in arguing a case for her dad. He raised a hand and jerked his neck toward the loading dock, beckoning for Grace to follow.

A MEMORY ✳ (HIM)

DEX GRINDS COFFEE BEANS in the kitchen wearing only his boxer shorts, feeling the Indian summer breeze flow through the open window and onto his skin. It is Saturday morning. Diana is asleep in the bedroom, a beauty to behold, and for the first time in his life, he wonders if he is in love. In all his years, he never thought it would happen, never once gave the possibility a fighting chance. For all that is wrong in the world—yes, it is getting more terrifying by the day, because the Queen shows no signs of backing down, and heterosexuals are on the verge of being all-out scapegoats for everything broken in society—this moment, as he breathes in the autumn air and pours the coffee grounds into the filter, knowing he has found something good, brings a sense of serenity he had no idea he was missing. This is what the homosexual majority has been telling him he has no right to have, to experience, to cherish. For thirty-six years—in just four days, the nineteenth of September, it will be thirty-seven—he let himself believe them.

A dove lands on the thin ledge outside the kitchen window. Dex is lucky to have a corner unit, even though the apartment is fairly cheap compared to the nicer ones around town. The dove flaps its wings, as if to dust them off, but stays on the ledge. Dex swears it sees him, and he waves, smiling. It is refreshing to feel silly once in a while. Diana has been nervous lately, due to Mandate 43, she says, and it has made him nervous as well. Today, however, the world is bright, warm, intoxicating—one of the last days of summer they will see this year.

Last night, he said "I love you" to Diana. Instead of saying it back, she had only smiled, then kissed him, then invited him inside her. Her sexual expression told him everything he needed to know, at least for that moment. He will try again this morning. He'll say it as she walks out the door, after they cook breakfast together, after they make love again.

No woman has ever said "I love you" to Dex in the romantic sense. He would admit only to himself it has been a life dream of sorts: to find heterosexual love, to hear the words of it flow from a woman's mouth, to share in something of that magnitude, even just for a moment.

Dex smiles, then starts the coffee. In the bedroom behind him, the covers rustle. Diana is awake. "Coffee's coming," he says.

But the bottle of cream in the refrigerator is empty, something he should have recycled yesterday but was too lazy to wash out. Both he and Diana love cream. It is a treat, a drop of richness with which to welcome the day.

He skips to the bedroom, throws on a shirt and his flannel pajama pants, then dashes out of the room, whispering, "Gotta get some cream. I'll be right back." Diana's feet move as she stretches to welcome the morning, but she says nothing. Coffee first, words later. In the two months they've been dating seriously, he has learned this is her daily order of operation.

On his way out, he glides his hand over Diana's overnight bag, which sits in a chair at his kitchen table-for-one. In five minutes, he will be back in the apartment with cream, ready to bring her coffee in bed. It will be a good day.

CHAPTER 54 ✳ (HIM)

THE MOUNTAINS SWAM UNDER THE HOVER JET, their rugged, snowy peaks cutting into the sky like godly spires. The steady *thwump-thwump-thwump* of the machine drummed in Dex's ears. Sheila sat next to him, staring out the window, over the jagged ridges. The colossal, ice-capped Mount Tasman was slowly overtaking the window in front of them.

"Take care of her, Dex," Stuart had told him in Franz Josef, sobbing into his shoulder. "Take care of my little girl. Tell her I love her more than anything in the world. And that I would have followed her to the end."

Stuart was a homosexual. An inspiring, good, and perfectly loving homosexual. He was a human being of the highest order, yet they had not cleared him for transfer to the mountain. The only thing he had to offer the future of the human race was love, but it seemed that was not good enough. It was a cruel verdict.

A black car was waiting for them at the fuel station in the tiny, soon-to-be abandoned town. The driver, a brown-skinned man with a tribal tattoo covering his face, approached the travelers, verified their identities, and delivered the news that would surely crush Grace to pieces.

"I'm sorry, but I have clearance only for you and the woman," the tattooed man said to Dex. He turned to Stuart. "You, sir, will have to stay." He explained the administration's decision, and Stuart accepted it with a stoic nod. Then he crumbled under his grief. Dex held him. When they parted, Stuart dug into his coat pocket and handed Dex a crumpled envelope.

"For Grace. From Linda." The envelope with the red kiss mark.

"I'll give it to her. And Stuart . . . thank you. For everything."

"Thank *you*," Stuart replied. "Thanks for not giving up on her. And on yourself, with all you went through."

"It happened because I ran in the first place. Fear won't get me anywhere, I've learned."

"Share that sentiment with my Grace, will you? She'd appreciate that."

"I think she's already living it," Dex said. He stood on his tip-toes and kissed Stuart on the forehead, hugged him again, and promised to contact him if it ever became possible. Stuart planned to attempt survival in New Zealand for as long as he could. If they never spoke again, the very least Dex could do was give the man's daughter love every day and do all he could to ensure she and the new child were happy.

Stuart managed to smile as Dex climbed into the black sedan with Sheila. They waved goodbye as it pulled away into a forest of sparkling, tangled trees.

Now, the hover jet. It sailed toward Mount Tasman, climbing over lush valleys and serrated peaks, giving Dex the most spectacular view of his life. He took it in, letting it wash through his soul, knowing it would be one of the last times he saw such beauty. But the ride was short. After only fifteen minutes, the hover jet descended into a shallow gorge just above the bush line, on one of the rocky crests leading upward.

"You ready, Dexy?" Sheila said, grinning. Her smile was, for the first time since he had known her, alive, touched by the anticipation of love. Dex felt the same type of smile form on his own lips. He looked out the window at the landing pad built into the valley. It was near a rectangular opening in the side of the mountain.

There, wrapped in a thick jacket with her dark hair sailing in the wind, was Grace Jarvis. Her belly was round under the coat, and she stood with the elegance and simple beauty of a woman on the brink of sharing life with the world.

CHAPTER 55 ❄ (HER)

THE COLD ALPINE WIND BEAT ON GRACE'S FACE, whipping her hair into a frenzy under the dazzling afternoon sun. It was glorious to be outdoors again, for what could feasibly be the last meaningful time in her life. She had grown accustomed to the ventilated facility air and artificial breeze on the deck, but no synthetic sunlight could compare to the real thing. It beat down on her face, her eyelids, her lips—a divine heat warming her entire being.

I hope our little girl can feel this someday.

She had asked—no, *begged*—Orion to let her accompany him to the hover jet platform so she could greet Dex and Sheila when they arrived. There was a part of her that still hoped, despite having no reason, to see her dad. She stood there, next to Orion's motorized cart, peering into the sky, searching for the source of that unmistakable vibration. They were getting closer.

Maybe the driver let Dad come. Maybe somebody remembered what it's like to act human, and they made an exception.

She would know in a matter of minutes. But she was determined to be happy and grateful, even if it was only Dex and Sheila on the hover jet. Orion had prepared her for it, so there would be no reason to mope. Dex was the baby's father, and he would be joining her in

Antarctica. That alone was reason to rejoice. They would be fighting together to save humanity.

And there it was: the hover jet, humming through the sky, appearing like a sparkle as the sun shone off its glass windows.

Grace smiled.

CHAPTER 56 ❄ (HIM)

THE HOVER JET TOUCHED DOWN on a cleared strip of the landing pad. Dex and Sheila looked at each other with exhilarated grins. Grace and the man she was standing with were no longer visible, as the hover jet had shifted its angle. The pilot kept its rotary engines running and jumped out to open the door for them. It was freezing up here, and the sleek black coat Stuart had purchased for Dex did little to ward off the alpine wind.

He followed Sheila out onto the cement platform. When they reached the other side of the hover jet, they both stopped, looking at their respective goals that were suddenly personified.

Wiping tears, Sheila dashed forward, and the mohawked man standing next to Grace ran to meet her.

Now, it was Dex's turn, but he would not run. He *could* not. Last time he had laid eyes on Grace, he had ripped her heart in two, ignored their shared plight, and decided to take the selfish road.

Seeing Grace now, he was ready to love her. But she had no reason to love him.

A MEMORY ✳ (HER)

GRACE GATHERS HER DARK HAIR into a ponytail, then realizes her face is far too round to have her hair pulled all the way back. She listens to the part of herself that says she looks like a five-year-old, shunning the trickle of confidence whispering that she has, in truth, become a beautiful woman.

Tonight is a party with Todd Bender, though she is starting to doubt they have any future together. Three days ago, Todd told her he might be developing a sexual interest in men, even though his TruthChip clearly labels him a failsafe. He was not convincing whatsoever, and Grace knows it's because his father is a priest who hates heterosexuals. Todd simply wants to have an easy, normal life, but the sad thing is that his effort to do so will be completely futile.

His friend Fletch is a pig, so if the party isn't any fun, she'll come home immediately. Being social tonight is important, because Grace feels she is disappearing into the world's woodwork, behind the dust trail of youth and hope and meaning. She grew up wanting to leave a mark on this ailing civilization, but if she is to be honest with herself, nothing in life has worked out in line with her idealism. All she has to do to remind herself of this is think about the Dyke Patrol and the fists beating down on her face that night, outside Pommie's Pub. That had shown her the real truth about things, hadn't it?

The Obesaland project is still under-funded, and she fears it will get the ax any day now. The Queen is on the verge of rebuilding a full-on dictatorship at a level not seen since just after the Bio Wars, and this time, there is no real reason for it other than for the government to have control. And her own life: over half her family supports the Queen's regime, even though they don't say it to her face, and Linda is her only close friend. Nothing is certain, except for this moment, this choice to take one night at a time and experience new corners of life while she still can.

For all she knows, joy is hiding in the shadows.

CHAPTER 57 ❄ (HER)

Dex Wheelock looked like a new man. He was bald now, standing in a black coat that hung almost to his knees. He stood with a new sort of confidence, which made him look taller, more dignified, like a man who had finally accepted the road he was paving through life as his own. Gone was the trembling man who had left her at Sterile Me Susan's.

Here was her daughter's father.

Only when tears froze on Grace's face did she realize she was crying. Her storm of emotions broke into a smile, and she moved toward Dex. She was self-conscious; walking was more like waddling now. But it was because of him, of them both. It was a million years ago, that night at Fletch Novotny's apartment. Now, it mattered not at all, and it mattered in every way. Here they were, on a hidden mountain ridge at the end of the world.

And then Dex was sailing toward her, crying, and there was no hesitation as he met her with a kiss. It was the longest, fullest, and happiest kiss Grace had ever experienced in her short, mystifying life, and for a second, it was all that mattered.

We're home, she thought as Dex pushed his body against her pregnant belly. Now, they were a family.

A MEMORY ✳ (HIM)

*D*EX FEELS HIMSELF *putting on a spray of cologne, his underwear, his pants, his shirt, a black stone necklace, socks, and shoes, but his anger and grief and fear and worthlessness are at the forefront of his consciousness, clear indicators that nothing about this night or life will be any different from what he always should have expected. He wants to hate Diana for leaving him, but he cannot, and this makes him angry, because he knows it was real love. If she left him because she was unhappy, that was for the best, because he wanted and still wants happiness for her. Yet the prospect that he was somehow a thorn in her life makes him sick to his stomach. To have been so duped into love feels like a razor cutting into his soul and removing the part that makes him human.*

And so he needs to feel angry at Diana. He needs to throw himself in the face of what they had together, succumb to what is sure to be another Fletch Novotny orgy. He had been an aimless man before Diana. He can become one again.

Dex tells himself there is a certain brand of contentment in aimlessness and complacency, outside the world of love and intimacy. If only he can find it and harness it, he can laugh the happy memories away, even make the thought of them, of anything better in life, a joke.

The way society is going, there will be no more chances to experience joy. That ship has sailed. He leaves his apartment building and walks into the night, resigned to endure a future of emptiness.

CHAPTER 58 ✳ (HIM)

"I'm so sorry," he cried in her ear. "I ruined everything."

Grace stroked his head. It was rough; he had been shaving it. "No, you didn't. You're here. That's all that matters. We're together."

"Your dad—"

"Orion tried everything, but they wouldn't have it. No homosexuals. They're transferring us all to Antarctica—"

"I know. Sheila told me. She knew all along. I should let her explain—"

"It doesn't matter. None of it does. Is my dad okay? Is he staying here in New Zealand?"

"If he can. He wants to disappear and try to survive what's coming. There's so much he wanted to say to you, Grace. He wants you to know he loves you *so much*. And he does. You're all he was thinking about."

"And my father?"

"I never heard. Your dad left, and your father never came after him."

They continued to hold each other. Dex glanced left, where Sheila and Orion were doing the same, whispering their own secrets to one another. Grace would have questions for Sheila, surely, but right now, it seemed to be the last thing on her mind. They would have time, at least before the baby came. *The baby.*

Dex pulled Grace's coat apart and put his hands on her swollen belly, feeling how warm, fluid, and incredible it was. He had never felt a carrier, never even seen one up close. It defied description for him, and the only thing he could think was, *This is why life is such a miracle. Why every single person is worth cherishing, no matter who they are.*

"It's a little girl," Grace said.

Giddiness colored Dex all over. He knelt down and examined Grace more closely. Then, still on his knees, he hugged her again.

"A girl! They told you?"

"When I got here."

"Do you have any names picked out?"

Grace shook her head. "I'm hoping we can do that together."

A minute later, Orion ushered them all onto the cart, and they drove through the opening in the cliff. Dex saw that a frame was built into the rock, hidden underneath a natural stone awning. From far above, if for some reason Frederik Carnevale opened the air space over his mountain, only the hover jet landing pad would be obvious, if it was not covered in snow. The scale of the man's rebellion left Dex mystified, awed, and grateful. He held Grace's hand on the cart, imagining the energy passing between them, into the soul of their unborn child. What he wanted to send to that little girl inside was hope—hope that her life would be a series of positive events, that all the things neither she nor her parents could control would still grant her the possibility of a future.

CHAPTER 59 ❄ (HER)

GRACE AND DEX EXCHANGED STORIES. That circumstances had intertwined to bring them full circle, back into each other's arms, was, according to Dex, a miracle. For Grace, being with him again was like breathing those precious moments of fresh air she had stolen on the landing pad, when he and Sheila arrived. He was a changed man, truly. When she had first met him, he had been comfortable in his own reticence, buried in a web of defense mechanisms that had kept him removed from the world and free of all culpabilities, save for those that mattered to him. Now, where Grace herself had swirled into fear and doubt, he had come alive. It was something he had simultaneously seen and heard on that dreadful train, as he was being cooked alive: a voice made of light. Even if their entire world were to go to hell, he told her, they would still be okay. His hopefulness was contagious, the exact remedy Grace needed to accept her losses without succumbing to despair.

In her room on his first night in the mountain, Dex handed her a crumpled envelope. It was light brown and heavily textured, folded from Linda's homemade paper, and sealed with wax. On the flat side was a bright red smear of lipstick—a kiss traveled across the world. Here in Mount Tasman was the last footprint of a friendship that had grown with them since childhood. The envelope unfolded into a flat sheet, and on its back side was a scribbled message:

One last kiss for the woman I will love forever and ever. Thank you for being my best friend. Be safe, and save our world.

Yours forever,
Linda

Grace held the note to her lips, and grief made of love ran from her eyes, onto her hands, dampening the paper. Memories of Linda were like bursting rays of light in her heart. Just as with her dad and even the rest of her family, the pure and perfect sensation was hers to hold, untouchable to the world. It would follow her to the end, even spread into new relationships brimming on the horizon.

Her life with Dex had only just begun. As the days passed, their happiness to have each other outweighed everything else. He was now learning to be a birthing coach to Grace in their Wednesday classes, and all of the other single women glowed over him. As Grace continued to grow and her due date approached, life was downright pleasant. Yet there was a through-line of anxiety in their exhilaration—neither one wanted to think what life would be like in Antarctica, and the only people they could speak with about it were Hilda, Orion, and Sheila. It would be winter there when they arrived. If the baby came on time, their hover jet would be landing when winter reached its most ferocious point: constant darkness, for over a month.

"But the Sanctuary has artificial daylight in the winter, from everything I've ever seen about it," Dex told Grace one evening, on the deck, ten days into his stay. "And there's a retractable roof where transport hover jets come through and land. You never really touch the outside. And it's huge. The size of a small city."

Still, there was the question that haunted Grace, late into those final nights of pregnancy. "But what if . . . what if those rumors you heard on WorldCom were true? What if none of that footage of the Sanctuary was real?"

Dex shrugged. "Then none of *this* is real." They were lying in bed, face to face, whispering the way they had once before, the previous December. This conversation seemed to repeat for them, day in and day out. Grace had become a worrier, and Dex was now a soother. "I think the Opposition explanation makes the most sense," he said. "It simply hasn't been in NRO hands, and they needed rumors to cover up the fact that they're losing the fight."

"God, I hope my dad stays down here," Grace said. "You don't think they'll blow up all of New Zealand, do you? You'd think it would be just the big metropolitan areas, right?"

"I'm guessing they'll want to maintain the environment as much as possible," Dex replied. "They can't possibly get reckless with nukes. I mean, the fallout and ozone depletion from a drastic attack would prevent us from going back and repopulating, at least any time soon. Plus it could mess with farming and crops for a good ten years or so."

"But the Sanctuary could sustain us for ten years, right? Maybe the counterstrike *is* going to be that huge."

Grace cuddled into Dex's arms. He kissed her matted hair, not caring that it probably felt dirty. Showers were limited to one every three days in Mount Tasman, which she guessed was a hint that her entire future would be a much rougher sort of survival. Life back home had been too clean, too easy. But she had her failsafe, which counted for more than she had dared to hope for.

SINCE HIS ARRIVAL, Dex had become obsessed with the Wall of the Future. He visited it almost every morning with Grace, brooding over Diana Kring's message and the two signatures she had signed. A trace of the old Dex showed up whenever they visited the wall. Guilt etched its way into his face whenever he saw Diana and Michael's names.

"She thought they were going farther into the mountain," he said one morning, chuckling at how ridiculous the idea now seemed. "Just like everyone else here."

"But she'll be at the Sanctuary. So will your little boy."

Dex must have sensed the worry under her voice, because he turned his head and looked Grace in the eyes. "Grace Jarvis, I'm *not* leaving you again. Don't even think like that."

"But what if . . . what if we get there, and you and she rekindle whatever you had . . . ?"

"You know, you're ridiculously emotional," Dex said, grinning. "Is that what being pregnant does to a woman? Maybe it's better the NRO made it illegal."

Mixing a laugh with a pout, Grace punched him on the shoulder. He was being honest, though; she could tell. It was that new light in his eyes. There was no need for him to disappear into self-protection anymore.

"If Diana is there with our son, and if he really is mine, then we'll cross that bridge when we get there. All I know is I'm here to be with you. Apart from having promised your father I'll watch out for you, I *want* to be with you. For what that's worth. But something tells me you'll manage to convince yourself otherwise."

"My hormones are crazy," Grace said, as if that settled everything.

Hundreds of names were staring at them, and Dex took her by the shoulder. "Come on, let's get dinner."

SHEILA WILLY WOULD BE STAYING at the Mount Tasman facility with Orion until it was time for the counterstrike. The mountain's staff had quarters separate from the maternity dorm, which, Grace noticed, helped sell the illusion that the facility went deeper into the mountain than it actually did. But Sheila and Orion often joined Grace, Dex, and Hilda for dinner. They shared the end of a long table at the back of the cafeteria, and somehow, the routine began to please Grace. Mount Tasman and the people in it were beginning to feel like home.

The days passed, one after the other, and many of them felt the same. Dex had remained convinced for the first three weeks at the mountain that Orion, Sheila, or somebody else would allow them to call out on a scrambled com line, but orders were strict; none of the refugees were allowed to make contact with the outside world. There was too much risk. Every day, Grace thought about her dad, father, brother, and nephew. Where were they? Had her dad been able to find a small house in New Zealand, where he could spend the rest of his days? Better yet, had he met new friends? And what about the rest of the family? Was Lars still marching with the Gay Youth, and was her own father still supporting it? Did he even care that his husband and daughter had become casualties of this atrocious battle for life? In a way, Grace felt the worst for her brother, Abraham. He had always been passive and devoid of self-confidence. Given the choice and a bit of encouragement, however, Grace thought he would have sided with the Opposition.

On the tenth of June, Sheila was admiring Grace's expanded belly. Hilda's too was getting large. Like most of the women who had not yet disappeared from the maternity dorm (Grace did not like to acknowledge these women, because the thought of their being duped threatened to crack her optimism), she and Hilda now had a glow about them that simply could not be suppressed. Their babies were coming, and an understood joy was bursting from their seams.

"One more stop, and then we all get a chance at a new world," Sheila said in a hushed, excited voice. "It seems kind of exciting now, doesn't it? I mean, living in a self-sufficient utopia built on two miles of ice? At the very least, all of us here are going to get a chance to experience something most humans in history would never have dreamed of!"

Orion gave her a warning look. "Shhh . . . too loud." Then, he smiled. "But I agree. And what's the worst that can happen? We go to the Sanctuary, finish out our years, and die?"

"Life is life," Hilda said. "And you know what? Spending it with you guys doesn't seem half bad. Better than the life I came from, anyway."

A moment of clarity warmed Grace, suddenly. Her friends were correct. This was an adventure to be embraced. What was meant to happen would happen. Maybe now she could be sure of that. She smiled, thinking of Marvel and Lieutenant Helio back in the ruins of Los Angeles, hoping they both had found some luck.

Dex grinned. "I don't know about you, but I'm excited to meet all these new babies. Isn't it crazy to think that they're all going to have their own unique traits? What was it Dr. Thrace said on Monday, Grace? That she liked to think we're all God's little puzzle pieces, or something?"

"She liked to think that if you could somehow combine every trait of every person who has ever lived and every person who ever will live, until humanity's end, you'd see the face of God."

The moment suspended itself as everyone, even Sheila, who claimed not to believe in any God, digested the idea. Then, the red-haired scarecrow woman grinned.

"You know, that idea isn't half bad. I like it. Makes me think of the baby they made me get rid of."

Orion lifted his mug of tea. "Here's to breeding."

Grace, Dex, Sheila, and Hilda raised their drinks in solemn response. "To breeding."

They drank.

CHAPTER 60 ✴ (HIM)

THREE DAYS BEFORE DR. THRACE PLANNED to induce labor, Grace's water broke. It happened in the bed she and Dex were sharing, early on the morning of July ninth. He was cuddling her, welcoming the new day. They were pressed together, warm under the covers, and he was aroused. He was kissing her neck when, suddenly, she jerked her head up in surprise and let out a sudden chirp.

"Oh!"

Dex felt the wetness on his thighs. Adrenaline rushed through him. "Is this it?"

Their two roommates, Erin and Rachel, woke at the noise. They realized what was happening and sat up in their beds. Dex jumped to the floor, forgetting his erection, and pulled the covers off Grace.

"Do you think it's happening? Should I call Dr. Thrace?"

Grace nodded. "It's just like they told us in class," she said. "I think this is it."

Here goes nothing.

Dex ran from the room, toward the hospital wing. Grace had passed her due date by nearly two weeks. The wet bed sheets came as no surprise, as they had been expecting labor for nearly a month. Irregular contractions had become increasingly intense over the past three weeks, but their daughter, whom they would name Leila, was stubborn. It seemed she wanted to stay inside Grace. They had decided on her name two weeks prior, on the deck while watching the artificial sunset. Today, finally, Leila was ready.

A nurse accompanied Dex back to the maternity dorm with a wheelchair for Grace. They brought her to Mount Tasman's medical wing, which lay on the other side of the facility's main hallway, just past the loading dock. Grace paced back and forth in the delivery room for the first three hours, while her contractions were mild. By the end of hour four, however, she had climbed into bed and was pressing her eyes shut with each one. Watching her go through this, Dex realized how powerful motherhood really was. It was a sacrifice of the highest order.

"They're coming in waves," Grace told him, trying to keep her breathing steady. She was gritting her teeth in pain. The waves were growing higher and closer together, yet she continued to refuse medication to numb the pain. She wanted to experience a natural child birth. "It's human to feel this," she whimpered at one point. "This is how it's supposed to be."

Two hours later, the waiting game was over. Grace was fully dilated—fast and lucky for a first birth, according to Dr. Thrace. She gave the directive. "You can push now, Grace. You're going to feel like it's all you can do anyway, so just follow your instinct."

"You're doing great, Grace! Breathe like we did in class. Slow breaths now, slow breaths." Dex grabbed her hand, and she batted it away in favor of scrunching her fingers into the bed sheets. But Dex only laughed, feeling such jubilation at her beauty that her refusal of his comfort failed to matter. "Come on, Grace! It's our little girl knocking on the world's door!"

"When did you get so goddamned *sappy*?" Grace exclaimed, then screamed. "God, it hurts! It fucking hurts! *OhmyGod—*"

She grabbed Dex's hand now and crushed it in her own. He cupped her head with the other, letting the sweat from her hair dampen his fingers.

Dr. Thrace and the attending nurse were waiting between Grace's spread legs, peering intently upward. "I see the head, Grace," the doctor said. "She's ready to come out!"

Now, Grace was sobbing, screaming, grunting, pushing with all her living power. "Dex! I feel her, Dex—oh my God oh my God *oh my God ohmyGod*—!"

Dex kissed Grace's hand, washing it in his own tears.

This is why humans are so incredible. Not because they can breed, procreate, give birth, but because of this! Of love. Of having come from nothing and having the ability to embody a beauty that nothing else in this universe can.

And Grace—

CHAPTER 61 ✳ (HER)

—CRIED OUT IN PAIN, AGONY, AND ABSOLUTE WILLINGNESS to push this baby out of her body. The pulsating heat between her legs burned like nothing she had ever felt before, stretching every part of her over torturous licks of fire. All she could think of was to push, push, push, and there was nothing else, no other goal. This was the brutal ache her entire life had built up to. Nothing had ever or would ever again compare.

She let out a guttural scream. Her entire body was tearing apart.

"Her head is almost out, Grace," came Dr. Thrace's voice from behind the sheet spread over her legs.

Dex kept her hand, but he leaned over. "Grace, she's out! I see her face! Holy God, I see her face! Come on, baby, you can do it! Keep pushing!"

Push push push push get her out get her out this is the most important thing you will ever do and you're doing it here in this mountain when nobody on the outside will ever be able to do this again push push push push ohfortheloveofGodPUSH—

And then there was emptiness and relief.

Sudden, dazzling relief.

The baby girl's head was out, and the rest of her tiny body followed like an afterthought. The placenta came out next as Dr. Thrace gave

Grace's belly a gentle push, and the contractions accompanying it were mild enough to be inconsequential. Other fluids followed, but nothing mattered anymore. It was over, and the sudden respite from the anguish was pure serenity. Things were happening around her: Dex had let go of her hand and was cutting a long strip of flesh connecting her to the baby (*the umbilical cord, what they told us about during class!*), and then the doctor was wrapping the baby in a flowing pink blanket.

Not just "the baby" anymore. She's Leila. Our beautiful Leila.

Leila was crying. It was the first effort of a new voice trying to find its breath. Dr. Thrace carried the infant toward her mother. In what seemed like no time at all, Leila was snuggled against Grace's bosom, searching for a breast. This was normal; this was okay; this was good. Grace let her breast free. Leila found it, began to feed.

Heaven. This is heaven.

What was behind did not matter now. All that could be was forward.

CHAPTER 62 ✳ (HIM)

IT WAS THE SEVENTEENTH OF JULY, and Dex was standing with an ink pen, in front of the Wall of the Future. Grace was next to him, rocking Leila gently in her arms. Like all the other women who had given birth in the past five months, she was about to disappear quietly from the hospital wing, without much ado. Their first week with Leila had passed unbelievably fast, and the hospital wing was already making room for more women, more births. This was the way of Mount Tasman, the way of the Opposition.

Sheila, Orion, and Hilda had visited them every day, and now, they stood behind the new family, watching, waiting for Dex to write the goodbye. He wondered how many other people who signed the wall had known what was coming. Judging by the enthusiasm in all the messages, it had been few.

Dex had always been simple, to the point. Now, he marked the passage of his family in the same way, careful not to let slip the secret of the Sanctuary.

Off to the final stop. Thank you for helping
our little girl see the world.
—*Dex Wheelock, Grace Jarvis, and Leila Jarvis,*
July 17, 2385

Three more women, none of whom were accompanied by a failsafe, had also given birth on the same day as Grace. Sally, Lacresha, and Elysia were their names, and they were accompanied by their infants Jos, Andrew, and Mary Ann. Each was standing near her own section of wall, accompanied by a small group of friends. This seemed to be the ritual: intimate goodbyes, as not to make much of a scene. Neither Dex nor Grace had ever spoken to them before today, but thirty minutes ago, while accompanying them to the blast door, Orion had encouraged introductions to be made.

They're going to be terrified when they realize there isn't anything but a hover jet past this door, Dex thought.

He was already preparing words for them, the same explanation as Sheila and Orion had given him and Grace. It seemed cruel to spring such a trap on new, innocent mothers.

"We'll see you when we see you," Sheila said. "I hope it's sooner rather than later." She flipped her bushel of red hair back with a hand and looked at Dex. "Honey, I'm glad you got another chance. Really glad. Keep your woman safe now, will you?"

To his right, Hilda was whispering to Leila in a gentle, childish voice. "Little Jane and I will be ready to follow you in a month, okay? Just a month! Remember to wait up for us, okay?" Leila's blue-gray eyes were wide and round, like Dex's own. She looked up at Hilda, who then glanced up at the new parents, grinning. "She's beautiful, you guys. Just beautiful."

They shared hugs. Dex combined Orion's hug with a handshake. "You'll be fine," Orion whispered. "These pilots work out of the Sanctuary, and they make this run all the time. They fly solid machines."

Soon, it was time to clear those who would remain out of the hallway. As was the rule, the door would open only when those left were the ones moving onward. Sheila and Orion could not stay, even though both were aware of what came next; controlling the blast door was not their prerogative. Sally, Lacresha, and Elysia, all three holding their babies, followed Dex and Grace to the door. Orion directed everyone else back down the hall, toward the sliding glass hatch that would lead them back into the maternity dorm. Far away, through that glass, as an alarm sounded and the blast door scraped open, the friends of the departing waved. Those departing waved back. Then, Dex turned to face what was ahead. The women followed suit.

They were only breeders with their offspring now, five adults and four tiny babies, facing what lay beyond the wall.

CHAPTER 63 ❄ (HER)

IT WAS A DIMLY LIT, MONOCHROME HALLWAY, stretching into the shadows. A voice from some hidden intercom instructed them to step forward. Grace had to pry her own foot off the ground to take that first step; the fear was suddenly paralyzing. If it was a hover jet pad they were going to depart from, it was different from the one at the mountain's entrance.

"Let's go," Dex said. As usual, Grace was encouraged by the newfound hope in his voice. She could see by the way the other three women looked at him that they felt the same. She clutched Leila, who started to squirm as Grace followed Dex across the blast door's threshold, into the darkness. She had so many questions, but it was not yet time to discuss Antarctica. The women next to them still did not know.

"This looks like the loading bay," Sally said once their eyes adjusted, sounding confused. Her baby, Jos, remained asleep in her arms.

As the door closed behind them, Grace noticed a pile of multi-layered hooded jackets. Winter in Antarctica could sometimes reach a hundred degrees below zero, or colder, without wind chill. She had seen pictures and video of the Sanctuary countless times, and, just as Dex had told her repeatedly, it had a retractable roof for its hover jet landing bay. Nobody would be exposed directly to the cold.

"Put the jackets on, please, for your own safety," the intercom voice instructed.

"Jackets? Why jackets?" Elysia said, but she found an adult sized jacket and put it on. Under it was a down body suit that would fit little Mary Ann. Sally grabbed a jacket and body suit as well, first bundling Jos, then herself. Lacresha looked uneasy. She picked up a jacket and body suit but did nothing with them.

"Come on, ladies, we should walk," Dex said. Perhaps it was the dim lighting or the eerie silence interrupted only by their footsteps, but he suddenly sounded nervous. At the end of the hall was another door. When they were twenty feet away, it opened. On the other side was a tunnel occupied by a chiseled man driving a motorized transport.

"Throw your bags on the back, please." He turned to Lacresha, who was simply carrying the jacket and baby suit the Opposition had provided for her. Andrew squirmed in her arms. "Miss, you're going to want your jacket. Make sure your baby is covered as well."

Lacresha hesitated before getting on the transport. "I'm confused about the jackets. I thought we were staying inside the mountain. . . ."

"Believe me, Miss, you're going to want to put those on. The mountain is cold this time of year."

It would have been easier just to tell everybody from the beginning, Grace thought, feeling sorry for all those who would have to face the deception this late in the game. She glanced at Dex. *Should we say something now?*

Dex seemed to have read her mind, and he shook his head. As planned, they would wait to discuss the truth with these women until they were on the hover jet, until it was obvious. With a mournful look of terror that suggested she had suddenly figured it out, Lacresha climbed onto the cart, set her baby on the seat, and donned the jacket. She grabbed Andrew again and put on his body suit.

"This isn't what I signed up for," she whispered.

Sally and Elysia seemed still to be in the dark as the transport zipped into the tunnel, taking them from the maternity dorm forever. Soon, they reached a final blast door, which looked identical to the one at the mountain's entrance.

It opened. Sally and Elysia gasped and descended into worried whispers. Lacresha remained stony faced as she stepped off the transport and walked forward, but Grace saw that her hands were pale, shaking. She was clutching little Andrew for dear life.

It was a cloudy day, and the mountains were rugged spires of black and gray. Just as Grace and Dex had suspected, a hover jet sat on the platform. Unlike the red transports that had lifted them to Mount Tasman from Franz Josef, this one was solid gray and large: a military transport, like the Sanctuary ones she had grown up seeing on the news. It was a high-speed Z-44 Falcon. She had given Lars a model of one for Christmas two years ago. He had begged and begged for it.

Oh, my God, it's all real now.

The landing pad was smaller than the one at the mountain's entrance. Grace guessed it was on an entirely different end of the mountain, because it was built on a rugged outcropping overlooking a craggy plummet to the death. She wondered how rock and snow avalanches had not demolished it. Then, she looked up and saw her answer: the landing pad lay nestled under two tapered sides of a small ridge, which created a diversion for anything that might fall from the mountain.

Two pilots dressed in tan uniforms were ready to help them aboard. One escorted the women, and the other threw their luggage into the cabin and began strapping it to the floor.

"But where is the other part of the mountain?" Elysia said, suddenly gasping in panic. "*Where are you taking us?*"

Grace and Dex exchanged troubled glances, then set the example by climbing onto the hover jet first. Seats with harness-like safety belts attached to the walls lined the length of the passenger cabin, and they took two spots near the rear, next to one of the hover jet's few windows. Lacresha followed, and Sally and Elysia came last. The two pilots ushered them aboard in silence.

"*Where are they taking us?*" Elysia said again, this time turning to Dex and Grace.

Grace buried Leila in her bosom to shield her from the cold air blowing through the open doors.

"The Sanctuary," she said. "The Opposition took it over almost ten years ago."

"That's a load of crap," Lacresha said. "There is no Sanctuary." But there was a spark of hope in her eyes.

Dex held up a hand to her. "Calm down. I found out through our friend Sheila before I came here, and your liaison Orion confirmed it. The Sanctuary really is in the Opposition's hands now, and they have weapons ready to blow the NRO to kingdom come. There've been rumors about the Sanctuary, because the NRO wants to cause as much confusion as possible to keep people away from the truth."

"The Opposition is *winning*," Grace added.

"They're bringing us there to wait for the world to recover," Dex continued. "And then the heterosexuals come back . . . and nature takes its course. Humanity goes on."

As the hover jet rose into the air, they all sat without speaking, avoiding each other's eyes, listening to its drumming rotors. It was too late for any of them to feel shame over being duped, to be afraid, or to speculate. They were sharing this last leg of the journey together, and they began it in silence. Grace looked out her window and saw the small landing pad disappear behind a cloud. Here it was: a new beginning.

Within minutes, they were flying for open sea, on a journey south.

CHAPTER 64 ❄ (HIM)

SOMETHING FELT SOUR, and Dex was getting nervous.

The moment the hover jet lifted off the mountain, a wave of horror washed over him. It was not simply the thought of flying for miles and miles over earth's last gap of ocean, into the belly of Antarctica's sunless winter, nor was it the fact that he would likely be stuck on a continent of ice until his dying day. It was the sudden, twisting realization he had been digesting for weeks, the one about which he had so tenaciously attempted to be optimistic:

We've been following this Opposition blindly.

He looked at Grace. Her eyes were closed, and she was cradling the bundled Leila to her chest. If there was doubt in him now, he could not show it. They were a family, and he was the role model of hope.

The hover jet raced onward, over the freezing water, which was growing darker and darker under the falling sun.

A MEMORY ✳ (HER)

*I*T IS THE SECOND NIGHT AFTER LEILA'S BIRTH, *and Dex is curled up next to Grace with his arm around both of them, asleep. His breaths come in slow, climactic waves, then release. They are a family, and he has come all the way across the world for her, already proven himself to be the kind of father only the luckiest child could have. Father, and husband? Grace may be able to get used to the idea, because in Antarctica they have restored, for better or worse, a tradition that has been absent for nearly two centuries: marriage for heterosexuals, for men and women who will bear children and recreate the human race.*

And here is Dexter Michael Wheelock, who survived death and still decided to risk his life for her. She leans over and whispers in his ear—

CHAPTER 65 ❄ (HER)

Through the small hover jet window, this is what Grace saw: a night sky, interrupted at the horizon by a low strip of blue-gray light—the inklings of a day. Whether it was the beginning of one or the end, she could not tell, for this was the season when the end of the world saw only darkness.

Antarctica crept into her life like a white snake under perpetual shadow, at first just a strip of ice on that dim and distant curve of the earth. Their pilots had turned off the hover jet's interior lights, which allowed what daylight there was to define the approaching landscape. Within ten minutes, they were close enough to see that the dark ocean was spotted with ice. It was broken at first, then became thicker as the continent drew them closer. Soon, the ice had taken over, and it was the black channels of open water that were fighting for space. There was enough light in the sky for Grace to make out some texture, even from the hover jet's altitude. Jagged spires were pushed together in some places, and in others, bergs jutted upward to form chiseled shelves. And then she saw it: a more substantial range of hills in the distance.

The mainland.

From what Grace knew, this vast world of ice grew substantially every winter, freezing outward and almost doubling the continent's size. The ice she now saw below was just that, the winter freeze. But those hills in the distance? That was land.

Grace wondered what the people would be like. Surely, there would be alliances; there would be enemies; there would be joy; there would be sorrow. That was life. *This* was life. She turned away from the window and prepared to nurse Leila. Once they arrived, there was no telling how long it would take for them to get settled enough for something as simple as a meal. As a precaution, she had three full bottles in her satchel in case breastfeeding became difficult.

Thirty minutes later, the sky was a burning purple, and the snowy hills beneath it were close, very close. This was it. Antarctica. Their new home. But what were those dots on the snow? Meteorites? Blotches of black, partially covered by snow, became visible as the hover jet descended to ground level.

When it happened, it happened swiftly.

The hover jet came to a stop, and the cockpit door burst open. Both pilots, now armed with sonic guns, rushed the main cabin. One opened the main hatch while the other pointed the gun at the nine passengers.

"Get up! Up, up, up! Move out!"

Jos, Sally's baby, began screaming as the freezing air hit him. The guard by the door pulled the mother and child out of their seat, threw them out the door, then turned to those who remained. For a moment, Grace only stared at Dex, who suddenly looked as though the world had come crashing down on his shoulders.

Through the jet's window, she saw that the sky had become blood-red. There were no words to describe how surreal the end of her life was about to be. There was no time to accept it. All she could do was hope to see the sun one more time before it happened.

Outside, Sally was shrieking. "There's nothing here! *There's nothing here!*"

Out went Lacresha, like a rag doll, then Elysia, who fell outward, stiff legged, and landed on her back in the snow. All the babies were screaming now.

"I love you," Dex whispered to Grace, just before setting his loving gaze on Leila. "And you."

Then, he jumped at the nearest guard, who shot the sonic gun at him and missed. It was a pitifully short fight, as Dex had no chance at victory. The guards pushed him out of the hover jet, and he fell out of sight. Now, it was only Grace and Leila, with guns pointed straight at them. The ripples of electricity inside those barrels were yellow, the color of death. They would kill her first, then her daughter. Was it worth it to give up now, or would it make her a better person to follow orders, leave the hover jet, and protect Leila, in however futile an attempt, to the very end?

Yes.

It was not a choice. There was no time to let the horror in. She kissed Leila on the head and stood up. On the way to the door, her neck tilted right, as if on its own volition, and she looked one pilot in the eyes, then the other.

"It was all a lie," she said. "Did the NRO know? Was there ever a Sanctuary?"

The pilot closest to her, looking defeated himself, shook his head. Then, he kicked her out.

Grace tumbled face first into the snow. Leila would have been crushed against her chest if not for the fluff of it. She heard the hover jet's pressurized door close behind her, then a rumble as it lifted off.

All five of the adults were in normal shoes and the silly coats they had been given. It had been pathetic, really, the ruse. What would a jacket have done, in case of emergency? The air was so dry and so cold that Grace had already lost all feeling in her face, fingers, and feet. She fumbled with Leila's hood until the baby all but disappeared into it. There was no hope, but she had to try, for Leila. It was automatic.

Dex threw himself around them both. "I didn't know," he

wheezed, over and over. In the distance, the horizon blazed like fire. Would there be sun, today? Or was it only going to tease them?

There was a heavy wind. They would not last long.

Lacresha was already running with Andrew toward the sunrise, as if to face their doom head-on.

"The NRO let the Opposition happen," Grace said to Dex. "To let us think we were the world's only hope. Carnevale led all this just to . . . funnel out the naysayers . . . so they could achieve their goal. But you know what?" The flesh around her eyes was already freezing.

"What?"

"I'm not afraid."

A MEMORY ❋ (HIM)

"I love you."

The whisper glides into Dex's ear, bringing him out of a dream. He had been on a boat with Grace, Leila, and, somehow, everybody who ever mattered to him. His mothers were on the boat. And Stuart, the Archers, even Lars. They were happy.

He doesn't open his eyes; they are too heavy. The room is dark, Grace is breathing under his arm, as is Leila, their daughter, who still seems like the most beautiful gift he could ever have asked for. Leila rustles under the covers for a moment, then settles again.

He has dreamed a thousand times of hearing those words come from a woman's mouth, yet he knows now he could have died a happy man never having heard them. Still, during this quiet night in the maternity dorm, inside Mount Tasman, lost in the middle of New Zealand's Southern Alps and awaiting transfer to Antarctica, Dex realizes just how profound they really are, and he believes them. Grace loves him, and he loves her, and they will now share that love with their daughter. What more can there be?

Another breath, and the sparkling sea encircles him again. He is back on the boat. They sail, laugh, and sing. It is joy.

CHAPTER 66 ✳ (HIM)

Dex stumbled with Grace toward one of the dark piles in the snow. Sally had run after Lacresha with Jos, who was already dead, and Elysia had disappeared onto her own final path.

All warmth had now sunk deep into Dex's core, leaving his skin in a painful freeze. Grace had begun moving to keep their heat as long as possible, so they could be together when Antarctica took them. There was no question in his mind to follow. His promise to Stuart held true, even now. This was his path. Grace was his path. Leila, too— she was their song to everything good in the world. Dex's thoughts were already becoming muddled, and all that mattered was that he would accompany Grace to the place where she would choose to rest. The nearing mound seemed to be her goal, an unspoken marker for the coming moments that would punctuate their lives.

As they staggered forward, Dex noticed the rocks were not rocks at all. They were bodies. Snow had drifted up and over parts of them, exposing only slivers of clothing underneath. Grace stopped next to the pile and fixed her gaze on it, gasping for breath.

Using his bare hand, which was frozen beyond feeling, Dex wiped off the buildup of snow and saw a human face. A man. Underneath him were two more, a woman and an infant. Had they piled themselves like this to keep warm? Or had the New Rainbow Order come here to make order of their genocide? Dex would never know, so he let the thought pass. Diana and Michael were here somewhere, but they had already gone forward, to that glorious light no evil could touch. Looking for them would not be necessary.

Clutching Leila to her bosom, Grace huddled next to the bodies, on the side shielded from the wind. She was beyond words now, so Dex simply crouched down and wrapped himself around her.

Clouds were blowing over them, creating a purple canopy above the prolonged sunrise, which had yet to come, which might never come while they were alive. Dex's muscles were beginning to seize beyond use, but he hugged Grace and Leila as hard as he could. His regret, his shame, his humiliation—all had passed. Now, he could only watch over the two most important people in his life and make sure they went in peace.

Grace was smiling, gazing forward, toward that bright spot beyond the expanse of snow. Dex turned to see what was bringing her joy.

There, just for a moment, was the edge of the sun. It caressed the sky, casting a momentary shaft of light into the approaching dusk. Then, there was an arc of color.

Impossible. There's no moisture in the air—

But there it was, nonetheless. Perhaps refracted through a cloud of blowing snow, perhaps by a miracle from the God who seemed to have abandoned them: a rainbow.

It was fleeting, like the sliver of sun, and then it was gone. But the colors had been there, all in a row—that universal symbol, God's promise that life would go on. Dex remembered sitting in church with his mothers, and he smiled.

Everything began to fade. There was nothing he could regret, because he had done his best. And there it was, what he had seen in the train car, that dazzling truth that had changed him forever, the hope that allowed him now to smile as well. Dex felt himself growing warm.

The frigid wasteland took them. Under winter's darkness at the bottom of the world, there was peace.

AFTERWORD

I HAD NOT PLANNED to write an afterward for this book or to explain it in any way, but when my editor Amy encouraged me to say something about it, I realized she had a good point. It wasn't fair to leave readers to make sense of something seemingly hopeless, to wonder what I meant by any of it. Was I making some sort of political statement? Why had I worked for two years on a book that ended in such a dismal fashion? Was I simply trying to dupe readers (or worse, alienate them) and be depressing? We already have the nightly news for that, don't we?

This book came from two separate snippets of reality: my (homosexual) friend's colorful use of the term "Stepford fag" and the National Organization for Marriage's 2008 ad campaign equating gay marriage to "a coming storm." Both these things made me laugh, but from them sprang questions: How would heterosexuals feel if they were the minority in a world filled with homosexuals? What would it be like for them to grow up? How might they fight for their own worth in a culture that deemed them lesser beings? These were questions I had never heard anybody wonder about, so I decided to wonder them for myself. Of course, it turned into a book.

At first, I thought *The Breeders* would be much funnier, a pure satire on what some people call "the gay agenda." As the ideas stirred around, however, I realized it might be more interesting to make it fit into the classic dystopian style made famous by *1984* and *Brave New World*, complete with the tragic ending. In context of this story style, I wanted to mirror my own experience of growing up "different" and having to deal with being part of an often-disdained minority. I thought about the times relatives threw around the word "fag" during holiday dinners, how it always made me want to crawl under a rock, and how it took me years to find worth for myself in a society where jokes were made about people like me. The idea of gay people taking over the world and wiping out heterosexuals was ridiculous from the get-go, but it provided an interesting stage to reflect on how it might be if current prejudices and socio-sexual norms were reversed. It wasn't long before I had flashes of a young woman bleeding during a family get-together, of one parent hating the woman's heterosexuality while the other embraced it, and of the woman (somewhere later in the story) sitting on a mountain ridge, pondering the life she left behind.

I knew almost immediately that these mountains would be in New Zealand, a place near and dear to me, and it was only a few quick mental hops that led me to the idea of Antarctica, a nearby continent that has always fascinated me. Inspiration for the Antarctic Sanctuary came from Alan Moore's *Watchmen* and *The X-Files: Fight the Future*, and it was the magic ingredient that gave me a story. The Sanctuary would be a farce, and my characters would be led on a journey of rebellion in an attempt to avoid Antarctica, only to be dumped there by the very people they thought were helping them.

This is when *The Breeders* became a bit more serious. I wanted to follow it through to the end in as emotionally honest a fashion as possible, yet I didn't want the ending to be hopeless. As it is now, it accurately reflects my own belief that even the worst in this life is merely a prelude for what is to come. At this point, I believe death might very well turn out to be a cosmic joke, that the final transition might be easier than any of us truly expects.

At risk of sounding like an author who presumes his work is worthy of post-denouement speculation, I'll share that there's more to the story than what made it into the book. Marvel, Exander, Linda Glass, Stuart, Lars, and Sam and Moses Archer have futures that are more fortunate than the one Grace, Dex, and Leila suffered. I could go into more detail, but I might write about some of them in the future, so I'll keep mum on the rest of their stories for now. On a broader scale, my fictional society doesn't stay in shambles forever. The genocide continues for quite some time, but like most terrible periods in human history, it comes to an end. I think the human spirit eventually wins out, if only in small ways at first. Perhaps it would be a new secretary general who works against the ideal of human extinction, or pockets of natives in the Unrecoverable Territories surviving and ultimately thriving. I envision human life on this hypothetical Earth going on with a lot of goodness until some greater natural force dictates its end.

Of course, you the reader are free to imagine anything you want; that is the delight of fiction. We get to project our own hopes, fears, and beliefs into the parts left ambiguous by the (sometimes cruel) author.

Now, another quick word about Grace and Dex, because they were the reason you are holding this book in your hands. Life dealt them some pretty crappy cards. They took the risk of hoping, and they suffered for it. But life is all about suffering, in my book. We can either rise above it, or let it destroy us from the inside out. The hardships we plod through can make us stronger, and by the time we actually die, perhaps we can be ready for it by knowing we have done our best. Grace and Dex did their best, and because I'm the one who wrote their story, I have the authority to tell you this: they went on, and they were dazzled beyond their wildest dreams.

Matthew J. Beier
Minneapolis, MN
September 30, 2011

ACKNOWLEDGEMENTS

THIS NOVEL WOULD NOT BE HERE without the help of many people. First, I'd like to thank my parents, Walter and Mariana Beier, for encouraging me since childhood to follow my dreams. They were and are the best parents I could have ever asked for. I'd also like to thank my siblings and brother-in-law—Amy/Steffen, Joe, and Mara—for their years of support and feedback. I also can't forget my nephew Lukas, and his soon-to-be-born sibling who doesn't yet have a name, who made the baby-factor of this book easier to write! In this same spot, I'd also like to thank Chad Aldrich, the first person to show me what it is like to fall in love. This book wouldn't exist without him.

Second, I'd like to thank my editors Amy Quale and Paul Whittemore for all their hard work helping to make this book presentable—and for telling me when and where I was veering dangerously off course. Next comes my line editor, Molly Miller, for making this book as shiny as possible. Any mistakes that remain are 100 percent mine. Also, thank you to my test readers: Mom, Mara, Amy, Laurena Bernabo, Philip Maret, Marina Baer, and Beth Varro.

For other necessary bits of time and input along the way, I'd like to thank (in no particular order): Melissa Oszustowicz, Robert Zupperolli, Weronika Janczuk, Melissa Sarver, Andrew Just, Jill Harmon, David Schall, Lizzie Engel, Jordan Wiklund, Kara Raymond,

Kristin Olson, Heather Tabery, Briony Bresnahan, Joe Gardner, Elysia Yeary, Erik Westman, John Cutrone, C. Ryan Shipley, Robin Beier, Debbie Crisfield, Will Ashenmacher, Leah Olm, Mike Hefty, Byron Elder, Jeffrey Harris, Ben Arfmann, Andrew Minck, Amanda Barthel, and Matthew Russell. I would also like to thank Miss Snark, Nathan Bransford, and all the other blogging literary agents out there who have helped fledgling writers learn how to write books.

Third, I'd like to thank my life inspirations: J.K. Rowling, Stephen King, Kazuo Ishiguro, Michael Crichton, Audrey Niffenegger, Suzanne Collins, Steven Spielberg, Chris Carter, Peter Jackson, Fran Walsh, Philippa Boyens, Alan Ball, Michael Bay, David Yates, Lady Gaga, and all the brilliant composers who wrote the film scores I listened to while writing this book.

Finally, I would like to thank you, Dear Reader, for giving me a chance, even if you ultimately decide I should have gone into finance, janitorial work, or anything other than writing. Please follow me on Twitter if you'd like, or feel free to contact me at epic@matthewbeier.com if you wish to share your thoughts on this book, your thoughts in general, or anything else you might have to say!

www.matthewbeier.com
www.twitter.com/MatthewBeier
www.facebook.com/MatthewJBeier
www.facebook.com/TheBreedersNovel
www.goodreads.com/matthewbeier

ABOUT THE AUTHOR

MATTHEW J. BEIER is a novelist, screenwriter, photographer, and graphic designer based in Minneapolis, Minnesota. When he was nine years old, the film adaptation of Michael Crichton's *Jurassic Park* (and, subsequently, the novel itself) inspired a passion for storytelling in him that branched in two directions: writing and movie making. This led him to film school at Chapman University in 2003, where he spent three semesters studying screenwriting, film production, and English before spending a final semester abroad at Victoria University in Wellington, New Zealand. When Matthew isn't working, he enjoys tea, exercise, watching films, and spending time with his friends and family.

CPSIA information can be obtained at www.ICGtesting.com
Printed in the USA
BVOW030227290513

321883BV00002B/46/P